COIN AND DAGGER

Jac Filer

Printed in the United States of America
Published in Hellertown, PA
Cover design and images by Angela Filer

ISBN 978-1-958711-76-7
Library of Congress Control Number 2023917704

For more information or to place bulk orders, contact the author or the
publisher at Jennifer@BrightCommunications.net.

Bright
COMMUNICATIONS
BrightCommunications.net

To my son, Kyle, for our countless hours spent brainstorming story ideas.
The journey has begun.

Chapter One

Capernaum, 27 AD

"No talking from this point forward!"

Simon offered only a nod in response, not wishing to mess up his first order on his first assignment.

He was determined to prove himself worthy to join the cause.

To complete what his father could not.

Just outside the city gate, Simon watched as Manaen took the upper road toward the sprawling estates on the hillside. When his mentor was out of sight, Simon followed until he reached his assigned place.

The western mountains hid the setting sun. Simon looked back and peered into their long shadows, stretched across the road. Nobody was approaching.

He retrieved tattered strips of linen from the brush and wrapped his head and face. He shed his outer cloak and stuffed it deep in the bushes. His old coat — now exposed — was streaked with stains and torn unnaturally, just as Simon had prepared it. He laid face-down between the road and the brush.

And he waited.

He forced his breathing into a calm, unnaturally slow rhythm and listened. In mere minutes, the expected footsteps reached his ears — the disciplined cadence of trained feet, accompanied by the lazy scraping of another set.

He dared not turn to look. He had to trust his ears.

And Manaen.

And the plan.

"What is this?" a voice that seemed hoarse from overuse said as the footsteps grew louder.

"Ignore it. Just a vagrant," answered a second, deeper voice in an unfamiliar accent.

"We never see vagrants outside the city gate. What if he was dragged here by a wild animal?"

"Look closer," the foreign voice urged. The sound was now directly over Simon. The slight warmth of a lantern reached him through his tattered coat. "He's wrapped in rags. You know what that means. Best to leave and not touch him."

"How could he have gotten here?" The question was distant and muffled.

"Maybe a wild animal. Maybe he got confused and wandered from hi—"

A wet sound, similar to a foot plunging into the mud, interrupted the man's words. A weak gasp followed, then a startled scream.

The thud on the ground was Simon's cue. He leaped to his feet and stepped over a fallen man dressed in the unadorned leather of a hired guard. Manaen was on top of the man, wrestling with the hilt of a blade buried in the man's back. Simon chased after the other man, who seemed slowed by his own excess weight and a heavy, embroidered cloak.

Simon reached the man with just a few long strides and shoved him down. He jumped on the fallen man and secured his arms.

"Give me your purse!" Simon spoke through linen that still wrapped his head.

"It's on my belt. Take it. Just let me go," the man's voice broke and strained as he spoke through gasps.

"Just your purse? What about the rest?"

"This is all I have!"

"For all that you extort from the people—*your people*—son of Alphaeus, I expect a chest full of coin!"

"Not here! Herod's portion stays in the storeroom. He sends his own officials to retrieve it. Please take this and let me go."

"I don't believe you." Simon gripped the man's arms tighter.

"Please. I want to live. I have no reason to lie. My extra is with the guard. Take it. I have nothing else."

"He's right," Manaen said as he walked to where Simon pinned the man to the ground. "I have the guard's bag. We're done here."

"Please. Let me go now," the prone man whispered from lungs still constrained by Simon's weight.

"You can go. We'll get to the storehouse another day." Simon let go of the man's arms and stood. The man coughed as he got his arms under himself and crawled forward. He tripped over his own cloak before finally pushing to his feet. He carried himself up the road on wobbly legs without looking back.

"You should not have said that, Simon," Manaen whispered after the man was out of earshot.

"Said what?"

"About the storehouse. It isn't wise to let them know our plans."

"Why let him go then?" Simon asked. "Unless as a warning to the rest of them."

"A warning, no. A harbinger, yes." Manaen held up an index finger in correction. "We want the others to be intimidated, not informed of our strategy. There is no need for words. The frightened traitor and the fallen mercenary that they find in the morning will be enough." Manaen turned and walked back toward the city without offering Simon an opportunity to respond.

———

Matthew winced and pressed a hand on his hip as he paced the floor in Samchai's meeting hall.

"I really don't understand why you expect me to solve this problem," Samchai said as he looked up at the toll collector across his desk. "Hire your own mercenaries according to what you find appropriate."

"It's getting harder to find guards who want to work in Galilee. The incidents are increasing, and the soldiers are demanding a premium," Matthew protested.

"So pay what it takes."

"And offset that against my remittance?"

"Of course not! We agreed on your remittance, for which you are accountable to me. Just as I am accountable to Herod, Herod to Quirinius, and Quirinius to Tiberius. Surely, you see why we can't just change your remittance on a whim. Neither of us has the authority to do so."

"So you expect me to just pay more for the same amount of protection? Protection that failed, I might add!" Matthew's face grew warm as he relived the memory of his recent assault.

"Failure that was on *your* watch, to be clear."

"*My* watch?!" Matthew's volume rose, but he no longer cared about niceties. "I hire guards for *protection*. Who is supposed to be watching who here?"

Samchai watched and waited as Matthew calmed his breathing. After a moment, Samchai continued, "I hope you don't rely on outbursts like that when you are at the toll booth. They make you look helpless and afraid. It's not an effective strategy." The tax farmer, paused a moment, then added, "And you will need all the strategy that you can pull together if you intend to collect enough to pay a premium for a new guard. You should also know that we will be supplying additional protection for the storehouse in light of the threat that you've reported. That expense will be shared equally by all publicans and added to your remittance."

"So that's the answer?" Matthew winced with a mix of frustration and pain as he pressed harder on his hip. "Squeeze more out of these people, keep less for myself, and send more off to Herod while more Romans occupy the city? The Galileans will see this only as a reason to fight harder. Surely you—and even Herod— must see that."

Samchai stood, "Are you not a Galilean yourself, Matthew Bar-Alphaeus?"

Unease welled up within Matthew as Samchai's searching eyes met his. He considered his response carefully. "By birth. But not in the way that you insinuate. I chose to bid for this role, and your own records show that I have fulfilled my duty honorably for many years." Matthew exhaled and forced steadiness into his voice. "And I've seen how their agitation grows. Maybe a stronger response is—"

Samchai held his hand up. "Yes, you *chose* this role. Perhaps because you fear the Romans more than you fear your own people. Then you must assume a stronger response would only mean cutting down the people. Then who would keep shipping moving? And more importantly, who would be left for you to collect from?" Samchai lowered himself to his seat. "As for your response, do what you've always done: Calculate your costs and let that guide your work. You are dismissed."

Matthew turned without speaking another word, even as the retorts he wanted to say filled his mind.

Fear the Romans more? The bandits know my name.

He left through the receiving room where two servants waited. They exited with him as he wrestled with the dread that any reprisal from the bandits would fall on him first.

Simon stood on the deck of a small merchant ship, loading sacks of grain onto a cart.

"Did you notice the extra security around the toll booth?" Thaddeus asked as he loaded a nearby cart.

"I really try not to see them—as difficult as they make themselves to miss."

"Well, something must have happened," Thaddeus pressed. "They wouldn't let me past to the docks until my father vouched for me."

"You? What makes you a threat to them?" Simon chuckled and regarded the youthful man with a smile.

"It's not just me. They are doing that to everyone. Didn't they interrogate you?"

"Like I said: I try not to notice them," Simon answered as quietly as he could.

"Easy for you to say," Thaddeus replied. "You're probably looking ahead to your big wedding. Only a week to go, right?"

"It won't be *big;* we're a simple clan. But I do look forward to getting home to Cana and enjoying some time with my wife."

"Enjoy it, you will!" Thaddeus continued as the men wheeled their carts down the ramp to the dock. "Maybe while you're gone, things will quiet down around here."

Simon didn't respond, and the men pushed their carts onto the shore where another team was loading a horse-drawn cart. They swapped stacked carts for empty ones and returned to the ship.

On the way back, Simon grabbed Thaddeus by the sleeve. "Listen," he said under his breath, "you can't be saying these things so freely. Not here. The ships have ears."

Thaddeus regarded Simon with searching eyes. "I'm just saying: Things have been a little interesting. First the Baptizer in Jerusalem, and now all these soldiers way out here in Galilee."

"The Baptizer is nothing." Simon shook his head and turned to load his cart. "He's loud now, but soon he'll wander into the wilderness where the Essenes wait for everyone else to do the real work."

"Really? Didn't you hear about the lightning and thunder when he baptized some Nazarene? If you can call it lightning and thunder, even. Some people are saying they heard the voice of God!"

Simon held up a hand to settle his young friend's excitement. "I was there, too. I saw it. That Nazarene is a distant cousin in my bride's clan—at least that's what her brother claims. Just a simple worker like you and me." He stepped toward Thaddeus and whispered, "Theatrics won't help our people. But that doesn't mean we are without hope—or a plan."

Mirroring Simon's hushed tone, Thaddeus asked, "What do you mean? What plan?"

Simon continued, "When I get back from Cana, things will be different. We can talk more then."

A week later, when his wedding day arrived, Simon reclined at the table with his bride and his guests. The main course was finished, and the servants were pouring after-dinner wine. A din of revelry filled the room, and Simon nearly missed the voice calling him.

"Simon!" the call grew a little louder. He looked around. The banquet-master approached with a cup in his hand and excitement on his face. "Simon. Stand up. Come here."

Simon pushed himself to his feet, stepped away from the table, and walked toward the banquet-master. The pair retreated from the hall to a quieter place.

"Everyone brings out the choice wine first and then the cheap wine after the guests have had too much," the banquet-master explained. Simon didn't understand why he had been pulled away from the table to hear that, and he tried to make his confusion obvious. The banquet-master continued without a pause, "But *you've* saved the best wine until now!"

"I don't understand," Simon responded.

"The wine! Can't you taste it? It's sweet and rich, nothing at all like I would expect from an after-dinner cup." He held out his cup, and Simon took a taste.

Simon returned the cup. "You're right. This is choice wine, but I have no idea where it came from."

"Did you not supply it? The servants are in the back preparing the cups now," the banquet-master gestured to the doorway behind him, "and they seem to have plenty!"

Simon peered past the man into the next room. Two girls ladled wine from stone jars into the cups.

"You do know how to take care of your guests!" The banquet-master squeezed Simon's shoulder.

"Aren't those the jars for the wash water?" Simon asked.

"Does it matter which jars you used, Simon? You did what it took to get the wine here, and that's what matters!" The banquet-master patted Simon's arm and walked away.

A man, about thirty years old, emerged from the back room and proceeded toward the banquet hall. When he turned enough for Simon to catch a glimpse of his features and his sun-bronzed laborer's complexion, familiarity struck him. It was the distant cousin from his wife's clan who had everyone talking after his moment with the Baptizer at the recent festival.

The laborer locked eyes with Simon as he passed, and with a slight smile, he nodded before he returned to the banquet hall and disappeared into the crowd.

Can he see my confusion? Read my thoughts? Simon returned his gaze to the servants drawing wine from the wash water, then toward the banquet hall, shaking his head all the while.

Simon wasn't sure how long he stood and pondered before returning to his wife's side at the table.

Chapter Two

Pain coursed through Matthew's leg, and comfort eluded him as he fidgeted on his stool. The seating—like everything else in the tax booth—was largely utilitarian. He shifted and extended his leg as far as the sore and stiff muscles would allow but found no relief. Even the tiniest movements stabbed at the inner workings of his knee.

All the toll takers were aware of the past week's robbery. When people awake to a murdered man on the road, it quickly becomes the news of the city. Still, Matthew tried to hide the extent of his injuries, fearing that he would be targeted again if he looked weak.

Walking with a crutch since that night, he made it a habit to arrive early to avoid being seen by too many of the day laborers. Lucian, his new personal guard, demanded a premium for the extra hours.

Matthew was grateful that Samchai ensured the booth had been reinforced with additional soldiery. *At least until Herod's administrators think the threat is gone.* Matthew could only hope that such a conclusion would be the result of an investigation. Maybe even a crucifixion or two.

The morning sun reflected off the lake as the fishermen returned to shore. Why they sometimes worked at night, Matthew didn't understand. He never cared to learn the intricacies of the trade, but he was here at the earliest part of the day so that he also would profit from whatever advantage they gained.

Two teams dragged their catch ashore and counted fish into their waiting carts. Matthew had seen the same scene hundreds of times, but he knew that today would be different.

The first team brought their cart past the toll booth on the way to the market. Matthew was familiar with these fishermen—a pair of brothers. Sons of Jonah of Bethsaida. He did not recognize the third man who accompanied them today.

The stranger was young but not youthful. His calloused hands and dust-crusted cloak suggested that his work was on the land, not on the sea.

"What is the count today?" Matthew asked.

"Only seventy," responded Andrew, the older of the brothers.

"So that will be one denarius."

"A full denarius?" the younger brother, named Simon, interjected. He was usually the more boisterous of the two. Matthew much preferred transacting with Andrew. "A week ago, you charged us half that when we were bringing in a catch of ninety! This is outrageous!"

Lucian took a small step forward, and Matthew appreciated the attentiveness. The guard's face was weathered and creased by a lifetime of service, but his stature had not suffered the impact of age. With a surge of boldness, Matthew sat as upright as he could without wincing.

"That was last week. Now, a denarius is the base rate. Surely, you've heard the news. These are troubled times. Officials in Tiberias have taken notice. Even they don't work for free."

"Don't make this about 'administration,'" Simon shot back. "It's clear you want to line your own purse. That's all you extortionists do!"

"Look around. You can see for yourself that there are more soldiers here. They need to eat, too!"

"So that's your angle! You find an opportunity to import a few thugs so that you can justify robbing us of our day's work!" The fisherman raised his voice and waved his arms dramatically toward Lucian as he carried on. "Maybe if these Romans would go back and find bread in their own countries, we would all have a little more."

Lucian took another step toward the trio, and one of the soldiers stationed at the storehouse approached.

Matthew was accustomed to these conversations, and his responses were well rehearsed. "I'm sure you don't want these men to have to justify their presence here, do you? A denarius is the price of peace in these difficult times."

"Peace?" The fisherman was shouting now, and Andrew grabbed his arm and pulled him back.

The stranger stepped in front of the brothers and approached the counter. Lucian neared within arm's reach of the newcomer and placed a hand on the hilt of his short blade.

"My friends have no desire to cheat anyone," the man said with measured calm in a Galilean accent. "We'll pay the denarius."

"Cheat?" The fisherman clearly wasn't done making his opinions known. "The only cheats here are the ones who hide behind the counter and these thugs!"

Lucian turned toward the brothers. The stranger did, too, holding up both hands. "Just pay him. We want to get on with our work," he said.

The stranger turned and addressed Matthew. "We'll pay what you've asked, and there won't be any further trouble." He reached out and placed a hand on Matthew shoulder.

Lucian unsheathed his dagger and knocked the man's arm away with the broad side of the blade. In that brief moment, a pulse that Matthew could not define coursed from his shoulder throughout his body. It was some kind of power, neither hot nor cold, just alive. Strength returned to his leg as pain dissipated from his knee. He moved his leg while trying to be discreet. No matter the angle, neither the pain nor the stiffness returned.

The stranger somehow ignored the soldier knocking his hand away. He offered no resistance and made no attempt to retaliate. "Be well, Matthew," he added.

How does he know me?

"Stand down, Lucian," Matthew finally said after taking in the moment. The older fisherman retrieved a coin from his purse and laid it on the counter. Matthew retrieved his ledger, a thin stone tablet coated in a layer of wax, from under the counter and recorded the payment while the trio proceeded to the market.

Lucian watched with unmoving intensity until they were out of sight.

―――――

"That wine at your wedding is all everyone is talking about," Thaddeus said as he and Simon loaded lumber onto a ship.

"I haven't been around to hear. What are they saying?"

"You've got to spend more time listening to the fishermen. They were all there. They said after the wine ran out, someone found more in the wash water jars."

"I remember—the banquet-master said something. I didn't really know what he was talking about. I just thought that was an odd place to store the wine," Simon responded.

"Some of the fishermen say there is another explanation," Thaddeus continued. "They said that the prophet they encountered at the Jordan River must have turned the water into wine."

"Prophet? You mean my wife's cousin? The one we saw with the Baptizer?"

"Yes! They said he worked a miracle."

Simon thought back to the wedding feast and recalled a mental image of the stranger in the back room and his knowing smile. "It doesn't make any sense. How can someone turn water into wine?"

"I don't know how it is possible," Thaddeus shook his head and hoisted a timber onto his shoulder, "but they say he was sent by God. All I know is they used those same jars to wash their hands when they entered the banquet, and there was only water in them at the time. Where else could the wine have come from?"

Simon hesitated as he considered the implications. "And you believe them?"

"I know it sounds crazy, but yes! I believe them. The scriptures tell of Moses, Elijah, and other prophets doing great signs. Why not a prophet in our time?"

Simon nodded, "Our time could use a prophet. The sooner the better. Look at us—breaking our backs to move this lumber carted here from Lebanon, going downriver to some rich man who has stolen up lands passed from father to son since the days of Joshua. And what do we—or any of our people—get besides tired bones and a coin purse subject to more imperial robbery?"

"Hello!" The voice came from behind Simon.

Simon's armful of lumber made it impossible for him to turn and answer. "This ship is at capacity. If you're looking for work, try the next dock."

"I'm not looking for work. I'm looking for you, Simon."

Simon's grip loosened, and his load started to slip. "I can't exactly step away."

"Of course. Meet me at the house of Simon Bar-Jonah, the fisherman, when you are done."

Simon stopped and set his end of the lumber down. He turned and watched the speaker leave. It was the now-familiar stranger from his wife's clan.

What could he possibly want with me?

"You're not getting paid to stand and gawk!" the worker at the other end of the log called. "Let's keep moving!"

Simon picked up his end and resumed carrying the load to the ship.

Beside him, Thaddeus said, "That was him! What did he say to you?"

"Only that he was looking for me."

"For what?"

"He didn't say."

———

After the workday, Simon walked an uneven, partially washed-out road along the shoreline past the active docks. He approached a half-sunken harbor—long ago abandoned to storm damage. He reached a teetering pier and climbed down a steep embankment. The sand had long since washed off the slope, exposing jagged rock. Once at the edge of the water, he stepped under the pier.

Manaen was waiting for him.

"With the festival coming, Quirinius will no doubt deploy additional troops to Jerusalem. It's time to finish the job we started here," Manaen said without a greeting. "Not just what we started, but what Judas Bar-Hezekiah started a generation ago."

"But Herod has stationed additional guards at the storehouse, and more soldiers are in the garrison," Simon answered.

"That's why we do nothing now; we wait until festival. You're good muscle, Simon, but you have much to learn about strategy. As long as we make Quirinius *think* there is no more threat here, he will override Herod's decision soon."

"How do we do that?" Simon asked.

"The less you know about that, the better, Simon. Just be ready."

"Of course. But there is one more thing," Simon continued.

"What is that?"

"Have you heard of a miracle worker arriving recently? His presence in Galilee might attract some untimely attention."

Manaen smiled, "I've not heard of any miracle workers, but perhaps I underestimated your acumen for strategy. If there is someone claiming to possess divine power, he might be of interest to Herod."

"What if his power is ... real?" Simon wished he could retract the words as soon as he said them.

"The pagans have their sorcerers, and they are all frauds. Judea has not seen a man of signs since the voice of God left our land hundreds of years ago. If we expect him to speak again, we must first drive out the Roman pigs."

Do I tell him about the wine?

"I understand," Simon said. "But you should know that this ... person has requested to meet with me."

"Good," Manaen added curtly. "You can find out more about how we might be able to use him as a distraction. And if for some reason there is any merit to the claim you have heard, he might be a useful addition to our cause."

─────

"I don't know how to explain it. I only know what happened!" Matthew paced the floor of his courtyard while Samchai sat and listened. He was grateful the tax farmer had decided to stay in Capernaum for a few days to oversee the implementation of additional security, but he remained frustrated with Samchai's dismissal of their best investigative lead yet.

"So let me see if I understand," Samchai said as he watched Matthew pace. "This stranger showed up, knew your name, and healed your injury?"

"Yes!"

"How did he do that?" Samchai asked.

"With a touch. I didn't ask for it or even expect it. He put his hand on my shoulder, and I was healed."

"But it was your leg that was injured. How did he heal your leg through your shoulder?"

"Again!" Matthew exaggerated his steps and flailed his arms. "I can't explain it, but that's what happened!"

"What you're describing sounds like a miracle, Matthew."

"I know it does. But look at me. You can see that I am walking well. Ask Lucian—he saw and heard the whole thing."

"Let's *say* that you are right." Samchai's emphasis on "say" was not lost on Matthew. "Suppose this man did somehow heal you miraculously. What makes you think he is the man who robbed you?"

"He knew my name even though he suddenly showed up in the city, just like the bandit addressed me by name. He must have known about my injury, too!" Matthew explained.

"The crutch under your arm could have given that much away," Samchai challenged him.

"I was seated at the time. He wouldn't have seen the crutch."

"You don't know what he did and did not see." Samchai held up a finger. "But suppose, for argument's sake, this was a genuine miracle. It still doesn't answer the question: Why would the man who robbed you want to heal you?"

Matthew threw his hands in the air. "I don't know! Maybe to make me think I can trust him. Or so he can get close enough to try an even bigger robbery. Motives and such are things for the administrators to figure out. But the two events are close enough together that it can't be coincidence!"

"Well, before I go back to Herod's office with wild speculative ideas, let's see if this new tighter grip on Galilee prompts him to say or do anything more. We'll need solid evidence before I can make a case to Herod."

"Of course," Matthew said with a nod and a sigh.

Samchai stood and exited the courtyard.

———

The slightest sunlight remained in the evening sky when Simon reached the fisherman's house. A woman tended a cooking pot in a shared courtyard. "You must be here to see the teacher," she said when she saw Simon.

"Teacher?"

"Jesus. The one from Nazareth. He is expecting you." The woman led Simon through the doorway into a small common room. The enigmatic stranger sat with a handful of local fishermen — all familiar to Simon. Thaddeus was also with them, and the young man stood and greeted Simon when he entered.

"I'm glad you decided to join us," Jesus said as Simon took a seat. "We were just discussing plans to go to Jerusalem for the upcoming Passover feast. You should come with us."

"Jerusalem? I made the pilgrimage for Tabernacles. And now, with a new wife, it's too soon for another trip. As much as I want to honor our traditions, the law allows me to stay here."

"If you're worried about bandits on the way, I'm sure our numbers alone will be enough to keep them away," Jesus responded.

Simon was stilled by his words. *Why bring up bandits?*

"Your wife can stay with my family while we are gone," the host fisherman — also named Simon — interjected.

"Why me?" Simon directed his question toward Jesus.

"Do you not want to see the kingdom of God?" Jesus asked.

How much does this man know about me? And how does he know it?

Simon spoke with caution. "I hear the temple is corrupted. And with the Roman occupation, Jerusalem hardly resembles the glory that filled it in the days of David and Solomon."

Jesus smiled, "I was not wrong about your passion. Besides, Simon, we should travel together since we are family now."

"Yes, I saw you at my wedding feast. I'm told you are my wife's cousin!," Simon paused.

Jesus didn't answer. He regarded Simon with open eyes and a straight face, as if waiting for him to say more.

"They say you are responsible for the wine," Simon added.

Jesus smiled again, more fully. "So you'll accompany us to Jerusalem, then?"

"How did you do that? The wine, that is." It was Simon's turn to be evasive.

"We saw the power of God descend on him in the Jordan," Andrew said. "I've never seen anything like it!"

"You have a lot of questions, Simon. If you come with us, you'll start to get the answers you're looking for," Jesus added.

Simon felt the words as much as heard them. *There is more to this man than the wine trick.* Somehow this Jesus knew Simon's deepest questions — perhaps better than Simon knew them himself.

The need to understand what Jesus knew overwhelmed Simon. "I'll go with you to Jerusalem."

Chapter Three

Two days into their walk, Simon and his companions found themselves deep in Samaria. Despite Simon's objections against going through Samaritan lands, Jesus had insisted on taking a direct route.

Among the less-than-dozen men in their party, they had only two donkeys to share the group's burdens. The consensus was to choose a route with shorter travel and less climbing.

Simon understood the logic but only reluctantly agreed. He was still unsure what to make of Jesus and his sudden appearance in Galilee, so he remained doubly alert as they traveled through hostile — *and unclean* — territory. He walked at the back of the group alongside Thaddeus.

"Your sword is sheathed and ready, right?" Simon asked in a near-whisper.

"Are you expecting trouble?" Thaddeus asked.

"We're in a nation of bastards. The better question might be: Aren't *you* expecting trouble?"

"This is just a pilgrimage. Who would see us as a threat?"

"Do you ever wonder if that is part of the problem?" Simon pressed.

"What do you mean?"

"I mean our people are too complacent. The Romans trample us underfoot, and even the priests don't speak out against it. Herod's a fraud — more desperate to prove his loyalty to Rome than to lead our nation. I'm done being crushed, and I'm doing something about it. You should join me, Thaddeus."

"Is that why you think Jesus called us on this trip?" Thaddeus asked.

"No. But it's why I'm here. The movement has already begun, and you can be a part of it. But I need to see if there is something to the power you say Jesus possesses."

"Well, you know about the wine; you were there," Thaddeus added. "And you saw what happened when Jesus went to the Baptizer."

The sound of approaching footfalls snared Simon's attention. The group had entered a rare shaded area under a rocky crag that rose above a small stretch of miles-long ridge. Now, with their small party hemmed in front and back, men descended from the slope before and behind them.

Simon turned and produced a dagger from his sleeve as two raiders neared. Linen wrapped their faces, leaving only their eyes visible. They were armed with short swords—not much larger than Simon's own blade. Thaddeus wielded a large knife—well worn from daily use, more a tool than a weapon.

The bandit nearest Simon swung his blade in a high arc. Simon ducked under the swipe and pierced the man's side with his own weapon. The marauder yelled and stumbled backward. Simon climbed on top of him and grabbed his sword hand. He smashed the man's arm into the rocky ground until his weapon dropped free. Simon retrieved the blade and stood, holding the man's own sword to his face.

"Let him go," a voice said from behind Simon. He turned to find Jesus—with the rest of the party gathered around him.

"There were more. Where did they go?" Simon asked.

"They retreated on their own. This one couldn't since he is hurt." Jesus reached a hand to the bandit. The man took his hand, and Jesus pulled him to his feet. The bandit rubbed his side beneath his right arm, where Simon had pierced him.

He was not bleeding.

"Simon," Jesus continued, "you have something that belongs to him."

Simon looked down at the blade, then up at Jesus. "These men are dogs, and they *attacked* us like wild dogs! Why should we let them go?"

"You want to see the kingdom of God, Simon? Listen and learn. Give this man back his sword. He won't be any further trouble."

Simon looked from Jesus to the bandit. The Samaritan's eyes reflected Simon's own confusion as he held out a hand. Simon turned the sword and offered him the hilt. The attacker took it and ran up the slope, disappearing behind the crag.

Simon stayed in the rear as they resumed walking. *So much for recruiting him to the cause ...*

"We learned more about this ... healer you told me about. I'm afraid there is no reason to inquire any further about him," Samchai said.

"No reason?" Matthew asked. "What do you mean?"

"They've already left for the festival, so we couldn't examine him directly. But under the auspices of taxation and census, I was able to get enough information from the wives of his companions. Apparently, he is a builder from Nazareth. He is probably in the city to find work."

"What's his connection to the fishermen? They are a loud rabble, and I don't trust them."

"There is much show and bravado in their grand protestation, but they always pay, do they not?" Samchai countered. "From what my sources say, they are all disciples of the Baptizer from Judea. He is not known to be a threat—just a zealous teacher calling people to repent."

His sources are women who would not be permitted to testify. How did he shake them down for information? "So that is it?" Matthew stood and threw his arms out wide.

"Yes." Samchai remained seated. "Don't be so surprised, Matthew. This is probably little more than a petty thief. It is not the sort of thing that Herod will put any more resources into."

"That's easy for him to say." Matthew's volume rose. "He wasn't the one who almost lost his life!"

"You're much more effective when you are negotiating. These outbursts do not suit you, as I've said before. Especially at your booth. As for me, my task here is done, and I will be returning to Tiberias." Samchai stood and strode toward the door. He turned and added, "I look forward to a return to normalcy here."

———

The temple shone brilliantly in the midday sun. Still, the grandeur of the Lord's dwelling place could not hide the blemishes that caught Simon's eye as they entered Jerusalem from the west. The palace, though not as grand as the temple, rose with opulence over the gate where they entered—a visible reminder of Rome's presence, further accented by guards who patrolled the parapets, the gate tower, and every other high point in the city.

The Antonia Fortress, where Rome garrisoned its soldiers in Jerusalem, braced the near corner of the temple court, adding to Simon's disgust. *Even the most sacred place in all the world is infested.*

Two of their party, John and Simon the fisherman, had gone ahead into the city to secure lodging. Simon couldn't remember ever seeing a crowd of this size, and he hoped that they would not be forced to spend their nights beyond the city walls.

The pair returned as they walked along the north wall toward the temple. "We've arranged a room in the Galilean quarter. It's good that we arrived early," John said.

"Thank you," Jesus replied.

Reunited, the group crossed the city to the temple steps. They passed under an archway and stepped onto the sprawling outer court. Roman soldiers patrolled overhead, walking along the porticoes accessible from their fortress.

Someday, we will topple this eyesore and rid the temple of its defiling blight.

"This way," Jesus said, drawing Simon's attention back to the ground level, where hundreds of people moved aimlessly in all directions.

They crossed to the far side of the outer court, seeing cattle tethered and sheep corralled in makeshift pens. The gate behind them was open, revealing more livestock on the pastures outside the temple walls.

Simon appreciated that despite the Roman occupation, the law was still alive and in practice. *It will be good to offer a proper Passover sacrifice.*

He had barely taken in the scene when Jesus started flailing a whip at the animals and their handlers. Sheep knocked their pen loose and funneled toward the gate while cattle pulled at their reins. "Get these out of here!" Jesus shouted as he rattled a cage of doves.

Merchants collided as they pushed away. Jesus toppled the table of a money changer, sending Roman denarii and Judean shekels alike across the stone floor in a hopelessly mingled mess.

"How dare you turn my Father's house into a thieving market!" he shouted as he continued to lash his whip.

Just when I thought he was averse to even the most necessary violence ...

The crowd pushed out of reach of the untamed whip while scholars and Pharisees — meticulous and outspoken defenders of Jewish laws and traditions — forced their way into the cleared circle from the colonnades.

"By what authority do you do all of this?" one shouted as he burst into view, adorned in all the customary accessories of the Pharisees, each piece steeped in tradition — phylacteries bound to his wrists and forehead, a blue mantle draped over his head and shoulders, tassels on his hem brushing the floor. "What sign can you show us?"

Jesus continued to usher the livestock toward the gate. Without looking back at his challengers, he responded, "Destroy this temple, and I will raise it again in three days."

"It took Herod the Great a lifetime to build all of this!" came a voice from the crowd. "How can you do it in only three days?"

Simon ducked under the flailing whip and got close enough to grab Jesus. "We need to get out of here. The walls have eyes, and these thugs will not hesitate to quell this mess hard. Think about this."

"Who are you?" came another shout from the crowd. "Where are you from?"

The last of the animals exited the temple court while money changers and visitors scoured the floor for fallen coins.

A loud wail rose from the ground only a few meters away. Simon turned toward the scream. A young boy in a simple tunic struggled in vain to pull his arm out from under a merchant's boot.

The boy opened his hand, and a fistful of coins fell to the ground. The man who had him pinned lifted his foot, and the boy rolled to the side. Jesus yanked himself free from Simon and picked the boy up. His arm fell at an unnatural angle at his side. Jesus placed his hand over the boy's arm, and the twisted expression on the boy's face settled into calm, then relief, then wonder. Jesus let go, and the boy gawked at his arm, then up at Jesus.

Simon grabbed Jesus' sleeve. "It will only get worse—for them and for us—if we stay and wait for the Romans to sort out this mess," he said. "We need to go *now!*"

The others joined them, and John said, "I'll show you where we are staying, assuming we are still welcome."

They crossed the temple court and exited under the arch. Simon looked back and spotted a small group of people pointing and following. Over the bustle of the crowd, he heard exclamations of "healer" and "miracle worker" even as he himself pondered the meaning of all that he had seen.

A group of teachers also stood by, watching them silently as they left.

———

With the festival week underway in Jerusalem, the bustle of Capernaum had quieted. Matthew still had a full day's work at the toll booth, but he had enough time to think.

About his harrowing robbery experience.

About the stranger who arrived right after.

About the miraculous healing of his knee.

According to Samchai's officials, the new arrival had gone to Jerusalem with some local laborers.

No doubt funding their excursion with my *coin.*

Still, he welcomed the reprieve. It afforded him time to recover his losses and ensure that Lucian was well compensated for his work. The guard was proving to be loyal, diligent, and alert.

At mid-morning, two fisherman wheeled a cart bearing the day's catch past the toll booth.

"Declaration?" Matthew asked as he picked up his stylus.

"Sixty," one fisherman answered.

Matthew started to scratch the number into a wax tablet, then stopped. He stood and peered at the cart. It was laden almost to capacity with larger-than-average fish.

"I would have expected a greater haul than sixty. You practically have the whole lake to yourself," Matthew said in a level tone.

Lucian positioned himself over the cart and gently moved the fish around with the tip of his knife.

Matthew stared silently at the fisherman.

"You're right," the fisherman said. "It's actually seventy-five."

"And they're some healthy-looking fish!" Lucian added while still poking at the pile.

"Well, for trying to evade fair payment of your due, your entire profit today is forfeit."

"You can't do that!" the fisherman pleaded as a look of dread washed over his face. "My children get half the bread they should since these new rates have begun. I just want to get enough to feed my family. Please! You must reconsider!"

Another guard approached the commotion.

"We all need to eat, too." Matthew said with a dismissive shrug as he gestured toward the guards.

"You look like you could do with a little less!" the fisherman said through a scowl. "These swine shouldn't even be here! If you would just—oof!"

Lucian's fist met the man's gut. He picked up the fisherman and shoved him toward another guard. "Take him to the garrison. We'll deal with him later."

The guard called to another, and together they led the still-hunched-over man toward the city gate.

The second fisherman, visibly younger than the first — possibly a son — stood silent and motionless as he looked wide-eyed at Matthew.

"Assuming there is no further protest, Lucian will see you to the market. And I remind you that your earnings today are forfeit."

The young man nodded and struggled against the weight of his cart as he slowly pushed it toward the town center.

"What is going on here?" called a man as two Pharisees, Hananai and Yoezer, approached. Matthew knew them well, as did all of Capernaum. Hananai spoke for the pair. "What authority do you have to arrest that man?"

"He defied a lawful order, issued by the authority of Herod's office."

"The only one who defies the law here is you. No, you don't just defy. You *defile*! There would be no Herod, no Romans, no pagan stain on our land if it weren't for you and your kind."

"If you are such an authority on the law, why are you not at the festival?"

"At this distance, the law does not compel our pilgrimage. We go when we can afford it, which has been more difficult since traitors like you have plundered your own people."

The word struck a nerve that Matthew couldn't identify. "What do you know of *plundering* people? What do you know of what I have suffered?"

"Sir?" Lucian had returned, no doubt hastened by the sound of a fresh confrontation.

"All is fine here, Lucian. These men were just leaving."

"It is you who should leave. Straight to the pit, you unredeemable traitor!" the Pharisees turned and left.

Matthew watched until they were out of view. The confrontations could have been worse. Much worse. Still, they left him more unsettled than ever.

———

Even after three days together in Jerusalem, Simon struggled to understand Jesus. There hadn't been another scene like the one with the money changers, but word of his healings began to spread. Each day it seemed more people were coming to him. As he sat with the teachers and the elders in the colonnades, he proved as insightful as the most learned scholars.

Now, on the third evening, Simon finally had an opportunity to approach Jesus alone. The others had retired to their mats, and Jesus sat by the lantern light in the common room of their hostel.

"May I speak with you?" Simon asked.

"Of course, Simon," Jesus responded.

"You often speak about the kingdom of God. And it's clear that you possess a certain ... power. Have you thought about how you might use this power?"

"What do you mean?"

"The times are evil. I believe that the Lord is preparing to break his silence and restore his kingdom. You've even said so. Will you join us?"

Jesus smiled slightly, with a look of great understanding on his face. Simon leaned in closer.

"Simon. Why do you think I've been sent by my father?"

His father? "You've come to restore the kingdom of Israel, right? To see the Romans out of the land and a son of David on Jerusalem's throne."

"The power you've seen is the power my father has given me. Just as my mission is to do his will."

"His will? To restore the kingdom, right?" Simon's heart sank. *Why is Jesus evading the answer?*

"The kingdom of God is not like the kingdoms of this world, Simon."

"I don't understand."

A man stepped into the common room from outside. "He's in here!" the man said, then promptly exited. A second man stepped through the doorway—clearly a Pharisee. A mantle adorned with flowing blue fringes rested on his head, and phylacteries were bound to his forehead and wrists. Simon had seen him seated among the most prominent teachers in the temple. His presence made Simon apprehensive.

"Teacher, I'm glad I found you. I've seen your signs and heard your teaching, and I would like to ask you more. We know by your signs that you have come from God. You couldn't perform these miracles without him."

"Who do you mean by 'we'?" Simon asked.

"I am one of the Sanhedrin. My name is Nicodemus."

The highest governing body in the temple. In all of Jerusalem. Simon felt the full weight of his error and stood. "I'm sorry. I will leave you to converse."

He had barely turned when Jesus responded, "Please stay, Simon. You should listen, too."

Simon turned, and Jesus gestured toward his seat. Without a word, Simon sat back down.

Two of the fishermen—John and James—entered from the bedchamber, visibly awakened. They sat, and Simon shook with agitation, wondering if he might get an opportunity to return to his own unfinished inquiry.

"I tell you the truth," Jesus said to Nicodemus. "No one can see the kingdom of God unless he is born again."

"How can that be?" Nicodemus articulated the question that was on Simon's own mind.

"Flesh gives birth to flesh, but spirit gives birth to spirit." Jesus responded.

Simon studied the Pharisee's face and saw the same confusion that he felt. *If a trained teacher can't figure Jesus out, how can I?*

"How can this be?" the Pharisee pressed. There was no challenge in his voice, only sincerity.

"You are Israel's teacher," Jesus answered. "Do you not understand?"

Simon looked to the fishermen, who didn't show any signs of comprehension either. Jesus, whatever his ideas were, would not be easily won over to the cause, though for reasons that Simon could not understand.

Still, the man's power was convincing, and that made him compelling even if his words were beyond Simon's grasp.

"... No one has gone into heaven except the one who came from heaven." Jesus was still speaking.

Why would he say such a thing? Simon tried to clear his mind and focus on the words that filled the room and captivated even the Pharisee.

"... God didn't send his son into the world to condemn the world, but to save the world through him ..."

Is that why he said "father" earlier? What claim is he making?

Simon threaded the strands of thought together. *If Jesus means to save the world, then he means to take on Caesar.* It was clear then that he would never join Simon's movement.

He came to lead a movement.

"... Light has come into the world ..."

Yes. Simon finally saw the truth.

"... Whoever lives by the truth comes into the light ..."

Simon knew what to do next. As soon as they returned to Galilee, he would seek out Manaen and tell him about what—rather who—he has found!

Chapter Four

Matthew stepped from his sleeping quarters to his receiving room. He was surprised to see someone seated there waiting for him. The man was very thin—almost gaunt. A simple stained cloak, threadbare at the elbows, hung loosely on his shoulders. His hair was tangled and unkempt. Clearly it had been some time since the visitor had a proper bath.

When the man turned his face to greet him, Matthew recognized him at once.

The man stood, and Matthew endured the unpleasant odor long enough to greet him with an embrace and a kiss.

"Brother," he said. "I am surprised that you would come here. I thought you would have made a home by the Dead Sea by now."

"Poke fun all you like, Matthew. The Essenes are wise in their own way. Much wiser than any Herodian. But one far greater than them—and us—compels my presence here."

"So you've come back the same way you left then, James? To condemn me for my station in society?"

"I've forsaken the luxuries of wealth and status." James stared emotionless into Matthew's eyes. "I've seen their power to defile the heart. But as I said, I've encountered a teacher the likes of whom we've not known since the days of Elijah."

"If it is the Baptizer that you speak of, word of him has already reached Galilee—with little reaction. Just another wild preacher who will no doubt end up isolating in the desert with like-minded people."

"You are far too worldly for your own good, Matthew, choosing expedience over truth, trying to buy your way into a society that will never truly be your own. Someday, the Lord will bring you to account. But to be honest, yes, I paid attention to the Baptizer. And if you had as well, you would know that even he spoke of a greater teacher to come. That teacher has now come, and he is the one I follow."

"And you think I, too, should follow this new … junior baptizer?"

"It is not accurate to call him a baptizer, too. He is much more. I saw when he came up from the Jordan how the heavens opened for him. Such a spectacle can't even be seen above our temple! He heals. And he teaches with such authority and wisdom that makes even the scribes and the priests awestruck. Even more strange, he's Galilean. He's returning from the festival as we speak. I made haste to get here so you might accompany me to the river to see for yourself."

A healer and a Galilean? Could it be ...? Matthew took pains to control his expression.

"James, I saw the Baptizer. I recall an unseasonable moment of thunder and lightning and thought nothing of it at the time. Still, I believe you are sincere in your hope. But suppose I meet this ... teacher, you call him ... Then what? I return to my duties; you return to your life of asceticism. What has really changed, except we've wasted time and lost revenue?"

"If your purse is what motivates you, then you are right," James responded. "Nothing will change. But I would not have come all this way to reach you if I thought this a waste to you. So will you at least give me the honor of accepting my invitation and come see this man for yourself?"

Matthew did not try to hide the smile that played across his face as he clasped his brother's shoulders. "You and I have made different choices, James, and we've led very different lives. Still, our father's penchant for persuasiveness did not pass you by. I'll meet this curious teacher."

Even as the words left his mouth, Matthew couldn't rid himself of the thought that this teacher might not be so unfamiliar to him.

Simon was grateful the return trip didn't pass through Samaria. He wasn't worried about his capacity to dispatch bandits as needed—even over the objections of Jesus. He was simply relieved not to have to enter such a defiled land.

They had traveled north on the far side of the Jordan as the cleansing waters of the river flowed between them and Samaria. They awoke in the small Perean village where they had sheltered overnight.

"Let's go to the river and baptize the people before we continue," Andrew said. The fishermen made a habit of following the practices of John the Baptizer, who had traveled with them for a time before going ahead of them.

"I agree. The people are eager," the fisherman's brother responded.

Simon looked around. "Where is Jesus? Is he still with us?" he asked.

"No." Andrew answered. "He left to return to Galilee. He followed the wadi." Andrew pointed to a valley on the far side of the river.

"We have to reach him!" Simon said. "He shouldn't be going through Samaria alone."

"Did you not see how he handled himself with the money changers?" Andrew answered. "He will be fine for the day while we baptize. We'll meet him by nightfall."

"The temple and the Samaritan wilderness are worlds apart," Simon pressed.

"Just a couple of hours, Simon. We aren't going to be far behind him."

Simon nodded and did not argue further. The idea that Jesus was vulnerable to their enemies was in his words, but Simon's real question remained unspoken. Jesus clearly didn't share his disdain for the Samaritans. *What if he is soft about Rome, too?* Simon had to be sure where Jesus stood to convince Manaen he was the messiah.

More importantly, he had to convince himself.

———

"We've been walking well over a day, and we're almost out of Galilee. This better be worth my time," Matthew scolded his brother as they approached the Jordan River. Lucian followed silently behind them.

Matthew and James reached the water's edge. A village sat just around a bend to the south, where a crowd gathered on the banks. Drenched people came up from the river below.

As they neared the crowd, the calls from the river grew clearer. "Produce fruit in keeping with repentance. A tree that does not produce fruit will be cut down and thrown into the fire!"

"This is the teacher you told me about?" Matthew asked. "He doesn't sound like a healer."

James stretched his neck to get a better view. "No, that is the Baptizer. I do not see the teacher."

The man in the river looked at them with wild eyes, his tangled, wet hair pushed back from his face. "You've come out from the cities to repent! Confess your sins and be baptized."

"Where is the other one? The one they call the Nazarene?" James shouted to the Baptizer.

"He has gone ahead to Galilee. While you are here, let the waters of repentance cover you."

"Repentance?" Matthew asked. "We are honorable public servants. What more must we do?"

"Public servant? A toll taker? You must not collect more than is required. As for this one," the Baptizer pointed toward Lucian, "avoid extortion and false accusation. Be content with your pay."

Matthew turned to James, "You brought me all this way to hear this? How can I pay Lucian, let alone pay my own expenses, if I collect only what Herod mandates? I would become poor myself!"

"You appeal to the word of Herod?" The Baptizer must have heard Matthew's objection. "By his greed, he extorts the people, just as by his selfish lust, he stole his own brother's wife. Turn from his evil ways and be washed in repentance."

"Sir, I could arrest him now," Lucian said to Matthew. "We are still in Galilee, and this man speaks against our king."

Matthew stood still as conflict stirred in his abdomen. "I should not have made this trip. Let's lodge in the village and return in the morning."

He turned toward the town without responding—or even acknowledging the Baptizer with a glance.

———

After a day's work, Simon walked the shore beyond Capernaum. A man emerged from the evening shadows and walked alongside him.

"I received your note," Manaen said. "You have news from Jerusalem?"

"It's that healer I told you about."

"I heard he made a scene in the temple courts."

"That news has reached you?" Simon's head jerked as he spoke.

"Our eyes and ears go far and wide. But the important matter is, were you able to win him to our cause?"

Simon searched for words. "We ... spoke. He knows the scriptures, but his passions are strange."

"So is he one of us or is he not?" Manaen did not hide his impatience.

"He speaks of the kingdom of God, but when I ask about it, he answers in riddles. Still, there is no denying his knowledge and power. He seems much more content to lead than to follow."

"Are you suggesting we step aside and let him take command?"

"If he is the messiah—" Simon began.

"That is a big 'if,' Simon—and a bold claim." Manaen stopped and faced Simon. "You might not be seeing clearly. We are too keenly aware of the corruption in the Sanhedrin, particularly among the Sadducees. But this man's stunt in the temple is likely to win him enemies among the Sadducees and Pharisees alike. And quite a few of the latter are ... sympathetic to our cause, if you take my meaning."

"I'm not sure I do."

"He has attacked the temple, but has he spoken out against Rome? I think you can understand our reluctance to count him a friend over an enemy. He is certainly no ally."

"But his power is—"

"His power is something we will deal with if it comes to that. Unless he decides to use it for the cause."

"Are you saying—"

"Let me make it clear, Simon. This man could fade into nothing, as so many others have. Or he could become a threat if he makes too many of the wrong enemies. It's too early to tell. But one thing is certain: We need to keep a close eye on him." Manaen clasped Simon's shoulders and looked directly into his eyes as he spoke.

Simon nodded in silence.

"You called for me?" Matthew asked as he entered the quarters of the garrison's captain.

"Yes," the captain responded, "Lucian reported the incident with the riverside preacher, as was his duty."

Matthew sat down. "And?" he asked.

"I've sent word to Herod. I trust he will be interested to question this preacher himself."

"Then why summon me?" Matthew asked.

"To corroborate Lucian's report. This Baptizer did speak against the king, did he not?"

Matthew thought of his brother's simple but sincere life choice. He thought about his disappointing failure to find the other teacher—the Nazarene healer.

But most of all, he thought about the Baptizer's words. *Have I been wrong all this time?*

He couldn't deny Lucian's account without suffering his own consequences. He chose his words carefully.

"The man expressed ... opinions freely. But just opinions. I heard no call to arms, no hint of rebellion."

The captain nodded. "Very well. We can take this to Herod's officials so they can present their findings. Follow me."

They left the quarters and walked to the more comfortably appointed manor house. It came nowhere near the splendor of the palaces in Sepphoris and Tiberias, but it provided more dignity to Herod's administrators than a utilitarian military outpost.

The captain led Matthew into the receiving room, while a servant rushed from an adjoining room to meet them.

"Cuza is not here," the servant said.

"When will he return?" the captain asked.

"I cannot say. He left in haste last evening. His son fell ill, and he went straightaway to find the healer who all of Galilee has been talking about. He heard that he might be in Cana and did not want to risk losing a day — for his son's sake."

Healer? Could it be ...

"When he returns, have him summon the publican, Matthew." The centurion indicated him with a nod. "He has more information about the Baptizer."

A young boy — about ten years old — emerged from the same adjoining room as the servant had.

"Is my father here?" the boy asked the servant.

"He has gone out to find the healer."

"I am well now. He does not need to find the healer."

"You were bedridden with a fever not even an hour ago!"

"And now it is gone. I can't explain it. I feel fine."

"Apologies," the servant addressed the captain. "I will relay your message to Cuza when he returns."

"Thank you." The captain turned to leave.

Matthew followed, his thoughts on the healer and the boy.

Chapter Five

Matthew sat at the tax collector's booth as the morning sun rose above the eastern mountains and brightened the lake. The day laborers had been processed, and now he waited for the night fishermen to return.

A man in a dyed and embroidered cloak approached from the gate, accompanied by the captain Matthew had met the day before. "You are the publican I was advised to meet. I hear that you encountered the Baptizer on the river?"

This must be Cuza.

"He spoke freely," Matthew began, then recounted what he had previously told the captain.

"I'm sure Herod will summon you should you need to testify at trial," the official said.

"Trial?" Matthew questioned.

"Of course. The Baptizer will have his chance to answer to Herod for what he has said. You should know that your report isn't the first," the official explained.

Matthew nodded, even as doubt tugged at his mind. *What makes this man such a threat? What is the official not sharing?* "Of course. I trust your son is well, then?"

Cuza had already turned toward the gate but hesitated at Matthew's words. "He is well, yes. Thanks to the healer."

"That's good to hear."

"You were there, right?" All formality evaporated as the official leaned on Matthew's table and his face brightened. "You were there when my son became well?"

"I did see him, yes."

"Do you recall what part of the day?"

Matthew paused a moment, then answered, "About the seventh hour, I think."

"It is true then! That is when I found the healer. He said my son would be well, and it was true, just as he said it!"

"This healer, do you know where he is now?" Matthew asked.

"He is coming to Capernaum. I thought he might have even arrived by now."

As they spoke, a toll collector at the adjacent booth motioned to a guard, who stepped into the path of a new arrival. "You're late, don't you think?" the toll collector told him. "All of the labor has been hired out."

"I'm not here to seek work. I've only come for my friends," the newcomer said.

The familiar voice registered, and Matthew quickly turned to see the Nazarene who had healed his injured knee. The man smiled knowingly at Matthew.

Speechless, Matthew was relieved when the Herodian administrator spoke first.

"My son is well, just as you said he would be! Thanks be to God!" the man said as he embraced the newcomer. "Have you come to heal others?"

"I've come because the kingdom of God is near," the healer said. He turned toward Matthew, smiled, and added, "There is much work to be done."

Then the Nazarene walked toward the shore as Matthew watched wordlessly.

―――――

"Look who's back!" Thaddeus said to Simon as they loaded sacks onto a small merchant ship.

Simon turned to see Jesus look their way and smile. He walked past the docks and approached the fishermen who had gone with them to Jerusalem as they tended their nets on the shore.

"You haven't said much since we returned," Thaddeus continued. "What do you think of him?"

Simon considered the question—and his assignment from Manaen. "He has given us a lot to think about."

"What do you mean?"

"I'm still trying to figure him out. He stopped us from harming the bandits in Samaria, but he wreaked havoc in the temple courts. Don't you find him confusing?"

"Sure, but what about the people who he's healed and the way he teaches? I'm sure it will all make sense if we watch and listen long enough." Thaddeus held out a hand toward the fishermen and said, "They seem to think so."

A crowd of townspeople stood around Jesus on the shore. Jesus got into a fishing boat and the brothers Andrew and Simon joined him, pushed out from the shore, and climbed into the boat with him. The people pressed closer to edge of the water.

"But what is he going to do with all of these people?" Simon watched Jesus and the crowd from the dock as he continued, "They're hardly the kind one would recruit for an army. Even if they were, does Jesus even seem to want an army?"

"Why would he need an army?" Thaddeus asked.

"Think about it," Simon said. "He keeps talking about the kingdom of God. How else does he expect to establish a kingdom? Herod and the Romans aren't going to leave without a fight."

"Is that why you follow him? To take up arms?"

"I will gladly do what it takes to rid our land of foreign rulers. If Jesus is the man to make that happen, I will be ready." Simon continued.

"But you said you aren't sure about his intentions," Thaddeus countered. "What if he doesn't raise an army? Then what will you do? You can't deny his miracles."

Simon watched the crowd disperse while the fishermen — accompanied by Jesus — rowed toward deeper waters. "Miracles or not, if he doesn't raise an army, someone will."

Thaddeus didn't respond, and Simon wasn't sure what to make of his friend's silence. *It's probably not a good time to suggest that Thaddeus meet Manaen.*

Weighing even heaver on Simon's mind was the fact that he was not any closer to figuring out Jesus' plan. He had nothing new to report to Manaen. He returned to his work: lifting sacks, moving sacks, dropping sacks. The activity did nothing to keep his mind from wrestling with the self-contradiction that Jesus represented.

A clamor rose on the lake, and the fishermen on shore hurried to their boat and pushed out. Against the high mid-morning sun, Simon could barely see what was happening. As best as he could tell, the first boat was close to capsizing.

"Leaky boat?"

Thaddeus turned and shielded his eyes. "Hard to say. Not much we can do from here, but the others should reach them in time."

The second boat came alongside the first, and all hands from both vessels struggled against the nets between them.

"They must have snagged a rock," Simon said.

Thaddeus continued to shield his eyes, "Or a big catch."

Simon shielded his own eyes and allowed them to adjust. Beyond the glare on the water, the fishermen were hauling in a big catch while both boats sank close to the water line.

The fishermen struggled as they pressed their oars and slowly pushed toward the shore.

"Should we go see what is happening?" Thaddeus asked.

Simon peered at the cart full of sacks yet to be loaded. "If we work quickly, we can be done before they get to shore. They aren't moving fast."

Simon lifted sacks and moved his feet with a surge of new strength. Where this vigor came from, he wasn't sure, but he gave it little thought as he and Thaddeus briskly completed the loading. By the time they finished, other workers were already hurrying off the docks toward where the fishermen stood in waist-deep water, pulling their vessels to shore, each boat requiring all their strength.

One fisherman collapsed. Simon got closer and peered through the crowd. The man was unhurt, kneeling in front of Jesus.

"Don't be afraid," Jesus said to him. "From now on, you will be fishers of men."

Thaddeus said to Simon, "What do you think he means by that?"

"I don't know," Simon answered. "But I need to find out."

———

James approached the tax booth, looking as unwashed as he did when he unexpectedly showed up in Matthew's house.

"You've come back, brother," Matthew greeted him.

"The teacher has made his home here, so this is my home now, too."

"So you come to me for hospitality?"

"Matthew, I have no need for comfort. I would rather sleep on my teacher's doorstep in the rain than be far away from him in a soft bed by a warm fire."

"He really has made that much of a difference to you, James?"

"You know that I forsook comfort long ago, when I first saw the corruption that it brings." James paused, but Matthew ignored the slight and waited for him to continue. "Now I am certain that I was right to do so. There is nothing left to hold me back from the coming kingdom. Clearly, I am not alone in my thinking." James pointed toward the shoreline. "There he is—Jesus. Look how the people follow him."

Matthew heard the din of the crowd before he turned to look. When he did, his eyes confirmed what his ears already told him.

At least two dozen people swarmed around Jesus, walking beside him. They appeared to be peasants; some of them walking with crutches, all of them joyous.

When Jesus and the crowd reached the tax booth, he greeted James with the familiar embrace of a brother. He turned to Matthew. "It is good to see you again. My friends are in need of another cart. Do you have one to spare?"

Lucian stepped toward Jesus, and Matthew held up a hand. The guard paused where he stood.

"Our carts are for official use only," Matthew answered. "Do your friends not have their own?"

"What use could be more official than the coming kingdom of heaven?" Jesus answered.

"I don't understand."

"In time you will, Matthew." Jesus smiled, and Matthew detected no deceit, only warmth. "The kingdom is near."

Matthew waited for Jesus to continue, but he didn't, so Matthew countered, "How does a cart help? You can't put a kingdom on a cart."

"But you *can* put an abundant catch on a cart. My friends cannot fit the day's haul on their own carts, so they need some help."

"How abundant?"

"Over two hundred fish."

"That's impossible! A good day isn't even half of that."

"Let us use your cart, so you can see for yourself and believe," Jesus continued.

The people around Jesus shouted at Matthew.

"It's true!"

"I saw them myself!"

"Too bad you'll just tax it all away from them."

Lucian looked to Matthew, his expression silently seeking further instruction.

"Leave their chatter alone and bring them the cart."

Lucian turned and went into the storehouse. A moment later, he emerged with the cart. Jesus wheeled it toward the shore just as the fisherman came up pushing two other carts stacked higher than should be possible with fish.

Matthew started a new record on his wax tablet. "This should be a prosperous day for all of us."

"You wouldn't punish us for a good catch, would you?" the fisherman who Matthew knew as Simon protested.

"It's simple math, really. Your license fee, plus a percentage of the catch. Seeing as you have the catch of eight teams here, it is reasonable to calculate your license fee accordingly." Matthew wasn't sure this was his best argument, but years of negotiation had led him to develop creative calculations.

"That's not fair at all!" the fisherman grew louder and waved his arms. "There are not eight teams here, just two that had a good day. We refuse to be extorted."

Lucian stepped closer, and a young man behind the fishermen pushed between them to the front.

Matthew recognized him as a dock worker. He panned the larger-than-usual crowd, which was about to swell even larger as Jesus and another group returned with yet another top-heavy cart.

"I'm sure we can reach a number that is fair for everyone," Matthew said.

Lucian shot him a questioning glance.

James leaned toward Matthew and said, "Remember the Baptizer's words, brother."

The rebuke was gentle, but it stung. *What does "fair" even mean anymore?*

Jesus stepped up to the counter. "Two hundred thirty-six fish total, from these two teams."

Matthew searched for the right words. *Had he heard our negotiation?*

"Sir, they need your answer," Lucian leaned in as he addressed Matthew softly.

Matthew nodded, said "Fine. Two teams. Two hundred thirty-six fish," and scratched calculations onto his tablet.

The Sabbath was only a day behind him, but Simon already felt the need for more rest. Since sundown, the people had been bringing the sick to the home of the fishermen where Jesus was staying. Simon had his hands full keeping the crowd in order.

It was close to sunrise when he had time to lie down, which he did right in the courtyard. He had hardly slept before the first light of dawn warmed his face. He rose only to find other early risers approaching the house from every direction.

He went into the house and found Andrew already awake and dressed. "Jesus is gone," the fisherman said to him.

"He probably had to hide to get some sleep," Simon answered. "What should I tell the people? They are already coming, no doubt to see him."

"I'll take my brother and go look for him," Andrew said. "Maybe you can have a normal day for a change."

Simon glanced toward the doorway. "Not likely."

He returned to the courtyard where about a dozen people gathered at the gate and announced, "The teacher has gone. He's not here!"

"But my child has a fever."

"Do not keep him from us."

"Where has he gone?"

"When will he return?"

The questions came all at once and compounded Simon's exhaustion. His eyes fought to stay open, and he barely noticed the man who approached the back of the crowd, then abruptly turned to leave again when the questions started. Simon recognized the finely embroidered cloak.

"You! Publican," he called. All the people turned in sudden silence. The departing man stopped but did not turn. Two men nearby moved to block his path. "You're not so big when you're not hiding behind your booth," one said.

"Let him come here," Simon called to them. The taunting man shoved the toll taker's shoulder, and he turned and walked toward the gate with slow, small steps.

"I just want to see the teacher," the tax collector said softly.

"He takes no payment from the people he heals so he owes you nothing," Simon said. "You've done enough harm to the people; now I suggest you go. I'm sure everyone here agrees that you do not belong here."

"Please, I do not mean to hurt anyone."

"Harm has been your way of life since you scratched your first ledger. There is no room for traitors in the coming kingdom. If you don't go of your own accord, I'm sure these people will make you go."

The toll collector held up open hands, and his eyes widened. "I don't want a confrontation. Please tell the teacher I came looking for him."

"Go."

The toll taker turned and left. The men in the back let him pass, and Simon watched until he was out of view.

Chapter Six

Matthew sat at his toll booth and settled with the fishing teams in the early morning, just as he had every day for years. It had been weeks since that extraordinary catch, and since then, life had returned to its usual unexciting routine.

The teacher they call Jesus was gone.

His fishermen companions had left, too, along with some of the dockhands and Matthew's brother, James.

What most unsettled Matthew was that the hope that had filled their town for a short while also seemed to vanish. The healings, the exorcisms, even the 236 fish, were all but forgotten.

I should be grateful. Money was flowing, and trouble wasn't. Herod had even called back the additional storehouse guards to redeploy them in the latest hot spot.

How could Matthew be grateful when he failed to thank the man who healed him and just as quickly disappeared? *If I see Jesus again, I will not miss another opportunity.*

Matthew focused on the task at hand: recording inventory for the grain vendor in front of him, who was no doubt eager to get to market and earn his coin for the day.

The grain vendor left, and two men wheeled a fishing cart up to the booth.

"You're coming in a little late," Matthew said as he looked up, then recognized the brothers, Andrew and Simon. "Have you brought the teacher back?" he added without masking his enthusiasm.

The brothers exchanged glances. Andrew held up a hand and responded, "Despite what happened last time, we can handle our own negotiations."

"We know you came looking for him before, probably trying to extort an 'underpayment' from us all," Simon interjected.

"Please do not judge. I just want to thank him," Matthew said.

"Thank him?" Andrew asked.

"Yes. When I first saw him, I had an injury, and he healed me. I didn't believe it at first, but then I saw what he's done for others —"

"You're saying he healed *you*?"

"Yes!"

The brothers exchanged glances again, and Andrew continued, "We need to get these to market. Fifty-one fish in all."

Matthew scratched his wax ledger. "You seem not to want to answer my questions, but if you see your teacher, let him know I'd like to see him. You might doubt me, but he would see that I mean no harm."

At that moment, Lucian stepped up from behind the fishermen, and Matthew couldn't recall when he had stepped away. "I think the teacher you're looking for is here, sir. I saw him sitting in a boat in shallow water talking to the people on the shore."

Matthew looked from Lucian to the brothers. "Well?"

"I guess you have your answer," Simon said, and the pair turned and walked toward the market.

Another merchant stepped up, and Matthew recorded names, quantities, and products without thinking about what he was doing. He looked toward the shore as peasants from the outlying villages scurried past. He saw the line of merchants and fishermen and wished for a moment's reprieve from his duties as the next one stepped up.

"Sir, if you have a matter to discuss with the Nazarene, I could summon him," Lucian said.

"Thank you, Lucian, but no."

Matthew spent the next hour barely aware of his work, until a large group approached from the shore. He searched their faces until he spotted Jesus, who was looking right back at him. James walked alongside him, as did some of the familiar fishermen and dockhands.

Impulse took over, and Matthew had no desire to resist. He stood, stumbled out of his booth, then ran around to the front. A shipper stood at his counter and watched, perplexed.

"Sir?" Lucian asked as Matthew hastened past the guard and into the crowd.

Villagers jumped out of his way, but one man stepped in front of Jesus and stood resolute: the young dockhand from the fishermen's house.

"Let him pass, Simon," Jesus said.

The young man looked to Jesus, then back to Matthew. He wore a stern, tight-lipped, narrow-eyed expression. He stood long enough that Matthew expected Jesus to instruct him again. After a moment of stillness, the young man stepped aside just enough to allow Matthew to stand before Jesus, still in arms reach.

Matthew walked up and threw his arms around Jesus, surprising even himself with the impetuousness of his action. "Thank you, teacher. Thank you for healing me."

Murmurs rose from the surrounding crowd.

"I didn't get to thank you before. I'm glad you came back," Matthew added.

"Your healing has only just begun, Matthew Bar-Alphaeus," Jesus responded.

"What do you mean? How do you know — "

"You'll know the answers in time. Follow me, and you will store up new treasures in God's kingdom," Jesus said.

The chatter from the crowd grew louder and interspersed with groans.

"This is not right!" The young dockhand called Simon spat. "How could a traitor be of any use in the kingdom of God? And what is this talk of healing?"

"I was injured," Matthew answered. "I had been attacked, and I was afraid, so I didn't tell anyone. But somehow," Matthew looked to Jesus, "somehow you knew and made me well."

Simon's fists clenched as Matthew spoke. When he finished, the young man shot back, "It's not right. There is no way."

Jesus turned, "Simon, I've called him just as I have called you."

"Well, I won't have it!" the young man turned and walked away.

Matthew called after him, "Please let me show you! I mean no harm. You will be my guests for dinner." He turned back to Jesus, "You, Simon, and the rest of your friends."

Matthew turned to the rest of the publicans at their booths and only then realized all commerce had stopped and the whole town stood watching him. "And all of you as well. Come and help me honor the man who healed me."

Turing back to Jesus, he said, "I will go and begin preparations at once."

Matthew retrieved his cloak from the booth and hurried toward the main gate, leaving his tablet and his records behind.

"Sir?" Lucian called from his position beside the booth as Matthew left.

———

Simon walked past the sprawling estates of the landowners. He hadn't been on this road since his first assignment for Manaen. He walked past the brush where he had set a trap for his target that night, and the image flooded his memory: the frightened face of the tax collector and the voice of Manaen instructing him to stop.

So much has happened since that night. The wine at his wedding. The commotion in Jerusalem. The fishermen, the healings, and the miracles.

What if Jesus had never shown up? How much more could I have done for the cause? Thaddeus surely would have joined us by now, and perhaps others. We might have even driven out the tax collectors. What if I had finished the task that first night, on this very road?

Instead, Simon found himself on the outside while the publican celebrated with Jesus. With the fishermen. With the people Simon thought were his friends.

He heard the celebration before the house came into view. He slowed his walk while guests passed him. Almost all of them wore embroidered or dyed cloaks. Some were accompanied by servants. Simon even noticed several women whose faces were made up with pigments and paints.

Just one affront to Israel after another.

As Simon neared the house, he hoped to get someone's attention — either Thaddeus or one of the fishermen — to try to make some sense of this spectacle. Peering through doorways and windows, he caught glimpses of his friends, but none noticed him. Guests continued to file past him and into the house. Voices approached from behind Simon. He strained to listen over the din of the party.

"He would dare to sit and teach in the synagogues?"

"The son of Mary is showing his true allegiance now."

"Surely this display will cause the people to abandon him."

The voices grew louder and mixed with the sounds of heavy footfalls on the hard packed road beneath them when Simon's attention was pulled away.

"Simon! I wasn't sure you were coming!" Thaddeus had come out of the house.

He must have seen me. "I'm not staying. And you shouldn't either."

"But Jesus would have us all here. He asked me to come get you."

"I want no part of this. I've never stepped foot into such a vile haven of indulgence and sin, and I am not going to now. Not for Jesus nor for anyone."

"You two!" came a call from Simon's right. He turned to see Hananai the Pharisee pointing a finger toward them. Three more Pharisees stood behind them. "You traveled with the Nazarene teacher. You are his disciples, are you not?"

Simon inhaled deeply and contemplated his words carefully. "We joined him on some travels, but as you can see—"

"Yes! We are followers of Jesus, the healer and teacher!" Thaddeus cut in, to Simon's surprise.

"Tell us: Why does your teacher eat with tax collectors and sinners?" Hananai asked.

"As I started to say—" Simon began before a different voice interrupted.

"It's not the healthy who need a doctor, but the sick." Simon turned toward the sound. Jesus was now standing behind Thaddeus. He continued, "I've not come to call the righteous, but sinners."

Simon was not sure what to say, and the silence that surrounded him suggested he was not alone.

"You should come in, Simon. There is a place for you at the table," Jesus said.

The Pharisees turned to leave, saying nothing. As they passed, the one in the back—Yoezer, to the best of Simon's recollection— stepped up to Simon and pressed something into his palm, meeting his eyes the whole time, then joined his companions and left.

"So are you coming in?" Jesus asked.

Simon clenched the crumpled parchment in his hand, shook his head, turned, and walked toward the town.

Down the road, he looked back to confirm that the house was out of view and nobody had followed him. He unfurled the scrap of parchment in his fist, turned it over, and read:

I've seen enough now. Have you?

Chapter Seven

Simon sat under the abandoned dock as the first light of dawn glinted off the lake. Footfalls across the gravel grew louder behind him.

"I was surprised to hear back from you," a familiar voice said. "I was beginning to think you had abandoned our cause."

Simon rose and turned toward Manaen. "Not abandoned. Just … looking at it a new way."

"Swept up by the Nazarene teacher? He is an enigma."

Simon tensed. "How do you mean?"

"First, he was with the Baptizer. I expected him to wander off with the Essenes. But instead, he surrounds himself with the lame and the lepers."

"He has … healing powers."

"But he has no strategy. He *proclaims* a coming kingdom, but his army is feeble. Ask anyone from Nazareth—there is nothing special about him."

Simon's fingers twitched. "I know what I have seen."

"Hmm." Manaen turned and faced the sea. "You defend him." He turned back and looked Simon in the eye. "Yet here you are. Why?"

"I want back in."

"So you admit that I was right?"

"I admit that he has done some … unexpected things."

Manaen snorted, "Well, let's hope he continues. In a way, your Nazarene teacher has helped our movement. Herod already locked up the Baptizer. It's only a matter of time until the Nazarene gets his attention, too."

"How does that help you?"

"How it helps *us*, Simon, is simple. Talk gets all the attention. We prefer to stay silent and let our *actions* speak for us. Are you ready to return to action?"

"I'm listening."

"Tiberias. Seek out a man named Jonah at the docks. He'll give you what you need."

"No king but God."

"No king but God."

Manaen climbed the embankment and walked toward town. Simon waited until he was out of sight and walked down the shoreline as the work crews arrived to begin the day.

He reached the harbor and strode onto a dock where workers were preparing a merchant ship.

"Where have you been?" Thaddeus asked as he secured ramps to the dock.

"Arranging future work."

Thaddeus stood, his expression sullen. "You don't mean — "

"There are docks in other cities." Simon leveled his stare at Thaddeus.

"You sure you don't want to stay and see where this goes?"

"I can't align myself with that traitor." Simon tied off one side of the ramp to a cleat and passed the rope across to Thaddeus.

"If you mean the publican, he seems to have walked away from that. I heard that it was quite a scene afterward."

"What's done is done. Some people can't be redeemed."

"But what about everything you've seen? The miracles, the healing — "

"No doubt, Jesus had made people more comfortable. Given them a little bit of hope. But ..." Simon looked down and shook his head.

"But what?"

"I just can't. Besides, we have a ship to load." Simon stood, lifted a sack from the cart behind him, and walked up the ramp.

———

Matthew took in the sights as he rode into Tiberias. The decorated columns and imported cedars were quite a contrast from the utilitarian stone structures in Capernaum. The opulence even outdid Sepphoris.

He rode down an avenue overlooking the sea. At the far end of the city, a road wound up the hillside toward expansive multi-tiered houses. Two guards met him a few strides ahead of the gatehouse. "State your business."

"Matthew from Capernaum. Samchai called for me."

The guard nodded at a junior officer, who brought his own mount before Matthew's party and led them to the smallest of several sprawling estates. A servant stabled their mules while another led them into the house.

They passed through a receiving hall with a high ceiling and large windows, into a smaller sitting room where Samchai waited. Matthew's secretary accompanied him while his driver remained in the waiting area.

Samchai sat next to a large desk, flanked by two men who Matthew took to be his scribes, judging by their pale complexion and embroidered attire.

"You've brought the records, as requested?" Samchai began without offering a greeting or even standing as Matthew entered.

The secretary stepped forward, opened a satchel, and laid two bound volumes on the desk.

Samchai picked up a tome and leafed casually through. Without looking up, he said, "I will have my accountants review these. In the meantime, four minas ought to be sufficient until a final tabulation can be made."

"Four minas?" Matthew threw his arms wide. "That is almost a year's worth of tolls!"

Samchai motioned toward a bench and looked silently at Matthew. Matthew processed his meaning and took a seat. The secretary sat on an adjacent bench.

"I don't understand the objection," Samchai continued. "You were awarded that term, were you not?"

"Yes, but it has already been posted for a new bid. You will fill the post in a matter of weeks!"

"What happens with your former post beyond your tenure is not your concern. Your obligation is immutable."

"I will cover the vacancy, but let the next publican close out the year."

"Why should I? You breached our agreement when you abandoned your post. When I consider the risk, especially after you invited all those day laborers and fishermen into your home—"

"Who I choose to entertain has no bearing on my work."

Samchai snorted, "You are terribly mistaken. Any sense of favor that these people perceive, they will use against you. Your ability to gain an upper hand or show a credible threat of force is gone. You might as well have put a box out for people to pay—or take—as they desired."

"Since I am no longer occupying the booth, I suppose you don't have to worry about that."

"Except that there appears to have been shortages and missed revenues on that day. No doubt more than one trader slipped past as your colleagues scrambled to mitigate your unexpected departure. Their own tills suffered because of it."

"They did not seem to be bothered when they sat at my dinner table. Perhaps they should check the purses of their own underpaid soldiery."

Samchai stood. "That is a bold accusation, Matthew. If you can back it up with evidence, I'm sure Herod would entertain a hearing. But if you are merely deflecting from *your* abdication of *your* responsibility, you would be wise to keep such thoughts hidden."

Samchai gestured toward the ledgers on his desk. "I have all I need today. I will call when the accounting is complete."

Samchai exited through a rear corridor while a servant crossed the hall and opened the door to the receiving room.

———

Simon took in the sights of Tiberias for the first time as he hauled a sack of grain down the ramp to carts waiting on the dock.

Multi-story buildings. Some framed in cedar, others with gilded ornamentation and polished stone. Beyond the harbor, an amphitheater rose from the shoreline — probably big enough to seat all of Capernaum.

Simon shook his head, disgusted at the concrete monument to Roman licentiousness and pagan debauchery.

So this is what Herod does with the wealth he siphons off his people.

The sprawling eyesore beyond the shoreline strengthened his resolve. He was sure he had made the right choice.

Now, to find this Jonah.

"I've not seen you here before." The man at the cart regarded him with narrow eyes.

"I was told I could find good work here." Simon dropped the sack on the cart. "I heard a man named Jonah is hiring."

The man chuckled and added, "You must be used to the small ports. Tiberias is no small city. 'A man named Jonah who is hiring?' That describes a dozen different men that I can think of. And I could come up with two dozen more with a little asking around. You'll have to do better."

"Hey — new guy. This isn't the synagogue — talk on your own time. We have a ship to unload." The worker who had arranged Simon's passage loaded a sack onto the cart as he berated Simon.

"Right." Simon nodded to the cart driver and walked up the ramp.

He returned with another sack of grain, and the driver said, "You might try Jonah the stone cutter. Local guy—he sounds like you. Start there."

"Thanks. I will."

"When your shift is over, of course," the driver said through a brief laugh.

"Of course."

———

After covering the cost of his passage, Simon's wage was just enough to secure a bed at the boarding house. The lodge was bigger than any in Capernaum or Sepphoris—almost comparable to Jerusalem. He found accommodation in the quarters where other workers—dockhands, stone and timber haulers, and builders—laid their heads, separate from the more spacious lodging of the traders and crafters.

It wasn't obvious to Simon who was who. All the workers wore the same undyed, unadorned clothing. There was nothing to differentiate one tradesman from another.

How to find the stone cutter?

More importantly, how to be sure he is the Jonah that I was sent to find?

For the first time, Simon wondered if Manaen had sent him to chase the horizon.

Two men about his age passed through the room, and Simon caught just a glimpse of a hilt beneath the trim of the first man's cloak. Simon did not entirely trust the image impressed on his mind, but he chose to believe that he saw a familiar dyed leather banding in that brief moment.

He caught up to the man and said, "I've just arrived in port today. I'm seeking a stonecutter named Jonah. Do you know where I might find him?"

The man looked Simon up and down, paying particular attention to his hands. "What need do you have of a stonecutter?"

The other man watched, silent and unmoving.

"I need work. A friend back home told me to seek him here." Simon hoped he was asking after the right Jonah.

"And where is home?"

"Capernaum."

The man nodded. "Capernaum?" He glanced at Simon's hands again. "You should understand that *stonecutter* is a crude designation. Jonah has no use for the unskilled. He's better described as a stone *shaper* – one who chisels and polishes with precision, until each stone is not just a building block, but a work of art. A thing of beauty," he stepped closer to Simon and in a near-whisper added, "fit for a king."

Simon locked eyes with the man. "I have no king but God."

The man's mouth curled into a slight smile, and he added an almost imperceptible nod. "I will take you to him in the morning."

———

Matthew woke in his own bed in his own home, barely aware of the return trip from Tiberias. The same thoughts that consumed him during the quiet ride flooded him anew as Samchai's unjust demand echoed in his mind.

Could I win an appeal? Would that just invite more trouble?

He considered the possible merits of Samchai's claim.

Did I say too much when I implied that there might be thieves among the publicans?

He hoped they would remember that not long ago they were his guests at a dinner given in honor of Jesus.

Jesus. The man who pierced his heart and first got him thinking about justice. About fairness. About honesty.

What if I had never met the man?

He could live the life he always had. He could prosper and enjoy favor. Perhaps there was still a way.

Could I buy back my office? Start over?

And if he did, he could still learn from Jesus.

The same Jesus who had called him *away* from his booth, his livelihood.

His security.

How much danger am I in now?

The Pharisees and the workers would not be eager to befriend him. Certainly, the bandits wouldn't leave him alone. Could he still count on his guards? On Herod's officials – even Samchai's men – to look out for him?

Where will I be safe?

Matthew endured the assault of his own thoughts and dressed. He strode to town, down the main avenue to the shoreline, past the merchants and traders surrounding the toll booths, paying for the privilege of doing business another day.

The booth where Matthew once sat remained unoccupied. The soldiers who once watched his back stood with other publicans, as dutifully as any other day.

Matthew rounded a bend and followed a side street to the home of Simon the fisherman. He crossed the small courtyard that Simon shared with other tenants and entered the simple structure.

Matthew was unaccustomed to such tiny, sparse quarters. There was no delineation of separate rooms—just a rudimentary bed in the far corner and a small dining table on the near side. A storage room, barely the size of Matthew's own wardrobe, stood open as the fisherman pulled out supplies.

"Have you seen Jesus?" Matthew asked.

Simon looked up and answered, "We just returned from Jerusalem yesterday. He must have gone out to pray, like he usually does."

"Jerusalem?"

"It would have been good to have you with us," a voice answered from the doorway behind him. Matthew turned and faced Jesus. "You should join us for the next festival."

"Join you? I rarely go to Jerusalem. And never for a pilgrimage. It is only by coincidence that I happened to be nearby when the Baptizer was active. My place is here. There is always ..." Matthew stopped as he realized that for the first time in his life, he had nothing to do.

He looked down, unsure how to continue. When he finally looked up, he asked, "Would a publican even be welcome?"

"There will be room for you in my father's house," Jesus replied.

"If Samchai calls to settle accounts—"

"Matthew, you are worried about many things. Remember what I said at your house about putting new wine only in new wineskins? It's time for something new."

"If I am gone when Samchai calls, he will assume my guilt. How is that just?"

Jesus put his hand on Matthew's shoulder. "You're just beginning to understand justice. Your understanding will increase if you join me. The festival is months away, but the synagogue is never far."

Matthew's mind filled with doubt, but he took a strange comfort in Jesus' words—a feeling that he had been missing for too long. He looked at Jesus and nodded.

———

"We have an opportunity before us," Jonah addressed the two dozen men seated on the hillside beyond the city walls of Tiberias. Quarried stones—roughly cut from the mountains behind Simon—

lay strewn about. Still, neither he nor any of those gathered had been given a hammer or chisel.

"Quirinius has been forced to deploy his resources to Jerusalem. Word is that Pilate has stirred up fresh unrest by parading images of the emperor through the streets. With the feast approaching, the governor is taking no chances." Jonah paced briskly across the front of the crowd as he spoke with forced restraint.

"We pray that the glory of the Lord will guard our brothers who fight for the land of our fathers in Jerusalem. But our work is here. And our time is now."

A younger man wearing a satchel stood and walked among the workers. He drew small, rolled parchments from his bag and handed one to each man. Simon took his, noted a stripe marked on the outside, and glanced around. A few parchments seemed to have names on them. The others hadn't opened their parchments, so Simon followed their lead.

When everyone had received his parchment, Jonah added, "These are your instructions. Do not discuss them nor share them with one another. The less each of you knows, the safer all of us are. Proceed to your assignment at the first hour after sundown. Match the symbol on your instructions to the mark on the building stone. The rest is written out for you."

The men began to rise as Jonah continued, "Of course, there is always risk that you might encounter imperials. Bloodshed might be necessary. Remember, we are at war with these pagans."

Murmurs of assent rose from the men gathered.

"We cannot let anything stop us. If we fail, we may not have another opportunity like this. Now let's get on with the day's work. No king but God."

"No king but God," Simon echoed with the others. He stuffed the parchment into his coin purse and lined up with the others to pick up his tools for the day.

———

Matthew sat and listened to the teachers in the synagogue. He was acclimating to the new routine—to spending more time around the teachers—but their words still escaped him. He stayed in the back of the assembly. His brother, James, stood with him despite his own preference for the front.

Matthew leaned toward his brother. "I haven't paid the scriptures any mind since we were boys. I will never understand this."

James stood listening in his simple cloak, his hair unkempt. His aesthetic appearance contrasted Matthew's own flaunted wealth and extravagance. In that moment, Matthew felt a pang of envy and wished he could trade his superfluous excess for his brother's simple wisdom.

"Understanding will come quicker than you realize. You walked away from a lucrative life when Jesus invited you to follow. Something prompted your change of mind."

"Well, it wasn't all of this," Matthew waved a hand toward the teacher at the other end of the hall. "Jesus didn't use lengthy readings and confusing proclamations and sayings from long-dead teachers."

For the first time, James turned toward Matthew. "What was it then? What made you get up and follow him?"

Matthew paused. He hadn't really thought about it. He knew he was compelled to listen to Jesus, follow him, and learn from him. But he hadn't considered *why*. "I can't really say. I've been hated by so many that it seemed odd to me that Jesus would want to have me around. He seems to have no profit motive."

"So that's it? You're simply *curious* why Jesus wants to have anything to do with you?"

Do I mention the robbery? The healing?

"Maybe that's not all of it. But I'm not sure what else it is. Why do *you* follow him? You and I are so different, after all."

"I've devoted my life to following the law and living by the scriptures. Sometimes, the Pharisees—as knowledgeable and faithful as they are—make it complicated. I guess Jesus makes it simpler."

"Then why sit in here and listen to the Pharisees and scholars at all?"

"There is value here. The scriptures are powerful. It is good that we hear them. The teachers are wise. Besides, Jesus spends his time here, so why shouldn't I?"

"But it seems he doesn't always see things the same way. He draws their ire." Matthew hung his head. "He invited all kinds of accusations on himself just by associating with me."

"Those are the moments when we must listen most closely," James said and put a hand on Matthew's shoulder.

Matthew looked up at his brother. "What do you mean?"

"The Pharisees think Jesus flouts the law, but he always has an answer. A *simple* answer." James pointed to the front of the assembly. "Watch."

Matthew turned. Jesus walked toward the front of the gathering, and the Pharisees eyed him with stern expressions. Jesus stopped and stooped down to address a man seated in the assembly. He helped the man to his feet and led him to the front.

The Pharisees conferred among themselves, and one called out, "Is it lawful to heal on the Sabbath?"

"They are challenging him," James leaned in and said.

Matthew peered more closely at the man with Jesus. His right shoulder drooped, and his arm bent at the elbow. Just barely protruding from his sleeve, Matthew saw thin fingers curled in on themselves.

"Is it lawful to do good on the Sabbath or to do evil," Jesus answered, "to save a life or to kill?"

"See," James whispered to Matthew, "he makes you hear the law a whole new way — not by adding to it but by making it simple."

Matthew motioned for his brother to be quiet while he strained to hear Jesus.

"… If your sheep falls in a pit on the Sabbath, you would pull it out," Jesus added.

The Pharisees exchanged quick glances. Their mouths moved, but Matthew couldn't hear their words.

Before the Pharisees could respond, Jesus spoke again, this time to the man standing with him. "Stretch out your hand."

The man slowly lifted his arm, first straightening the shoulder, then the elbow. His hand emerged from his sleeve, and his fingers straightened and stretched. The muscles in his forearm, which had been bone wrapped in skin, appeared to grow. The man held his hand before his own startled face as he splayed his fingers and balled them into a fist over and over, like an infant seeing his hand for the first time.

"That man used to beg," James said, "but now he can work."

Matthew nodded at his brother's words but kept his eyes on the Pharisees who had huddled in closer among themselves while the rest of the people surrounded Jesus and the latest beneficiary of his healing.

———

The sun had fallen behind the mountains in the west, with only the faintest glow still glinting off the sea of Galilee. Simon didn't know the lay of the city, so Jonah assigned him to a post on the perimeter of the action.

From there, Simon could see the edge of the administrative district and the operatives stationed there. Traders and publicans still walked the streets, but Simon and the others had been given strict orders to ignore any passersby and focus only on the mission.

But it was a mission that Simon knew nothing about. He knew only that he was the first line of defense if any soldiers converge on an alarm. His task was to cut them down from behind when they passed.

Away from the city's center, the occasional soldier passed across the road that led to the main caravan route at the north end of the sea.

Routine patrols.

Light from two lanterns flooded the road and grew brighter. A patrol stopped the new arrivals for a moment before they continued on the main road right toward Simon.

Simon knew the city enough to know they were not going toward the common inn. *They must be the personal guests of someone in the city.* As they neared, Simon walked toward them, blending in with passersby. When he got closer, he spotted the unmistakable mantles and phylacteries of the Pharisees — two of them — accompanied by a pair of servants. As he passed, he recognized them from Capernaum.

What are Hananai and Yoezer doing in Tiberias? These pious guardians of the law despise all things Roman. The other Pharisees would ostracize them just for setting foot in this unholy place.

Not unlike his decision to walk away from Jesus, after he made himself a friend to traitors.

Simon glanced back. They were walking deeper into the administrative district.

Could they be part of the plot?

Not likely. No Pharisee would involve himself so directly in bloodshed.

Simon turned and followed, matching their pace.

Simon passed the next operative, who glared at him with accusation. They dared not speak to each other, but Simon understood.

There was more foot traffic deeper in the city, and Simon was grateful for the cover. He kept his eyes open for other operatives despite knowing that he would recognize few of them anyway.

Each building was larger and more ornate than the last as he approached the central hub of the city, the offices of the chief tax farmer and Herod's officials. He reached a walled compound that encircled barracks and adjoined a near-palatial building, which Simon assumed was used by Quirinius and other Roman elites when they visited.

The Pharisees seem to know where they are going.

He sparsely noticed the mason's mark on the cornerstone of the building, but it was enough to remind him that another operative was nearby.

If I have trouble, I have help.

Simon slowed. The Pharisees stopped at a gated entryway to a large, well-appointed building. Simon wondered if this might be the home of Herod himself, or at least a prominent administrator.

Could this be about the Baptizer who Herod had imprisoned?

Two servants from the estate conferred with the visitors at the gate. Simon's attire marked him as out of place in this part of the city. He affected a limp, a hunch, and a stagger and moved closer.

An estate guard stepped into the road. "Get your vagrancy away from here," he barked and shoved Simon.

Simon hit the ground hard and laid still for a moment before making a show of working clumsily to his feet. As he did, he strained to listen.

"We've come to see Benaiah."

"Is the secretary expecting you?"

"No. It is about the Nazarene — the one who follows the Baptizer's work."

"So make an appointment."

"I'm afraid urgency demands haste in this matter. This Nazarene is an even greater threat than John was."

"To you, perhaps. But how does that concern Herod?"

"It concerns us all. If we are to work together to rid ourselves of a common threat, it demands discretion. An appointment in daylight hours would compromise us both."

Simon got to his feet and glanced toward the gatehouse. The servants were leading the Pharisees inside.

Simon shivered. Jesus kept unsavory company, but what did the Pharisees expect Herod's office to do?

Imprison him?

Execute him?

Simon limped back the way he came. When he turned the corner and was out of sight of the gate, he righted himself and walked as briskly as he dared without attracting unwanted attention.

Chapter Eight

Simon woke with the sun and left the boarding house. He hadn't heard how successful the previous night had been, and he didn't ask. The presence of familiar faces told him enough. He was content not knowing more. He was too preoccupied with what he *did* know.

And there is nobody I can tell. At least not here.

Simon looked up the road toward the stonecutter's shop on the hillside. The soldiers in the city center were more visible and more numerous.

Or maybe he was simply more attentive.

He hesitated, then turned and followed the road downhill to the docks.

Soldiers lined the pier, and workers crowded around them as two officers attempted to shout order into the chaos. Simon fell in line behind the mass of workers.

Behind the soldiers stood several well-dressed men. One conferred quietly with a Roman centurion.

The sounds of a scuffle and an argument emerged from the front, but the words were lost in the noise. After a moment, two decurions forcefully led a man past the line and away from the docks. His face bore fresh bruises, but Simon still recognized him from the stonecutter's home. One of the well-dressed men followed them, accompanied by two more soldiers.

Simon did not turn to watch.

The line advanced slowly while impatient merchants waited with their ships.

When Simon neared the front of the line, a soldier approached him. "Show me your hands," he ordered.

Simon held out his hands in front of him. The soldier turned them over and back with a not-so-subtle show of force.

"Open your bag," he barked.

Simon was grateful that he traveled with sparse supplies. He was even more grateful that he had shredded last night's parchment and scattered the fragments to the wind.

He unfastened a small purse and untied it to show the Roman the few denarii inside.

The soldier looked at the coins and furrowed. "Is that all you have?"

"Yes. Now please let me work so I can fill it."

"What is your name?"

"Simon of Cana."

"Cana? What are you doing in Tiberias?"

"Returning from a family matter to my work. These ships do not load themselves, and these merchant aren't going to do the heavy lifting."

The soldier straightened and looked down his nose at Simon for a long moment.

"Go on," he said, waving Simon past.

Simon descended to the pier and began inquiring after the ships until he found the first one bound for Capernaum.

—

Matthew woke and left his estate. He was greeted by scattered campsites outside the city. In town, the crowd on the main avenue was larger than usual.

These weren't the ordinary workers and fishermen making their way to the docks. These were travelers. Some were hunched or debilitated, wheeled in by others on carts. Many carried wailing children. Outside the city, a band of people covered in rags huddled together.

Matthew looked down as he passed the tax booths. Merchant ships waited outside the harbor while passengers spilled out of moored ships onto the pier.

When Matthew reached the home of Simon the fisherman, he found Simon's wife preparing bread in the courtyard.

"Has Jesus been here today?"

"They left early. Follow the crowd. I'm sure you will find them."

Matthew nodded his gratitude and turned toward the docks. Travelers still poured off the pier and walked along the shoreline past the edge of town. Matthew filed into line and was soon knocked from behind. He stumbled forward and turned. A young man who Matthew recognized to be a resident knocked into him again, obviously with intention.

"Go back to your padded comforts, publican. You don't belong here."

"I've left that post. I'm going to see the teacher."

"There's no way for a traitor like you to find favor. A good man like Jesus would want nothing to do with you."

The man elbowed Matthew in the ribs as he passed.

Matthew rubbed the bruise on his side, but the soreness that weighed on his mind was more severe.

Why does Jesus want me around?

Did Jesus really think that there was hope for him? Or was his friendship misguided?

Matthew's head ached as answers eluded him. He forced his feet forward and followed the crowd. He didn't know why they all came. Sure, many were obviously sick or injured. Others seemed to be afflicted with evil spirits. It was clear what they wanted.

What Matthew wanted was far from clear.

And what does Jesus want with me?

That was the most troublesome question. Every other question brought Matthew back to that one.

The crowd slowed as they squeezed past a narrow bend where the vegetation neared the water and tightened the shoreline. Some trampled a new path where they could, but the going was still slow and tedious.

Ahead, more people cascaded down the plain from a neighboring village and filled the open space, moving as a swarm toward the water, wading into the sea up to their chests to where Jesus stood in a small boat. His fishermen companions stood in the water and steadied the craft while the sick, lame, and afflicted were undeterred by the water between them. They came up to him, and he turned none away. Matthew couldn't get close enough to hear, but he eyes told him everything. Bent backs and limbs were straightened with new strength. Wailing children were calmed, and seized people settled.

There was no malady that this man could not heal.

Except, perhaps, the weight of guilt.

Confusion and doubt rested heavy on Matthew's mind and shoulders. He watched and hoped until he no longer knew how long he had stood on the shore.

———

Simon paced on the deck of the merchant ship. The delay with the soldiers at the docks left him agitated, but no amount of agitation made the ship move faster.

I have to get to Jesus before the Pharisees and their unlikely allies do.

Soon, the coastal mountains gave way to a cove. But the scene was anything but the familiar wild grasses and open plain.

Instead, the hillside was alive with movement. Bodies — hundreds of them — converged from the shoreline and hillside paths toward Capernaum as the town barely came into view. From this distance, he saw no trouble, no suggestion that the people might be fleeing.

Returning his attention to the cove, Simon realized they were not running *from* anything, but *toward* something.

Toward *someone.*

A man stood in a small boat several meters off the shore. People splashed into the water toward him. His features were indiscernible at this distance, but Simon was certain this could only be Jesus.

A new worry overtook him. *How can I reach Jesus from the port in Capernaum?* The crowds and the extra distance would cost him hours.

As the vessel entered the harbor, Simon fixated on the scene on the neighboring shore until Jesus was out of sight.

The ship reached the docks, which were unusually barren for midday. Only a small crew, already hard at work unloading another vessel, was present.

"Time to finish earning your passage," the shipmaster said as he walked past.

They dropped the ramp, and Simon secured the ship to the pier. Wagoners wheeled their carts onto the dock, and Simon unloaded cargo as fast as his muscles allowed.

The lack of dockhands lengthened his workday. By the time he finished, Simon estimated he had just enough time to reach the cove before sundown.

Simon walked briskly along the shoreline, beyond the abandoned docks and the town. Beyond a narrow shore buttressed by a steep cliff face, he encountered people returning to Capernaum.

Has Jesus already left?

The mood was joyous, and Simon listened carefully to the conversations — to proclamations of healings and of evil spirits driven away. Simon pushed against and through the crowd as it grew thicker.

"You're going the wrong way," one person said as they bumped shoulders.

"The healer has gone for tonight," another added.

Urgency drove Simon forward as he cut between bodies with determined force that knocked more than a few passersby into a stumble.

He emerged onto the hillside cove where people moved in all directions. The fishermen were tying off a boat at the far side, but he saw no sign of Jesus. He increased his pace, absently bumping into others.

"Simon! You've returned," a familiar voice called from behind. He turned without slowing down as Thaddeus strode quickly toward him.

"I thought you had gone to Tiberias."

"I did, but something happened, and I needed to get back. Where is Jesus?"

"Simon, what is going on? After your outburst over the toll collector, I thought you were done with him."

"Maybe so. But I still need to find him."

"He's gone up the mountainside alone. To pray, he said. And I'm not telling you any more until you explain what is going on. What is with your sudden change of mind? I know how these Zealots work, and—"

"Zealots?" Simon bristled. "This has nothing to do with them. I just need to find Jesus."

Thaddeus clasped his friend's shoulders. "This has everything to do with them. I might not know the Zealots well, but I know *you*, Simon. You would not set foot in Tiberias unless you had a worthy cause. What have they put you up to?"

Simon put up his hand and nodded. He stepped closer to Thaddeus and lowered his voice. "You're right, in a way. The Zealots *did* send me to Tiberias. But I returned on my own—to find Jesus. I've learned that he is in danger."

"From the Zealots?"

"No. From the Pharisees. And the Herodians."

"That makes no sense. They despise each other!"

"I don't understand it either, but I know what I saw." Simon paused, taken by a new thought. "Did Jesus somehow anger those tax collectors gathered at the publican's house?"

"No. The publican still follows, but he mostly keeps to himself. Spends some time with an odd ascetic. They might be brothers. But Jesus has been frustrating the Pharisees."

"How so?"

"He healed a man on the Sabbath. In the synagogue. While the Pharisees stood nearby."

"But the Sabbath law says—"

Thaddeus held up a hand and interrupted, "And Jesus had an answer for that! He has an answer for everything."

"Still," Simon stood quietly for a moment, "why go to Herod's men?"

"I don't know. Herod locked up the Baptizer. Perhaps they think they can persuade him against Jesus. Now help me understand something."

Simon cocked his head. "And what is that?"

"What made you come back?" Thaddeus asked. "You were so angry when you left. Why not just leave Jesus to whatever fate he earns?"

Simon felt more than heard the question—like a punch to the gut. His fingers fidgeted, and he looked down. "I wish I knew. I don't like the company he's chosen, but I don't think he should die. There's something about his power that I don't understand. And now, there's even more that I don't understand."

"We should camp here if you want to find out. I'm sure Jesus will be back to healing and teaching at first light."

———

Matthew awoke as first light struck the waters of Galilee. He twisted in a futile attempt to alleviate the soreness in his shoulder and looked with confusion at the simple canopy over his head. He sat up and untangled his cloak, which had twisted around him seemingly in all directions at once.

"How do you do this? I feel terrible."

"Comfort has been your way for far too long," James said as he exited the tent. "You'll grow accustomed."

"I plan not to have to." Matthew stepped into the open air. Several dozen tents were scattered across the plain, and scores of people slept on the ground protected only by their cloaks. Most of them stirred with the sunrise. A couple of men—the fishermen who seemed to never be far from Jesus—walked among those gathered, carefully regarding the people with intention.

Andrew approached. He seemed to hurry when he recognized Matthew. "Jesus asked that you come and meet him. Both of you."

Matthew looked to his brother, then back to Andrew.

"Yes. You and you." Andrew pointed to each of them. "Come with me."

Without a word, Matthew and James left their tent behind and followed Andrew across the plain and up a winding hillside path.

They reached a small plateau where Jesus sat with a few others. The men wore the plain cloaks of fisherman and laborers, and Matthew recognized most of them from his days at the toll booth. One man — a little older and dressed like a merchant — looked as out-of-place as Matthew felt. His presence was a small consolation.

After a moment, Andrew's brother came up the same path with two more men following him.

"No. What is he doing here?" one said as he pointed directly at Matthew. It was the dockworker who was always quick to interfere.

"He's here for the same reason you are, Simon," Jesus said in a calm voice. He spread his arms wide. "For the same reason all of you are here."

Simon crossed his arms.

Jesus continued, "My Father's kingdom is upon us. I've prayed for him to show me who he has appointed to send forth and proclaim his coming kingdom."

The others glanced around with as much confusion and curiosity in their expressions as Matthew felt.

"He has given me you," Jesus said. Matthew looked to see who Jesus had indicated, but Jesus had his hands clasped before him.

"Which one of us?" A man unfamiliar to Matthew asked.

"All twelve of you."

"No! This can't be," the dockworker called Simon said as he uncrossed his arms and pointed toward Matthew. "I can't work with that traitor."

Matthew stood and held his hands out. "I don't know what deep offense I've caused, but if I have wronged you, I will compensate you."

"What deep offense? I've seen Tiberias — the monument to defilement that Herod has built. It's an homage to our oppressors that they fund with the tolls that you and your kind extorted from the rest of us." Simon turned to Jesus while keeping his accusing finger leveled at Matthew. "How can one who has spent his whole life building up the devil's kingdom proclaim the kingdom of God?"

Matthew stepped closer and pleaded, "Please. Let me make right whatever it is that I have done—"

"You *can't* make it right. Don't you see? You can't undo the damage that is already done."

Jesus stood and stepped in front of Simon, clasping his shoulders. "He has been chosen, and so have you. You have much to learn about my Father's kingdom—all of you do."

Jesus stepped next to Simon and faced the dozen gathered. "Stay close to me. Listen and learn. My Father's kingdom is like nothing in this world. Someday you will all understand."

Matthew's guilt weighed heavily. Simon was right. *How could I undo all of the wrong I have caused?* It wasn't like he could go to Samchai and demand repayment. Even if he compensated Simon for whatever injury he claimed, he couldn't repay everyone.

So much squandered wealth.

Too much squandered time.

A squandered heart.

All in vain pursuit of peace and security.

But Jesus always seemed to be at peace. And full of wisdom. And compassion.

Why would he want me around?

"He's here!" a voice called from the path. After a few brisk footsteps, a young boy came into view, pointing at them. Several other boys followed close behind. "Tell the others that I found the teacher!"

Jesus looked across the twelve and said, "Let's get to work," and he followed the boy toward the shore.

Simon sat on the now-familiar hillside and listened while Jesus taught the hundreds now gathered. At least, he tried to listen. His attention was back in Tiberias, where he witnessed the secret liaison between the Pharisees and the Herodians.

The previous evening, he had only a moment to warn Jesus. It was impossible to say more. What little he shared would have to be enough. Even when the crowds dispersed, there were still a dozen sets of ears present. Including the toll taker.

Especially the toll taker.

So Simon watched and listened. He looked over the crowd, most of them poor, traveling with what little they had for a chance to be healed.

Some left right away after being freed from their illnesses, but most lingered to hear more about the kingdom that Jesus taught.

A kingdom that Simon couldn't understand.

A king needs to be wary of his enemy, ready to conquer! Who has ever ascended to the throne by praying for his enemies? Certainly not David, according to the Psalms.

Jesus showed no inkling of raising a sword. Yet somehow, he still attracted enemies.

Enemies who had become unlikely allies.

Did Jesus even take my warning seriously?

Jesus *acted* undeterred, but he hadn't returned to the synagogue since Simon's warning.

So Simon vowed to be Jesus' eyes and ears—and his sword if necessary. The Pharisees had not bothered him here on the hillside. They would have been conspicuous, unlike the Romans, who have been known to disguise themselves as peasants.

Simon carefully scanned the crowd.

In one face after another, he saw desperation, longing, and hope. No hint of anger. No signs of plotting.

With every twitch or gesture that Simon spotted, he scanned for a like response. Any sign of a coordinated attack. But the unusual movements he saw, he could only attribute to evil spirits or illnesses.

When and how will Jesus' enemies strike?

Will he take up a sword in his own defense?

When evening approached, Jesus descended the hill to make his nightly return to the city, where he rested in the home of Simon the fisherman.

It was always a lengthy endeavor because people swarmed him for healing. This night was no exception. Like each night before, Simon, Thaddeus, and the rest stayed close. Simon kept a hand on the hilt of the dagger beneath his cloak, prepared for any danger. He trusted Thaddeus did the same.

Simon walked a couple of paces behind Jesus so he could see all that happened. He made sure the toll collector was in his line of sight, too.

Pray for your enemies.

That's what Jesus told them. Matthew stood as a constant reminder to Simon that his enemy was real. He was one cog in the crushing machinery of Roman oppression, his extortion of excess breaking the backs of the Jews, ensuring their enemies would always out-resource them.

Simon dreamed of doing many things to Matthew and his kind, but praying for them wasn't one of them.

Still, Matthew bought daily provisions for their group.

Probably a feeble attempt to assuage his guilt and make token restitution for a debt he cannot repay.

Simon was so consumed by his thoughts that he hardly noticed when they reached Capernaum. A contingent of Roman infantry stood on the shoreline, the piers, and even the ships that had been moored for the night. Half a dozen soldiers broke off and approached the disciples.

"State your business here!" the lead soldier demanded.

"This is our home!" Simon the fisherman countered without hiding his indignance.

The soldiers eyed each of them carefully and looked at Matthew — who still wore the attire of the business class — with particular curiosity.

"You're the strange teacher that everyone is talking about," one soldier said.

"If you know who I am," Jesus responded, "then you know this is our home."

The soldiers glanced at each other and stepped aside. Simon looked over his shoulder as the disciples passed, and he kept glancing back as they walked to ensure that they weren't followed too closely.

The main avenue bustled with even more soldiers, plus a few officials who were engaged in spirited discussion with the tax collectors. Simon recognized none of them from Tiberias and was glad for that. He spotted a notice posted by the tax booths but could not read it from this distance.

Matthew pushed to the front and walked ahead of the group. He approached one official and asked, "What is going on here? This is more soldiery than the garrisons can hold. Why have you brought them here?"

The official shook his head. "Matthew," he said with obvious familiarity, "you must know that things have gotten … difficult in Tiberias. There were some incidents led by Galileans against some of Herod's holdings in the city. This," the official waved his arm, "is merely the standard response. All the towns and villages on the shore also experience the same.

"Of course, none of this should surprise you," the official continued. "It hasn't been so long that you've been away from your post that you would have forgotten how things work, including the increased tolls that will be necessary to pay for the damage done."

Simon wanted to speak up, but doing so would risk exposing his part in the operation in Tiberias. He stood silently, hand on hilt, hoping—even praying—that Matthew could talk his way around this.

"Surely you're not assuming that Capernaum had anything to do with whatever happened!" Matthew's voice rose as he spoke.

"Herod is covering all possibilities," the official replied. "For me personally, it seems curious that as soon as you abandoned your post, Tiberias felt the impact of *emboldened* agitators."

Simon stepped to Jesus' side and said, "Let's just leave."

"When our friend is done," Jesus said.

"He's hardly my friend."

Jesus turned to Simon. "Someday. Let's go."

Matthew left toward his grand estate. Simon followed Jesus to the fisherman's house, where he would get no sleep as long as the city was teeming with Romans.

Chapter Nine

"We seek the Nazarene healer."

Simon jolted awake at the voice. Pain tore deep into his shoulder as he pushed into the solid stone against his back. He squinted against the bright sun laying low on the eastern horizon while he hastily rose to his feet.

He was scarcely aware of his surroundings but had drawn his dagger by the time he stood. He heard the scrape of sword against scabbard before his eyes adjusted to reveal two town elders standing before him. He did not recognize the elders, but from their dress he concluded that they were not Pharisees. A Roman soldier stood next to them, with his sword drawn.

Simon gripped his weapon more tightly. "You've come to arrest him?" he asked. "Why? He's done nothing wrong."

The soldier stepped closer to Simon. "You would dare to interfere with a lawful arrest?"

"Stand down, soldier," the seemingly older elder said. He addressed Simon, "You misunderstand our intentions. We were sent for the healer because he is needed."

Simon lowered his weapon, still gripping it tight at his side. "How do I know this isn't a trick?"

"There is no ruse! Marcus, the centurion who commands the garrison, sent us. His most faithful servant has taken ill, so he calls for the healer."

"And you think that I would just walk Jesus into this trap by sending him with you to the enemy's stronghold?"

"No," the elder pleaded. "You have it all wrong. Marcus is honorable. He acts with justice and has been a friend to our nation. He even built our synagogue."

"Built with the ill-gotten gains that he and all the Romans have extorted from us. If not for them, we could build a hundred synagogues!"

The soldier stepped forward again. "Why shouldn't I arrest you for sedition?"

"Stand down!" the elder said with increased exasperation. "We're here for healing, not to start a war!"

"We'll go," a voice answered from behind Simon. He turned to find Jesus approaching from the doorway.

"But these men would have you killed!" Simon protested.

The elders exchanged curious looks.

"No, Simon. These men are sincere," Jesus said. "I'll go. You should come with me."

"Into the enemy's lair?"

"To see the kingdom of God coming to fruition." Jesus turned to the elders and added, "Please lead the way."

———

Matthew woke and dressed with haste. He did not engage with his servants as he gathered his cloak and left the estate alone.

He had no guards. No servants carrying ledgers nor driving carts.

No purpose.

He had walked away from everything because of this Nazarene who healed with a touch and spoke of compassion and forgiveness.

The workers who follow him did not seem to want to forgive me.

Matthew did not blame them, but he had no idea how he could make it up to them, much less convince them that he had changed.

What will it take?

As Matthew approached the city gate, his brother, James, met him on the road, joined by another of Jesus' followers—a man called Judas. Judas was one of the twelve that Jesus had called aside the other day, and he was the only one beside Matthew who wasn't a laborer or fisherman.

"We thought you might have returned home," James said.

"Jesus wants you to join us."

"Where?"

"Not far. He has been called to the garrison."

Matthew shivered briefly as he recalled his last meeting with Samchai. The tax farmer had no problem exerting his authority over Matthew in a manner that Matthew felt as punitive. "That can't be! He has done nothing to deserve being taken in."

"It's not like that. Someone there needs healing."

"And Jesus agreed to go?"

"How is it any different from Jesus agreeing to be *your* guest?" Judas retorted with sharpness.

Matthew bristled and straightened. He nodded and followed his brother.

They reached the main road, where Jesus and the others waited with two local elders.

They followed a side street to the Roman compound built into the city wall. The gate to the compound stood open, flanked by two soldiers. The bunkhouse where they were headed was small, but as the only two-story structure in Capernaum, it looked imposing by comparison.

An administrator stepped out of the bunkhouse to meet them, accompanied by a decurion. "Marcus has asked that you not trouble yourself, Lord. He says that he is not worthy to have you come under his roof."

The words of the administrator stung Matthew's ears.

Why?

Jesus had been a guest in his home. *Am I more worthy than this Marcus who sends others to speak for him? Or have I been blind to my own lack of worthiness?*

Jesus hadn't been back to his estate since that first celebration.

Surely, he would be more comfortable there than in the simple home of a tenant fisherman.

He pushed his troubled thoughts aside and listened while the administrator delivered the centurion's message.

"Just say the word, and my servant will be healed. I am a man under authority, with soldiers under me. When I give one an order, he does as I command."

Matthew felt a new sting—the sting of loss. He had once ordered others, wielding the sword of Rome to pad his own purse.

Now my voice means nothing to these people.

And the people who exercised authority over him made sure he knew it. With no capacity or authority to exert his own will, he felt exposed and vulnerable.

Only this enigmatic teacher and a handful of laborers stood between Matthew and abject ruin.

Do they care if I suffer?

"Never have I witnessed such faith in all of Israel!" Jesus turned toward Matthew and the others and the dozens more that he only now realized had emerged from the city to see what was happening.

To the administrator, Jesus said, "Go tell Marcus that I have heard his request, and his servant is well."

Matthew wasn't sure what just happened, but a touch of hope creeped into his thoughts. *If Jesus would care to heal a Roman's servant, perhaps he will care enough to give me purpose, too.*

———

Jesus led the men back to the city gate. A crowd pressed behind them as travelers left their camps to converge on Jesus, adding difficulty to an otherwise simple trip.

Simon's attention was on the crowds emerging from the city itself. Several people—even women and children—made a hasty exit as shouting and clamor increased behind them. Not much farther back, Roman soldiers snapped bands of leather to drive them away.

Simon's hand found the hilt of his dagger, and he pushed through his companions. A hand grabbed his cloak at the shoulder, and he jerked his head around to find Thaddeus gripping him.

"You can't do this. It's too risky."

"They have no business driving *our* people out of *our* town!"

"Didn't you see what just happened? Jesus healed one of their servants."

"That's all the more reason for the people to be reassured that we are on their side!"

Thaddeus spun Simon around and grabbed both of his shoulders. "Simon. You know I love our nation, and I want just as badly as you to see God's kingdom restored. But sometimes you are blinded by your passion!"

A fresh wave of shouts—louder than before—erupted behind Simon.

After a moment, four Roman soldiers burst through the crowd, plowing and toppling bodies with their shields. The crowd tumbled backward and knocked Simon off his feet. Thaddeus still gripped his shoulders.

The two fell, Thaddeus atop of Simon. They scrambled to their feet, and Simon checked his belt. He was reassured to feel his weapon was still there.

The soldiers led two bound men toward the barracks. Simon thought that one looked familiar, but he had no time to examine his face more before he was lost behind the crowd.

"Does anybody else want to question the terms of our occupation?" a centurion barked as he stepped into the gateway and addressed the incoming crowd. "We have a ship headed to Tiberias. You can make your plea to Herod."

"We have no king but God!" Simon shouted with a renewed forward push. He could barely see the main avenue, where Romans ringed the toll booths and servants were resetting and reloading toppled carts. Soldiers bound two more men. Simon knew their faces from the docks but not their names.

"Simon, we're not going to get in there," Thaddeus said from behind him.

"And we don't need to," Jesus added as he stepped alongside Simon. "Let's go out with the people and see the kingdom of God."

Simon shook his head, but before he could protest, Jesus had already turned and was walking away from the town. Against his internal reluctance, Simon followed.

As they walked, Matthew approached Jesus. Simon strained to ignore the background noise and hear the toll collector.

"We could go to my estate," Matthew said to Jesus, but loud enough to be heard easily over the crowd. "There is plenty of room for our group to eat and rest. And ..."

Matthew hesitated, and Jesus turned to face him but didn't say anything. Matthew continued, "... I want to repay these people, somehow."

Jesus smiled and offered Matthew a comforting nod.

Simon had no interest in entering the toll collector's home. He still felt stained from his trip to Tiberias.

Now we're about to go to a traitor's home to be his guest?

Simon slowed his steps and let the crowd fill the space between Matthew and himself. They passed several houses belonging to wealthy landowners and traders. Each teemed with Roman soldiers.

The soldiers stood in pairs at each pathway, blocking access to any home or stable along the path.

Simon assessed the crowd. By numbers alone, they could overtake the Romans and claim the whole hill, even though these people were not warriors.

Jesus would never direct such an action.

Simon pondered the enigma of Jesus anew. His miracle-working was undeniable and unmatched. Yet he never used that power to advance against the enemy.

Perhaps he is waiting for the right time.

Simon recalled something Jesus said on the hillside the other day — something about the meek being favored and inheriting the Earth. Simon's attention returned to the present when they reached the path to Matthew's estate. No soldiers stood watch.

Did Matthew dismiss them?

No. Nobody was departing.

Why do they not afford this home the same protection as the others?

Jesus looked back and motioned for Simon to make his way to the front. He pushed through layers of bodies until he reached Jesus. Matthew led the group into a receiving room and through a side corridor into a banquet hall.

Simon remained near the door while others filed past. The crowd packed themselves into the hall, into the courtyard on the other side, and even filled the receiving room behind them.

"He has gone out of his mind," a voice behind Simon said. He turned to the sound and saw the familiar face of Jude, Jesus' younger brother, who was turned away and speaking to the rest of his brothers.

Before Simon could acknowledge him, two men led a man with clouded eyes through the doorway. "Let us through! We're here to see the healer!" they shouted as they wedged through the throng.

Two Pharisees, neither of whom Simon had seen around the synagogue, followed in their wake, straining to see inside.

Simon barely had a clear view himself when the blind man reached Jesus. Jesus clasped the man's temples and shouted, "Be gone, tormentor, and let this man see and speak!"

The blind man buckled over and grimaced. He writhed just a moment, then righted himself and opened his eyes to reveal clear, brown irises. He embraced Jesus and shouted, "Praise be to God! Thank you, Lord, for restoring me!"

"He's the possessed one!" The shout came from behind Simon in a voice that carried the accent of Jerusalem. Simon turned as a Pharisee pointed at Jesus. "He drives out demons by the prince of demons!"

Jesus called from the banquet hall. "How can Satan drive out Satan?" he challenged them. "A kingdom divided against itself cannot stand." Simon turned back and realized Jesus was looking directly at him. "A house divided against itself cannot stand."

Why direct that comment at me? It was Jesus who brought a traitor into the group – perhaps he should save his admonition for the tax collector ...

... the tax collector who seems to have been abandoned and cast aside by the Romans.

As Jesus spoke, something tugged Simon's sleeve, "Simon! Please help us!"

Jude had finally noticed him.

"You're close to Jesus. Go in there and bring him out. We're begging you!"

"I don't know if I can persuade him."

"Please. We are his family, and we need him to come home and care for his mother and stop this … Please. Just let him know that his mother and his brothers wish to speak with him. Surely, he'll listen to that much reason."

"I'll try."

Simon forced his way into the banquet hall.

"Teacher!" he called. When Jesus turned, Simon continued, "Your mother and brothers are outside to see you."

"Who are my mother and brothers?" Jesus responded.

Simon didn't know how to respond. The curious look on his face must have been evident. Jesus continued with a flourishing wave of his hands around the room. "Here are my mother and my brothers. Whoever does my Father's will is my brother and my sister and my mother."

Simon looked back at Jude and shrugged. Jude hung his head and turned away.

The Pharisees let out an exaggerated gasp of disdain. "Did he really say such a thing?" one shouted. Simon was too bewildered to engage their indignation, even while he pondered their question.

How could Jesus keep such strange company and say such peculiar things while asserting that a house divided cannot stand?

———

Matthew surveyed the crowd that filled his banquet hall, receiving room, and courtyard. He pushed his way to an open window. Outside, crowds fanned out in every direction all the way to the road.

He fought against the swarm to get near Jesus.

"Teacher! There are too many. They cannot all see and hear you, and my land cannot accommodate them."

"We'll return to the shore then." Jesus turned to John and James. "Go and prepare our boat."

As the pair muscled toward the door, Jesus told Matthew, "Send the people to the shore. I will speak to them there."

Matthew called over the crowd, "Go to the shore. Jesus will not be staying here. It is time to leave this house!"

Few people seemed to hear him. Even fewer heeded him.

With every step, Matthew pushed whatever bodies were before him. "It is time to go! This is my house, and you need to get out! The teacher can meet you at the shore."

The shoves had little effect as the mass of bodies pressed back from the outside.

Just beyond the doorway, Matthew spotted Simon, the angry dockworker. He preferred to avoid the young man but had no choice in the moment.

"Simon, help me send these people away. Jesus is taking them to the shore."

"Is that one of his *brothers*? The tax collectors? Who next? Prostitutes?" two Pharisees in the crowd shouted, seemingly to anyone who would listen. Matthew gave Simon a puzzled look.

"They didn't like what Jesus had to say. They aren't enamored with his host either."

Matthew bit back a retort. "Well, Jesus wants to get back to the shore. Help me get these people out of here."

Simon turned toward the crowd. "It is time to return to the shore!" his voiced boomed, startling Matthew. "Jesus will see you there."

"Thank you," Matthew said to Simon.

"I'm not doing this for you."

The people slowly retreated. Many looked back. After a moment, Jesus exited and stepped in front of Matthew. The people let him pass, and Matthew and Simon both fell in line behind him.

"Here is the man who rejects his own mother to keep the company of tax collectors," an agitating Pharisee said as Jesus passed. "He is not worthy to be called 'teacher'!"

Matthew kept his head down, expecting to be taunted, pushed, or hit at any moment. But no action—not even a word—came against him. The crowd that followed behind them created some separation between him and the Pharisees, for which he was grateful.

The main avenue toward town was still filled with soldiers, though the chaos from earlier appeared to have settled.

Jesus addressed his disciples. "Andrew, get your brother and come with me. We'll go through the city. The rest of you, take the people on the hillside road outside town to the other side."

Matthew turned to Simon, who was already calling to the nearest of the crowd. "You heard him. We'll take the road, not the shoreline. Follow us."

Simon turned and led the procession past the garrison and around the edge of the city without acknowledging Matthew—or anybody else.

Matthew bit back more words and quietly hoped for a time—soon—when he could speak his mind to this young man.

The road was rocky and uneven and at points too narrow. Matthew walked in silence, not understanding why Jesus would choose this over the comforts of Matthew's spacious home. Of course, the size of the crowd made the hillside practical for teaching.

But in the quiet times, when it is just our small group, why not seek a little comfort?

Before it is gone.

Matthew no longer enjoyed the security of hired guards who had the authority to enforce the rule of Roman law.

With his resignation, his income—legitimate and questionable alike—was diminished.

And now Samchai threatened to impose further penalties on what remained.

Familiar fears rose to the surface of his mind.

How much can I stand to lose? And how will I replace my losses by following Jesus?

Matthew reached the hillside, where the people were already spread far and wide across as if taking seats at a Greek theater. Poor and sick, widows and orphans, laborers and those unable to work—they had nothing to lose, for they had nothing at all.

Nothing except the hope that they found in this Nazarene teacher, himself a poor laborer like them, but with wisdom and a presence that Matthew could not express. He was unlike anyone Matthew had ever met.

Matthew was fascinated by Jesus. And it utterly terrified him.

At the foot of the hill, crowds pressed tightly on the shoreline. Matthew descended the slope with awkward caution. As he neared the base, a boat pushed off from shore, carrying Jesus and his fishermen companions. They set out just beyond reach of the people who waded into the sea toward him. Some of the other chosen twelve stood in waist-deep water and assisted them safely back to shore.

Matthew wondered how he fit with this group. His skills had no use here. He kept his feet firmly planted on dry ground and watched as Jesus directed John and James to stop the boat. James dropped an anchor.

Jesus sat facing the shore and began to speak. The crowds moved closer together until they were pressed tightly, spanning the shoreline, and standing dozens of bodies deep on the hillside—all with silent attention fixed on Jesus.

Matthew heard a stirring nearby, and Judas, another one of the twelve, pushed through and stood beside him. Judas' hem and feet were as dry as Matthew's own.

Jesus was nothing like the teachers that Matthew recalled from the synagogue in his youth. They read the scriptures and appealed to the sayings of the scribes and teachers that had gone before them.

No, Jesus tells the people stories. When the stories are done, he tells them more stories.

Jesus told stories about sowing seeds and pulling weeds. About sun-scorched plants and scavenging birds. About growing grain and plants so big that birds make their homes in the branches.

"Do you understand any of this?" Judas asked him.

"I've never been a farmer. I'm sure these stories make more sense to these people."

"Look at how they listen. They cling to every word he says."

Matthew took another look at the crowd, surprised to entertain a new thought.

Envy.

Hope, peace, joy. On face after face, he saw the way everyone regarded Jesus with … expectation.

But what do I expect?

He expected his way of life to continue to crumble beneath his feet until he had nothing left.

"So why do you follow him?" Judas' question startled Matthew.

Has he been reading my thoughts?

"Samchai asked me the same question. And I don't know if I can answer. All my business sense says this is a waste of time and resources. Still, there's something about him. I guess it is the way he sees me so honestly—different from all the officials, tax farmers, and traders. But I can't say how he does it or what it means."

"Do you think he could be the messiah?"

"Every would-be messiah that I've seen stirs up problems just to fix them. But Jesus—his talk of the kingdom of God is … different. And the healings. Who can explain them? But who can ignore them? Maybe you can help me understand. Tell me why *you* follow him."

"I'm probably more like you than like them," Judas said and gestured toward the fishermen. "Except I've followed a few of those would-be messiahs."

The revelation surprised Matthew, and he was sure his face did not hide it.

Judas added, "They all let me down, usually by getting crucified. Maybe Jesus will let me down, too, if I give him enough time. But like you said. He's different."

The mention of crucifixion prompted a new pang of fear. Matthew had been around the Romans long enough to know that when one threat caught their notice, they were sure to eliminate their target *and* any who might continue his efforts.

Herod was already holding the baptizer that first drew everyone's attention to Jesus.

Could he be next? Could all of us be next?

Matthew's attention was yanked back to the moment when two of the twelve, Philip and Nathaniel, approached them, dripping with sea water from the waist down.

"Jesus wants you both to get to the boat. He's taking us across the lake."

"To Tiberias?" Matthew asked without hiding his surprise or apprehension.

"No. To the east."

They turned back, and Matthew and Judas followed. Matthew was relieved that they were heading away from Tiberias, but it wasn't enough to assuage his growing fear.

"Are publicans permitted to get their feet wet?"

Matthew bit back a reply to Simon's barb. Instead he made a show of getting his feet and his hem wet as he climbed into the boat while the fishermen steadied it. He was sure that his clumsy effort revealed a lack of experience with boats.

Matthew unsteadily righted himself. Even with the fishermen holding the boat, he couldn't acclimate to the movement of the vessel.

"Teacher! Let me come with you!" A young man emerged from the crowd and approached the boat. His attire suggested that he was suited to life in the synagogue.

"Foxes have holes, and birds have nests," Jesus answered the man. "But the Son of Man has no place to lay his head."

Matthew turned to Judas. "Even answering a simple request, he uses riddles and stories."

"But do you understand the riddles?"

Matthew thought of the life he abandoned. He was despised, but he could purchase enough security to ensure his comfort. He never lacked for food nor a comfortable place to rest his head.

Now, he had forsaken all of that to follow this teacher—even onto a boat in the evening—unable to rest in his own home. He was still despised by the people, except perhaps the men in the boat.

Most of them, anyway.

Matthew nodded to Judas. "Yes. I understand it all too well."

The fishermen pushed the boat off the shore, and Matthew gripped the side as they rocked on the surface of the water.

Jesus was already seated near the stern, enjoying the meager comfort of a small mat where he rested his head in a way that seemed impossibly unnatural. Yet, Jesus rested as if he enjoyed the comfort of royalty.

Even if Matthew had a place to rest his head in the boat, he would not. He focused his sight on his own feet as daylight dimmed. He felt each lap of the water's surface against the side of the boat. He didn't need to see it, too.

Darkness took over, and Matthew lost track of time. He couldn't gather the courage to look toward the stars, nor anywhere at all beyond the edge of the boat. The rocking seemed to grow more intense, but he wasn't sure if it was a trick of his own mind.

"What was that?" someone let out—Matthew couldn't tell who—and a new dread overtook him as the exclamation confirmed his own experience.

A cold gust sprayed Matthew's face, and he ducked as low as he could go. Water splashed over the side, drenching him head to toe.

Where is Simon's callous mockery now?

The boat lifted and then suddenly dropped. A wave breached the edge and collapsed on Matthew's head. He gasped and was surprised to feel the boards of the boat still beneath his legs.

He wanted to cry out but was too paralyzed with fear to speak. Over the howl of the wind and the crash of the waves, he barely heard the others saying all the things he wanted to say.

"Has it ever been this bad before?"

"We should have waited until morning to set out."

"Is there anything we can do?"

"How can you sleep! Teacher, don't you care that we are going to drown?"

Matthew wasn't sure who spoke that last, but he was alarmed that Jesus could somehow sleep through the chaos. "Please, help us," he added, though he was sure nobody could hear his weak plea over the voices of the others and the noise of the storm.

"Quiet! Be still!" The unmistakable voice of Jesus cut through all the other sounds. The boat dropped hard onto the surface as if the wave it was cresting had simply dissipated underneath it.

Matthew's bones jolted, and his stomach churned. He heard his own groaning and only then realized that the wind was gone.

He stayed low and looked up, barely able to make out the others in the moonlight. As far as he could tell, they were all still present. Jesus stood in the spot where Matthew had last seen him drifting into sleep.

"Why are you all so afraid? Do you have no faith?" Jesus asked. Nobody answered.

Matthew considered the fear still pounding as his heart thrummed within his own chest. "Who is this?" he heard someone say. He thought it might be Simon, but without the angst that usually characterized his tone. Instead, the man sounded just as fearful as Matthew felt. "Even the winds and the waves obey him."

Matthew nodded and allowed himself a moment of relief that Jesus had somehow calmed the storm.

If only he could have the same effect on my crumbling life …

Chapter Ten

As the sun breached the eastern hilltops, the disciples steered their boat toward a small inlet nested between steep cliff-faced hills. The cliffs cast long shadows across the boat while waves cut gently into the rocky wall.

A small stream fed the inlet. A village was barely visible where the stream disappeared beyond the rising hillside. Across the valley, a herd of pigs freely roamed a neighboring hill.

Simon fought back a foul taste at the mere sight of pigs.

After sleeping in Tiberias then entering the home of a tax collector, Simon was unsure how much more uncleanness he could endure. He longed for a mikvah, a ritual bath.

I'll never find one in pig country. I don't even know why we are here.

A wild howl returned his attention to the moment. The scream endured beyond the normal capacity of human breath. A man raced toward the shore from the shadows of the steep hills to their left.

At least Simon thought it was a man.

The man's hair was long and unkempt, tangled with dirt and debris. He wore only a shackle on one ankle. The binding was misshapen and dented, with the remains of a broken ring protruding from one side.

A layer of dirt failed to mask the long gashes splayed across the man's torso, arms, and thighs—too many to count. Some had long been scarred over, and others seeped with freshness.

In contrast to the man's appearance, he ran with strength and vigor toward them. As the fishermen exited the boat and pulled it aground, he approached near enough for Simon to discern raw fear in his eyes. Wide open and alert, they signaled a sharp mind trapped behind layers of torment.

"What do you want with me, Jesus, son of the God most high?" The man stumbled and fell face-first into the gravel as Jesus stepped out of the boat. Unhampered by the blow, he cast a pleading look at Jesus from his prone position. "Swear that you will not torture me."

Torture? Jesus never raises a blade to another—even when he should. How deluded is this man that he fears violence?

Then a larger question invaded Simon's thoughts.

How does he know Jesus at all, let alone recognize him while our boat is still offshore?

"What is your name?" Jesus asked as he stepped closer to the man. Simon and the others remained in the boat.

"We are Legion," the man cried into the gravel while resting his face on the ground. "Please do not send us away or torture us. If you must drive us out, send us into the pigs!"

"Go!" Jesus said.

The man rolled onto his back and wailed a strong howl, even more powerful than the one that announced his arrival. Almost at once, the sound of his voice was overtaken by the squeals, grunts, and shrieks of the nearby pigs. Simon hadn't spent enough time around pigs to know their natural sounds, but he was sure that the terrible grating in his ears was not natural. He was even more sure what the pigs did next was not normal either.

Crashing hooves joined the torrent of sound, followed by pounding waters. Even as the boat sat aground, waves struck with force and breached the edge, jostling the disciples.

As Simon watched, dozens of pigs raced down the steep hill toward the water. Simon wasn't sure if pigs could swim, but these pigs began to panic in the rough sea. Porcine bodies piled up in the water as more trampled over them and into the deeper waters of the sea beyond.

As the last of the pigs scrambled down the hill to their deaths, the man lay exhausted on the shore, panting, his eyes open and lucid. He turned over and looked down at his own body, then promptly stooped and hunched in a tight posture, suddenly aware of his shame.

The toll collector removed his embroidered cloak—the most richly made garment in the boat—and tossed it to the man.

Jesus was the first to step ashore.

As he did, dozens of men ran down the banks of the stream from the village above.

"What have you done?"

"You've made our pigs mad!"

"Do you have any idea what we have lost here?"

The healed man faced the villagers and said, "This man is sent from God. Look! He has freed me!"

"Who are you? What power have you unleashed on us?" the villagers persisted.

The man stepped between them and Jesus. "Look and you will see! He has released me from the evil spirits."

"But he must leave!" The villager nearest Jesus turned to him. "You must go! You cannot stay here."

"Please don't send him away," the healed man pleaded. "He is a good man. Look what he has done for me!"

To Simon's surprise, Jesus said nothing in his own defense. He turned and climbed back into the boat.

"Please let me go with you!" The formerly possessed man stepped into the water and grabbed ahold of the boat.

Jesus turned to him and said, "Go and tell your family what the Lord has done for you and how he has shown you mercy."

Simon turned the words over in his head as they left the shore.

Mercy. Accepted by one and rejected by many.

Simon hoped that Jesus would soon move on to the real work of the kingdom of God.

Mercy will only get him killed.

Despite the bright midday sun, Matthew felt the chill of the unimpeded breeze. With his cloak gone, he had only a thin undercoat to protect him. He held it tight and tried in vain to find relief from the wind.

"Why did we come all this way only to turn back?" Nathaniel asked.

"It seemed like a lot of wasted time," added Judas. "We couldn't even set foot on the shore without being turned away."

"Not like Capernaum," Simon said. "There you have enough followers to raise an army!"

Matthew looked intently at Simon; all the others had stopped their conversation and regarded the young man, too.

Jesus broke the silence. "I've chosen you—each of you, all of you—not an army. Today, you saw power that no army possesses. A man too strong for chains was conquered by mercy, not by the sword."

"But that's not the way the Romans work," Simon answered through a scowl as he turned toward Matthew.

"Why do you still hold that against me?" Anger welled up within Matthew. "I've left that life behind, and it has cost me!"

"Cost you what? A cloak far nicer than the ones who made you rich could ever own?"

"Simon, there is so much that you *don't know* about what I have paid—and continue to pay!"

"What I do know is this. Everything you have paid was first paid by others. That's something *you* will never understand. You'll never grasp how much *I* have paid!" Simon's face reddened as he spoke, and Matthew shivered—more from fear than cold.

"You *all* still have much to learn about the cost of following me," Jesus interjected, and Matthew was grateful that he did. "Don't be surprised when men reject you, just as they rejected me. But know that your Father in heaven sees you. Let that priceless treasure be your reward."

Neither Simon nor Matthew—nor any of the others who were all listening intently—argued further.

Jesus continued, "Today's journey is not wasted, as you will soon see."

———

Jesus instructed the fishermen to steer away from the docks, toward the hillside. A crowd waited by the lake, and shouts rose from the onlookers up the hill. More people rose from their slumber and strode, pressing one another, toward the shoreline.

How many more people have come since we left?

The boat reached the shore, and one onlooker in particular caught Simon's eye. A synagogue leader named Jairus—a man Simon recognized—shouldered his way to the front of the crowd. His robes and obvious status did little to compel others to step aside as all attention remained on the boat.

Simon closed his eyes and thought back to Tiberias.

Did I see Jairus meeting with the Herodians?

He didn't think so, but couldn't shed the last threads of doubt.

James and John maneuvered the boat to ground, and Jairus pushed back against the pressing crowd to maintain his position in the front.

Two fishermen stepped off the boat and secured it with stakes. Jesus followed them off, and the crowd pressed closer.

Jairus, with a clumsy manor not suited to his station, lurched forward and dove to the ground at Jesus' feet, hugging his ankles.

Hand on hilt, Simon scanned the crowd. Jairus appeared to be alone, but the Herodians—and their Roman overseers—were not above trickery in these situations.

"Please come quickly, teacher. My daughter is dying," Jairus pleaded, still prostrate. He looked up. "She is at my home. Please come right away. I know you can make her well."

Simon and the rest climbed out of the boat while Jesus helped the man to his feet.

Simon looked from face to face — forlorn and hopeful alike — for any threat.

Jairus cut through the crowd along the shoreline toward Capernaum while Jesus followed. Simon tried to keep up, but the movement of the crowd slowed him. Bodies pressed from all sides, and Simon became more distanced from Jesus.

I can't protect him.

A hand squeezed Simon's right arm, and he tried to pull free while maneuvering his other hand toward his hilt. He could do neither as the grip tightened against his resistance.

"I thought I might find you here," a voice said behind his ear.

Manaen.

"We need to talk."

Simon tried to step away, but Manaen held tightly, and two more hands grabbed his other arm. The crowd bumped and knocked past them.

After most of the crowd passed, the men led Simon down the shoreline to the familiar old dock. They eased their grips but did not let go. Simon chose not to resist.

A few slower-going people still moved past them as Manaen climbed down below the dock. At the other man's prodding, Simon followed, and after a moment, the second man — who Simon was finally able to see but did not recognize — followed.

"We've not heard from you since Tiberias," Manaen began. "You left with such haste that we were worried you might compromise our plans."

"I left because an urgent matter came up. But make no mistake, I was glad to leave such a defiled and unclean place," Simon answered.

Manaen chuckled. "I appreciate your distaste for the city. But I don't understand what matter was so urgent that it reached you then and there. And how? Why would you risk the lives of your brothers and all that we fight to accomplish?"

Should I tell Manaen about the plot against Jesus? What if he's also a part of it?

Simon knew that an alliance between Zealots and Herodians was unlikely. Still, Jesus had a knack for uniting people in unexpected friendship.

And earning himself unexpected enemies.

"It was a personal matter — not relevant to the movement."

"When a key lookout post is abandoned and an operative disappears as suddenly as he arrived, it is of *significant* relevance!" Manaen stepped closer, almost nose to nose with Simon. "Some say you could be a spy."

Simon bristled. "Who would say such a thing? You know my loyalty, Manaen. You've seen my work. No king but God!"

"Your past accomplishments are the only reason that I even bother to have this exchange. Others would just as soon cut you down," Manaen responded. "Still, your actions in Tiberias raise a fair question. This teacher that you've been following — one who has refused to take up our cause, I might point out — has shown himself to be a friend to tax collectors and now even to centurions!"

"He heals without regard, true. But all he talks about is the kingdom of God. His command over the spirits and over illness testifies to his power."

"If he is proclaiming God's kingdom, why keep the company of traitors?" Manaen challenged. "Why provide comfort to the enemy? Why sail east to unclean lands? *We* are God's chosen people, Simon. Your teacher seems to miss this important truth. I've heard the grumblings of the Pharisees and the teachers of the law."

Maybe Manaen really is in on the plot?

"What are you saying?" Simon forced an accusing tone as he spoke.

"Your teacher seems to have amassed quite a following. That much is obvious. But it is *equally* obvious from the company he keeps and the people he attracts that his following will never amount to anything resembling an army."

"I don't see why that's a concern," Simon replied.

"Then you've been blinded, Simon." Manaen paced as he added, "Whatever sort of messiah your teacher thinks he is, as long as people follow him, they will be following him on a road to nowhere.

"We need as many able bodies and willing hearts as possible if our movement is to prevail," Manaen continued. "The increased taxes and the presence of more soldiers mean that *now* is the time to win people to our cause, while Rome's actions impact them *personally. Now* is the time for you to make the right choice, Simon."

"Choice?" Simon wasn't sure what he was being asked.

"You can return to the movement and help us establish a *real* kingdom."

"And if I remain with Jesus?"

"Then you will be working against us. We will raise our army with or without you and your teacher. When we do, don't think the favor he has shown the enemy will be forgotten."

Simon stared at Manaen for a long, silent moment.

He's not part of the Pharisee's plot.

But he's just as dangerous. Perhaps more so.

But do either of us understand what Jesus is doing?

"You'll have my answer in due time. But now, I must return home to my wife," Simon said, then climbed the embankment and returned to town.

―――

Traveling gave Matthew a strange sense of relief. Despite the simple accommodations in the villages and the lack of familiar comforts, he was glad to be away from Capernaum and the constant reminders of his past.

Of my seemingly unfinished business with Samchai.

Matthew was certain his records were in order, but not certain that would be enough.

How else could he conspire against me with the backing of Herod's office?

His thoughts returned to the moment as they approached Nazareth. Matthew had never visited the tiny town, preferring the large cities on the ports and trade routes.

The houses were among the most rudimentary he had seen— loose stonework patched with dried mud. There were few signs of commerce. Most of the houses surrounded small garden patches— little more than enough to feed a family. Women and children tended the gardens.

"Where are the men?" Matthew asked.

"You shouldn't really expect much from Nazareth," a voice called from behind him. Matthew turned and saw that Nathaniel had been the one to respond. Without furthering the dialog, he turned ahead.

"To answer your question," Jesus added, "most of the work is in the larger towns: building projects, farms, wine presses. The men go out from Nazareth to find work. We'll lodge until the Sabbath. Then we will meet them in the synagogue."

"This small town has a synagogue?" Nathaniel asked.

"Don't be surprised, Nathaniel, that even in the smallest villages the word of God is honored."

They moved among the houses on unpaved streets. Even the main street that divided the town was little more than a wider version of the dirt paths that partitioned the garden patches.

Women and children glanced up from their work as they passed. It was a noticeable contrast from the excited swarms that typically greeted them.

A man just past his prime sat on a boulder outside one house where two children about nine or ten years old gathered lentils. The man waved but said nothing.

"Why is that man not off working like the others?" Judas asked Jesus.

"Let's find out," Jesus responded.

"Peace to you!" Jesus called as he approached the man, his disciples close behind him.

"Peace," the man responded in a hoarse whisper. "They tell me you're a teacher now. And a healer," he coughed.

"And you were a proficient metal worker. You've … rested from your labors?"

"What choice do I have? Since I fell ill, the heat chokes my breath. Even here in the cool air, I can't draw enough air to walk."

"Do you believe what you have heard?"

The man nodded wordlessly, and Jesus stooped and placed one hand in the middle of his back. He placed his other hand on the man's chest and said, "Your disease is gone; your lungs are free. Breathe the breath of life."

The man inhaled, sputtered, and coughed again. After a moment, he inhaled again, his chest rising with strength as he breathed deeply, audibly. "I haven't felt this way in a long time," he said with volume and clarity that made him sound twenty years younger.

The boy in the garden turned, dropped his basket, and ran over.

"Father, what happened?" He turned to Jesus. "Is he well?"

"He is well."

"Yes, I am well. Go and get your mother." The man stood and stretched life into long-idle legs. He clasped Jesus' shoulders. "Thank you, friend." He kissed Jesus on the cheek and turned to the doorway where his wife now stood.

———

The synagogue in Nazareth was smaller than Matthew's house but was still the largest, most prominent structure in this town. The men had returned from their work, and the entire village of several hundred gathered to listen to the teachers.

Matthew was grateful to be around people and have something to do. The week was uncharacteristically quiet. Apart from the metal worker and a few children, nobody had sought Jesus out.

After a young teacher of the law finished expounding on the writings of the prophet Isaiah, Jesus took a place in the teacher's seat. The people murmured among themselves while offering skewed glances to the disciples gathered near the back of the room.

Jesus taught from the Psalms, songs about finding refuge in the Lord. He spoke of David's troubles and the dangers he faced with such vivid detail that it sounded as if he had been there. The room stilled to complete quiet and rapt attention as he spoke.

They've ignored Jesus since we arrived. Why regarded him with such acute notice now?

When Jesus finished teaching, the murmurs rose again, louder than before. Some hollered at Jesus. One man who stood near the disciples turned to them and asked, "Where did this man get these things?"

"What do you mean?" John asked him.

"We've never heard these teachings. Where do they come from? And the miracles that we have heard about. Where do they come from?"

"Do you not believe?" John pressed him.

Another man joined the conversation. "He is just a builder, no different from us. What is there to believe? He's Mary's son, along with James, Joseph, Simon, and Jude. His sisters live among us."

Mary's son?

It was an unveiled slur, a challenge to the legitimacy of Jesus' teaching and miracles.

To the legitimacy of Jesus himself.

Cold expressions worn by the other disciples showed that they heard it, too. Young Simon the dockhand wore a particularly fierce scowl that failed to veil the deep well of anger inside him. Thaddeus stepped to Simon's side and placed a hand on his shoulder.

Matthew scanned the crowd, looking for Jesus. He found him walking along the side wall toward the disciples. The insults and offenses followed him.

"This is unlike anything we have seen," Simon the fisherman said with exaggerated alarm when Jesus reached them.

"Only in his hometown is a prophet without honor," Jesus responded with consoling eyes. "Still, what you've learned here is not wasted, as you will see in time. For now, we need to return to Capernaum."

Jesus and the disciples neared the end of their two-day walk home from Nazareth. As Capernaum came into view, a messenger on horseback came out to meet them.

"Which of you is Matthew, son of Alphaeus?"

"I am Matthew."

The messenger eyed Matthew up and down and scanned the rest of the group. His eyes darted between Matthew and Judas. Matthew looked down and understood the messenger's doubt. *A plain cloak.*

"So you say. Samchai requests your immediate presence. He has been waiting too long here, and his patience grows thin," the messenger said. His hands were empty.

No documents or orders?

"Where will I find him?"

"At the home of Jonathan." Matthew knew of the younger toll collector, whose estate was not far from his own.

Matthew turned to Jesus. "Please excuse me. I must go."

"We will all go," Jesus responded.

Simon looked at Jesus with wide-eyed, mouth-agape shock. Jesus offered only a passing glance in response.

"Let's go, then."

Matthew followed the messenger to the city, with Jesus and the others following close behind.

They passed the city gate and approached the estates of the landowners on the outskirts, then followed the first offshoot to a large dwelling. It was smaller than Matthew's home but newer and more visibly adorned.

Samchai and Jonathan met them on the road, flanked by two Roman soldiers. Samchai looked up and down at Matthew. "You have gone even farther than I would have expected in renouncing your office."

Jonathan chuckled, and Matthew felt a nudge at his right shoulder. He briefly glanced sideways. Simon had come around to the front of the group, a stern expression in his piercing eyes and squared jaw.

"Someone else needed my cloak more than I did," Matthew said, held out his hands wide, and smiled.

"Perhaps I was right to fear that you had absconded after our last meeting."

"Absconded? I traveled, and now I've returned." Matthew looked to his left and right, indicating Jesus and the others with flair. "Surely, you have heard that we are not difficult to find."

Quiet laughs rose behind Matthew, but Samchai set his face hard against any mirth.

"And surely you've been *funding* this excursion quite generously, seeing it has cost you your cloak," Samchai said.

It was the Romans' turn to laugh.

"But enough with the banter," Samchai said with forced formality.

"Shall we meet, then?" Matthew responded, then turned to Jonathan, "I trust you have suitable space for our conference?"

Samchai held up a hand in front of the junior toll taker. "This won't take long. Right here will be fine." He held out a small codex, bound and sealed.

"I've reviewed your accounting and compared the shortages tabulated by others. Another mina is required to settle the discrepancies."

"A full mina? How is that possible? I told you that my books are clean, and all payments have been made. Let me show you." Matthew broke the seal and opened the codex, which contained only the tabulation provided by Samchai. "Where are my books?"

Samchai looked surprised. "Surely you kept your own copies. The ones that you gave me are in safe keeping in the official records store of Herod's office."

Those are my only records. What a costly error.

"I'll expect full payment by the end of tomorrow," Samchai said as he looked across the group that stood wordlessly around Matthew. "I trust you haven't spent it *all* in the course of your ... activities."

"You will have it," Matthew added with forced calm and a touch of defeat. He turned and started down the path.

"One more thing," Samchai called from behind him.

Matthew turned back. He noted that Simon remained in the rear of the group, still facing the tax farmer and his guards.

"There is the matter of interest on the balance as well. Jonathan will see to it that it is collected from your ... beneficiaries ... in due course."

Matthew said nothing as he turned back toward the road.

"What did he mean by that?" James asked him.

"It means the price for living in Capernaum just went up. For all of us."

Chapter Eleven

As the sun rose over the eastern mountains, Simon loaded lumber from a northern trade wagon onto a docked ship.

"Simon!" a voice called from behind him. He turned his head as far as his load allowed. In his periphery, Matthew approached.

"Not here. Not now," Simon grunted while he passed lumber down the line of workers in choreographed rhythm.

"I only need a moment."

"I don't have a moment."

"What do you mean?"

"I don't pay you to talk!" came a bark from the top of the ramp.

"That's what I mean," Simon said through clenched teeth, still passing timber as quickly as he received it.

"Please. I need your help!"

"And I need to work! I had to pay an hour's wages before I could even come to the docks. I haven't earned anything for myself yet."

"That's not how it's done!" The exaggerated incredulity in Matthew's voice matched the flail of his arms.

"It is now. Go. We can meet this evening at the fishermen's house."

"Very well then."

Simon assumed by the silence that Matthew had left. He didn't bother to check as lumber continued passing through his hands.

––––––

Simon approached the fishermen's house, where Matthew, Jesus, and Judas sat in the courtyard.

"Good. You're here. Time is running out!" Matthew said as he stood and approached Simon.

"Time for what?"

"I have to settle with Samchai, and I would like you to accompany me."

"I've worked all day. I paid a toll before beginning work and a *double* toll when leaving all because of whatever dispute you have with this Samchai. Now you expect me to be *more* of a nuisance to him?" Simon clenched his fists and paced the courtyard.

Matthew stepped out of his way and sat back down.

"I don't expect you to do anything but keep me from going alone."

"Until he changes the terms. Or his soldiers cause trouble. Or any of a dozen other reasons why you want me close. I can't help you. This mess has already cost me enough."

"Yesterday, you were the quickest to help," Jesus added. "You were the one who stepped to Matthew's side."

Simon took a deep breath and forced calm back into his voice. Jesus was right. Arguing with him would likely be fruitless, but Simon didn't want to give in too easily. "Yesterday, trouble came to us, and I responded. That doesn't mean I want to go looking for it."

Jesus stared wordlessly at Simon for a long moment. Simon thought better of adding to his defense.

"There will be no trouble. I want this to be done, too," Matthew offered. "I will pay what Samchai has asked, and the matter will be settled."

Simon looked from Jesus to Matthew, then back to Jesus. Jesus nodded with a slight smile.

"Let's go then," Simon sighed.

They left town in silence and walked toward Matthew's estate. There was no activity around Jonathan's land as they passed.

If Samchai and his men are expecting us, they don't show it.

Simon stopped at the doorway when they reached Matthew's home.

"Please, come in and have a seat," Matthew implored.

Simon stopped short of the entrance. "You invited me for a purpose. Let me stand watch. At the door."

"Very well."

Simon stood facing the road. Matthew emerged after several minutes carrying a purse. They walked in silence to Jonathan's nearby estate.

Samchai and his Roman guards met them on the path.

Simon stayed close to Matthew but made no movement toward his hilt.

"One mina to settle the accounts for good." Matthew held out the purse.

Samchai took the bag and opened it. He peered inside and nodded, then handed the bag to a guard, who stowed it in a larger sack.

The guards kept their attention on Simon while Samchai handed a rolled, sealed parchment to Matthew. "Your receipt."

Matthew opened the parchment. Simon was relieved that he didn't have the naïvety to stow the document without examining it, as he was expecting the publican to do.

Simon glanced across Matthew's shoulder to confirm for himself that the receipt was correct and complete. He looked wordlessly at Matthew.

"Very well," Matthew said to Samchai. "Our business is concluded then."

"I should hope so," Samchai responded.

I wish it were so ...

Simon bit back words. He placed a hand on Matthew's shoulder and turned to leave. His jaw ached with tension as Matthew walked beside him.

When they reached the main road, Simon said, "He's not done."

"What do you mean?" Matthew sounded perplexed. "The account is settled."

Simon kept his eyes on the road. "They are never done until they are stopped."

After a long silence, Matthew said, "I should thank you for accompanying me today."

"I didn't do this for you."

———

The meeting with Samchai left Matthew feeling uneasy. Simon's comment didn't help, but Matthew couldn't confidently challenge the young man's assessment.

He might be right.

Matthew remained wary as they entered Capernaum and strode down the main avenue. They turned down a side street ahead of the toll booths that partitioned the commerce and shipping district from the residential areas.

It was evening, and the normal workday was over. Activity at the toll booth was sparse.

One guard locked eyes with Matthew, prompting him to look away as they turned the corner. Twice he looked back, and twice he confirmed that the Roman's eyes followed him, but his feet did not. Matthew allowed himself a small feeling of relief.

They reached the home of Simon the fisherman, where Jesus and the rest of their companions prepared for the evening meal.

As Matthew reflected on his brief exchange with Simon and their obvious differences, he noticed for the first time the composite makeup of Jesus' handpicked group of close friends.

What a contradiction.

They were more than just fishermen and dockhands. There was the older, more business-minded Judas. Then the young traders, Philip and Nathaniel. Of course there was Matthew's own brother, James, who had forsaken earthly comforts and lived his own simple quest for personal piety. If not for Jesus, Matthew was sure his brother would have joined the Essene community by now.

A publican might be the greatest contradiction of all.

Matthew didn't share in the tedious life of fishermen and laborers. He didn't embrace the law with the fervor of Simon and the other young men.

As one who lived indifferent toward the law while he pursued his own comfort, he felt starkly out of place.

Even in a room that barely contained the group, he felt alone.

I don't belong here.

Nor did he belong where he once was.

So he reclined at the table—surrounded by men but utterly lonely.

"The harvest is ready, but the workers are few," Jesus said while they ate.

Harvest is months off. The field hands have barely finished sowing.

Matthew glanced around. The other faces at the table confirmed that he was not the only one who didn't understand.

"The Lord of the harvest is sending you as workers into his fields."

"Teacher, harvest is still months away!" Thomas spoke up. "Where is there a ripe field?"

"I'm sending you out among the lost sheep of Israel. Go into the towns and villages and proclaim, 'The kingdom of heaven is near.' Heal the sick and the lepers. Raise the dead and drive out demons."

"How can we do these things?" asked Judas. "We have seen *your* power to heal sickness and command evil spirits. That's why we follow you. But *we* don't have your power."

Jesus turned to Judas. "The authority that I have been given, I now grant to you." He met each pair of eyes in succession and continued, "Use it. Do not go into the Samaritan or Gentile villages, but only to the lost sheep of Israel. Take no coin, no bag, not even an extra tunic. When you enter a town, search for a worthy person and stay as his guest ..."

Is it too late to back out?

Some of their travels had been less comfortable than Matthew would have liked, but this was different. Could he endure not being able to depend on his own resources?

If I stay, what could I return to?

With Jesus and his companions gone, Matthew would be vulnerable to Romans and resentful Galileans alike. He resigned himself to going along with the mission.

I hope Jesus knows what he is doing.

Simon listened with anticipation while Jesus described the task ahead. He thought about his self-shortened assignment in Tiberias and the doubt Manaen expressed over whether Jesus could truly lead a coalition — an army — against the evil of this world.

It's finally happening!

"Be on your guard against men. They will flog you in their synagogues," Jesus said.

Simon remembered the Pharisees who came to Tiberias to meet with Herod's men.

Finally, we will expose the corrupt and rally the righteous!

"There is nothing hidden that will not be made known ..." As Jesus continued, Simon's eagerness grew.

No more secret meetings and scribbled notes.

No more lurking in the shadows.

Jesus was ready to proclaim God's kingdom — loudly and in bright daylight.

Then Manaen would have all his questions answered and doubts assuaged.

When Manaen adds his coalition to the army that Jesus gathers, not even Rome will be able to stop us!

"... and anyone who does not take up his cross and follow me is not worthy of me ..."

What? Take up a cross?

"... Whoever loses his life for my sake will find it ..."

Simon's heart sank.

What is Jesus saying?

A moment ago, he was rallying the people.

Sure, people die in war. It's part of the risk. Part of the honor.

But taking up a cross? That can't be right.

Simon had committed his whole life to fighting against Rome and their torturous oppression. He wouldn't rest until the Romans were gone, never to raise another cross again.

Simon tried to quiet his mind while he listened even more intently to Jesus. Maybe this was just another strange riddle or a reminder of the enemy's brutality.

Of the urgency of the mission …

As Matthew and Thaddeus walked, their journey took them away from the sea, toward the villages in Galilee's northern foothills.

Matthew was grateful to have a companion who seemed thoughtful and reasoned—but also fully capable in the face of physical danger.

What value do I bring to this excursion?

"Why do you follow him?" Matthew blurted the question without any preface or warning.

"You mean Jesus?" Thaddeus responded, seemingly to fill an otherwise awkward silence while he contemplated the question.

"Right. What made you decide to follow him?"

Thaddeus kept his gaze on the road ahead, as if considering the question for the first time. He began with hesitation, "I suppose part of it is my distaste for the Romans. Part of it is a desire to see things get better for us—our people, I mean. More than one would-be savior has promised all of this if I would just take up a sword for Israel."

"That doesn't sound like Jesus at all."

"That's the point. Jesus is different. It's not that I didn't care about the revolutions or Israel's fate. It's just that I saw a lot of talk and a lot of failure. Jesus isn't full of bluster. He lets his simple stories and miracles do what the Zealots couldn't do with all of their bravado."

Matthew shivered. "You've been involved with Zealots? In my experience, nobody dares speak of these things."

Thaddeus turned and answered, "Not involved, but always adjacent. And invited. Of course, nobody would mention such things around you—nor any publican."

Matthew nodded. "That still doesn't explain how you came to follow Jesus."

"I first saw him with the Baptizer. It was quite a display; people are still talking about it. But it was the story from Simon's wedding that got my attention."

"Simon? The angry one?"

Thaddeus chuckled, "Yes. I suppose you could call him that. At his wedding feast, Jesus turned water into wine. I didn't believe it at first, but all the fishermen saw it, and I trust them."

"That was it? A story was enough?"

"No, there was more. When we went to Jerusalem, Jesus had a strange authority about him. I can't describe it. It was the way he taught—and even challenged—the experts."

"Then what?"

"I heard the parables and saw the healings. I was struck by how simple it was for him. He just *touched* sick people and made them whole, with no spectacle, no extortion. Simply healing because he is kind."

"Yes," Matthew reflected on his own miraculous healing. "He does have a unique kindness."

"Is that what drew you to him?"

"What?"

Thaddeus smiled, "I told you my story; now I want to hear yours. What makes a publican leave his comfortable station to follow a poor healer?"

The question pierced Matthew, and he looked down, trying to bury his sorrow. "I suppose I am not a … typical follower. Not like the rest of you."

"Because you were a toll collector?"

Matthew nodded, "I don't really belong with the group."

"Where do you belong?"

"Nowhere now." Matthew paused. *How much do I share?* "Let me just say that Herod's officials in Tiberias didn't take kindly to my decision to vacate my post."

Thaddeus nodded, and Matthew saw deep thought behind his eyes.

"But *something* made you decide it was worth it."

"It started with my brother. He had heard of Jesus and tried to convince me to join him. He and I were always so different. Then when I met Jesus myself, he didn't treat me with hostility and resentment the way the workers and fishermen do. And he didn't dangle reminders of power and influence in front of me the way Herod's men do."

"What do you mean?" Thaddeus appeared thoroughly engrossed in Matthew's story. He even tripped as they walked.

"I mean, it seemed like Jesus came to Capernaum just to find *me*. I finally *belonged* somewhere."

"Didn't you say you feel out of place?"

"With you and the others, yes. Not with Jesus."

The men reached a small village nested in a clearing. Two dozen or so basic, one-room, stone structures were visible. Household garden patches grew between the small buildings where goats roamed freely.

"We're going to see if performing these healing miracles is as easy as Jesus makes it look," Thaddeus said.

Some children spotted Matthew and Thaddeus and ran between the buildings and out of sight. After a moment, two women came from behind one of the structures, accompanied by a graying man who leaned heavily on a crutch. The man took slow, awkward steps on a leg that clearly refused to straighten.

Perhaps a break that healed poorly?

"What do you want with us?" the old man asked with unmasked suspicion.

"We bring good news," Matthew responded. "The kingdom of heaven is near!"

"We have no king but God here," the man responded. "And you are late!"

Matthew was perplexed, and he was sure his face did not hide it.

"What my friend means," Thaddeus interjected, "is that we have come to *give*, not to *ask*."

"What about your friends who were just here two days ago?" the old man asked.

Matthew responded, "What friends? We—"

Thaddeus held up a hand. "We come with the power of the one who sent us—the power of the kingdom of heaven. Let me show you."

Thaddeus clasped the old man's shoulders. The man dropped his crutch, but Thaddeus did not let him fall as he held firmly and prayed in a barely audible whisper.

The women gasped and looked down. Matthew followed their gaze to the man's foot, which now faced forward. The man planted his foot firmly and shifted his weight onto his newly straightened leg. His eyes widened, and he threw both arms around Thaddeus and kissed his cheek.

"You mentioned others who have come through here?" Matthew asked.

One of the women answered, "Yes. Just yesterday. They said the Romans are on the move, and we must be ready to fight. Our husbands left with them. Are they part of your party?"

Thaddeus looked at Matthew, and Matthew shrugged.

"We are not with them," Thaddeus began. "We were sent by Jesus of Nazareth to proclaim the kingdom of heaven. If someone in your village can take us in, we will wait until your husbands' return."

"Most of the men have gone," the woman responded. "They answered the call to arms."

"You will be my guests," the old man offered. "You have earned that much. While you are here, there are a few other ailing and injured people who were unable to go. Can I bring them to you?"

"Yes," Matthew spoke up, grateful to contribute to the discourse. "We will gladly heal them."

The old man nodded and turned, leaving his crutch where it had fallen. "Follow me. And while you are here, tell me more about this kingdom of heaven."

———

Simon and James followed a creek into the western mountains. Simon was grateful to have a quiet companion, but he was apprehensive about James' relation to the toll collector.

They neared a settlement beyond a bend in the creek, with wood-and-stone buildings clustered closely together. The buildings were modest, but of slightly better quality than Simon was accustomed to seeing.

The huts surrounded a larger building—not a full two stories high, but noticeably taller and wider than the rest.

Probably the synagogue.

"Which of us does the talking when we get there?" James asked.

"I've never been one for much talking," Simon responded.

James chuckled, "Me neither. It was hard to get a word in with my brother around."

Simon felt a pang of distaste at the mention of Matthew. "You two are quite different. How did that happen?"

"Our father was a wealthy aristocrat. He was honorable, but his resources clearly helped him gain favor. Matthew is older than me, and he learned our father's ways a little too well. When he built up his own fortune, he seized a chance to purchase an office as a publican."

"What about you?"

"I was disgusted," James said. "The more my brother bought into Roman ways, the less I wanted to be around him. I saw the suffering of the people they extorted. Then to see them throwing their coin around for extravagance, women, and drink ..."

James looked away as his voice trailed off.

"Why not take up arms?" Simon asked.

James' head jerked, and his eyes pierced Simon. "Against my brother?"

"Against the Romans."

"Arms are for the angry. I wasn't angry; I was heartbroken. I had compassion for the people who suffered under this system, but also for my brother. He was lost and misguided, not evil.

"That's when I decided to throw off material comfort and live by fasting and prayer. I first heard the Baptizer preach near Jerusalem. I was about to leave the city and see if the Essenes might welcome me. I had a long wait to prove myself worthy, so I listened to the Baptizer.

"Then another came; the Baptizer called him the Lamb of God. When he was baptized and came up out of the water, the light of heaven and the voice of God came down on him."

"That's how you met Jesus?" Simon eagerly took in the story, his own memory of that moment so fleeting.

"Yes. And I knew I had to make peace with my brother—and rescue him from his own folly. I kept the simple life, but hoped I could somehow persuade him to listen."

Simon's mood leveled as the conversation turned back to Matthew.

Misguided or not, he's still a collaborator with the enemy.

"But as I said," James continued, "I'm not one for much talking. It's your turn."

"What?"

"Where did you come from?"

Simon hesitated. *How much would James share with his brother?*

"I'll just say that unlike you, I *was* angry."

"And now you're not?"

How do I answer that?

Before Simon could respond, two men emerged from the village and met the pair on the path.

"What brings you this way? And where are you from?" one of them asked.

"We're from Capernaum," Simon answered. "We need food and shelter."

"There are no trade routes or roads out here. Are you lost?"

"Not at all. We are messengers, sent to announce that the kingdom of heaven is near."

The man's eyes widened as Simon spoke, but his voice was heavy with suspicion. "Then perhaps you should meet the teachers."

The men led Simon and James into the village. They passed a cluster of homes and approached the large structure at the center. The walls were solid at the far end. Columns supported the roof on the near end and the sides.

A teacher sat at the far end, reading from a scroll to several dozen men who stood and listened. Simon recognized the words of Moses. Others continued to arrive until over a hundred men were shoulder-to-shoulder under the canopy.

"This can't be mere fortunate timing," Simon leaned in and said to James. "Do you think these people have been called together because of us?"

"I'm sure we will soon see."

"We have sojourners among us!" The teacher's voice echoed from the front of the colonnade as he indicated Simon and James with an open hand. "Tell us, friends, from what school do you teach?"

Simon didn't understand the question. "What school?"

"Are you students of Hillel or Shammai?"

Simon looked at James, who offered only a silent shrug in response.

"We are sent by Jesus the Nazarene to proclai—"

A shriek pierced Simon's ears and swallowed his speech. A disheveled man who was obviously not fond of bathing pushed past the crowd toward them.

Some onlookers attempted to restrain the man, but he shook them off like pests. Others scrambled out of the way of his reckless charge, until Simon and James found themselves alone and encircled by the villagers.

The unkempt man made his way to them unimpeded and collapsed. "You must not speak that name!" he shrieked.

"Come out of this, man!" Simon shouted back.

"Please don't kill me!"

Simon raised his voice as loud as he could. "By the authority of Jesus of Nazareth, God's chosen, come out of this man and be gone."

The man collapsed in silence, and his forehead smacked the stone floor.

James stooped down and placed a hand on the man's back while the crowd slowly tightened around them.

"I have never heard of this Jesus the Nazarene," said the teacher, now standing in the circle with a scowl on his face. "Clearly, he is a magician and an agent of Beelzebub. And now you've brought the devil's work to our sanctuary."

Agent of Beelzebub? The devil's work?

The circle of onlookers closed in, and Simon felt like the air was being choked away.

"Seize them," the teacher said as he turned. Almost at once, multiple pairs of hands took hold of him.

Chapter Twelve

Matthew sat on a boulder near the outskirts of the village and recounted the stories he had heard from Jesus. He knew he didn't tell them as well, much less correctly remember half of what he had heard.

Still, the people listened.

The few men present were sick and injured — left behind by the war party when they joined the call to arms. Now they stood — strengthened and healed — hungry to hear more about this kingdom where the lame walk and the blind see. Matthew couldn't remember the last time he felt such a sense of belonging.

If only I could stay.

Even the sparse bedding and the repetitive, bland diet of bread and lentils no longer made him long for the comforts of his former life.

This is all the life I need.

Matthew finished relaying another parable. A boy, no more that twelve years old, spoke up. "This Jesus. Is he the messiah?"

Matthew wasn't prepared for the question. "He is God's messenger, sent to proclaim His kingdom."

"So does he work for the messiah?"

Another boy, a year or two younger, interjected, "My father left to work for the messiah. Is that who Jesus works for, too?"

The older men moved about and admonished the boys for speaking out of turn. Still, the bell had been rung, and it echoed in Matthew's mind.

Messiah. Is that how Jesus sees himself?

If so, what a strange strategy. Jesus promises to set captives free, but isn't that just his term for healing the sick?

What could I be missing?

Matthew was relieved when Thaddeus came alongside him and addressed the crowd.

"Jesus has come to proclaim the good news of the kingdom of heaven. And what is this good news? That our sins are forgiven.

By his healing—healing that your village has experienced, he has proved his authority to forgive."

"And then what?" The older boy asked, earning another admonition from his elders.

"Then the righteous will produce good fruit, like a healthy vine produces grapes. You don't harvest grapes from the thorns, do you?"

"What thorns?"

The boy is persistent.

"The false teachers will be exposed because they produce no fruit, but only thorns that tear and pierce the workers."

Matthew recalled hearing this lesson from Jesus, but it sounded different coming from Thaddeus.

Is he speaking of the sword?

Is that what Jesus really meant before?

What else have I missed?

The distant sound of approaching voices drew Matthew's attention to the road. At once, the conversation stopped, and the whole gathering turned in unison.

Women emerged from their gardens and homes and walked briskly toward the road. The men and children followed close. Matthew fell into place behind them, and Thaddeus walked at his side.

After a moment, a party of two dozen men came into view. One by one, women ran ahead and embraced them. Several women walked cautiously, growing unsteady with each step. A few sank to their knees and sobbed.

A muscular man with bronzed skin spoke over the shoulder of his wife, who clung to his neck, and addressed the village.

"They were better prepared for us than we expected. Too many of us didn't make it back. Simeon and Ezekias were captured. Others weren't so fortunate."

The crying women wailed even louder.

"Who recruited you?" Thaddeus called from the back.

"We answered a call to help in Chorazin. Who are you?"

Their venerable newly healed host stepped around the crowd and walked up to the returning villagers. "These are our guests! Look at me!" He indicated his healthy leg with a flourish of his arms.

"Guests? Times are too dangerous to entertain strangers," the man retorted.

"But look at me! I am well! They healed me—all of us!" The old man waved his hand toward the crowd as several heads nodded.

"Then we have more able bodies to fight when the Romans retaliate. It will only be a matter of time before they track us here from Chorazin." The man looked around as he spoke. His eyes met Matthew's, and he locked his gaze into a scowl. "Or perhaps they already have."

The man gently nudged his wife aside and strode around the crowd, keeping his eyes on Matthew.

Matthew's mind flooded with panic

Can I run? Hide? Or ...

Grapes. Thorns.

"No!" He shouted while the man was still several meters away. "Let our results testify to our intentions. We've brought healing to your village, not a sword."

The villagers who had stayed behind, even the boys who spoke out of turn, came near to Matthew and stood around him. He continued, "Do not let the thorns of anger pierce your hearts as a sword pierces the body. The kingdom of God has come with the power to heal, comfort, and forgive."

Standing only an arm's length from Matthew, the man raised an accusing finger that almost touched his nose. "This one is a liar and an agent of Rome! I have seen you, publican. You waited until our village was defenseless so you could come and take what little we have for your Roman dogs."

The old man stepped between them. "Listen to what he says! You are wrong. This man has taken nothing. He has brought healing, and we are his witnesses."

"He is a deceiver sent by Rome. First, he extorts the poor, and now he comes to perform tricks and tell us to lay down our swords so we can wait defenseless to be trampled."

"No," the old man's features betrayed his dread. "Please examine for yourself the miracles they have done. There are no tricks here."

"And let our guard down? Even if his miracles are genuine, anyone who teaches our men to lay down our swords while the enemy gathers strength is not *for* us, but *against* us!"

With that outburst, the man shoved the older man aside with one arm and four calloused knuckles hurtled toward Matthew's eyes.

Ropes bound Simon's wrists and ankles and held him slumped over a large boulder. The solid stone pressed against his ribs. Simon could breathe; he wasn't stretched as the Roman savages stretch their victims across a crucifix. But he could move only enough to breathe, not to resist.

His ribs would show bruises by the time the ordeal was done. And it would be done.

Just endure the lashings. All forty-minus-one.

"Do you have anything to say for yourselves before you receive the rod of correction? Do you wish to repent of your sorcery?"

Simon couldn't see the speaker, but he knew it to be the voice of the first teacher they encountered — the one who ordered them to be seized.

Simon, with a hoarse whisper, coughed out indiscernible words. The tension in his arms and shoulder eased, and he pushed himself up on his forearms. That was all the ropes would allow.

"How can Satan drive out Satan?" Simon asked, recalling Jesus' answer to the same accusation. "A house divided against itself cannot stand. But authority over spirits has been given to us by the one who sent us and stands as proof that the kingdom of God has come into your presence.

"We've done nothing wrong, but by binding us and accusing us of evil, you prove your own guilt as you deny the Spirit of God, who rests on the one who sent us. It is you who must repent and be saved — not from the destruction of the body, but from the one who can destroy body and soul."

The people roared with one voice, and the ropes yanked Simon's forearms out from underneath him. His chin struck the stone hard, cracking a tooth as his mouth clenched shut, just missing his tongue. His chest smacked the slab and forced the air from his lungs.

As Simon fought to reclaim his breath, he heard a whistle grow louder behind him, a musical prelude to the sting across his exposed back. He gasped, unable to cry out. He heard the cries of his companion, James, and knew that he had been struck as well.

"One!" the unified voice of the crowd responded.

Another whistle. Another sting.

This time, Simon had enough air to cry out.

"Two!"

The blows came faster now.

"Three."

———

Matthew opened his eyes. Blurred light entered only the right, while swelling and darkness pushed back against the left. He moved his head around until a face—at least he hoped it was a face—filled his tiny field of vision. He forced his good eye open a little more until he finally recognized Thaddeus looking down at him.

"He's awake," his friend called.

Matthew propped himself up on his elbow. His head ached at the movement, but his body felt only the stiffness of age and poor bedding.

After a few soft footsteps, the old man came into view. Matthew fought the aches and forced himself upright. His host handed him a cup of wine. Matthew drank. It was weak, but welcome to his parched throat and warm to his stiff muscles.

"I told the others that you would leave as soon as you are able," the old man said with visible sorrow.

"What happened? How long was I asleep?"

"Several hours," the old man responded. "You apparently are not conditioned for taking such a blow."

Matthew started to shake his head, but the throbbing, coupled with a pain now shooting down his neck, forced him to stop. "No, combat has never been for me."

"And you happened upon an angry combatant who still felt the raw wound of losing a battle."

"I hope you've calmed him down. Or otherwise dealt with him."

"Words were exchanged, but no more blows," the old man explained. "He finally saw the truth of my healing—and the others. That is why he agreed we could host you until your health returns."

"That's it?" Matthew was confused about the arrangement.

"They've allowed us to stay," Thaddeus added. "But only as long as we must. They still don't trust outsiders, and they fear Roman reprisal."

"But that has nothing to do with us."

"Please put that aside," the old man pleaded. "Go in peace as I swore you would. You have been a friend to me, and you brought healing—and hope—to my home. Now do me this one final honor of allowing me to keep my oath to my people."

Matthew nodded through more pain. "I understand."

The old man handed him a small loaf of bread wrapped in cloth. "God be with you."

"And may His blessing rest on your household."

Thaddeus helped Matthew to his feet, and they exited the one-room home. With Matthew's good eye, he watched the simple gardening and household activity that had been the familiar picture of daily life in the village for the last time.

Thaddeus placed a hand on his shoulder and walked to his left as they descended the narrow trail. Matthew took what solace he could, knowing that his friend guarded his blind side.

Simon and James shook their sandals and stepped onto the path beyond town. Shouts of protests rose behind them, but neither man looked back.

Simon had nothing more to say, and he was sure James had even less to express. Turning back would be painful. Simon's tunic rested delicately on the wounds that traced lines across his back from top to bottom and still seeped, grabbing at the fabric like a patch of briers.

The pair carried their cloaks, unwilling to burden their wounds any more than necessary. Simon shivered against the chill of the evening air.

"Can we reach the next village before sundown?" James asked as their legs carried them slowly.

"I'm not even sure how far it is," Simon responded.

They reached a bend in the road circling a small incline. Beyond the curve, a field of scrub grass spanned to their left. Across that, a shallow cliff rose about ten meters above them.

As they pressed on, a voice called from the base of the cliff, "Unclean! Stay away!"

Simon turned and winced as threads pulled at scabs and reopened his wounds. Two figures huddled in a crook in the rock, covered in dirty rags — even over their heads and hands.

James stepped off the path and proceeded toward the figures.

"We are unclean! Keep your distance," a strained voice called from under the rags.

"Where are you going?" Simon asked. "We don't have much time to reach the next village. Especially in our condition."

"I am going where we were sent," James responded as he moved toward the people with surprising speed.

Simon didn't try to match his friend's pace, remaining all too aware of the fresh wounds of his own torn flesh. As Simon's lacerations protested with resistance, he considered a new thought.

These rag-covered people are in even greater pain. Lepers.

Their flesh was subjected to wounds that would not heal and forced them into isolation where they were unable to work or even care for themselves.

James was just a couple of meters away from them while Simon strained to push his legs through the pain.

"Unclean! Please go," one of the figures coughed with a voice so strained that Simon could not tell if it was a man or a woman.

"We have good news. The kingdom of God is near," James said as he stepped within arm's reach. A third figure emerged from a cave opening that had previously been obscured from Simon's view.

"God has forgotten us!" one of the lepers protested.

"No," Simon responded. "He has sent us in His power to make you well. Do you believe?"

"Yes," the one who had stepped from the cave answered. This figure was noticeably smaller than the others and spoke with the clarity of a young female.

She couldn't have been in this colony long.

"By the power of the God of Israel and His servant, Jesus the Nazarene, we declare that you are clean. Your faith has made you well."

The figures looked briefly at one another, then the young one unwrapped her hands from the rags. The skin beneath was smooth and clear, and she kept exposing her skin up to her elbows.

The others followed, and they also revealed hands and arms without blemish. At once, they tore at the strips of linen wrapped haphazardly around their heads. They revealed disheveled hair and dirty faces, but their skin was otherwise whole.

They gazed at one another first with shock, then smiles.

One, a man, leaped to his feet and hugged Simon. Simon winced and gasped as the force of the man's embrace sent pain deep into his open wounds.

The man jumped back and threw up his hands. "I'm sorry! What did I do?"

"It's not your doing. Just dealing with a wound or two."

Ironic. These lepers stand healed while my own back still bleeds.

"Where are you going that brings you by our colony?" the healed man asked.

"We are returning to Capernaum. And we must continue before we lose more daylight."

"The next village is hours off; it was our home. You won't reach it. Please be our guests tonight. We cannot offer you comforts, but you'll be safe here."

"Thank you," Simon said.

James added, "In the morning, let us accompany you to your village so you can present yourselves to the elders and priests."

"And on the way," the man responded, "tell us more about this kingdom of God that makes the unclean whole."

———

Simon awoke in his own quarters in Capernaum, feeling like he had slept for days after being exhausted by the beating and the journey. James was still asleep on the floor of his room.

Simon stepped through the door and was greeted by the rising sun. He roused James, and together they walked to the house of Simon the fisherman. Inside, Jesus sat with the rest of the twelve. Simon surveyed the room. They were the last to arrive.

"I thought I would have to go and fetch you," Thaddeus said.

"The return journey was a little slow," Simon responded.

The men sat and listened to the stories already underway. Some reported whole towns believing and entire families healed. A few had been chased from the villages without an opportunity to offer so much as a blessing.

Matthew spun a verbose account of healing and teaching, followed by fear and betrayal. His face showed bruises and swelling that evidenced his ordeal. Simon took little solace in knowing that his party was not the only one met with violence.

He struggled to find sympathy for Matthew, who clearly absorbed the force of the outburst—not for what he had done in the village—his work there was noble. But simply for who he was.

Would anyone assault me on mere recognition?

The room turned to Simon and James for their report. James told of the small leper colony who had been healed—all of them—and restored to their village.

As James spoke, Simon stood and shed his cloak and coat. He lifted off his tunic and turned his back to his companions.

The room grew silent. Simon turned to Jesus. "It was everything you said it would be."

Jesus nodded without a word, and the sullen expression on his face did not change.

Simon put his tunic and coat back on and returned to his seat.

The disciples in collective silence glanced around at each other.

"What comes next?" The question came from Simon the fisherman.

"Let's get to our boat. I know someplace we can go," Jesus finally answered.

"But what about the people?" Andrew protested.

"You've done much to announce the kingdom, and you've done well. Now we must withdraw for a short time. You need a chance to eat and rest.

"You must also know that while you were away, my cousin, John—the Baptizer—was executed by Herod.

"His followers have told me that word of our work has reached Herod, too. Now he is seeking me out. Some people say Herod is afraid that John might have returned from the dead, but I have received this news directly from the ones who buried him."

"So Herod has heard of our miracles and thinks John somehow defies his sentence?" Judas asked.

"That's why he wants to see me," Jesus continued, "to be sure that I am not John."

"The whole region knows that you are not John!" Andrew insisted. "Why ask for proof?"

Tiberias!

The nighttime visitors!

Simon stood and said, "You can't go see him! We will not let you."

Jesus remained seated and looked up at Simon with compassion and sadness. "I don't plan to go. You shouldn't be so quick to worry. As I said, we will eat and rest by ourselves. There will be more to do when the time is right."

Chapter Thirteen

Jesus led the group to the dock. They approached the toll booths, and two soldiers stepped onto the road in front of them. Jonathan, the young toll collector, addressed them. "You know how this works. Half upfront before you begin your work."

"That's outrageous!" Simon the fisherman responded. "We have no way of knowing in the morning what the day's catch will be. Besides, we aren't even taking our nets out today."

Matthew wondered if his own demands had been as bad as Jonathan's.

It does sound outrageous when you're just an observer.

The young toll collector continued, "That's why it is only half up front. If you have a light catch, there is nothing more to settle."

"Unless you decide to change your mind while we are on the sea! Where is the fairness in that?"

"Herod has been *made* to pay for extra policing; it shouldn't surprise you that the money has to come from somewhere."

"Then let Herod pay for it out of his own fat!"

The guards stepped toward the fisherman. The other Simon, the dockhand, moved to the front with his hand tucked in the folds of his cloak. Matthew's unease grew. Heightened unrest meant more than the obvious eyes were watching. A small crowd of onlookers formed nearby.

Jesus stepped between the two Simons and faced the toll collector. "There will be no catch today. Let us go to our boat so we can travel."

Travel? Jesus didn't say we were traveling, did he?

The toll collector nodded, and the guards eased their stance. "Five denarii for the group," the publican said to Jesus. Jesus nodded to Judas, who stepped forward and paid for the whole group.

They passed the toll booth, and several people from the crowd followed after them.

"Are you leaving?"

"Where can we find you?"

The people were anxious for Jesus to stay, despite his visible fatigue.

So somber, too.

A small group followed as Jesus led them with uncharacteristic quiet.

One man, beyond his youth but not yet old, came alongside the group as they walked. He grabbed Simon's arm from behind and asked, "Are you men in trouble with the locals?"

Simon turned abruptly, and his eyes widened.

Fear.

After a long pause, Simon answered, "We made it past, didn't we? There's no trouble here that we can't handle."

The man maintained a firm grip on Simon's arm.

"That's ... reassuring."

Simon didn't respond as he jerked his arm out of the man's grasp, turned forward, and kept walking.

The man glared at Matthew as he passed. Simon looked back for a moment.

The group filed onto the dock and into the fishermen's boat.

"Go east," Jesus told them. "Let's get to a quiet place and get some rest."

Several dozen onlookers watched them go. A few ran down the shoreline as if to race with the boat.

The man who accosted Simon was nowhere to be seen.

Matthew looked to the young man who sat quiet and wide-eyed in the boat, staring absently at his own feet. "Who was that man who approached you?"

Simon looked up. "You know how these things happen. There's always someone who's trying to learn what Jesus is all about."

"But you recognized him."

"It's a small city. I've seen him in the streets before."

It's not easy getting this one to talk. "It must have been a memorable encounter for you to react as you did."

A scowl settled over Simon's face. "Jesus is right. We need to rest." He bundled his cloak together and tucked it under his shoulder while he awkwardly laid his head down.

Well after midday, the boat approached a cove, isolated from the nearby towns by the terrain itself.

"Bring the boat to shore here," Jesus directed the fishermen. They turned and aimed for a gently sloped length of shore.

Water hit the hull with a steady rhythm. The sound was soon covered by distant voices from the shore. Matthew tried in vain to find the source of the voices, but the natural rock formations obscured too much.

Perhaps some of the people really did race the boat down the shoreline.

The four fishermen climbed out and pulled the boat to shore. As the rest stepped onto the pebbled beach, dozens of people descended from the surrounding hills. Jesus, still visibly exhausted, stepped into their midst. Almost at once, they surrounded him, as they so often had on the shores by Capernaum. Jesus ascended the slope and sat down on a level boulder.

The trail of people continued to pour into the cove from the small roadways. But now they came from both directions.

"We have to stop this," Philip said while the disciples watched the spectacle from the shore. "Can't they see the teacher needs rest?"

Matthew barely heard him as he focused on the swelling crowd. "This is more than were in Capernaum. Where do they come from?"

"I don't know," Philip answered. "None of us will get any rest if we let it continue." Philip climbed the hill toward Jesus, who was already speaking to people seated around his feet.

Matthew chased after him. "Stop it? How do you think we can do that?"

Matthew stumbled more than a few times as he climbed, dodging a cross-current of bodies as men, women, and even children pushed through and around the crowd for the best position to hear Jesus.

Climbing high enough to see beyond the seaside ridge, Matthew got his first look at the villages scattered across the otherwise barren landscape. People continued to emerge from everywhere, walking—even running—with purpose toward the cove.

More were still arriving when Matthew reached Jesus. Philip was several paces ahead of him. Jesus shared the familiar blessings that Matthew had grown accustomed to hearing in every new setting. Still, they challenged him every time.

"Blessed are the poor in spirit ..."

"Blessed are the peacemakers ..."

When have I ever been any of these things?

Witnessing the hubris and covetousness of the toll taker as an outsider had opened Matthew's eyes to new truths. And he felt the sting of Jesus' words more sharply than before.

How could I ever become the kind of person who Jesus speaks of? How could I ever be blessed?

"Blessed are those who hunger and thirst for righteousness ..." Jesus continued to the attentive crowd.

Matthew understood that hunger and thirst more than ever. He hoped if he followed Jesus long enough, he could eventually discover whatever elusive teaching would satisfy his hunger.

"It's too late in the day for this," Philip interrupted when he reached Jesus' side. "Send these people out to the villages so they can buy themselves something to eat."

Jesus looked up from where he sat, his eyes full of compassion as always. "Or you could give them something to eat. Where should we go to buy bread?"

Matthew scanned the villages across the ridge. *All the bread in the countryside will not be enough.*

Philip waved a hand toward the sloping shore and protested, "Eight month's wages wouldn't be enough to buy each of these people a single bite!"

Matthew turned back toward the crowd. It had swelled to even greater numbers during his climb.

Thousands! The theaters in Tiberias don't draw a crowd this big.

Andrew climbed the hillside and joined the conversation. "This boy has five small barley loaves and two fish. I can't speak for anyone else, but these people seem to have rushed here—completely unprepared. There's no way this little bit of food will go far in this crowd."

"Have the people sit in groups of fifty," Jesus answered. "Then you will feed them."

The surprise and confusion on his friends' faces assured Matthew they were as taken aback as he was. "How is that even possible?" he blurted out.

Jesus smiled with weariness.

Is he frustrated with us or just tired?

"Please have the people sit down," Jesus repeated.

Matthew looked to Philip and Andrew and shrugged. They branched out into the crowd, calling the other disciples to help them organize the throng as they went.

Simon was slow to leave the boat, the strange encounter with Manaen still on his mind. Simon still owed him an answer.

Will I remain with the movement or go?

Yet here he was on the shores of ... he wasn't sure where they landed, only that they had gone east, away from Capernaum, away from Tiberias.

Away from the action.

Maybe simply making this trip already answered Manaen's demand. But at what cost?

Simon hoped that Jesus would fully reveal his purpose soon.

Manaen isn't the only one with unanswered questions.

Simon returned his attention to the moment as the hillside quickly filled with villagers and travelers. Jesus sat on a boulder near the top, with most of their companions nearby. He climbed toward them, weaving awkwardly around the hundreds who packed onto the grassy slope. Nearer the top, movement stilled, and the travelers sat in clustered groups—about fifty each.

"Good! There you are," Thaddeus called as he walked toward Simon. "Jesus needs your help."

"What kind of help?"

"He wants us to have everyone sit down so he can feed them."

"Feed them? There are thousands here! How does he expect to do that?"

"How does he do anything he does?" Thaddeus leaned in close to Simon. "About that encounter in town—the others are asking questions."

"It was nothing," Simon answered.

"I know better than that, Simon."

"Just be glad that you didn't get into this movement like I did."

"Does that mean you're out now?" Thaddeus asked.

I wish I knew. "In or out, right now I'm here."

"Then let's get to work." Thaddeus turned away from Simon and called instructions to several families who clustered nearby.

Simon turned the other way and was greeted by a mix of hope, confusion, and wonder on the faces around him.

"Are you with the teacher?" one older man asked him. "We've traveled a long way to hear him. Why is he running away?"

Another question I'd like answered, too ... "However he's done it, he has brought us here," Simon hoped that his tone conveyed more assurance than he felt. "He asks that everyone sit down to eat."

"But we did not expect such a long journey, and we have brought no food."

"I'm sure the teacher has a plan." *I hope there's a plan.* "Sit here— and your family, too. And the rest of you, gather here." Simon called to others nearby and gestured for them to assemble. "Just as you see them doing. The teacher will speak when he is ready."

Simon moved on to other groups as he made his way down the hill. Most had already formed their own clusters. By the time Simon reached the base of the hill, much of his group was making their way back to Jesus. Simon began the ascent to join them.

As he neared the top, Jesus held up a small basket of loaves and looked to the heavens. "We give thanks to you, our Lord and God, for your daily provision," Jesus shouted. He set the basket down, pulled out a loaf and tore it in half, giving a portion each to two of his disciples. "Go and feed the people," he told them.

Another loaf torn and another pair sent out. Then another, until finally, Simon was handed a half a loaf alongside Thaddeus. He turned to feed the people seated nearest to him, but they were already eating. Somehow, they seemed to have enough.

Maybe they brought some bread with them?

Simon moved further down the hill to a cluster of families who looked up at him with anticipation. These people looked weary and more than a little desperate to eat. The men of the group stood, and Simon tore off portions of the loaf for each of them. Each man continued to divide the bread and share with his family, while Simon kept breaking off portions until he handed the last chunk to the last man standing.

The people already seated each held a full portion, and some voraciously bit into their bread.

Where did it all come from?

Simon turned to Jesus, who had begun to descend the hill toward those who were not yet eating. Simon went to him, and Jesus reached into his basket and handed Simon another loaf, which he took to a nearby group.

How did he get more?

Simon broke a piece off the loaf and handed it to one man. He watched closely as the man shared with his family. Nobody reached into their own cloaks or added their own bread. They ate only what Simon had given them.

He looked to the loaf in his own hands. *It's torn, but is it less than it was before?*

Simon continued to break and share, break and share, until this group was fed, and he turned to find Jesus. The disciples were almost at the bottom of the hill when Simon met up with Jesus again. Jesus reached into his basket, pulled out a smaller basket filled with fish, and handed it to Simon. "Now, pass these out."

Simon took the basket and stepped into the nearest cluster of people, who were still filling up on bread. He reached blindly into his basket and handed out fish without paying any mind to what was in his own hand.

He looked across the field. Each of his companions had their own basket, and each made their way from cluster to cluster, toward the spot where Jesus had first sat to teach.

When Simon reached the families nearest the top, he shared the last of the fish from his basket, only then realizing that he hadn't reached the bottom before. Jesus returned to his place, and the other disciples gathers around him, each wide-eyed with awe.

"How ..." Simon started, but Jesus held up a hand and stopped him.

"Now take your baskets, each of you. Gather up the pieces and let nothing be wasted."

Several of the men groaned, and Simon realized that he himself had not yet eaten. Still, he turned and made his way into the crowd. Many had already left, and others stood and walked toward the villages. Simon went to their vacated spots and picked up half-eaten fishes and chunks of bread far larger than he expected.

"Your teacher is a prophet, isn't he?" One man said as he approached Simon.

"You can judge that by what you've seen and heard," Simon answered.

"What I have seen and heard is more than just a prophet. I have seen a man who should be made king!" The man's voice rose with his proclamation, and others nearby heard and approached them.

"Is he to be king? Is he the messiah who will throw off the shackles of Rome?"

"He must be king. Who else but God's chosen one can do what he has done?"

Another man grabbed Simon by his cloak. "Take us to him! Let us be there when he claims his throne!"

Simon forgot his hunger as he fed on their hopeful demand.

King. That would silence Manaen.

And show that Jesus holds more power than Herod.

More power than Caesar!

But how many times has Jesus rejected this idea?

Maybe now he's ready!

"I can't speak for the teacher. Let me finish this task, then we will hear more of what he has to say."

Simon stepped away and proceeded down the slope, picking up bread and fish scraps along the way. He reached the shore where the others stood, each carrying a basket full of scraps.

"These people are ready to make Jesus king!" Simon told them.

"Can you blame them?" Thomas answered. "How long has it been since they have eaten this well?" He gestured to the baskets.

Simon considered the mounds of food that they held. He didn't remember bringing even a single basket full of provisions onto the boat.

He turned. The rock at the top, where just a moment ago Jesus had sat, was now empty. The last of the people stood and returned to the road as their shadows stretched far beyond them.

James and John came down the hill.

"Let's get the boat back on the water before it gets too dark," John said.

"Where is Jesus?" Thomas asked.

"He will meet us. He said to get in the boat and go ahead of him back to Capernaum."

Simon felt his hunger again, as the hope and expectation of the previous hours suddenly left him.

What king hides from his subjects?

The people are ready!

I am ready.

Why isn't Jesus ready?

Chapter Fourteen

Only the moon was left to cast a dim glow on the lake. Matthew wasn't sure if he preferred the dimness to the full visibility of daylight. But he was certain of one thing: He preferred to be on land.

The faintest firelights were still visible, and Matthew had no way to determine how far from shore they were, or even which direction they were facing. The wind became stronger and cooler as the journey progressed.

Matthew let his thoughts take him back to the miracle on the hillside.

A miracle that I was invited to be a part of.

After a lifetime of taking, Jesus used me to give.

Matthew still couldn't understand how — or why — he had been chosen.

"Have you ever seen anything like that?" he blurted out to nobody in particular.

"We're trying to sleep."

Matthew wasn't sure who answered, but he was undeterred. "It's easy to see why the people were so excited."

"Yes. They were excited. And now they are sleeping."

Matthew grew flustered. "Am I the only one who's amazed by what we experienced?"

"No. But you are the only one here who can't relate to those people."

Matthew had no trouble identifying the speaker this time.

Simon. Angry as always.

"You haven't known the hopelessness that so many of them know," Simon continued. "You haven't experienced their fear and worry. You take a simple meal for granted. They don't. They don't take sleep for granted either."

Simon's words pierced Matthew — not with guilt, but with insult at the young man's assumptions about him. "What do you know of what I have known and experienced? My station might have been different from yours, but I have sacrificed much to be here with you — with Jesus."

"How much of what you had was ever really yours?"

A cold gust of wind slammed into Matthew's face and body, chilling him deeply.

A fitting complement to Simon's words.

"Simon, why must we go over this again? I've opened my home to Jesus' work. I've paid for our travels — yours included. I know I can't pay back all that I have taken, especially since Samchai has taken so much. But Jesus has shown me a new way of living. I am just as happy to give what I have left to whatever he is doing. I have no desire to go back."

"No desire?"

"None."

"When Jesus takes the throne, what will you do then?"

"What do you mean?" Matthew asked as another gust of wind blasted him, bringing a splash of cold water over the edge of the boat and into his lap while the boat swayed.

"When he is made king, he's going to need administrators and such, maybe to collect tribute from the Romans for all they have taken from us." For the first time in this conversation, calm entered Simon's voice.

Matthew was confused. "King?"

"It was all the people were talking about," Judas added.

Whoever is trying to sleep must have succeeded or given up by now.

"That's because they understand what a true ruler — a *benevolent* ruler — is all about."

Matthew bit back a retort. Another gust rocked the boat harder than the last time. Matthew grabbed the edge of the boat and tumbled backward, unable to resist being tossed around by the unstable vessel.

"If we don't make it to shore, all your arguing is going to be pointless. Come give us a hand with the oars," Andrew called as he strained against the force of the water.

Matthew stumbled and fell to his knees, unsure of what to do even if he could get to someplace where he could help. Another set of hands grabbed him and lifted him up, helping him to a seat next to John, who moved aside to make room on the oar for him.

"Just do what I do. Remember — push with me, not against me," the fisherman said as he grabbed hold.

Matthew felt the oar jerk toward him, and he almost lost his grip. He barely stopped the handle from pummeling his midsection. Almost as quickly, the oar flew away from him, and he gripped and pulled to hang on.

"*With* me, not *against* me," John repeated.

Matthew grunted and tried to mimic John's movements. His whole body swayed with the back and forth of the oar, and he felt like his own arms were contributing nothing.

After a few repetitions, he found the rhythm—and an inner strength that he was certain was an illusion.

When he found the confidence to turn his eyes to the lake, the shadows of the moonlight played unnaturally across the water toward the shoreline. Firelight from a coastal village blinked in and out of view.

Matthew looked up. The moon, unobstructed by clouds, reflected its fullest light on them. He looked back toward the shore, and the shadow moved again in front of a distant firelight. He let go of the oar and screamed. John kept rowing, and the handle came back around and slammed Matthew's gut, knocking him from his seat.

"Why are you screaming?" John asked.

Matthew fought against his cloak and finally got an arm underneath to bear himself upright.

"Because we're about to die! An angel of death is coming for us!"

"What are you talking about?"

The force of the water passing under the boat slowed, and Matthew realized that they had all stopped rowing. He scanned the coastal village until his eyes caught the moving shadow. It was closer now and clearly man-shaped.

"Right there!" Matthew pointed at the figure. "The ghost!"

Several others cried out, masking the howl of the wind.

Andrew barked instructions, and as a group, they clamored to the oars and resumed rowing.

In the brief quiet that followed, a familiar voice carried across the air. "Don't be afraid. It is I."

Jesus!

The oars slapped the water.

"If it's you, Lord, tell me to come to you on the water!" Simon the fisherman called back to the barely visible figure.

"Come," the distant phantom responded.

The fisherman rose from his seat and threw his legs over the edge of the boat. Matthew hunched low and covered his head with his hands, expecting the whole boat to capsize.

Instead, the boat remained still, except for the gusts and waves that continued to determine its course. A hand tapped Matthew's shoulder, and he watched as the fisherman walked across the water to the strange figure. The wind had carried their boat closer — close enough to finally see that it was Jesus who walked toward them. Another wave smacked the boat hard and knocked Matthew off balance. When he righted himself, Jesus was pulling the fisherman out of the water.

What did I miss?

Jesus kept an arm around the coughing — and drenched — man and walked with apparent ease toward them until he reached the side of the boat, where Andrew pulled them in.

The fisherman collapsed on his seat, and everyone sat in stunned silence while Jesus found a seat of his own.

"There is nothing that this man cannot do," Matthew whispered to himself.

———

The shore was empty when they landed. The crowd that saw their boat off several days ago was nowhere to be found. Further up the shoreline, the docks bustled with the usual comings and goings of daily life.

Matthew was glad for a moment of normalcy.

But how long will it last?

He wasn't sure if he would ever know "normal" again.

Soon the crowds will find Jesus again and then what spectacle will we witness?

And what new trouble will we all experience?

Matthew wanted to be done with Samchai. Done with Herod.

But Jesus will keep drawing their attention.

As they walked down the shore, past the docks, and into town, everybody went about their daily lives.

Normal never looked so strange before. Perhaps people are losing interest?

If only they could have seen Jesus walking on the water!

Still, they saw him feed thousands. They *were* the thousands!

Of course, they'll be back.

For today, Matthew was grateful to be on land as he retreated to his own estate.

Matthew woke with the sun the next morning. He exited his home and quickly encountered a small group of travelers—maybe ten in all.

"Is the teacher with you?" a middle-aged man asked.

The quiet didn't last long at all. "Didn't he return to his own home?"

"We don't know. We saw him here with you before, but the other day he vanished from Bethsaida, and we are all looking for him."

"He came back yesterday, but he's not here. Have you looked in town or by the shore?"

One of the two younger men toward the back said, "We'll go tell the others," and ran with purposed speed toward the road.

"Others?" Matthew asked the one who spoke for the group.

"Like I said, we have been looking for the teacher. If he came back with you, then he must be close. When did he get back? We saw him stay behind when your group left, but in the morning, he was gone. He could not have walked here so soon."

"Let me tell you about it on the way," Matthew answered. "I think I know where to find him."

Matthew led the travelers through town and past the docks, toward the shore where Jesus preferred to teach. On the way, they encountered a stream of people walking toward the synagogue. Matthew turned and followed.

The messengers must have made good time ...

A group of men huddled together on an old, abandoned pier. One caught sight of Matthew and followed him with his gaze. The onlooker did not attempt to hide interest.

Could this be one of Herod's men taking an interest in Jesus?

Matthew turned his head just enough to get a look at the man. Nothing about his dress suggested he was from Herod's office—or from Tiberias at all.

Definitely a local.

They walked on, under the man's scorching gaze.

At once, Matthew's memory stirred.

That's the man who confronted Simon when we left.

And Simon still has not spoken about it.

Matthew looked back and confirmed what he sensed. The man still watched. Just as quickly, Matthew faced forward again. He reached the synagogue. The crowd already swelled beyond the perimeter of the canopy. He maneuvered around the front where Jesus spoke from the teacher's seat. He scanned the faces and spotted all four fishermen—and Judas and Thomas.

When he found Simon, he pushed through bodies toward him.

"Simon," he called as he approached.

The young man looked up and promptly looked away.

"Simon, I need to talk to you!"

"I prefer that you don't."

"Simon, at some point, we need to get past my life as a publican. *You* need to get past it."

"You have no place to tell me what I need!"

Matthew wanted to keep the argument going, but the immediate matter pressed on him. He pulled Simon through the crowd toward the edge. Simon gave less resistance than he expected. "Perhaps not," Matthew conceded, "but I still need to speak *now*. About something happening *now*. The man who confronted you before—he is watching us."

"A lot of people are watching. Jesus is back."

"But he was specifically watching *me*," Matthew's insisted. "I know you know him, but I need to understand, is he a threat?"

"You're a publican. You should know that you are more threatened than you realize—especially now that the Romans seem to have withdrawn from you. Jesus might want you around, but that doesn't mean you're making friends elsewhere." Simon paused and looked closely at Matthew, but his characteristic scowl had given way to a shadow of fear. "As for the man you saw—he is *my* concern. But *don't* let him see you talking to me. Besides, we have a new problem. Jesus doesn't seem to be making any friends today either."

"But the people love him! The came to my door looking for him this morning!"

"And now they are demanding a sign, and Jesus is refusing. It's something about the bread they ate. Watch and listen."

Simon was unsure what he missed while the toll collector distracted him. The man might have walked away from his thieving ways, but he still had a mountain to climb to earn Simon's trust, much less friendship.

He certainly wasn't about to tell him who Manaen was—or how they were connected. Simon finally got the verbose publican to stop talking and turned his attention back to Jesus.

"... I am the bread that came down from heaven," Jesus said to the crowd.

How much did I miss?

Behind him, a man called out, "How can he say that? He's just the son of Joseph. We know his mother and father. 'Came down from heaven?' That's absurd!"

Matthew turned and shouted, "If you had seen what he could do, you would take back those words. He heals disease and casts out devils. He feeds many with little. He even walks on water and commands the winds!"

"Let the hecklers go." Simon stepped between Matthew and the stranger.

"But these people need to know what he has done!" Matthew said. "I don't know your story, Simon, or where you came from. But I thought I had everything until Jesus came along and showed me what I was missing. Now, my eyes have been opened to a new truth. And I want everyone to know it. Don't you want that, too?"

How dare he question my story! And to try to elicit sympathy! He has only crushed others for his own personal gain! "You have no idea what has been taken from me. And you have no place to question my motives. Now hold your tongue long enough that I can hear what Jesus is saying!"

Simon crossed the synagogue floor away from Matthew. Murmurs hit his ears as he moved through the crowd. "How can he give us his flesh to eat?"

"What a strange thing to say."

"This teacher has stopped making sense."

Several onlookers left the synagogue altogether. Simon strained to hear Jesus and pushed closer to the front.

"Whoever eats my flesh and drinks my blood remains in me." Jesus' voice echoed louder as the crowd thinned.

What else have I missed?

"Your forefathers ate manna and died, but anyone who eats this bread will live forever."

"This is a hard teaching. Who can keep up with this?" a voice shouted from behind Simon.

He turned and took in the nearly empty synagogue. Of the hundreds who had gathered, only a few dozen remained.

Simon turned and walked straight toward Jesus. Most of his companions were already at the front with him. The rest of the crowd dispersed, and Jesus and the disciples left the synagogue.

As they walked, Simon came alongside Jesus and said, "I don't understand what you're doing! Two days ago, these people were ready to make you their king. Why say all these things to send them away?"

"Does this offend you?" Jesus asked.

"It confuses me! Thousands of people stood ready to carry you to Jerusalem — to the palace. They've seen your power, and they want you to *use* it. *We* want you to use it!"

"What if you see the Son of Man ascend to where he came from?" Jesus asked him with a calm that made Simon self-consciously aware of his outburst.

"We want you to ascend to the *throne*! Isn't that why you're here?" Simon forced some calm into his response.

"What kind of king talks about eating flesh? You're wasting your time if you follow this man!" The familiar voice came from behind Simon. He turned to see a group leaving the synagogue behind him.

Manaen.

"There's still time to find a *proper* messiah — one who would make a powerful king!" Manaen shouted without looking back.

Simon clenched his fist until his fingernails cut his palms.

I can't reveal my association with Manaen. And he knows it!

Simon turned back and noticed Jesus had stopped. He waited until the onlookers had passed, until only the twelve were left with him.

"You don't want to leave, too, do you?" Jesus asked as he looked at each of them one by one. Simon was pierced by his kind — but knowing — gaze.

Silence hung for a moment before Simon the fisherman answered, "Where would we go? You have the words of eternal life. We believe that you are God's holy one."

The twelve looked back and forth at one another, nodding with assent.

Jesus' face relaxed into a slight smile as he looked again to each of them. "Haven't I chosen all twelve of you? Yet one of you is a devil."

A devil? Which one does he mean?

To Simon, the publican was the obvious answer, given his lifetime of service to the Roman pigs.

But Matthew defended Jesus just now. I'm the one who challenged him. Could he mean me?

The question plagued Simon as they walked. He kept to the back in silence.

Chapter Fifteen

Matthew hadn't acclimated to boats and was certain that he never would. Still, he was relieved that the waters were calm, and they had enough daylight to complete their trip.

To where, he was unsure. For months, Jesus had been leading them up mountains and on long journeys — even as far as Tyre. Matthew was glad to be back in the familiar surroundings of Galilee.

Still, questions weighed on his mind.

"Teacher, why do you keep dismissing the crowds? Even when they are reluctant to leave, you press them with teachings that are too difficult," he asked Jesus.

"What do you mean?"

"Remember the five thousand? They were happy to have the bread you gave them, but then you challenged them for wanting only bread. Will the same thing happen with the last group — the ones you just sent away after feeding them, too?"

"Matthew, it's like I told them: No one came come to me unless the Father draws them."

"But they *did* come. Thousands of them! Why send them off? Why go to all the trouble of teaching and healing if you're not going to gather a following? It seems the more we do, the more we are hated. What's the point?"

Jesus remained calm. "As I asked before, do you want to leave? You've all been chosen, and you've all stayed."

But I never really answered. Only one — Simon the fisherman — had spoken up. Now, it was Matthew's complaint that prompted the question. *And now he is asking me.*

Just me.

"No, I don't want to leave. I have nothing to return to. I'm still despised by the people, and the ones I thought were friends ..." Matthew didn't want to finish the thought. He was not accustomed to being so exposed. And here in the boat, he had no place else to go.

"Here are your friends, Matthew." Jesus waved both arms out in an open gesture. Matthew scanned the other eleven. He met young Simon's eyes; the young man wore a stern expression of disapproval and shook his head. Matthew looked down.

Jesus continued, "It's like I taught you before. Those who give only to please men will have their reward. I've come to do the will of my Father, not to please men."

It's like he knows my thoughts.

Matthew kept his head down and remained quiet for the rest of the trip.

___

The men docked on the far side of a plain on the western shore.

"Look! It's the teacher!" The shout came from the hillside, and several people ran into the nearby town.

The fishermen were securing the boat when dozens of people emerged from the town and raced down the shoreline toward them. Matthew wanted to get off the dock and onto dry land, but the crowd blocked his way.

Jesus stepped out. Before he could step off the dock, three Pharisees descended toward them. They walked with exaggerated purpose and held their heads aloft with pomp.

"We've been hoping you would come to us," one of them said — an average-sized man with gray streaks in his beard. "We've heard all about your miracles and healing. What great sign from heaven have you brought to our town?"

Jesus sighed and gestured toward the lake. "You look at the morning or evening sky, and you know if it will be a fair day or a stormy one. Why can't you interpret the signs of the age? You are a wicked, adulterous generation, and you will be given no sign except the sign of Jonah."

Without another word, Jesus turned and climbed back into the boat.

Matthew stood dumbfounded; his companions were equally speechless. The Pharisees wrinkled their brows as they watched Jesus leave. The townspeople looked on with a mix of bewilderment and anticipation.

The disciples glanced at one another. One by one, they returned to the boat. Matthew offered a slight smile and a nod as he met one old man's forlorn gaze, but the confusion remained on the man's face. Matthew walked on.

I don't understand either.

The fishermen untied the boat and pushed out onto the lake. Matthew fixated on the people on the shore as they rowed away.

"We didn't even stay long enough to buy bread," Thomas said behind him.

Matthew turned toward the others. "We didn't stay long enough to do anything at all!" he exclaimed. He looked toward Jesus. "This is what I don't understand. Why come here only to walk away? If we're doing the Father's will, why are those who know the scriptures best always the first to challenge us?"

"Beware the yeast of the Pharisees," Jesus answered him, "and that of Herod."

The words stung. Matthew was the only one in the boat who had ever given Herod any deference—and all of them knew it.

"Is that why we didn't buy any bread?" Philip asked. "There was something foul in the yeast?"

"At least we might still get home in time to get to the market," Judas added.

"Why are you still talking about having no bread?" Jesus interrupted. "Don't you remember feeding five thousand with five loaves, or four thousand with seven loaves? And all the leftovers you gathered?"

The group nodded. "Twelve baskets," someone mumbled.

"Then how do you not understand that I'm not talking about bread when I say 'be on guard against the yeast of the Pharisees'?" Jesus added.

James, Matthew's brother, spoke up. "He means their words."

Philip cut in, "Like when he told the others that what comes out of their mouths makes them unclean."

Matthew looked back to the shore. It was barely visible, and the people had scattered. Still, the image of wide-eyed faces watching them leave remained in his mind.

How has the yeast of the Pharisees affected them?

_____

Months of travel were taking their toll on Simon. They had ventured as far west as the Great Sea and visited most of the towns on the eastern shore of Galilee, and now they were headed to the northern limits of Herodian territory.

The physical rigors of traversing the mountains and valleys did not wear on Simon. Nor did being away from home because his wife was one of more than a dozen women who recently began to accompany them.

What is the point of all this traveling?

Much of the past year seemed to make sense at first. Jesus was healing people and feeding them. He was strengthening bodies and filling hearts with hope all at once.

The perfect plan for raising an army. Until he sent them away.

The religious leaders and the Herodians alike were determined to stop him—even if it meant killing him. He would need to hold on to every follower and all the influence he could to have any chance against the reach and influence of those currently in power.

They had picked up some benefactors in Magdala and a few dozen faithful followers from various villages. But they were nowhere near replacing the numbers that they had lost. *It's a long walk to the next village ...*

Simon approached Jesus at the front of the group and asked, "Why have you been sending the crowds away? When there were thousands, they were ready to declare you king."

"Simon, when I sent you out, it was to proclaim the kingdom of heaven," Jesus replied.

"That's why I don't understand. We proclaimed the kingdom, but when the time came to establish the kingdom, you walked away. All those people were willing to make you king. But now where are they?"

"Remember what I have taught these crowds," Jesus began. "Not everyone who says to me 'Lord Lord' will enter the kingdom of heaven—only the ones who do the will of my Father."

"Couldn't we teach them? Train them? Push out every influence of Rome so our nation can honor God? This is what I have been fighting for my whole life!" Simon didn't try to hide his frustration.

"Simon," Jesus turned and looked him in the eye, "watch out for false prophets. They come in sheep's clothing, but they are wolves. Learn to recognize them by their fruit."

What false prophets? Does he mean the Pharisees?

"Teacher, my back is covered with the scars I suffered at the hands of the Pharisees. Obviously, I know how corrupt and self-serving they are."

"Be wary of the false prophets that you have known for a long time. It's like I taught you before: You don't pick grapes from thorn bushes. A bad tree will bear only bad fruit. That's how you will recognize them."

Simon held his questions. *No matter how I ask the question, he refuses to answer ...*

Jesus stopped and turned to address the group as a small village came into view. "You twelve," he began while pointing to Simon and the others he had chosen in Galilee, "Let's go off to this clearing to pray. The rest of you, go ahead to the village to buy bread and arrange lodging."

The disciples followed Jesus up a gently sloped gravel trail to a rocky clearing overlooking the grassy terrain below. Jesus sat on a large boulder, and they circled around him.

He seemed to fix his gaze for a particularly long moment on Simon before panning the group and asking, "Who do people say I am?"

"Herod's people thought you were John the Baptist, raised from the dead!" Nathaniel answered.

A few of the group chuckled, but Simon thought of the lengths to which Herod would go to silence his enemies. He saw no humor in the moment.

"I've heard people say Elijah, and even Jeremiah," John added.

Jesus nodded as the answers kept coming. He looked around again.

Is he waiting for me to say "King" so he can admonish me in front of the whole group? Simon took a breath as he prepared to answer, but Jesus spoke before he could form the words.

"What about *you*?" Jesus continued, letting his gaze rest a moment longer on Simon. "Who do you say I am?"

"You are the Christ!" The answer came from behind Simon. He turned to see Simon the fisherman on his feet, "You are the son of the living God!"

They all turned to Jesus with expectant expressions.

"You are blessed, Simon Bar-Jonah. This was revealed to you by my Father in heaven. From now on, you will be called Peter, for it is on this rock that I will build my church."

Build a church? What happened to building a kingdom?

"This revelation," Jesus added, "is for you alone. Do not tell others."

"How can we proclaim the kingdom without telling others?" Simon asked. "That's still the plan, right? The kingdom of heaven?"

Jesus offered Simon a compassionate smile. "Since you insist on knowing a plan, I will say this. The Son of Man must suffer and be rejected by the elders and the chief priests. He must be killed and on the third day raised to life."

Simon had uncovered the plot by the Pharisees and the Herodians. He knew the danger. *Why would Jesus say it* must *happen?*

Before Simon could protest, Peter stepped forward and stood directly in front of Jesus, "Never!" he began. "This will never happen to you!"

Jesus responded, "Get behind me, Satan! You are a stumbling block. You do not have the things of God in mind, but the things of men."

Peter stepped back, eyes wide and wet. The rest watched Jesus in silence.

Simon wanted to say everything that Peter had said. *Then the rebuke would have been mine.* Just as it had been earlier.

The things of God ...

The things of men ...

Grapes ...

Thorns ...

Two men approached on the path. "We've made accommodations. The people are eager to hear what the teacher has to say."

Jesus followed them and gestured for the rest to join them.

How long will their eagerness last once they hear what Jesus has to say?

They entered the village and found the people already gathered on a nearby hillside. Simon surveyed the buildings. *No obvious synagogue.* A few multi-room structures sat amid a haphazard layout of one-room shelters.

The people led Jesus to a large boulder. *This must be the place for the town's teachers.* Even as people still filed onto the hillside from their homes, Jesus began laying hands on the sick and injured.

Simon struggled to listen as Jesus began teaching. He had heard the familiar blessings and parables so many times. Instead, the words Jesus just spoke in the clearing repeated over and over in his mind.

The son of man must be killed.

"Blessed are the peacemakers ..." Jesus continued

What peace could he make by getting himself killed?

For a conquering king to make peace, he must first dispatch his enemies.

Watch out for false prophets ...

Simon still couldn't decipher that riddle.

Do you pick grapes among thorns?

Simon tried to will the thoughts from his mind and focus on Jesus' words in the moment. *Maybe he will say something to unlock these mysteries.*

"If anyone would follow me, he must deny himself and take up his cross daily," Jesus said to the crowd. Their sudden discomfort was visible.

He is going to drive these people away, too – along with their hope – with all this death talk.

"Whoever wants to save his life will lose it, but whoever loses his life for me will save it."

The people stirred, and grumblings increased across the crowd. Simon wanted to silence Jesus. *But then what?*

He grew restless as Jesus continued. *They need to hear hope – or better – a call to action!*

"What good is it for a man to gain the whole world, but lose his soul?"

From the corner of his eye, Simon caught a nearby figure running off and down the hill, toward the village. He turned. It was Matthew, the tax collector.

Probably running from his guilt. Simon had no interest in trying to understand a traitor's mind and turned his focus back to the crowd.

"If anyone is ashamed of me and my words, the Son of Man will be ashamed of him ..."

Is Jesus admonishing the one who left? Or the one who stands here wishing to silence him?

Thorns.

Grapes.

What will it take to understand these riddles?

Matthew was finally out of earshot.

Why are Jesus' words so piercing now, in this place and time?

Here, on the cusp of Judea's reach, on the doorstep of the pagan world of the Romans, these people had nothing. *They've always had nothing.*

Until Jesus showed up.

Jesus and the rest of us will move on, and these people will still have nothing.

Except whatever hope and healing Jesus leaves behind.

Matthew examined the simple huts and meager gardens. A new realization snared him.

I envy these people.

But he was more like them than he had ever realized.

Maybe I'm the one who has always had nothing ...

Only now did he finally realize it.

"Are you alright?" A voice came from behind him.

Judas.

"I think so," he answered, "maybe even for the first time."

Judas gave him a puzzled look. "We should get back. Jesus will need our help soon."

Matthew nodded and followed his friend back to the hillside as the villagers dispersed and returned to their homes.

Chapter Sixteen

A week had passed since Jesus began fixating on dying.

The son of man must be killed ...

Whoever seeks to save his life must lose it ...

He must take up his cross ...

Simon turned the words over in his mind, hoping to find some other meaning.

The fervent, eager crowds were gone. Now they traveled further away from the familiar shores of Galilee. Only Jesus' closest companions — with their wives and a handful of others — remained with him. They continued south until they reached Mount Tabor.

Where God's people triumphed over the Canaanites.

If only Jesus had an army ...

The sun sank behind the mountain and cast long shadows across a cluster of villages on its gentle eastern slope.

"Should we go to the villages to find shelter for the night?" Philip asked.

"No. Camp here," Jesus answered. "Stay by the stream tonight. Remain here until I return."

Simon guided a mule to a small clearing and unpacked their tents. He turned to Thaddeus. "Another mystery. Where could he be going while leaving us here?"

Jesus called the brothers James and John, and Simon the fisherman — whom Jesus now called Peter — to join him. The four walked toward the mountain.

After they were out of view, Thaddeus turned to Simon. "Can they reach the top before nightfall?"

"Maybe," Simon turned to the peak and shielded his eyes, "The terrain looks easy enough. But it doesn't explain why."

"Why they're going?"

"Why they're going. Why take just those three. Why all this crazy talk about dying. Jesus practically raised an army. But where are they now?"

He threw down another tent and let out a sigh. "Jesus has power. Nobody can deny the healing, the bread, the winds, and waves. We even saw that power in our own hands, and I was willing to endure flogging and take up a sword because I believed in him."

Thaddeus helped Simon unroll the tent. "We're all willing. That's why we're still here. When Simon—Peter—called him Messiah, Jesus *didn't* deny it."

"That's my question! What messiah asks his followers to take up crosses? A messiah should call his people to *arms*! You don't become king by sending your people to die. You become king by making the *enemy's* people die!"

Thaddeus dropped the tent and stood. "Then why stay? You left once and came back. What keeps you here now?"

Simon looked down. "I don't really know. At first, I thought I could recruit Jesus. I wanted to keep him close so we could turn his followers into an army when the time comes.

"As confusing as he has been in recent days, I guess it's his power—the miracles. They keep me here. Maybe he'll build a new army—not out of the weak and the sick—but from the laborers— the poor, but strong. People like us—worn down by Roman rule."

Thaddeus offered no response but nodded cautiously to Simon's left. Matthew approached.

"A villager is looking for Jesus. Do you know where he is?"

Simon turned toward the mountain and gestured to the trees. "He's in there somewhere." He turned back. "What does the villager want?"

"His boy needs healing."

"He might have to wait until Jesus returns."

"Should we at least try?"

Simon shook his head. "You've never lifted a fishing net, nor a building block. What are you suggesting we try? I've seen plenty of miracles. We all have. But right now, what can we do but wait?"

Matthew bristled, "And we've both *done* miracles. Remember our earlier missions? Instead, you bring up this tired line about my past again. We came from different places, but for two years, I've been on the same journey as you. You might say that I've given up more!"

Simon's arms tensed as he stepped from his half-hoisted tent toward Matthew. "Is *your* back striped with scars from—"

A clamor across their camp caught his attention. Heavy footfalls approached, accompanied by a cry for help.

A young boy — no more than seven or eight — ran through the camp with an unsteady stride. His legs bent at unnatural angles, and his knees, strangely, were unmoving.

Yet he ran somehow — faster than his twisted legs should have allowed. He knocked over a half-pitched tent before slamming into several disciples and stumbling toward a sharp embankment above the stream.

As the boy passed, he peered at Simon with an expression of dread while spittle flew from the corner of his mouth and his hands twitched.

Three men ran after the boy. "Please stop him! He is going for the water! Don't let him get there!"

Nathaniel and Andrew joined the chase just as the boy tumbled down the rocky embankment and plunged into the stream below.

"No! He can't swim! Somebody help him! Get me a rope!"

Simon ran toward the commotion before he realized it, and Philip was not far behind the men, a rope in his hand unspooling behind him.

They reached the bank. The boy's arms thrashed in the water, and his head dropped below the surface a few times.

In a single motion, Andrew threw off his coat and cloak. He scrambled into the deepest water, where the boy continued to convulse.

The men from the village took the rope from Philip.

"Help us hold on!" one called out as the others took an end of the rope and stepped out into the shallow rapids several meters downstream from where Andrew fought his way through the churn toward the boy. Simon and the others added their strength to the rope while the man — the boy's father, he assumed — shouted further instructions.

"Go now! We can hold you!" The two men waded until the water reached their chins and swam toward the boy and Andrew, who had almost gotten close enough to grab him.

The three men grabbed at the boy's arms in succession, but the child shook free each time. Andrew briefly disappeared beneath the turbulent surface. After a moment, his head shot up from the water followed by both hands, with a firm grip on the boy's ankle.

"No!" the father shouted. "Don't turn him over. He will drown!"

Andrew's arms and chest bulged as he fought to maintain his grip on the unnaturally strong boy. The boy kicked and pulled against Andrew's grasp, while the other men threw the rope across his body and secured it around his arms and chest.

The boy strained against the rope, and Andrew let go of his foot and tightly embraced the boy. Andrew kicked his feet to stay afloat, and he squeezed the boy tightly through labored grunts. The others looped the rope around the boy several more times and secured the loose end.

The boy stopped his thrashing—whether from fatigue or defeat Simon couldn't tell—and the men pulled him to shallow water while Andrew held the boy's head above the surface.

The boy's head rested on Andrew's hand, eyes and mouth half-open.

Is he alive or dead?

The disciples pulled the rescuers up the bank, and the boy's father rushed to meet them. As Simon heaved, his shoulder collided with the form behind him.

"Oof."

Simon glanced back. Matthew stood behind him, adding his own strength to the effort.

When the last rescuer climbed up, the disciples dropped the rope and let out a chorus of sighs.

Matthew caught Simon's eyes and lifted his hand. "I should—"

"Don't." Simon waved a dismissive hand and turned back to his now-collapsed tent.

Andrew called the group together. He found his coat and put it on over his wet tunic. He stood with the boy's father, who held his now-sleeping son.

"Please stay in our village tonight. You are our guests. I insist"

Nathaniel answered, "Your offer is kind, but our teacher instructed us to wait here."

"You're disciples of the Nazarene, right? We've heard of his healings. Where is he?"

"He went up the mountain," Nathaniel waved his hand toward the summit. "But he didn't say for how long."

"If you've just arrived and he's going the peak, he won't be back before daybreak. Please come and share a meal with us before dark."

The disciples nodded in agreement and gathered their belongings.

The village was a short walk up a well-worn foot path around the base of a hill sitting opposite the mountain.

As they walked, the man introduced himself as Josiah. They reached his village and sat in a courtyard surrounded by several simple one-room houses.

A fire blazed in the center, and several men reclined nearby. Two women tended boiling lentils and a bread oven in a shared kitchen.

When everyone was seated, Josiah said, "As you have seen, my son suffers with seizures and convulsions. An evil spirit torments him. It's been with him since birth. It's even seized his tongue."

Josiah's gaze followed the sparks and embers that danced off the fire.

"Usually, he just collapses and goes rigid. But when his tormentor is alarmed, it throws the boy into the fire or the water. This hasn't happened recently. Perhaps the evil spirit noticed your arrival." Josiah scanned the faces of the disciples and stopped at Andrew. "It must know that you come with power. Can you help him?"

Simon searched his friends' faces for any sign that he was not alone in his doubt. Just days prior, he would have gladly cast the evil spirit from the child. They all would have. But Jesus' strange new talk of dying made him question their purpose.

What if we have no power left?

Andrew answered, "We will help your son. Bring him to us in the morning."

When morning broke, the disciples gathered in the courtyard. They were met by the men of the village and residents from neighboring settlements.

Josiah exited his home, guiding the boy by the hand. Color had returned to the boy's face overnight, and he walked on his own, watching with wide, expressionless eyes.

Andrew, Philip, and Nathaniel approached and laid hands on his head while Simon and the five other disciples circled around them. Doubt and hopelessness welled up in Simon.

What if we fail?

Philip spoke with force. "Identify yourself, demon! In the name of the Most High, I demand that you leave the boy."

The boy opened his mouth and moaned as his arms stiffened.

We are fools to think we are stronger than this spirit.

Philip continued, "In the name of Jesus the Nazarene, I command you to release the boy!"

The boy coughed and spit at Philip. Philip stumbled backward, and the boy trembled. Matthew reached a hand toward the boy while Andrew and Nathaniel shouted commands.

"Identify yourself!"

"Be gone!"

"In the name of God Almighty!"

"Release the boy!"

They shouted over each other. Simon fixated in silence on the strange scene. He had witnessed such authority in Jesus, and he had even wielded power over evil spirits himself.

Power that's gone as quickly and strangely as it had arrived.

His doubt grew while his companions twisted their brows into worry and anguish. The boy collapsed, rigid and twitching, and the villagers broke their silence.

"What fraud is this?"

"You are powerless without your teacher."

"How do we even know he sent you?"

"Maybe he is a fraud, too!"

Josiah's face paled. He collected his son and pulled the boy away from the agitated crowd.

Simon shouted, "Nothing you say is true! We *have* seen God's power, and we've *wielded* his power. It's your insults that interfere. No wonder God has closed His power off from you!"

A hand on Simon's shoulder pulled him from the center of the fray. "You can't say these things." Thaddeus was stern, but kind as he spoke.

An older man from the village called back, "What do you know of the things of God? By what authority do you dare speak of His power?"

"What is happening here?" The question came from behind Simon. The growing crowd turned toward the voice and hurried past Simon and the others.

Simon turned as the people swarmed Jesus on the path. A distinguishable but indescribable vigor was evident in his face, his eyes, and even his gait. Peter, James, and John followed behind, and their own eyes seemed lost in thoughts beyond the moment.

People shouted over each toward Jesus until he held up a hand and asked, "What are you arguing with them about?"

Josiah pressed through the throng. When he emerged, he looked at Jesus with a wide-eyed mix of awe and desperation. "Teacher, my son is possessed, robbed of his speech." Josiah recounted the same horrors that he had shared the previous day until he was choking on his words. With a heavy sigh, he looked down and said, "I asked your disciples to drive out the spirit, but they could not do it ..."

Jesus' eyes revealed only kindness as he listened. "Oh, unbelieving generation," he responded with a touch of sadness. "How long shall I put up with you? Bring the boy to me."

The crowd parted, and two men carried the fatigued boy to Jesus.

At the sight of Jesus, the boy jerked away and landed in an awkward heap at Jesus' feet, knocking one of the men into the crowd. The people pushed back as the boy convulsed and rolled on the ground. Simon pushed closer to the center of the mass of bodies. Foam flew from the boy's mouth as he spasmed.

Jesus turned to the boy's father. "How long has he been like this?"

"Since childhood. If you can do anything, please help us."

"If I can? Everything is possible for the one who believes."

Jesus' words were directed at the boy's father, but Simon felt them like a blow to the sternum. Ever since Jesus started talking about crosses and dying, he wasn't sure what he believed — if anything at all — about Jesus.

Please give me a reason to believe.

Josiah cried out, "I *do* believe. Help me in my unbelief!"

Yes, help us all in our unbelief.

Jesus stooped down, grasped the boy's shoulders, and spoke with force and authority. "You deaf and mute spirit! I command you to depart from this boy and never return to him. Be gone from here!"

The boy let out a piercing shriek and threw his head back in a violent convulsion. He collapsed, and the color drained from his face while murmurs rose from the still-growing crowd.

Is he still alive?

Jesus took the boy's hand and lifted him to his feet. His father met him with a smothering embrace.

Josiah's eyes filled with tears as he looked up at Jesus. "Thank you. Please come, rest, and eat."

The villagers returned to their homes while Jesus and his disciples followed Josiah.

Away from the onlookers, Simon approached Jesus and asked, "Why couldn't we drive the spirit out?"

Jesus regarded Simon with kindness. "This kind can only come out by prayer."

"I don't understand. We've driven demons out before. What's different about this one?"

"It is because you have little faith. Consider this mountain, Simon." Jesus waved a hand toward Mount Tabor. "With faith as small as a mustard seed, you could command this mountain to move. Nothing will be impossible for you."

Simon returned to the courtyard in silence.

Have I given up?

Nobody spoke to him as he sat in silence.

Am I the only one with these doubts?

Jesus sent the disciples ahead to Capernaum while he stayed behind with Josiah and his son.

On the road, Thaddeus came alongside Simon. "I heard what Jesus said to you. Do you really think you just need more faith? Several of us tried to drive the spirit out of that boy, but nobody succeeded. It's not only you."

"Maybe. But I didn't really try to help. I doubt it would have made a difference."

Simon paused, but his friend did not reply. Agitated by the silence, he continued, "I know everyone who tried failed, but they still tried. Maybe Jesus is right; maybe I just don't believe."

From behind the pair, Matthew interjected, "I tried, but I didn't get much of a chance. Maybe if I had gotten to him first, I could have helped him."

Simon stopped and turned. "Do you really think that you could have done better? None of us had success. *None* of us."

A shocked expression came over Matthew's face. "I cast demons out and made lame men walk by my own hands when we were out near Chorazin. Why shouldn't I believe that I could do the same thing again?"

"Because it's not the same!" Simon let his volume rise unchecked. Matthew held up his hands and stepped back.

The group circled around them. Before either continued, Peter interjected, "We weren't all there, but perhaps if we were, we could have healed the boy."

"So that was the problem?" Judas joined the argument. "All we needed was *you*?"

"Why were you up on the mountain anyway? What did the rest of us miss?" Thomas pointed an accusing finger toward Peter.

"We can't say," added James, "until it is time."

John nodded.

"Why are you two always acting as if you're better than the rest of us?" Thomas redirected his pointed finger toward the brothers.

"At least they were gone at Jesus' request." Andrew stepped between Thomas and the pair. "Where were *you* when I jumped into the water?"

"We all had a part in the rescue!" Matthew flailed his arms. "Not like the next day when everyone gave up too soon on healing the boy. I didn't even get a chance to—"

"To what?" Simon cut him off. "When have you ever helped anyone but yourself?"

"Do you know how much I've lost following Jesus? The tax farmers have withdrawn their protection. My household is at risk. Yet I am still here *trying* to do some good."

"Do good? You built your wealth by *taking* from these people." Simon waved a hand toward the others. "You've kept people like these villagers—that young boy that you pretend to care about— mired in poverty while you flaunt your excess and hide behind the sword of Rome. Why? So Herod can get fat, and Caesar can overrun more kingdoms."

"This isn't about Herod and Caesar! It's about us ... about our calling to—"

"*You are not worthy of this calling!*" Simon shouted. "Why should Jesus want *you*? You've always been a traitor! I don't know if we'll ever know who is the *greatest* among us. It might not be me, but you are certainly the *worst!*"

Simon felt all eyes on him as his outburst ended as abruptly as it began. He saw Matthew open his mouth to respond, but before the words came, a voice interjected from behind. "I expected you to be farther along." Jesus had caught up to them.

The sudden silence weighed on Simon, and he looked down. Anger that raged just a moment ago gave way to a flood of shame and regret.

How much did Jesus hear?

Jesus continued, "That was quite a clamor. I could hear you long before I could see you. What were you arguing about?"

Nobody answered.

"Let's keep moving. We need to get back to Capernaum."

The men resumed walking, leaving the conversation behind.

Only Jesus broke the silence. "The Son of Man will be betrayed into the hands of men. They will kill him, and after three days, he will rise."

Simon tensed. He glanced at Thaddeus, who responded only with a subtle shake of his head. The rest exchanged puzzled glances, but nobody spoke.

Simon spent the rest of the journey formulating a plan.

Return to the Zealots.

Prepare for a more capable messiah.

One who is willing to fight and not just surrender and die.

They reached Capernaum and proceeded toward Peter's house. At the customs booths, Matthew's former station was occupied by a familiar face—Malchus, the younger brother of Joses, a prominent toll collector in Tiberias. The young man had been present with his brother and father at the feast Matthew had thrown in Jesus' honor.

He's finally earned — more likely purchased — some success of his own.

Malchus regarded Matthew with narrow eyes and clenched jaw as they passed. More ominous was the way the guards eyed them. They watched more intently than Matthew had ever seen. Matthew averted his eyes when he met theirs.

They reached Peter's house, and Jesus called the twelve together in the common room. "What were you arguing about on the road?"

The disciples looked at each other in silence. Matthew hoped that someone—anyone—would speak up. He scanned the room, and his eyes met Simon's. Simon's brow furrowed as he fixed his stare at Matthew.

Jesus sat on the ground and searched their faces with kind eyes. "You've had trouble understanding these past few days. So let me say it this way. If any of you wants to be first, he must be the very last."

The disciples exchanged more puzzled looks, and Jesus called toward the door to the courtyard, "Come in here." He nodded and waved an inviting hand. A boy—barely old enough to speak—approached Jesus.

Jesus put an arm around the boy and continued, "Whoever welcomes one of these little children welcomes me. And whoever welcomes me welcomes the One who sent me."

The boy in Jesus' arms was barefoot and wore a simple tunic in sore need of washing.

He will never be more than a laborer or fisherman. He will probably never read.

Yet, the boy looked at the disciples with innocence as he leaned into Jesus. There was no judgment in his eyes, only wonder. He was one of the least.

But he doesn't know it.

Matthew recalled how he'd surrounded himself with influential people—other toll collectors and tax farmers. He had made allies in Tiberias and Sepphoris.

With his wealth, he could buy pleasure, influence, and security. He had bid a hefty price for his old toll booth, but his investment paid off a hundredfold.

What is it about Jesus that drew me away from that?

Compassion?

Compassion was absent from all of Matthew's dealings. The Pharisees and the labor class alike judged the company he had kept.

How fickle my allies turned out to be.

They were swift to render their own judgment when he stepped away from the life of influence and comfort.

I must not have been useful to them any longer.

But this boy knew nothing of greed, power, influence, judgment, nor fear.

Fear.

Fear had driven so many of Matthew's decisions. Fearing the oppressors, he found a way to join them. Fearing his own people, he hid behind the oppressor's sword—a privilege for which he paid well.

Still, it wasn't enough. He recalled the robbery that nearly cost him his life—and did cost him a sizable purse. That memory had kept fear in the forefront of his mind.

Until Jesus came along.

This same Jesus who talked about betrayal and dying with no hint of fear or reservation. Now he welcomed an insignificant child without judgment.

How much must I give before I am as free as this child?

Matthew was snapped from his reverie when one of his companions stomped toward the door. He looked up just as Simon exited. He heard more footfalls above him.

"You should follow him," Jesus said.

Matthew looked toward Thaddeus, Simon's closest friend. The man started to rise before Jesus held out a hand to stop him.

"Not you, Thaddeus." Jesus turned and held an open hand toward Matthew. "You."

That can't be right.

Jesus must have seen the confusion in his face. Jesus nodded at him, "Yes. Go."

Matthew crossed the courtyard and climbed the stairs. Simon stood on the roof with his arms crossed, facing the sea. He turned at the sound of Matthew's heavy footfalls. "I didn't expect you to come after me."

"I didn't expect to be sent. But here we are."

Simon's arms dropped to his side. "Jesus sent you to find me?"

Matthew nodded.

"What is he doing? Everything I thought I understood no longer makes sense."

Matthew detected the resignation in Simon's voice. For two years, the man had been openly hostile toward him. Now — for the first time — the hostility was gone. "We all have questions, Simon. Seeing that little boy made me understand mine."

A perplexed look crossed Simon's features. "How? You can't relate to his poverty and need nor to the toil that he'll grow to face."

"By contrast, the boy knows nothing of my fear! The more threatening the Romans became, the more I worked to appease them. When Jesus stood that child up before us — in that moment — I wished I could *be* him. I wished I could be the boy who didn't know the sleepless nights, the conflict of compromise, the knowledge that I could never truly *trust* the people around me. I wished I could forget all that I knew."

Simon closed his eyes and clenched his jaw as Matthew spoke. He let out a breath. "I hardly had a childhood. My father was caught up in the uprising of Judas Bar-Hezekiah. He wasn't directly involved. He had no blood on his hands — at least that's what my mother told me — but it didn't matter. Rome crucified him all the same. Those savages didn't care. And what's worse, they carried off my sisters. I have no idea what became of them, and I try not to dwell on the possibilities ..."

Simon inhaled deeply, then continued, "When Jesus brought that boy forward, I saw peace in his eyes. I wanted to go back and find that serenity myself, but I can't go back."

Matthew's thoughts churned with this new information. For two years, he had walked with Simon and the others, but he was just now learning who he really was. *How do I even respond to this?* Silence stretched between them.

Simon turned and again faced the sea. "You talk about fear. When my father and sisters were taken, I was determined not to be afraid of the Romans. So I learned to fight. And from that moment on, I spent my whole life fighting.

"When Jesus started talking about dying, it made no sense. I was ready to *fight*—to rally everyone behind Jesus and drive the Romans out for good. But he talked about surrender. I planned to walk away when we got back to Galilee. To get back to the real fight. But that boy ..."

"The real fight? What do you mean?"

"To take up arms with like-minded men who would be willing to fight."

"You mean to join the bandits?"

"Not just bandits. Don't confuse us with roadside thugs who take from their own people. We choose our targets more carefully."

"*Us?* So you're already one of them—a Zealot?"

Simon faced Matthew and nodded.

Matthew recalled his own terrorizing encounter with Zealots. The tax farmers—and even Herod—were little help. The Romans seemed not to regard an isolated encounter as worthy of their hearing, much less their response.

"I'm ... familiar with the Zealots—"

"I know." Simon looked Matthew in the eye. All anger and condemnation were now gone from his voice, his gaze. Matthew saw sorrow in the man's eyes.

"How?"

"I was there."

The robbery?

Matthew opened his mouth to speak, but no words came.

"You're angry. I understand. I was angry, too. I was angry at the Romans who tore my family apart. I was angry at the poverty and hard life of everyone around me. And I was angry at you and others like you for using our suffering for personal gain.

"When I first decided to rob you, I wanted you dead. I wanted to send a message to Herod and the Romans—let them know what it's like. But you were so fearful in that moment, so I thought maybe your fear would spread if I let you live." Simon turned and faced the sea.

"I hoped that you would give up your toll booth and others would think twice. I didn't count on you buying more security."

"A man *died*. There is blood on your hands. And don't dismiss him as a mere thug. Ask yourself, what chance does *his* child have now? I bought more security to keep it from happening again!"

As Matthew spoke, he heard the irony of his own words:

I bought more security …

He'd never considered it that way. For two years, he'd carried his resentment of that robbery. He'd dreamed of justice. He never thought twice about paying more guards—and funding them through steeper tolls on the fisherman and traders.

Is my coin purse so different from Simon's dagger?

Each of them had tried—and failed—to secure the peace that had always eluded them.

Simon stood motionless, his back toward Matthew. Matthew wondered what was going through the younger man's mind.

Does he also realize how alike we really are?

Maybe the strange teachings they'd absorbed over the past two years were finally starting to make sense.

Does Simon also see the equal futility of both coin and dagger?

Matthew broke the silence of their mutual reverie. "Friend," it surprised him to hear the word in his own voice, "I forgive you."

Simon inhaled deeply and turned to face Matthew. "And I forgive you, brother." He stepped forward, hand outstretched. Matthew returned the gesture as they clasped forearms, then shoulders.

Simon continued, "What's next?"

"We have preparations to make. We won't be in town long." Jesus stood on the stairs with his hands clasped and just a hint of a smile.

How long has he been standing there?

"Let's go. There's a lot to be done."

Chapter Seventeen

Weeks had passed since Simon made his peace with Matthew. Somehow, that meeting compelled him to stay around. Though he still had no love for the Romans, he now questioned his own reliance on the sword.

It helped that life had returned to normal. Peter and the others were out on the sea each day while Simon and Thaddeus worked the docks.

And Jesus continued to teach them in the evenings.

Always about forgiveness.

Jesus had just finished another lesson, and the people left the hillside where more and more of them were spending their evenings. Jesus' recent teachings turned over in Simon's mind—again. He had forgiven Matthew—even found some empathy for him.

But how can forgiveness defeat Rome?

If Jesus is meant to be the messiah, what does that word even mean?

Simon hoped that with one of these parables, Jesus would help him understand—help them all understand.

At least he stopped obsessing over his death. The people must have noticed, too. The crowds were growing again.

As people dispersed, a few men moved against the flow and approached Jesus. "We're preparing to go up to the Feast of Tabernacles," Jesus' brother Jude said when they reached him. "Come with us."

Jesus gestured toward the people leaving the hillside. "I'm not done my work here."

"Let them see you work your miracles in Judea. No public figure acts in secret. Show yourself to the world!"

Jesus placed a hand on his brother's shoulder. "Any time is right for you. The world doesn't hate you the way it hates me. You go to the feast. I'm not going up to this feast yet." He kissed his brother's cheek and turned away.

After Jesus' brother left, Simon asked, "What do you mean the world hates you? The crowds have been growing every day. Word of your healings and teachings is spreading again."

"Remember what I said when we fed thousands on the shore? It is the same now. People are getting their fill, but not many would count the cost. It is different in Judea. People will be looking for me, but for a different reason. We'll go quietly, after all the other pilgrims have left."

Simon bristled at Jesus' mention of costs. *Is he back to talking about dying?* "You want to go to Jerusalem after the caravans are long gone? You're asking to get robbed along the way if you do that. It isn't safe!"

Jesus offered a slight smile, "I'll have you and the others. It will be enough."

―――――

The next morning, Simon scrawled a note on a scrap of parchment. He approached the docks and placed the note in the hands of a boy. He whispered instructions and watched as the boy followed the shoreline beyond his sight.

He spent the day reliving his recent conversations with Jesus. *Why take this unnecessary risk? What does it have to do with Jesus' recent talk about dying?* Every scenario he imagined ended in failure—or worse.

Simon collected his wages and went to Peter's house. Matthew waited in the courtyard. He stood when Simon approached.

"Jesus asked us to prepare to go up to the feast. We'll leave after the Sabbath."

"I need to talk to you about that." Simon drew close to Matthew and spoke in low tones. "It's too dangerous to travel then. There might be a way that we can make the trip safely, if you are able to help."

Matthew wrinkled his brow. "I don't understand."

"I don't want to say too much because I am unsure of a lot these days. But I know the bandits will be out, and they'll have no trouble overpowering any small parties they encounter. They *might* be persuaded to leave us alone—for a price."

Matthew's expression turned to exaggerated shock. "Are you suggesting we *pay* for protection? That's criminal!" His arms flailed wildly as he spoke. "Jesus will never go for this!"

"I'm not asking for his permission. In fact, I'm not asking anybody but you to be a part of this. Not even Thaddeus."

"Because you want me to pay these ..." Matthew shook his hands, and his voice escalated in agitation. "... these thugs?!"

"You have as much blood on your purse as I have on my scabbard. It's the least you can do to make restitution." Simon turned to leave, then stopped and turned his head. "If you are really with Jesus, you'll see the wisdom in what I am asking."

_____

The next morning, Simon passed the docks and followed the uneven road to the abandoned pier. He knew from his many trips to this place that the active harbor was out of view. Still, he looked back. He reached the dock and climbed down to the water's edge.

An unfamiliar man stood waiting.

Even in his coat, the man's frame was visibly muscular. His features were hardened and bronzed by daily exposure to the sun and wind, but still full of youth and vigor. Simon estimated that the man was not much older than he was.

"I was expecting Manaen. Who are you?"

"When Manaen got your message, Simon of Cana, he brought it to me. You've become something of a concern to our movement, and I thought it would be in our best interest to sort out this confusion myself."

Simon tensed and stood silent. *What did Manaen say about me?*

The man continued, "To answer your question, I am Jeshua, son of our fathers, Abraham, Isaac, and Jacob."

Simon's heart skipped. He had heard of this Jeshua. Others in the movement had adopted his moniker, but he was said to be the first to call himself a son of the fathers — *Bar-Abbas. How deeply have I gotten myself entangled?*

"So why are you here instead of Manaen?"

"Simon," Jeshua gently shook his head, "the road to Jerusalem is long and not well traveled now that most of the pilgrims have already gone. Your request — bold as it is — requires someone with influence that reaches well beyond Galilee. But before we discuss what I can do, there is the matter of your teacher."

This was a mistake. But it's too dangerous to back out now. Simon answered, "He is kind and wise. He heals people. He gives people hope. They love him."

"Not everyone sees him that way, Simon. That might be true in Galilee, but in Jerusalem, even now, there are a few in the Sanhedrin who would rather see him silenced."

"You've spoken with the Sanhedrin?"

"Like I said. My influence reaches far. Still, I am willing to hear you out." Jeshua sat on the gravelly slope under the dock and gestured for Simon to do the same. "When I first saw how the people gathered around your teacher, I had great hope. I saw a man who could sway many to his cause. That's why Manaen compelled you to recruit him — an effort in which you failed, I might note."

Simon drew back. "It was hardly a failure. Jesus speaks of a different kind of kingdom. And he has shown power even over the forces of nature. I don't pretend to understand it all, but he always seems to know what he's doing."

"But all of that does us little good, Simon. And don't think that I haven't heard about Jesus bringing a toll collector into his fold. How can we be sure this isn't some treachery by Jesus — by *you* — to root our people out and hand them over to the Romans?"

The insult — *the accusation* — cut deep. Simon breathed slowly and searched for a careful response. "Jesus has shown no interest in doing anything but helping people. He hasn't professed enmity to Rome, but he hasn't declared allegiance either."

Jeshua nodded as Simon spoke, and his eyes pierced the younger man with scrutiny. "Very well. I will ensure that your party is not harassed from here through Perea. Cross by Jericho and make the climb from there. I'll have eyes on the road.

"You might still encounter some random thugs and desperate bandits. But those types are few and scattered and act alone. They are not a part of us. The size of your party should be enough to deter them.

"As for our men ..." A stern, emotionless gravity washed over Jeshua's face, and he added, "... they will require compensation. You are asking them to forgo their livelihood. Thirty shekels, delivered to me, at this place tomorrow."

Thirty shekels? Robbers wouldn't get half that if they stripped us down to our tunics!

"We could *buy* a guard for that amount. Besides, it's much more than we carry. And how do I know your men will listen? I can offer you five shekels."

Jeshua let out a derisive laugh. "They will listen because it will be worth their while. Besides, you're only calculating the cost of your wares and your purse. Factor in the cost of shed blood, broken bones ... or the cost to your wife if you don't return. Still, I'm fair. So twenty-five, as a show of goodwill."

Simon clenched his fists and fought back the urge to hurl Jeshua down the slope onto the watery crags below. "Five tomorrow — my show of goodwill. The other twenty when we return." Simon stood to leave.

"Very well," Jeshua nodded as he stood, too. "But one more thing: I can see you safely *to* the feast. Once your teacher is *in* Jerusalem, I cannot help him."

Simon turned and left without so much as a clasp of the man's shoulders.

———

Matthew tensed as he neared the toll booths. *It would be nice to have another route to follow.*

Ever since the group returned to Capernaum, the tax collectors whispered among themselves when he passed. Even the guards stopped to scrutinize him.

Just like every day. How would they answer if I confronted them?

Only a nagging thought that confrontation would be futile gave Matthew a measure of restraint — and preparations for their oddly timed trip to Jerusalem.

Why would Jesus want to go at such a time? Simon's right. It isn't safe.

Matthew reached Peter's house and found only Judas gathering provisions for the journey. The fishermen were still on the water, and Jesus preferred to spend his time on the outskirts with the people.

About mid-morning, Simon entered from the courtyard. *Unusual that he's not on the docks.*

"It's done — what we discussed."

Judas emerged from the storeroom. "What's done?"

"A family matter." Worry played across Simon's features.

There's more weighing on him.

Matthew gestured toward the door and said, "About what we discussed..." He exited and turned toward the stairs. Simon followed.

They reached the roof, and Simon said, "They won't take less than twenty-five shekels. I convinced them to accept five now and the rest when we return —"

"Twenty-five shekels?! That's extortion!" Matthew flailed his arms, and his voice cracked as he spit words. "Why would you agree to such a price? Don't you realize that is more than we even carry?"

"I said as much. But ... it was the best I could do."

"Maybe you should learn a little about negotiation before you make any more deals! Why would you think I would agree to such a price? You don't speak for me!"

Simon's fists clenched. He set his jaw and turned away. Matthew let the silence hang between them.

"It got complicated," Simon continued without turning to face Matthew. "I called for Manaen, but it went higher."

"Higher? What do you mean? Who?"

"I can't say."

Matthew grew frustrated with Simon's evasive half-answers. *Unless …*

"How do I know you didn't arrange this steep price yourself? You've been critical of my wealth—"

Simon turned and faced Matthew, his face flush and his voice firm. "I'm critical of how you *got* your wealth. But I promise, none of what I am asking is for me—at least, not in the way you imply."

"What do you mean?"

Simon sighed and relaxed his shoulders, "I mean my family is not safe. If I don't pay as I promised, I expect them to retaliate."

Matthew wanted to chastise Simon, to point out that he was only inviting more trouble by making this deal. But the fear in his friend's face was all too familiar.

Would I have done any differently?

Matthew offered a silent nod, which Simon returned. "We have even more to do now than before. Bring your wife to my estate. She can stay until we close this deal. My servants will ensure that she is cared for, and I'll hire a guard."

"Thank you." Simon clasped his hand and then turned toward the stairs.

Matthew turned to follow. Judas stood at the top of the steps. *How long has he been there?*

"Someone is here calling for you. He says he needs you to return to your estate at once."

Matthew pushed Judas aside and hurried to the courtyard, where one of his servants waited with a rolled parchment.

"Men from Tiberias arrived this morning," the young man said as he held out the document. "They wish to speak with you immediately."

Matthew took the scroll and examined the familiar seal. *Samchai.*

Matthew climbed the slope to his homestead as briskly as his legs allowed. He approached his house while a servant led a horse to the watering trough. Two guards waited alongside the road. He recognized one as a recent addition to the toll booths.

Matthew dismissed his messenger and stepped into his house. Samchai waited in the receiving room, accompanied by his personal guard and his secretary. Matthew didn't extend a hand, and Samchai seemed unaffected by the lack of greeting as he stood and addressed Matthew.

"Matthew, son of Alphaeus. It has been some time." Samchai's gaze was soft, but alert.

"Why are you here? My debt is paid, and another has taken over my toll station. What further business could we possibly have?"

Samchai smiled mirthlessly. "I am here on behalf of Cuza, secretary to Herod Antipas. You might have heard there has been growing unrest in Jerusalem. Pilate blames the Galileans for stirring up dissension."

"What does that have to do with me? Those thugs have harassed me as much as they've harassed the Romans."

"Nevertheless, you've chosen to walk away from your very profitable arrangements with me and take up with the Nazarene teacher."

"The very same Nazarene who healed Cuza's son!"

"And Cuza's wife, as I'm sure you know, because she has been traveling with your party. But did you also know that he has since written her a divorce decree? He hasn't taken kindly to his wife spending so much time away from the palace. Strange, how this Nazarene has a way of enticing people to leave their comforts ..."

Joanna. She's paid for as much of our travels as I have. Maybe more.

Samchai paused and examined Matthew's expressions. Matthew fought to suppress any sign of reaction. Samchai continued, "And that brings us back to you. You are often seen with him and a not-too-small number of fishermen and laborers, the sort of men who are strong enough—and foolish enough—to rally to violence."

"My teacher heals people. He feeds them. He doesn't stir up dissent."

"Nevertheless, if he were to do so—once his army has grown large enough—how valuable would a toll worker be to his cause?"

Where could this discussion possibly be going? With more caution in his voice than he meant to betray, Matthew asked, "Valuable how? No Zealot would trust a toll collector. And I promise I have no love for their ways either."

Samchai nodded. "I thought you would say as much, and I believe you. But convincing Herod is another matter. So I've been sent to inquire and to provide ... assurance ... that your knowledge of our systems and our people is not at risk of ... compromise."

Is Samchai making a threat? Matthew held his breath while trying to speak past his fear, which he was certain Samchai — or at least his guard — could plainly see. "You have my word. It has been two years since I surrendered my duties, and you've had no trouble from me nor from my teacher. Isn't that enough?" Matthew regretted the question as soon as he spoke it.

Samchai laughed, "Matthew, you've grown naïve since you left. I fear that this 'teacher' is not making you any wiser. The question of your involvement in any fomenting sedition was posed to me because of our history. I called on you, hoping you might be able to ... persuade me that there's nothing to worry about."

There it is. He's asking for a bribe. Matthew wondered if Herod's office had even contacted him, or if this whole story had been engineered.

Do I ask Joanna? It doesn't matter. If Herod is unaware of the inquiry, Samchai will be sure to make him aware if he doesn't get his way.

Matthew crossed the room to a doorway leading to the courtyard. Samchai came alongside him, offering a nod of assurance to the guard who jerked to attention. When they were beyond prying ears, Matthew narrowed his eyes and turned to Samchai. "What persuasion do you have in mind?"

"Two minas ought to be sufficient."

"Two minas? That isn't possible. You know that I am not still lining my coffers."

"Still, you make do with what you've accumulated. I can't imagine you've exhausted your reserves. After all, you've always been a prudent, sensible investor."

"I can offer you fifty denarii to be gone from my life for good."

"I expect a less insulting offer from someone with your negotiating experience. One mina. Plus collateral."

Fear and rage stirred discomfort in Matthew's chest, but he held back.

Samchai has the upper hand.

Samchai continued in an even tone, "You have a daughter of marrying age. Simeon has been a loyal guard," Samchai gestured toward the receiving room. "I'm sure he would treat her well."

Matthew clenched his fists and fought back tears. His mind raced with questions and resigned hopelessness. More than hopelessness. Regret.

How many years had I been too busy to even remember she was here?

He shivered when a new thought invaded his mind.

What did Simon say before about his sisters?

He exhaled loudly, fully aware that his attempt to hide his emotion was futile.

The silence hung in the air for a long moment, then Samchai added, "I wouldn't have expected you, of all people, to be lost for words. I trust we understand each other."

Matthew turned and entered the house. He refused to even look at Samchai as he found a servant and asked her to summon Hannah.

When his daughter came to the receiving area, Matthew gave her a long embrace. "You will be well cared for in Tiberias. Samchai's people will ensure your comfort," he whispered.

I hope I am right.

He stepped away from his daughter and turned to his manager. "Please retrieve a mina from the storeroom."

Matthew hoped the upcoming feast, the trip to Jerusalem, or whatever healings, miracles, and wisdom Jesus had to offer would restore his peace—a peace that he thought he knew, but had somehow been swindled from him.

Samchai and his men returned to their cart. Hannah looked back with uncertain eyes as they guided her out the door. As they approached the stable area, a goat brushed Simeon's boot. The guard responded with a swift stab of his sword into the animal's neck.

Matthew's heart sank deeper still.

Chapter Eighteen

Simon waited for Jeshua under the abandoned dock. Doubt nagged at his mind. *There's too much at stake to back out now.*

With Matthew's report of the tax farmer's renewed interest in him — in all of them — the stakes continued to climb.

He prayed that Jesus would amass an army so vast that neither the Zealots nor the Herodians would dare take action against them.

A voice interrupted Simon's contemplation. "It's dangerous to daydream. A foe would have your throat — especially if he knew you were carrying what I trust you have brought for me."

Simon startled and jumped to his feet, unsheathing his dagger as he turned. He paused at the familiar face of Manaen. He had come alone.

"I was expecting Jeshua. The one called Bar-Abbas. My pact is with him."

"Jeshua's questions about this matter have been satisfied ... for now. He's entrusted me to complete the agreement that you began with him."

Simon studied Manaen thoughtfully. *How deeply entangled has he gotten? This is no longer the impetuous young man who first recruited me years ago.*

"You doubt me, Simon? You know I've always kept my word. Has this Nazarene teacher of yours gotten into your head?"

Simon's arms tensed. "This has nothing to do with Jesus. I called on you as a favor to a friend, and I am willing to compensate you well. But you sold me out to your Bar-Abbas. He threatened me, you know."

Manaen's face softened. "Of course, I apologize that he would give you such a stern warning. We never want to harm our own. Bar-Abbas doesn't know you like I do, and he only wants to ensure that our movement is not ... compromised."

"Neither do I, and neither does Jesus."

"Then why follow him, if you're not seeking some kind of change?"

"It's still change—just not the way you envision. Jesus works differently. Like I've told you before, he has real power. I've seen the miracles, the healings. He speaks with authority."

"The Pharisees would disagree. And I'm sure you know that many of them are sympathizers—if not full-fledged adherents—to our cause. Yet, your teacher has managed to make enemies of them by flaunting the Sabbath regulations. If he would only be so bold toward Rome, toward Herod—"

"He has spoken against the corruption in the temple." Simon recalled his first trip with Jesus to Jerusalem. *I had so many questions then, and even more now.*

Manaen arched his brows and nodded. "A valid criticism, indeed. But it's not enough. So again I ask, why follow him? What's his plan?"

If only I knew the answer.

Simon searched his mind. He had no idea what Jesus had planned. At every turn, the Nazarene did exactly what nobody expected. *There's only one way to find out.* "I don't really know. He doesn't talk about plans—just the kingdom of God. He speaks in parables. It's different, and there's much I don't understand. I only know that—for reasons I can't explain—I must follow."

"Very well," Manaen nodded, "I'll collect your deposit and leave you to your journey."

Simon untied a bound purse from his waist and handed it to Manaen. Manaen took the purse and felt the weight in his hand without opening the packet before dropping it into his own satchel.

Manaen pulled a leather cord from his bag, more than a meter long, braided with red threads. Fastened to the end were seven bronze spearheads. *Roman. Military-issued.* Simon made no attempt to hide his confusion.

"Take this. Fasten it to your cart. You won't have any trouble."

Simon took the braid with a nod and examined the spearheads. *No need to ask where these came from.*

"Just one more thing," Manaen added, "a personal question. How is it that a laborer like you can give up your ... pursuits ... and still fund a transaction like this?"

Simon stiffened. "You accused me of collusion, of giving your secrets to our enemies. This," Simon pointed to Manaen's bag, "proves otherwise."

"So your toll collector friend has become your benefactor. I should have charged you tenfold." Manaen turned and climbed the slope. Simon sat and watched the sea as he waited for the man to be gone.

———

After a day's journey, Jesus and the disciples reached Kafr Kanna, where the road would take them east across the Jordan River and into Perea. James and John, leading the party, turned toward the east.

"Stop!" Jesus called from the middle of the group. "We will take the south road."

"But that takes us through Samaria. We can't do that—especially during a festival," James objected from the front.

"I have sheep in other pens. We go south."

Matthew shook his head; he glanced around and confirmed that he was not the only one. *This is strange – even for Jesus.* A hand landed on his shoulder. He turned, and Simon silently gestured Matthew to come aside.

They stepped off the road and walked in waist-high grass. Matthew offered the younger man a smile and a shrug. "I guess there is more than one way to avoid bandits."

Simon didn't laugh nor even show a hint of a smile. He whispered, "Do you think he knows?"

"Well, your tassel certainly had most of the men talking. But still, don't you see it? The way he looks through us—it's like he knows our minds, our hearts, our bowels! That's what made me pay attention to him in the first place—not the healings or any of that. It was the way he saw me at the toll booth. Like he saw my fear but refused to condemn me. I didn't understand it then, and I don't understand it now. But somehow, I know less fear with Jesus than when I am surrounded by armed guards. I'm glad to be done with them and with Samchai, and the rest of the Herodians."

"No matter. As long as Jesus keeps insisting on going through Samaria, we're on our own."

Matthew hung his head. He hardly heard Simon's comment as his mind returned to his last meeting with Samchai. A new fear washed over him, but not about their trip to Jerusalem.

What if Samchai isn't done with me?

———

The next day, they reached the border to Samaria and continued south. After several hours, they arrived at an inland trade route from Caesarea and the Great Sea. Jesus sent two of their companions ahead to find accommodations in the villages.

The party was nearly fifty strong, but with the lack of travelers on such a heavily traveled road, the villages ahead appeared well suited to accommodate their numbers.

Simon walked in silence. Thaddeus had tried to engage him, even bringing up the bandits on their last trip through Samaria. But Simon dismissed his friend with a story about his wife being unsettled over his decision to travel again.

It's not a lie. She did initially object to Simon's insistence that she take shelter in the toll collector's household.

Still, he couldn't let Thaddeus know about the deal he made with Manaen. *With Jeshua Bar-Abbas.*

As they continued deeper into Samaria, Simon pondered Jesus' reason for bringing them this way. *Is he trying to avoid trouble with bandits?* Simon preferred their company to defilement of the Samaritans any day. At least the bandits — most of them, anyway — were fiercely loyal to Judea; to the God of Abraham, Isaac, and Jacob; and to their fellow Jews.

Could Jesus really be the messiah if he breaches custom after custom? Still, Simon had witnessed too many miracles to consider leaving now.

Not that I could ever return to Manaen after all that has happened.

Simon was jolted from his reverie when the two messengers returned. He was too far back to hear their conversation with Jesus, but they waved their arms in dramatic fashion and spoke rapidly.

Those closer to the conversation grew flush. Their brows furrowed, and they clenched their fists. John shouted, "Let's call down fire on them!"

James added, "Show them your power!"

A few others murmured assent. Jesus turned sharply toward the brothers and ordered, "We will not. And you will not make this suggestion again." When everyone was silent, Jesus turned back to the messengers and gestured further instruction to them. The pair went ahead of the party down the inland road.

Simon made his way to the front and came alongside Jesus.

"A show of power could help us — especially among our enemies. Besides, what if we are not welcomed in any village? It could be dangerous to camp in hostile land."

Jesus turned and regarded Simon with his always-kind eyes. "Simon. You once called the toll collector your enemy. Do you remember what I said to you then?"

"That it is the unwell who need a physician."

"That's right. As I taught you before, don't fear those who can kill the body. And don't resist an evil man. Instead, pray for those who persecute you."

Simon looked to the ground without responding.

"You might not understand now, Simon. But soon you will. A time is coming when you *must* do all I have taught."

"But ... what about your kingdom?"

"You will see me come into my kingdom, Simon. When I do, you'll understand."

Simon wondered how many others heard their conversation as he left Jesus' side and returned to the back of the group.

———

The disciples passed through Samaria without incident, followed by an uneventful two-day journey through Judea to Jerusalem. If there were any raiding parties on the road, they stayed hidden.

Maybe the spearheads actually kept them away.

They ascended the road toward the western gate into Jerusalem. Crosses lined the road, some empty, others still bearing rotting carcasses. On a few, men gasped and strained against their ties and the splintering wood. The affront to Simon's eyes was matched only by the assault on his nose. He had heard stories of Pilate stirring up dissension with his brash decisions.

Does the Roman prefect agitate our people on purpose?

What does Jesus plan to do about it?

Camps were set in and around the surrounding villages and across the open land north of the city. Arriving mid-festival, they would have difficulty finding reasonable accommodations.

Still, Jesus seemed undeterred. He sent two messengers — the same two who went ahead of them in Samaria — to a nearby village to arrange shelter. Most of the party followed them, leading the pack animals and carts away from the city.

Jesus instructed the twelve to remain with him, and they entered the city. They had not been back since the Passover feast two years ago.

Jesus made his share of enemies then.

The Pharisees objected to his Sabbath healings. The priests questioned the authority of his teachings. And everybody — most notably the Sanhedrin — certainly remembered how he challenged the money changers.

Simon recalled his meeting with Jeshua Bar-Abbas and the reminder that they would be on their own inside Jerusalem.

Jerusalem must not have forgotten the impact Jesus made the last time he was here.

They passed through the gate, where the opulent palace built by Herod the Great loomed over them. A newer-looking guard tower and the prominent presence of Roman soldiers suggested that Pilate had taken up use of this space.

The scene renewed and refreshed Simon's anger.

Men exposed to the sun, the wind, the birds, and their own shame are left to die on crosses while these heathens parade around God's sacred city as if they somehow have the right to be here.

Is Jesus as disgusted at this sight as I am?

They proceeded along crowded roads. Simon and the others had a hard time keeping up with Jesus as he moved through the mass of bodies with ease and purpose toward the temple.

They climbed the steps and entered the bustling outer courts, packed with festival goers. Simon kept his eyes on Jesus as they crossed the outer courts.

Commerce has not slowed down since our last visit.

They walked along porticoes that were filled with teachers and hearers. Jesus found them space, and the disciples filed in behind him as a teacher closed a scroll and concluded his homily.

Jesus seized the opportunity and began to teach the gathered crowd. His words were familiar to Simon; he had heard them all throughout Galilee—strange words about blessing the poor, the hungry, and the meek.

Meekness.

Simon thought about the notion that setting aside power could somehow lead to blessing. The crosses, the guard towers, and the troops garrisoned in the Antonia Fortress just outside this sacred ground all reminded him that the Romans were eager to put their own power on display.

How can meekness be a blessing against such a show of force?

Simon's mind returned to the moment when chatter rose among the listeners.

"Whose school does he follow?"

"He didn't say."

"How did he get such learning without having studied?"

Jesus answered them, "My teaching is not my own. It comes from Him who sent me ..."

Simon strained to hear Jesus over the growing murmurs.

"… but he who works for the honor of the One who sent him is a man of truth."

The chatter grew louder. *What did I miss?*

"… not one of you keeps the law. Why are you trying to kill me?"

The crowd roared as one.

"This man is possessed!"

"Who is trying to kill you?"

Jesus was speaking, but his words didn't reach Simon. As the crowed settled to listen, he once again heard Jesus.

"… If a child can be circumcised on the Sabbath, why are you angry with me for healing a man on the Sabbath?"

The crowd drowned Jesus' words out with another clamor. Simon looked around with hyper-vigilant attention. The commotion attracted others who closed in under the colonnade. Simon focused his hearing on nearby voices behind him.

"Is this the one they are trying to kill? Yet he speaks publicly …"

"Do they say he is the Christ?"

"But we know where he is from!"

Even over the noise, Jesus answered the newcomers. "Yes, you know where I am from. But you do not know Him who sent me. I know Him because I am from Him …"

Jesus kept talking, but Simon no longer heard him over the crowd as they left their places and closed in on Jesus. Simon pushed through them along with the others. Peter, James, and John had been much closer and got to him first. They led Jesus to where Simon and the others stood.

A group of Pharisees had taken an interest and asked the crowd what Jesus was saying. One called for temple guards to arrest him.

"You will look for me, but you will not find me!" Jesus called to them.

More questions rose from the crowd. "Where does he intend to go?"

"Will he go and live among the Greeks?"

If only I didn't have all the same questions.

The twelve surrounded Jesus and led him down the steps and into the throng of merchants and pilgrims swarming the outer courts. They pressed through hundreds on the winding roads of the lower city to the Essene gate.

After they passed the city walls, Simon approached Jesus. "These people are not our enemies. Why rile them?"

"As I told them, I am here because of He who sent me."

"Yet you say they are trying to kill you? The more you say it, the more ..."

"Simon, be at peace. The time has not yet come. There is still more work to be done. Now let's go to where our shelter has been set."

——

Weeks had passed since Jesus was nearly seized at the feast. The pilgrims had returned to their homes, and lodging was widely available in Jerusalem, but Jesus insisted that they remain in Bethany.

Matthew did not object. The town wasn't poor like so many in Galilee, and they could easily walk to Jerusalem. They enjoyed the benefit of proximity to the city, without the trouble that came with being *inside* the city.

Ever since Samchai's threat, Matthew was reluctant to spend much time in the presence of soldiers.

They aren't hard to find in Jerusalem.

Jesus made a daily habit of going into the temple to teach. Some Pharisees and chief priests continued to challenge him, but Nicodemus, who was still a member of the Sanhedrin, assured him there was not a consensus to have him arrested.

Matthew took little solace in assurances.

I've seen how quickly the powerful can turn.

Still, the people kept coming out to hear Jesus, and their party had grown from fifty to twice that in only a few weeks. Even bigger crowds gathered daily in the porticoes.

The disciples were with Jesus in the temple courts as he spoke to the several hundred gathered. Matthew listened in earnest, as Jesus taught about being slaves to sin ... having no place in the family ... being set free ...

I always thought I had freedom.

Matthew had built up his wealth through shrewd dealings. Walking away from that life was hard, and now Samchai had taken his daughter—a daughter who, for years, Matthew had been too preoccupied to notice.

What else might Samchai notice that I have missed? What can stop him from continuing to take?

No matter how much Jesus spoke about freedom, it eluded Matthew.

Maybe freedom isn't for people like me.

Matthew focused on Jesus and his words, unaware of the crowd until a wave of agitation rippled through the people.

"Samaritan!"

"Now we know that you are demon possessed!"

Several chief priests made their way toward the growing clamor while the accusations swelled and echoed off the high stone walls.

"… Never taste death? Are you greater than Abraham?"

"Who do you think you are?"

Jesus raised his voice over the crowd as he continued, "Your father Abraham rejoiced at the thought of seeing my day …"

The people rose to their feet. Matthew struggled to stand as bodies pressed from every direction. Shouts rose nearby, but Jesus only spoke louder.

"I tell you the truth. Before Abraham was born, I AM!"

Matthew couldn't believe his ears. *Did he really just say that?* Whatever holdouts remained among the Sanhedrin surely would be swayed against Jesus now.

Even Nicodemus might withdraw his support.

How many more powerful people will turn against Jesus? Against all of us?

Matthew had no time to deliberate over their future as a wave of bodies surged toward the front of the portico, knocking him to the ground. Matthew dodged feet on every side, while hand after hand picked up stones where they lay, and the mass of bodies pushed toward where Jesus stood.

After several failed attempts, Matthew got his legs under him and stood. His eyes followed the movement of the crowd, but he could not locate Jesus.

He ran behind the crowd as they crossed the outer courts, and some went east while others went south. Beyond the temple grounds, the crowd scattered even more.

Did Jesus manage to escape?

And for how long?

That evening, the disciples gathered again in Bethany. Nervous chatter filled Matthew's ears.

But can I tell them how much is really at stake?

Apart from Matthew, only Simon knew about the threats from Samchai.

Shortly before nightfall, Jesus entered the village from the direction of the Mount of Olives, situated about halfway between

Jerusalem and Bethany. He was accompanied by James, John, and Lazarus, a young man from their host family.

Peter paced among them, agitation obvious in his speech. "We can't let this happen again. We've got to stay close to Jesus and be ready to protect him at all costs!"

"Our numbers aren't great enough," Simon countered. "Can we convince him to return to Galilee?"

Before anyone could answer, Jesus reached them. "There is still more work to be done here. But for tonight, let's rest."

For the next several mornings, Jesus didn't go up to the temple. He remained in Bethany, teaching a small gathering of people who had joined them in recent weeks. More came to hear him each day.

Like the Galilean hillside.

It was a new morning, and more people came in from Jerusalem. Matthew recognized more than a few faces.

Jesus led the crowd out of town toward the Mount of Olives. More continued to join them, pledging to follow.

As they approached a neighboring village, Matthew's attention was diverted by a messenger approaching with haste from Jerusalem. "I'm told I could find the Galileans here!"

Simon stepped to Matthew's side, and the party stopped and turned.

The man was accompanied by two others.

No temple guards, though.

"Which of you is Matthew, son of Alphaeus?"

Matthew stepped forward. "I am."

"Your presence is required in Capernaum," the messenger said and handed Matthew a scroll. The seal faced upward. *Samchai. Again.*

The messenger added, "I am charged with ensuring your return."

Chapter Nineteen

In the days since the incident at the temple, word of where Jesus was staying continued to spread. Each day, more people came from Jerusalem and the surrounding villages to hear Jesus teach.

Matthew was too preoccupied with his own predicament to notice, much less pay attention to anything Jesus was saying.

Samchai's men had found accommodation in Bethany, having dismissed any suggestion of staying in Jerusalem, where they could find more suitable lodging.

They must not want to lose track of me.

He had pressed them about Samchai's intentions — with Simon's help. They had no authority to arrest him — here nor in Galilee. Yet they were compelled — by duty or fear, Matthew could not tell — to not return without him.

Matthew read and reread the message. It made no mention of formal charges — not even a suggestion. It was just a vague mention of further discrepancies to be reviewed.

Matthew contemplated sending the men away and abandoning his estate to Samchai. That would be easier than drawing out a slow bleed of his wealth, as Samchai seemed prepared to do.

This is where I belong now. With Jesus.

But his thoughts returned again to Hannah.

What will become of her? She might be gone, but will they punish her if I fail to return?

Matthew couldn't allow his self-absorbed agenda to cause him to overlook his daughter's needs.

Like I've done her whole life.

Plus, Simon had pleaded with him to accompany him and bring his wife to safety.

Is any place still truly safe?

No temple guards had come searching for them after Jesus' latest controversy, so it was safer here.

At least for the moment.

Thaddeus and James, Matthew's brother, had agreed to accompany Matthew and Simon on the trip to Galilee.

Jesus seemed troubled at their pending departure. Matthew couldn't get the image out of his mind. The sadness in his teacher's eyes. Disappointment, but no anger, only kindness.

Always kindness. Always compassion.

So different from the shrewd tax farmers and financiers he had surrounded himself with his entire life.

Jesus accompanied them as they made their way north to a westbound trade route. A multitude followed. Every day, more people joined their numbers. Matthew longed to stay and just ...

As they passed more villages, others came to join them.

"I will follow wherever you go," one eager young man declared.

Jesus stopped and regarded the man with the same, all-too-familiar sad kindness. "Birds have nest, and foxes have holes. But the son of man has no place to lay his head."

While I return to a home that might no longer exist.

The man hung his head and turned away as Jesus called others to follow him.

"Let me first bury my father."

My father taught me everything I know about commerce and negotiation.

"Let me say goodbye to my family."

Did I even have a chance to say goodbye to my daughter?

Jesus answered them, "Let the dead bury their own. Anyone who puts his hand to the plow and looks back is not fit for service in the kingdom of God."

As the villagers turned and walked away, Matthew felt their disappointment, which only added to the weight of Jesus' words.

Does he mean me?

No!

Matthew wasn't going back to his old life.

He wasn't looking back.

He had to answer this summons and then he would be back.

Surely, Jesus must know this ...

They reached the road where they would part company.

"We will return," Matthew said as he embraced Jesus.

"I know you will."

"I'm sure you think—"

Jesus held up his hand. "Go. And return quickly."

Then Jesus turned toward the people who remained with him and said, "The harvest is plentiful, but the workers are few. I am sending you out like lambs among wolves ..."

Matthew and the others continued down the road. Within a minute, they could no longer hear what Jesus was saying.

———

After four days, they reached Capernaum. They approached Matthew's estate and found the homestead overrun with soldiers. Matthew glared at the messenger who had traveled in near silence with them. The man shrugged and gestured toward the house.

Simon stayed close by Matthew's side as they quickened their pace and entered the receiving room.

Matthew could not find a familiar face among the servants and soldiers. A man not half his age approached him. "Son of Alphaeus, you have returned. Please wait here, and I will call for Samchai."

Matthew threw his arms in the air. "You tell me to wait here? This is *my* house!" and stormed past the man. A young man dressed in the leather armor of patrol forces stepped into Matthew's path and grabbed his shoulders.

Before Matthew could react, Simon lunged forward and punched the man in the jaw.

Thaddeus leaped for him, but two more soldiers descended on Simon and grabbed him before his friend could reach him.

"What is the meaning of this?" Matthew boomed with a mix of belligerence and incredulity.

"I'll explain."

Matthew looked toward the doorway to the main quarters. Samchai emerged.

"Your questions are understandable, and you must know that I do not wish for there to be any ... trouble." Samchai's eyes shot toward Simon for a moment.

"No trouble? You're tearing my house apart! What reason do you even have to be here?"

"As my message described, we've encountered additional discrepancies —"

"Discrepancies? What is this? More extortion?"

Thaddeus and James exchanged curious glances.

Samchai smirked. "Matthew, if you wish to make a formal charge, I could refer you to the office of Antipas. Or perhaps Quirinius." Samchai paused before continuing. "Or you can hear what I have to say."

"Very well. But let my friend go. There will be no trouble." Simon steeled his jaw and remained unmoving as Samchai nodded and the soldiers unhanded him.

They went through another doorway into the courtyard. Samchai and the four disciples sat while two soldiers remained standing on either side of the tax farmer.

"It has been two years since you've left your post here, Matthew."

"And I paid my debts—even the bribe that you extracted."

"Again, if you wish to levy charges, there are means to do so. As I was saying, since your time here, the toll collection in Capernaum has become markedly more ... profitable."

What point could he be leading to with this talk?

With a shake of his head, Matthew responded, "That's to be expected. With Tiberias built, more trade must be coming through the harbors."

"It's not that simple, Matthew. Tiberias has been populated for some time now. You only prove my point that, for years, you were undercollecting."

"I collected what was required of me. If your office asked for too little, that is *your* concern, not mine!" Matthew felt flush, and Simon's twitching hand told him he wasn't alone in his reaction. He gave his friend a quick glare. *No more. Let's just get through this.*

Samchai laughed and shook his head. "But it *is* your concern, Matthew. My calculations are based on what you had done the prior year. According to Herod's office, other ports saw a marked increase in revenue. It is only a matter of time before Quirinius questions the disparity."

Matthew was used to negotiating with merchants and laborers, traders and fishermen, but he found Samchai impossible to read.

How much does Quirinius actually know? How much of what I am hearing is even true?

"And if he does, I'm sure that's a question he will ask of *you*. It is no longer my concern."

Samchai leveled his gaze at Matthew. "If the anomaly is in any way related to what you've kept for yourself or—more likely—what you've allowed your Nazarene rabbi and his local fishermen to keep, I assure you it will be your concern entirely. Still, there are more expeditious—and less troublesome—ways to resolve this."

Here it comes.

Samchai leaned forward. "I am prepared to settle this matter for the four minas that you have on hand. I'm sure Quirinius will be satisfied that any further inquiry would be a needless expenditure."

Does Quirinius even know about this?

"You broke into my storeroom!?"

"I acted under the auspices of Herod's office."

"And where is my *wife*?" Simon was on his feet and halfway to the tax farmer before the soldiers stepped in front of him. Thaddeus grabbed Simon from behind and pulled him back.

"My messengers came ahead of me. By the time I arrived, only your people were here," Samchai said to Matthew, without turning to acknowledge Simon directly.

Simon turned to Matthew and added, "We have to go. Now." His face was red, and his shoulders were visibly tense even under his cloak.

Matthew held up a hand. "We still have this unresolved matter of four minas—"

"Now! There is nothing more to resolve." The soldiers moved closer to Simon as his volume increased. "This isn't a negotiation. They won't stop until they've taken everything. That has always been the way with these imperial pigs."

The soldiers moved to seize Simon.

Samchai called out, "No! If he wishes to leave, let him leave. As for our ... resolution," Samchai addressed Matthew and leveled his tone, "your friend is right. I did not come all this way to negotiate."

———

They left Matthew's homestead and followed the road toward the city proper. Simon walked behind the others, dagger unsheathed, looking back frequently. None of Samchai's guards pursued them.

"Do you think that talk about Herod was just a ruse?" Thaddeus asked as he came alongside Simon.

"There is only one way to know for sure, and it would be too risky to try."

They walked on in silence as Simon turned the question over in his mind.

The disciples reached the city, and Simon returned his blade to his sheath before they entered the gate. They followed the main thoroughfare toward the docks. As they neared the toll station, a toll collector nodded toward them, prompting two guards to step into the path.

The toll collector was first to speak. "State your business."

Simon pushed past his friends to the front of the group and placed a hand on the hilt of his blade. "You can see that we are not here on business. Clearly, we've brought no cargo to ship nor wares to sell."

One guard stepped toward him and unsheathed his own sword. Simon turned in response to a hand on his shoulder.

Matthew regarded him with imploring, yet confident eyes. "Let me handle this."

Simon nodded and stepped aside.

"As you well know, we are not strangers here. We've come to call on a friend. As to any allusion you make to ... business, I suggest you consult with Samchai directly. We have just come from meeting with him, and I can assure you that all open business matters have been resolved. Now unless you wish to tarnish your young reputation with further brash displays of intimidation, you would be well advised to step aside. For twenty years, I stood where you stand now, and I can see that you would be wise to learn a little diplomacy."

Simon studied the young toll collector as Matthew admonished him.

He won't know what kind of world he's stepped into until it is too late.

The publican stole glances at his books, at his guards, toward the docks. When Matthew finished, the young man gave his guards a curt nod, and they returned to their stations.

They left the toll booths, with Simon taking up the rear and regularly glancing back.

They reached Peter's house, and a flood of relief washed over Simon. His wife was across the courtyard, assisting Peter's wife and mother-in-law with meal preparations. He ran to her and pulled her into a long embrace. She buried her face in his cloak and shook as she quietly sobbed.

"I saw men coming up the road, and I didn't know why they were there. I thought someone had turned you in—turned us in. I posed as a servant and went out into the fields until I could get to the road. I didn't even tell anyone I was leaving. I was too scared to be seen."

Simon exhaled heavily, "It is okay that you left. But now we have to leave here, too. All of us. It isn't safe here anymore."

James objected, "We could get back to Jerusalem to gather the others if we travel light. When we get Jesus and the others back here—"

"No!" Simon cut him off. "What you've already seen is only the beginning."

"They let Matthew go. And you—despite your temper." James' volume rose uncharacteristically as he continued his rebuttal, "If they had a reason to arrest us, they would have done so."

"I'm not worried about arrest." Simon turned to Matthew as he spoke, silently pleading.

Am I the only one who understands the danger?

"Then what you are saying makes no sense!"

"No," Matthew interjected. "Simon is right. We'll go at first light."

Simon pulled his wife to his shoulder, and she began sobbing again.

They took the long route back to the Jordan River, following the primary trade routes around the north side of the Sea of Galilee. With Matthew's help, Simon had managed to convince the others that spending as little time as possible in Herod Antipas' jurisdiction was in their interests.

Even though Herod isn't our biggest threat right now.

They lodged in the cities as they traveled south along the river, until they reached an eastward route that led to where they could cross the Jordan into Judea near Jericho.

They stopped in a village to buy food. As they inquired around the town, people came from their homes, calling others into the streets.

"You are Galileans."

"Are you with the Nazarene?"

"Is it time?"

"My son has fallen ill. Can you heal him?"

Before Simon could sort out all the voices, Matthew stepped toward the crowd. "Yes. We are with Jesus of Nazareth. You've heard of him?"

A roar of excitement went up from the crowd. Simon had difficulty hearing one person over the next and threaded together fragments of recollections as they hit his ears. Accounts of messengers coming ... proclaiming the kingdom ... driving out an evil spirit ...

"Bring your son forward." It was Thaddeus who spoke. A man carried a limp young boy—no more than six years old—in his arms and handed him to Simon. The boy was warm to the touch. Thaddeus laid hands on the boy, followed by James, then Matthew.

Thaddeus prayed out loud, "Lord almighty. By the power that You've placed on Your chosen one, Jesus, and he has imparted to us, make this child well."

Simon closed his eyes and let the words of his friend's prayer fill his mind.

The boy tensed in his arms and moved his limbs with haphazard and seemingly purposeless motions. Simon loosened his firm grip on the boy just slightly. He felt the child's fever dissipate as strength seemed to move through him.

Our first healing – my first healing – since before our failure at the mountain with the demon-possessed boy.

For a moment, he forgot about Matthew being robbed of his wealth and status ... about Manaen and Jeshua Bar-Abbas and their thinly veiled threats ... about their inability to pay the debt that Simon had incurred.

He winced with fresh regret as he considered anew the danger they were all in. *It's my debt, but they'll come after any and all of us.* Just as quickly, he forced his thoughts back to the moment at hand, happening in his arms.

Yet somehow ... Jesus still works his power in us. The kingdom is near. These people know it, and I am in the midst of it.

He didn't care if he never saw Galilee again. They had to get back to Jesus and see this through ...

Chapter Twenty

Matthew, Simon, James, and Thaddeus reunited with Jesus and the others in Bethany. Matthew was relieved to be in the company of his friends again—and encouraged to learn their numbers had grown.

Despite the healing miracles and similar accounts from the others, the weight of his losses gnawed at his mind and distracted him as Jesus taught the growing crowd with his familiar parables.

Jesus brought the twelve together early in the morning. They left the home of Mary and Martha, Lazarus' sisters who had hosted their stay in Bethany, and set off toward Jerusalem. Matthew had not been in the city since they barely escaped with their lives months ago during the Feast of Tabernacles.

Now, his life was all he had left.

They reached the Kidron Valley, and Jesus led them north without crossing.

"Are we going into Jerusalem?" Matthew asked Jesus.

"When it is time for the feast, we will go. But not yet."

The temple mount came into view across the valley as they climbed a gentle slope into a well-tended grove of olive trees. Even at this distance, the reflection of the morning sun off the gilded facade of the temple multiplied its brilliance. Jesus led the group to a clearing large enough for them to gather comfortably. *They seem to know this place. They must be making themselves at home here.*

Jesus continued beyond the clearing while the others stopped. Matthew started to follow but paused when he realized that nobody joined him. When he looked back over his shoulder, most eyes were on him.

"We'll pray here," Andrew told him.

Taking his cue from the others, Matthew sat with his back to a tree and let his mind wander. In the haste of their trip to Capernaum and back, he had spent little time in prayer. Even the recent healing of the sick boy couldn't draw his mind away from everything that had happened with Samchai. He tried to pray but couldn't sift the words from his crowded thoughts.

Do I even know how to pray?

Matthew wasn't sure how much time passed before Jesus returned to the clearing. The other disciples started to rise as they finished their own prayers. Matthew pushed himself up and stumbled toward Jesus. "Teach us to pray!" He shouted with a little more desperation than he intended.

Jesus smiled and waved for the others to gather closer. "It's not difficult. When you pray say, 'Father, hallowed be your name. Your kingdom come, give us each day our daily bread. Forgive us our sins ...'"

Matthew heaved and gasped as he broke into heavy sobbing. He stumbled away from the gathering, toward the road. Jesus' voice trailed off behind him. Soon, heavy footsteps followed, and he felt a hand on his shoulder. He turned to find James, his brother, regarding him in silence.

"I have nothing left!" Matthew rasped through labored breathing. "Never in my life have I had to ask for *bread*. And now ..." he brought both hands to his face and turned to leave.

"And now ask. And it will be given." It was the voice of Jesus. "Suppose a friend comes to *you* and asks for bread—even in the middle of the night. You don't turn him away. Because of his boldness, you give."

Again, a hand came to rest on Matthew's shoulder. He looked over, and Jesus clasped him firmly by both shoulders and continued, "How much more will your Heavenly Father provide His Holy Spirit to all who ask."

"No," Matthew shook his head, "No. You were right before. I am not fit to follow you."

Jesus didn't answer. He just looked as if waiting to hear more.

"You said that anyone who looks back could not follow you. But I left, and now I have nothing. I deserved to lose everything. And now I don't fit anywhere."

Jesus put an arm around Matthew's shoulder and led him down the road while the others followed in silence. "You have everything you need, Matthew. The Feast of Dedication is not far off. You will see."

The following morning, Jesus and the disciples entered Jerusalem through the south gate and immediately encountered a raucous scene. A crowd gathered around the Siloam pool, facing outward.

Some men tried to push through, but failed each time as the crowd repelled them violently.

Simon stood as high as his toes could lift him and took a quick scan of the chaos. The ground had been cleared on the slope beyond the far side of the pool and cut stones sat around the perimeter of the clearing. The whole area was strewn with spades and picks.

He strained to hear the voices coming out of the fray as more residents converged on the scene.

The mass of bodies was so great that they could not reach the road without getting swept into the movement of the crowd. With each step forward, they were pushed aside or backward. Bodies pressed against Simon. He glanced around and barely caught sight of Jesus and the others as the movement of the masses pushed them farther apart.

Even through the shouts, Simon heard the fall of boots on stone — dozens, perhaps more — and looked up the road toward the temple. Several columns of Roman soldiers marched into the fray. Leading with their shields, they plowed bodies indiscriminately, knocking people off of the road left and right.

They shouted orders to clear the way as they pushed closer to the Siloam pool. As the soldiers advanced, Simon struggled against the surge and toppled backward into the bodies behind him. As one mass, they fell. They pushed against each other and the still-parting crowd as they jockeyed to return to their feet.

Simon stood and scanned the crowd but did not see Jesus nor any of his friends. The column of soldiers moved within a couple of meters, and one nearby man pounded a fist in vain on a passing soldier with an indiscernible shout. The soldier shoved his shield into the man's chest. He tumbled into Simon, knocking him off his feet a second time before landing on top of him.

Simon struggled to get an arm under him and push up enough to keep from suffocating.

The man rolled off Simon, and Simon got to his feet and helped him up. The man gasped for air as Simon took his arm.

Simon pulled the man away from the road and asked, "What is going on?"

The man inhaled sharply, waved a hand in the direction of the crowd, and rasped, "Can't you see? We're trying to stop the Roman's from further defiling our city."

Simon looked back toward the pool. Two rows of soldiers formed a pathway for others to pass through the crowd. Laborers filed down the makeshift aisle and around the pool to the excavation site on the far side.

Lines of people, still held back by Roman sentries, hurled insults as they passed. Some threw rocks at the laborers. A soldier smacked the broadside of his sword across the temple of one taunter, toppling the man.

Then he spotted a familiar face among the heckling crowd.

Manaen.

Simon pushed toward the road, toward the temple, away from crowd, leaving his questions behind.

He shoved through the tide of bodies still surging the opposite direction as he made his way deeper into the city. He had no idea if the others were ahead of him, behind him, or trampled underfoot.

At least I know where to find them if they got through here safely.

Simon continued toward the temple as fast as the packed street would allow him.

Simon reached the steps and ascended to the outer temple courts. It was early in the day, and compared to his last visit to the temple, the crowd seemed sparse. Still, Simon observed the customary comings and goings at the tables of the money changers, vendors, crafters, and traders. He scanned for any sign of Jesus and the rest, but he did not see any of them.

Simon turned back toward the stairs as Manaen stepped onto the concourse. They met eyes.

This is no chance meeting.

"I see you've come back," Manaen said as he approached. He moved closer to Simon and lowered his voice before continuing, "Yet on your last trip Galilee, you neglected to pay your debt."

"That trip was unexpected and unplanned. Besides, Jesus didn't make the journey with us. Our deal was for *his* protection."

"Jeshua doesn't see it that way. When we heard of your brief stay in Capernaum, he even sent a few of us to collect from your toll taker friend. We were disappointed to find that someone had already picked the carcass of his estate clean."

Simon regarded the man with a set brow, but he did not speak. After a tense moment, Manaen continued, "You shouldn't be surprised, Simon. And *I* do not believe that you are. Your collusion with that traitor is apparent. For you to abscond without paying your debt—"

"Abscond? There was no collusion. The Herodians betrayed one of their own and extorted him of all he had. It's you who shouldn't be surprised."

Manaen regarded Simon with questioning eyes.

Had he not considered the possibility?

Manaen shook his head and snorted softly, "That's a creative story, Simon, but far-fetched, even for greedy Herodians. Meanwhile, your teacher continues to stir up the masses, but for what ..."

As Manaen spoke, a new commotion erupted on the temple courts. A wave of people crossed the outer court with haste, calling and pointing as they moved. Manaen stopped speaking and let his gaze follow the crowd. Simon also turned toward the commotion. To his left, a crowd gathered under the porticoes at the eastern wall. He gave a quick glance back at Manaen and turned to follow the crowd. Manaen kept pace as they neared the throng.

So he did make it to the temple. Jesus was speaking to a growing gathering. Several Pharisees stood off to the side, shouting back at him—although what they were saying, Simon could not hear.

The stir grew louder as he continued to push through, until he was finally close enough to make out Jesus' words, "... I and the Father are one!" A new roar swept across the crowd. The Pharisees pointed at Jesus, and people spilled over each other while they picked up every loose stone among them.

"Is this your idea of a messiah, Simon?" Manaen shouted right next to him. "He makes no move against Herod, but he is quick to turn his own people away. Payment or not, your teacher will not be safe anywhere. And I should also remind you that *we* have eyes *everywhere.*"

Simon turned and started pushing into the bodies between him and Jesus, but a hand hauled him back. He found himself nose-to-nose with Manaen. "If we weren't on sacred ground, I would cut you down for this treachery. Others among our ranks might not share my reservations."

A piercing pain shot into Simon's hip as Manaen finished speaking. He flinched and stumbled backward. Manaen flashed a wide-toothed grin, then turned and left.

Simon looked back toward where Jesus had stood a moment ago and could not see him. He pushed deeper into the crowd and moved under the colonnade where others streamed toward the gate. He let the flow of the crowd guide him, his hip stinging him anew with each step.

Beyond the gate, people dispersed in all directions. *But did Jesus get away?* Simon shielded his eyes from the morning sun and peered across the valley toward the olive grove where he had prayed with Jesus just the day before.

He inhaled deeply and sent up a wordless prayer as he followed the road along the temple wall back toward the village where they had been staying.

Simon followed the road as quickly as his hobbled steps would allow. More than once, he stumbled as he looked back with regular frequency. To his relief and surprise, he reached the village. He looked around and saw no sign of Manaen—nor anyone who might have followed him. With that danger gone for the moment, he limped along, even more acutely aware of the pain searing his leg.

He reached the home of Mary and Martha, where the sisters moved with frenetic energy as they packed wares into a crate. Their brother, Lazarus, helped James and Thaddeus load packs onto a mule.

Martha ran to Simon and grabbed his shoulders. "Jesus has decided to leave. He said to meet him on the other side of the Jordan."

"Where are the others?"

"They've all gone ahead," Thaddeus answered without looking up from his task. "We stayed behind to wait for you. How did we get separated when we got into the city?"

Simon rubbed the wound on his hip and clenched his teeth. "I'll tell you more on the way. But for now, let me say that we've got more enemies now than even Jesus may realize."

Chapter Twenty-One

Matthew woke to the usual sight—people bringing the sick and possessed from the nearby villages. Jesus had decided to remain outside of Judea, east of the Jordan, but news of his presence and healings reached far, judging by the number of travelers.

Even in the early morning, a crowd already surrounded Jesus, and he did not shy away from them. Matthew's own spirits were lifted as people came from all directions. He sat with them and prayed with them, almost too engrossed in them to realize that his former ties to Samchai, to Herod, to his estate, and to his wealth seldom entered his mind anymore.

Even Simon has stopped fretting over Manaen and his recent threats.

The disciples tended to the masses flocking to see Jesus. Matthew was first to notice a large party approaching on the road coming up from the Jordan. Several wore the customary long-fringed mantles of the Pharisees. Matthew counted at least a dozen, but he did not see anyone among them dressed in the leather of the temple guards.

He went up onto the hillside beyond the city, where Jesus sat teaching and healing the people who came to see him. Their numbers had grown beyond what the city could contain. Tents dotted the landscape surrounding the city and the nearby villages. As Matthew neared, he heard the familiar teaching that Jesus shared, "… I will tear down my barns and build bigger ones. I will store all my grains …"

Matthew knew the parable well; he had heard it many times. Each time, it reminded him of all that he had lost—for a moment he felt renewed grief. *Is this worth what it has cost?* He had convinced himself many times that it was. *Why do I feel more doubt today?*

He pushed deeper into the crowd until he reached Simon.

"A group from Jerusalem is coming. Possibly Sanhedrin."

"They have no jurisdiction out here."

"I didn't see any temple guards. I have no idea why they would be out this far."

Jesus' voiced boomed over them, "Therefore, do not worry about your life …"

186

"We need to get him away from here!" Matthew raised his voice as he grabbed Simon's cloak at the shoulder and pulled him deeper into the crowd.

They pushed their way to the front where Peter, John, and James sat listening.

Matthew called to Jesus and waved for him to join them, but he continued speaking to the crowd, "Don't be afraid. Your Father has been pleased to give you the kingdom ..."

Matthew, undeterred, stepped up to Jesus. As soon as he did, a pair of hands yanked him back. He stumbled off his feet and landed on Peter, who pushed to get out from under him.

"You can't pull him away from the people!"

"But there is trouble!"

"What kind of trouble?"

"I think the temple officials have finally found him."

"He won't leave! You know that!"

"Then help me convince him!"

"It won't work. You've been listening. And now look," Peter threw his hands out in a wide flourish. "This is what he lives for. He won't turn these people away."

Jesus stepped to Peter and placed his hands on the disciple's shoulders without any interruption to the cadence of his teaching, "... You must also be ready, because the Son of Man will come at an hour when you do not expect him."

Peter turned and looked at Jesus. "Are you telling this to us, or to everybody?"

Matthew didn't wait for an answer. He turned and pushed back through the crowd toward the city.

When he reached the gate, the visitors were close enough that he recognized the familiar face of Nicodemus among their number. Relief washed over Matthew as he stepped out onto the road to greet them.

———

Later that day, as the disciples ate, they were joined by Nicodemus and another Pharisee—unknown to Matthew—named Joseph. Matthew was surprised to hear that the stir that Jesus had caused in the temple wasn't the biggest news of recent weeks.

Nicodemus recounted, "You saw the protests at Siloam. A few of the Sanhedrin were quick to associate you with the agitators, given the timing of your arrival. The festival got out of control, and more than a handful are blaming you."

"What do you mean?" Simon interjected. "We were hardly in Jerusalem for a day before we were chased out."

"I know this, but still ..." Nicodemus fidgeted as he spoke, seemingly searching for words to continue. "The tower at Siloam — the one that was being built to support the planned aqueduct — fell and crushed the workers. The Romans say it was sabotaged — especially with the increased Galilean presence in the city."

Nicodemus paused and buried his face in his hands. Joseph and the others with him looked down in silence. After a moment, Nicodemus lifted his head and continued, "They waited in the temple courts, in plain clothing, just like last time. Only this time, they weren't just armed with clubs. When a group of Galileans came into the courts, the Romans were ready with their swords. Dozens of men were cut down. No trial, no crucifixion, just carnage. Right there in God's house."

Nicodemus dropped his head to his hands again.

Simon stood abruptly and made for the exit without looking back. While Matthew kept one eye on Simon, Jesus addressed Nicodemus and Joseph. "What do you think? Were these Galileans worse sinners than all the other Galileans because of how they suffered?"

Simon stopped in the doorway and turned as Jesus continued, "I tell you, no!" Jesus looked at each person present: disciples, Pharisees, and others. Matthew felt his thoughts — his very soul — laid bare when Jesus met his eyes. Judging by other reactions, he was sure he was not alone in this feeling. Jesus settled last on Simon, still standing in the doorway. The young man's customary defiance vanished, and his shoulders sank when he met Jesus' stare.

Still fixed on Simon, Jesus added, "But unless you repent, you will all perish, too." Simon's eyes clenched in a tight grimace. Jesus continued, "Or the eighteen who died when the tower of Siloam fell on them ..."

Matthew jolted. *Nicodemus hadn't shared a number, had he?* He turned his attention to Jesus, who again scanned the faces present as he added, "... do you think they were any more guilty than everyone else living in Jerusalem?" This time, Jesus settled on Matthew as he spoke, "Again I say no! But unless you repent, you will all perish, too."

Matthew's blood chilled. He felt naked and exposed. He was sure that all eyes were on him, but as he looked around the disciples —

and even the Pharisees — only exchanged puzzled looks with one another.

He looked toward the door; Simon had slumped against the wall. His friend looked at him with wide eyes, as if begging him to run. Matthew wanted to get up, but his legs did nothing. He returned his friend's imploring look. Simon responded with small soft steps as he made his way back to his seat.

It was only then that Matthew realized that Jesus had resumed talking. *How much did I miss?*

"... I've been looking for fruit on this fig tree for three years now and still haven't found any. Cut it down ..."

Matthew's stomach turned as he listened to Jesus, clutching his abdomen. Around the room, several faces filled with pain — a few even with tears. When Mattew met Simon's eyes again, Simon dropped his head.

"... one more year. I'll dig around it and fertilize it some more. If I see fruit next year, fine! If not, then cut it down."

Peter, John, and even the visiting Pharisee, Joseph, spoke over one another as they addressed Jesus with questions. Matthew stood and walked to the door on shaky legs that felt like they would collapse under the weight of his burdens. Outside, he heard footsteps close behind him and turned. Simon rushed toward him, his face reddened despite the cool air.

"Does he know?" Simon threw his hands out to the side as he spoke, his voice barely more than a rasp.

"He must. But I don't know how."

Simon offered no reply. He looked down and shook his head.

Matthew continued, "We have to tell him. He's not safe anywhere." They walked away from the house. To where, Matthew wasn't sure, as his mind searched for solutions. "What if we go. You and me. We're the ones that Manaen is after — "

"Unless he was one of the ones cut down in the temple."

I hadn't considered that possibility. After a pause, Matthew continued, "We don't know, and it is too risky to find out. We have to assume we are still marked men. Even if Manaen is gone, that still leaves Jeshua Bar-Abbas. And I can't go to Tiberias or even Sepphoris for help at this point."

"Where is there left to go?"

"North. Into the villages and towns. There are still more who haven't heard, and the time is drawing nearer."

Matthew startled at the voice. *Jesus. How much did he hear?* He turned and his teacher—his friend—regarded him with kind eyes and a slight smile.

"I ..."

"We should not have put you in danger." Simon offered as Matthew fumbled for words.

Jesus' smile seemed only to increase slightly. "We'll set out in the morning. Prepare your things."

Matthew opened his mouth to speak, but no words came out.

"Oh, and you should know that this has always been the plan." Jesus turned and walked back toward the house without waiting for a response.

As weeks went on, Simon became less preoccupied with Manaen and his threats. He had no idea if his former friend and mentor had survived the massacre in Jerusalem, and it would be too risky to draw attention to himself by asking around.

It helped that their travels north along the Jordan had been filled with healings, driving out demons, and receptive ears taking in every word Jesus spoke.

Perhaps Jesus can still raise an army after all.

They stopped at a village near a river crossing on the border of Galilee. All the apprehension that Simon had left behind suddenly returned. Philip and Nathaniel had gone ahead to make preparations in the town, and now they were returning as Simon and the others approached.

"We've secured rooms. But their questions are ... unusual."

"In what way?" Jesus asked.

"They want to know if we're all Galileans."

"Could it be because of what happened in Jerusalem?" Peter asked.

The hair on Simon's arms and neck stood up. *Or it could be because Manaen — or worse — has been out looking for us.*

"Some Pharisees seemed very interested in our group, too," Philip added.

"Then I'm sure we'll have a lively discussion in the synagogue."

Simon studied Jesus. *Does he ever worry, even a little bit?* He saw only conviction and resolve in his teacher's expression.

As they entered the town, several Pharisees waited at the perimeter.

"Leave this place," called one with a gray beard before Jesus even reached them, "Go somewhere else. Herod wants to kill you."

Simon exchanged glances with Matthew, then looked at the others, searching for any sign of recognition. Jesus was quick to respond, "Go tell that fox 'I will drive out demons and heal today and tomorrow, and on the third day, I will reach my goal. I must keep going today and tomorrow and the next day. Surely no prophet can die outside of Jerusalem.'"

The Pharisees exchanged puzzled glances among themselves. "What is he saying? Jerusalem is a five-day journey from here."

"Perhaps he is lost."

More chatter rose, and Peter stepped forward, but Jesus put out a hand and held him back.

Simon couldn't listen to what was said next. In his mind, he repeated Jesus' words over and over. *"No prophet can die outside of Jerusalem."*

Thaddeus stepped to Simon's side. "What's wrong?"

Only then did Simon realize that he had clutched his gut and was hunched over.

"Let's go."

Simon turned and stepped away from the crowd while Thaddeus followed him. They walked until the voice of Jesus was faint behind them, and Simon looked up at his friend.

"I've done something terrible. I thought it was done, but now Jesus is talking about dying again."

"He's done this before. I don't understand it. I don't think any of us do, really. He seems to be invoking the prophets ..."

"It's not that. He sees things. He knows things."

Thaddeus looked at Simon with a quizzical expression. "Well ... of course. That's why we trust him, even if it doesn't make sense ..."

Simon held up a hand. "There's more. I've put him in terrible danger. I have to leave. It's the only way to keep him safe."

The confusion on Thaddeus' face grew more pronounced. "I don't understand."

"Remember our last trip to Galilee? When Matthew was plundered by the Herodians?" Simon paused, waiting for acknowledgment.

"Go on." Thaddeus nodded.

"There's more to those events. Parts you don't know ..."

Simon told Thaddeus about Manaen and the protection money. About Jeshua Bar-Abbas and his threats. About their inability to pay as promised. About his encounter with Manaen in Jerusalem.

Simon's voice rose, and his cadence quickened as he spoke. His hands trembled by the time he reached the end of his story.

Thaddeus let him speak without so much as raising a finger to pause for a question. When Simon's words finally caught up to the present day, he inhaled deeply and slowly let out a breath.

Thaddeus finally spoke. "So you think leaving will keep Jesus safe?"

Simon nodded, his voice too weary for more words.

"Look at our numbers," Thaddeus added. "At every town and village, more join us. Dozens were following Jesus when we left Jerusalem. Now hundreds follow him. We're all safe together. But if you leave, the Zealots will cut you down for sure!"

Simon nodded. *Thaddeus isn't naïve to the Zealots, even if he never got involved. But he doesn't really grasp how demanding and persistent they can be.* Still, Simon was too weary to argue, so he turned and walked toward the town center, where Jesus was still engaged in lively discussion with the Pharisees.

The following day, Ananias, a local Pharisee, invited Jesus and the disciples to eat. Matthew and the other eleven joined them, while people from the city and the surrounding villages continued to come to see Jesus.

The Pharisees didn't say much, to Matthew's surprise. Still, they watched Jesus closely and stole glances among themselves as he spoke. Matthew had been present when Jesus quickly silenced their bluster the day before, and he expected more of the same. But they remained uncharacteristically quiet, so Matthew watched them as closely as they watched Jesus.

A group of people came in off the road and approached Jesus. At their center was a man who was visibly suffering. His extremities were swollen to the point that his skin looked as if it were on the verge of bursting.

Jesus looked first to his host, then to the other Pharisees and asked, "Is it lawful to heal on the Sabbath or not?"

Matthew had been present for several Sabbath healings throughout Galilee. *This is when they will finally challenge him.*

But the Pharisees said nothing.

After a moment, Jesus went to the man, placed both hands on his head, and prayed. There was no mistaking the sight. The man's swelling subsided as quickly as a torn wineskin, revealing well-muscled forearms. The pained grimace that was etched into the man's face eased. He embraced Jesus, kissed him on both cheeks, and left—bounding on strong legs and shouting praises to God.

The Pharisees still sat in silence. Matthew scanned their eyes. *What could they be thinking?* Years of haggling, dealing—and even coercion—had trained him to see fear, deceit, doubt, and more in people's faces.

No reaction at all? Am I looking at dead men?

Jesus continued to engage them, "If your ox or your son falls into a well on the Sabbath, you would pull him out immediately, right?"

There it is! Matthew detected the change in Ananias' breathing, the tensing of his shoulders.

Jesus stood and walked around the room, stepping over and between the legs of the men reclined at the table. All eyes were on Jesus when he reached the head of the table with awkward, clumsy steps.

He stopped behind a man who had not been present the day before. He didn't wear the mantle of the Pharisees. From his dress and his rings, Matthew took him to be a merchant—and a successful one at that.

Jesus addressed the room, instructing everyone to choose a place at the table appropriate to their station. Matthew looked around as Jesus spoke. Pharisees, fisherman, merchants, crafters, all at the table. *Nobody seems out of place.* The puzzled looks on all their faces told Matthew that he was not alone in his confusion.

He turned his attention back to Jesus, who was still speaking. "… don't invite your friends or your rich neighbors." Jesus eyed the wealthy merchant, prompting the man to look away. "… invite the poor and crippled, and you will be blessed …"

Heads turned more quickly as everyone—even those who knew Jesus best—exchanged glances in search of understanding.

Matthew didn't keep his eyes still either. A growing crowd of people outside stopped to listen. Some of them were waving others over.

Matthew turned back to Ananias. The crowd had caught his notice, as well as that of his merchant friend. A smug expression, hardened as stone, rested on the Pharisee's face. It remained there even as Jesus continued speaking.

Does he not see the offense that's filling the room?

Matthew thought back to the parties that he had hosted. He had entertained prominent dignitaries from Sepphoris and Tiberias. Plenty of food, drink, and other indulgences flowed freely to all who wanted them.

And now he sat as a lowly guest—without home or resources— in a house of wealth and prominence. *Could I have used my own wealth better?*

He glanced back again at the growing crowd outside. *If only Samchai hadn't extorted everything from me. What I could do for these people …*

But would *I?* He wanted to think so. *Then why do I empathize with the Pharisee and the merchant's self-assurance? Am I really any better than they are?*

He turned his attention back to Jesus and listened for any bit of assurance and hope to settle his growing doubt.

"… Go out to the roads and the country lanes and have them come in …"

The people who I have always shut out. Worse, the people who I extorted to pay for the feasts, the wine, the indulgence.

"… Not one of those men who were invited will get a taste of my banquet."

Matthew felt Jesus' words as if they were delivered by a punch in the gut that jolted him from his self-absorbed thoughts. The rumbles and raised hands that went up at the other end of the table told him that he wasn't the only one who felt the strength of Jesus' rebuke.

Chapter Twenty-Two

Simon was jolted from his sleep when two hands yanked him from his mat. He tried to get his feet under him, but a blow to the back of his head toppled him to the ground. As he rolled to his side, his cloak tangled around his head, obstructing his vision.

Arms — at least two sets — gripped his legs, and hands clenched his shoulders. As his assailants lifted him unevenly from the ground, he turned to free his hands but couldn't get past the layers of his cloak. He couldn't tell if his cloak was being held in place or he was just hopelessly tangled.

Not that it matters. They were moving, and Simon's bones jostled and stung with each step. More than once, his hips smacked the hard ground. As they moved, his forehead collided with something solid — wood or stone, he could not tell. The pain from the blow sent tension down his neck, even as the back of his head continued to throb.

A cool breeze met the exposed skin of his leg. He knew that they had taken him from the house.

But who are they?

Simon didn't know, and the pain in his head didn't allow him to think much about the answer. The realization that his life was in danger filled every corner of his mind.

Simon struggled with all his strength, but the grips against him only tightened in response. Through the tangled cloak and over his own pulse pounding in his head, he heard the occasional grunts of his abductors, but he couldn't make out any other sounds.

At last, their movement slowed, and Simon fell hard to the ground as all his captors' hands let go at once. The landing forced his breath from his lungs, and a new pain shot from his spine to his head.

Simon grasped against his cloak and fumbled to get his hand to his face. Fingers — not his own — pulled at the cloak tangled around his face. A sharp jerk twisted his head, and the muscles in his neck strained to hold together before his head fell back and made hard contact with the rocky ground beneath him.

Simon smelled blood and opened his eyes. The sky was still dark, and it was impossible for him to make out the face — or faces, he couldn't tell — in front of him. He strained to keep his eyes open, but weariness and pain won over as his eyelids closed again.

"Did you think you could run forever?"

Simon didn't recognize the voice.

"Your teacher doesn't travel with stealth. You should have known that if you got anywhere near Galilee again, we would find you."

Simon opened his mouth, but only a wordless rasp escaped his lips.

"There's nothing more for you to say, Simon. You betrayed your people and cost us much. But don't worry. We'll take care of your publican friend, too."

"I ..." Simon couldn't form the words even if he could find them.

"You know how this works, Simon. We have no king but God. First, you got into a deal with that Herodian swine. And now your teacher makes enemies everywhere he goes. Herod wants his head. The Jews call him a blasphemer."

The throbbing in Simon's head settled slightly, but he still couldn't identify the speakers. He opened one eye again as the first light of dawn breached the horizon, but his vision was blurred, and the man before him seemed — to Simon's limited sight — to have his head covered.

The man continued, "His trouble will find him out in due time, I'm sure. But for today, I am here to exact justice on *you*."

Powerful hands gripped Simon's shoulders and yanked him to his feet. He tried to stand, but his legs could not hold him. The men gripping his cloak were all that kept him from collapsing again.

Yelling and footsteps approached — from what direction, he could not tell. The voices grew louder, but his eyes still refused to cooperate. Pain seared Simon's forehead when he tried to open his eyes. As suddenly as he had been pulled to his feet a moment ago, the hands at his shoulders released him, and he dropped to the ground even harder than the first time.

Simon opened his eyes to the underside of a tent canopy. Blurred faces surrounded him, and his shoulder and head burned with pain.

"He's awake!" The speaker sounded young — no more than a child.

Simon's mouth felt dry, and he fought through the discomfort to speak, "Did they get Matthew?" The words were little more than a rasp, and Simon's throat grated with pain.

"I am here. And so are the rest."

"What happened?"

"Who were those men?"

"Are there more of them?"

I know these voices. Friends. Simon was grateful to be safe for the moment. *There's so much they don't know. So much they need to know.* He strained to answer, but he could not find the strength.

"It's okay, Simon. You don't need to speak." The unmistakable voice of Jesus was a welcome sound to Simon's ears.

Hands gripped his head, and Jesus whispered a barely audible prayer.

The pain left Simon's head, then his shoulder. Even the bruises on his hips stopped aching.

Simon opened his eyes again, this time to the kind face of his teacher. The wisdom in those eyes told him that there was nothing more that he needed to explain.

Simon's peace was interrupted when a voice called, "You Galileans — you need to leave this place!"

Simon looked past Jesus. They were sitting on the outskirts of the city. Ananias approached from the town, flanked by the rest of the Pharisees.

"I warned you about Herod! And now you invite this trouble on our city!"

Jesus stood and waited for Ananias to reach him. "This is not about Herod. Not that I need to tell you as much. Still, we will be on our way this day."

What does he mean by that? Did someone tell the Zealots where we're staying?

The raised voices drew villagers and others who had been following Jesus from their tents and shelters across the plain. The crowd let out a collective gasp when Jesus announced his intention to leave.

"Who were those men?"

"Can we come with you?"

"Where are you going?"

"Will those people attack us, too?"

The people shouted over each other. Some directed their questions to Simon, but most called out to Jesus. Simon was relieved when Jesus turned and addressed the crowd even as more people continued to emerge from their homes and tents. "If anyone does not hate his mother and father, his wife and children, his brothers and sisters, even his own life, he cannot be my disciple."

Simon thought of his own wife. Too many times, he had to leave her behind for months at a time. He knew she supported him, but for how much longer? He thought of the Zealots—Manaen and the others. He had considered them brothers, but they nearly cost him his life.

Did I really count the cost before following Jesus?

No. Not at all.

And now it was impossible to return to his old life. *But even if were possible, would I?*

The Zealots had nearly ended his life, but Jesus healed him. *Even after I put him in danger with my foolish plans and short-sighted deals.*

He didn't understand much, but he knew he would follow Jesus anywhere.

"... Anyone who does not take up his cross and follow me cannot be my disciple ..."

There it is again. The talk of crosses and dying.

So much had happened to Simon since Jesus last spoke this way. He couldn't understand it, but he hoped it would somehow make sense whenever Jesus was ready to ... *ready to what?* Simon had no idea what he had planned.

"... If salt loses its saltiness, how can it be made salty again?"

He had to follow Jesus and see for himself—and be a part of— whatever he had planned.

For days, Jesus led the disciples with determined persistence. They stopped only to eat and sleep as they made their way south along the Jordan River. With each village they visited, the crowd grew larger. Matthew never tired of hearing the same familiar parables over and over at each stop.

Every time Jesus spoke about lost sheep or coins, people gathered their belongings and joined them. By the time the Dead Sea was in sight, there were hundreds with them. They stopped at a settlement just east of the Jordan River.

The town swelled with visitors as dozens traveled up the road from the Jordan. Matthew was relieved to be surrounded by so many people—visitors and new followers alike. Simon's attackers hadn't appeared a second time, but he suspected they would search for another opportunity. *Better that we're not so isolated.*

Jesus led the people to an open hillside outside of town while Matthew turned his attention to the new arrivals, scanning faces for any sign of recognition. He quickly spotted the telltale blue mantles of approaching Pharisees — but no Nicodemus or Joseph.

Matthew went into the marketplace to a fruit vendor near the main road. He kept his ear trained on the visitors as they passed.

"I don't know which is worse anymore: these Roman swine or the Galilean troublemakers who keep instigating them."

"Every time this happens, they squeeze us harder with more taxes."

"It looks like we've found the next mob."

"Look at them: women, children, poor, crippled. These are the ones who follow that Nazarene."

"Let's hear for ourselves what he's telling them now. Maybe we can lead a few of these misguided people back to the law."

Matthew walked among the fruit carts until he could no longer hear the Pharisees. He purchased some figs and returned to the hillside.

When he arrived, he watched the Pharisees toward the back of the crowd, standing and waiving arms toward Jesus as they discussed something among themselves. Matthew couldn't hear their words, but their expressions made it clear they did not approve of whatever Jesus had to say.

The crowd began to disperse, and Jesus was preoccupied with babies as mothers lined up to give their children a moment with him.

This will take hours. Why does he spend so much time with children?

He reached Jesus and the other disciples and passed the figs around to them. As they walked back toward the town, a young man stood by, seeming to wait for them.

His face was familiar. *Had he been traveling with Nicodemus before? Or did we see him that day we were praying in the olive groves?*

The boy was well dressed, and his hands were smooth. He seemed to have come of age recently. He had no family with him, as far as Matthew could tell.

"Good teacher! How can I have eternal life?"

The boy spoke with the accent and cadence of the educated. It puzzled Matthew that someone of his status would travel beyond the Jordan to learn from a teacher of peasants.

Peasants like me.

Matthew allowed himself a moment to miss all the wealth and comfort he had lost. Still, he didn't blame Jesus, or even his deal with the Zealots.

Jesus patiently entertained the boy's question. "... You know the commands. Do not commit adultery; do not steal; do not murder; honor your mother and father."

"All of these things I have done since I was a boy."

Matthew stifled a laugh. *Isn't this young man* still *a boy?* His mirth was short lived, though, when he reached the realization that he had defied most — perhaps all — of these commands before his encounter with Jesus.

Why did Jesus choose me, of all people? Were the Pharisees right to consider me beyond redemption?

Jesus continued, "Sell all you have and give the money to the poor. Then come follow me."

The boy was pale to begin with, but what little color there was drained from his face when Jesus spoke. His eyes widened, and he hung his head.

Matthew's own mind was pierced as he watched the young man drop his shoulders and slowly turn to walk away.

Remembering what he had seen in the villages, he wished that he could have sold his estate and given money to all these poor people. It pained him more deeply than ever to realize that all he once had was now in the hands of Samchai and Herod's men.

What a waste.

As Matthew watched the man go, his companions — first Judas then Peter — asked Jesus more questions. He had questions, too, but his feet carried him toward the road.

He quickened his pace and chased after the younger man.

"Friend! Don't go!" Matthew called out.

The young man stopped and looked back. He waited while Matthew continued toward him with brisk steps.

"I know what the teacher asks sounds costly," Matthew said as he reached the man. "But I promise you it is worth it."

"But my family ... my estate ... it's too much. I can still help the teacher — even the poor — still do good ..."

"It's more than that," Matthew added to fill the pause even as he searched for words. "There is no need to say it. I know. I once thought the same way. It's taken me years to finally see, and I still don't understand it all."

The young man looked up. "Years to see what?"

"What it really means to be rich! I had my grand estate, wealth, important friends. I could buy whatever indulgence I wanted."

"But I have no interest in indulging. I just want to keep the law and prosper—and see my people prosper."

"In that way we were different. Still, we are more alike than you know. I thought if I just gave a little out of my excess, that would be enough. I thought I could follow Jesus and still hold on to everything else."

The confusion grew more apparent in the young man's wrinkled brow.

"I held feasts; I paid for lodging; I thought I was using my money well. I saw miracles and healing and hope. But still, I always thought I could go back to my estate if this didn't work."

"What made you stay?"

"Everything was taken from me. A lifetime of dishonest gain extorted by treachery. Perhaps it was God's judgment, and well deserved. I could no longer contribute funds to Jesus' travels like I did before."

"So what did he do?"

"He healed even more people! He went to more villages! He spread even more hope. That's when I finally understood."

"Understood what?"

"That I couldn't *buy* hope and peace. That was a truth I could only see when my purse and coffers were empty. *That's* why Jesus tells you to give everything to the poor. Not because he needs it or even because they need it," Matthew paused and clasped the young man by both shoulders. "But because *you* need it."

Discomfort overtook the young man's face as he looked down and grimaced as if pain seared his bowel. Matthew wanted to keep going, keep shouting all the great things he witnessed as his words spoke even to his own mind in ways he had not considered.

The young man stood silent for a moment without lifting his head. Matthew inhaled deeply and continued, "You must know that it wasn't until I met you that I saw how free I truly am now. I don't even know your name, but I know that I want you to taste the same hope and peace that I know. And I know Jesus wants the same for you."

"My name is John, but I am called Mark."

"Well, John … Mark. Consider Jesus' invitation."

John Mark hung his head again. "I'm sorry, it's too much—" he clasped Matthew's forearm without looking up and turned back toward the road.

Matthew watched him walk away for a moment and turned to go back to town. Jesus was watching. *How much did he hear?* As Matthew approached, a smile formed across Jesus' face.

Jesus clasped Matthew's shoulders and pulled him into an embrace without saying a word.

They walked back to the house together, joined by Peter, Judas, and the others who had stayed behind.

After they ate, a servant working in the boarding house came to them. "I have a message for Jesus the Nazarene."

Jesus got up and followed the servant from the room. When he returned after a moment, his expression had changed. Concern played across his features.

"What is it?" Peter asked.

Jesus returned to his place and sat. "Lazarus is not well."

"Our host in Bethany?"

"Yes. His sisters have sent for me."

The elation that had filled Matthew since his encounter with John Mark subsided, replaced with a new burden of grief and urgency. One young man had walked away earlier, despite his pleading. He had to speak up for the one who sought Jesus out.

"What can we do, teacher?" Matthew stood as he spoke. Several disciples startled and shifted, and Matthew realized how abrupt his proclamation must have been. He leveled his tone and added, "Surely we can't just let him suffer and die!"

"This sickness will not end in death. But it is for God's glory, so that the Son of God may be glorified through it." Jesus looked around the room at each of his companions as he spoke.

"So we should go!" Matthew waved his arms as his volume increased again.

Jesus remained calm. "We should finish our work here first."

Matthew realized that all eyes in the room were on him. *Do they not see the urgency? Do they not understand? Why is Jesus so calm?*

He knew asking Jesus to explain would only invite more confusion.

So he sat.

And he pondered.

———

Two days later, after teaching and healing the continuously growing crowd on the hillside, Jesus returned to town and called his disciples together to eat.

Nobody had asked Jesus anything more about Lazarus in the past day. Simon had grown frustrated with Jesus' evasive answers. He assumed they all had.

Simon was content to remain east of the Jordan—far from the hired daggers of Jeshua Bar-Abbas in Galilee. Removed from the growing agitation with Pilate in Jerusalem. Witnessing daily healing miracles. Losing count of a growing throng of followers.

They might even outnumber the first group in Galilee.

The group ate in silence until Jesus spoke up. "Let's go back to Judea."

Simon dropped his bread as images of the angry crowd in the temple and his encounter with Manaen in Jerusalem crossed his mind.

"Go back?" He stood and said, "The last time we were there, the Jews tried to stone you."

"Twice!" added Philip.

Other voices joined the protest, and Simon struggled to hear all that his friends said, his head lost in his own recognition of the danger ahead of them.

Jesus stood, and the group grew quiet. He said, "There are twelve hours of daylight. The one who walks by day doesn't stumble because he has the light. But when a man walks by night, he stumbles."

Simon looked around the room. It was filled with furrowed brows and tight lips.

I guess we're all confused.

After a silent moment, Jesus continued, "Our friend Lazarus has fallen asleep, and I am going there to wake him."

"Let him sleep then," Phillip responded. "He'll get better."

"Remember the centurion?" Simon asked, as he glanced around the room with a pointed finger. "His servant got better. And you didn't even have to go to him. So you don't need to go to Lazarus either." He looked around again. *Not even a single nod of assent?*

Jesus gestured silently for Simon to recline. Simon looked around, this time more purposefully. No one else was standing. He gently lowered himself to his place at the table.

Jesus resumed speaking. "Let me say it another way. Lazarus is dead."

The insight struck Simon. *How did I not understand that is what Jesus meant?*

Jesus continued, "I'm glad that I was not there, for your sake, so you may believe. But let's go to him now."

"Why?" Simon jumped back to his feet. "There is nothing more we can do for Lazarus, but what about all of the people here and all we can do for them?" Simon waved a hand around the room and added, "What about us?"

Thomas rose to his feet and stepped to Simon's side. He turned to the group and said, "Let's also go, so we may die with him." Then he turned and exited the room.

Wide eyes stared in silence at Thomas as he left, but Simon did not turn to look himself. He hung his head and lowered himself again to his place at the table.

Whether at the hands of the Manaen and Jeshua, Pilate, or the priests and scribes, he was certain of one thing. *Thomas is right.*

Chapter Twenty-Three

Jesus and his disciples arrived at Bethany with about fifty people from the villages of Perea following them. As the sun neared its midday peak, their destination came into view.

As they approached, several figures came down the road toward them. Simon recognized Martha, but not the woman and two men who accompanied her. Martha moved ahead of her companions and called out, "If you had been here, my brother would not have died."

Jesus met her eyes. "Your brother will rise again."

"I know he will rise in the resurrection at the last day."

"I am the resurrection and the life. The one that believes in me will live, even though he dies. Do you believe?" Jesus spoke with calm assurance. Simon thought of all the times that Jesus spoke about death. He had never betrayed a hint of worry. Only hope.

Do I believe? Simon hadn't considered the question in this way before. He had seen too many signs—too much power—not to believe. He had experienced too much kindness and love—even after the ones that he thought were his allies tried to kill him—not to believe.

But what *do I believe?*

Could Jesus cheat death somehow?

Martha turned back, and the group followed her toward the village. They had barely resumed before a crowd of perhaps a dozen or more emerged from the village and approached them.

Mary, Martha's sister, ran ahead of them. She reached Jesus and collapsed at his feet with the same type of cry that her sister had uttered only moments before. "Lord, if you had been here, my brother would not have died." She shook and heaved with deep sobs.

The men who accompanied her reached them, and Simon didn't recognize any of them. Their cloaks were lightly embroidered, but not dyed. Their dress suggested they were merchants from Jerusalem. Each of their eyes swelled with tears.

Jesus' speech cracked as he asked, "Where have you laid him?" Tears filled Jesus' eyes, too.

"Come and see," one man answered and gestured toward the hillside below Jerusalem.

Tears ran down Jesus' face, and he let out a loud sob.

Simon jumped at the sound. He had never seen Jesus in this state before, and a wave of doubt knocked the air from Simon's lungs.

Is Jesus doubting his own strength? Is he powerless against death, just like we all are? And what danger have we placed ourselves in by coming back to Jerusalem?

Simon turned his attention to the whispers of the men from Jerusalem who walked with Mary. "Couldn't he keep this man from dying? Isn't he the one who opened the blind man's eyes?" Still, knowing that he was not alone in his doubt gave him little solace.

Jesus sent the group who followed from Perea ahead into the village to make provisions for their stay. Two of Mary's companions accompanied them, and the others led Jesus and the disciples off the main road onto a small well-worn path toward the hills.

They passed a grove of freshly pruned and well-tended fig trees before they reached a steep, rocky embankment.

They followed their guides past a steep rock formation that rose sharply into to a near-vertical wall and stopped where a large boulder sat against the cliff face.

Tears returned to Jesus' face, and a new tremor shook his shoulders as they neared the tomb. With a deep breath and a heavy sigh, Jesus looked to the men and said, "Take away the stone."

Martha stepped in front of him. "But is has been four days. The odor will be unbearable."

Jesus spoke with his customary calm assurance. "I told you that if you believe, you will see the glory of God." He gestured toward the stone and nodded at Martha's companions.

Two men pulled their cloaks up over their mouths and noses and pushed the stone to the side. The whole group stepped back.

Simon struggled to keep his balance as others shifted against him.

He brought his sleeve up to his face but detected no odor at all. He scanned the cliff face for another stone, scarcely aware that Jesus was speaking.

Have they brought us to the wrong place?

He found no other obvious openings and no blocked tombs.

"Lazarus, come out!"

The force of Jesus' voice startled Simon, and he jerked his head back to the cave before them. A young man stumbled out, slipping over the linens that wrapped his feet.

He held out wrapped hands in front of him and guided himself along the cave wall. Linen wrappings covered his head and face. The group stood in collective silence as Mary and Martha stumbled to their brother's side and embraced him.

"Take off the grave clothes and let him go," Jesus said with measured calmness.

Martha unwound the wrappings from Lazarus' head, and the young man put his hands over his eyes. The visitors from Jerusalem encircled him.

Jesus turned to his disciples, said, "Let's go and eat," and walked back toward the road.

———

Jesus and his disciples stayed several days at the home of Mary and Martha. Jesus spent his days teaching on the outskirts of town. Simon used this time to go around the village, listening to the farmers and merchants.

The construction of the aqueduct in Jerusalem had been delayed several times. With each incident, more crosses were erected, and more men hanged to die.

Simon learned that from the west a traveler could smell the carnage before he could see the crosses. Each piece of news added to and reshaped the questions that danced in Simon's mind.

Could Jesus raise those crucified men like he did Lazarus?

Did Manaen somehow survive?

And if so, do we still need to worry about him?

"It's getting out of control," one crafter shared as Simon helped him load his cart to take to the Jerusalem markets.

"More soldiers than ever are garrisoned in the Antonia Fortress. And now, Pilate himself has come in from Caesarea to put a stop to any rebellions. Your group is Galilean. Surely, you've heard all of this."

Simon detected the hint of suspicion in the man's tone and paused before responding, "The whole village is talking about Lazarus. You've no doubt also heard the stories of healing from everyone here who follows Jesus. Don't you think he is more interested in life than in death?"

A slight smile crested the corner of the man's mouth as he eyed Simon with piercing silence. After a moment that seemed like a season, the man nodded and returned to loading his cart. Simon bid him off and walked back to the house of Martha and Mary.

Visitors from Jerusalem streamed into the village. The mourners had gone days ago, but for every person that left, ten more arrived. *News about Lazarus — about the one who raised him — is traveling far and fast.*

Simon spotted the mantles of two Pharisees just above the heads of the crowd. He tried to quicken his pace, but the slow-moving bodies in front of him made catching up impossible.

It made no difference. As he continued toward the sisters' home, it was obvious that the Pharisees were set on the same destination.

Simon reached the path leading to Martha's family estate and broke into a run, dodging pilgrims and visitors both coming and going. As he reached the main house, Mary came out to greet him. "The teacher is looking for you. They are waiting."

"They?"

"Jesus, your other companions, and two Pharisees who have come to see him."

Mary led Simon through the courtyard to a large room. When he entered, he was relieved to see the familiar faces of Nicodemus and Joseph.

Nicodemus sat at the far side of the room facing the rest as if he were teaching in the synagogue. The others seemed not to notice Simon's entrance. All eyes were fixed on Nicodemus as he spoke.

"... the Sanhedrin has eyes all around Jerusalem. That's how I knew I could find you here. We must assume that high priest Caiaphas and his supporters know you are here as well."

It sounds like he is just getting started. Simon found space near the door and sat.

Nicodemus continued, "It is no longer safe for you as long as you are in Jerusalem's reach. The Sanhedrin is convinced that Pilate's grip will only tighten if your following grows any larger. The story of Lazarus is spreading to every street in Jerusalem and every village in the countryside. Caiaphas has made up his mind to stop it."

"Why would the Romans care that a dead man has been raised?" Simon didn't think he had missed much of Nicodemus' speech but wondered if he was not in time to hear a key detail or two.

"As far as we know, they don't care. The Romans have had their hands full with increased policing ever since construction began on the aqueduct. Most of the agitators they've rooted out have been Galileans."

Simon recalled his confrontation with Manaen during the Feast of Dedication. *Could he have been captured, or even crucified?* He dismissed the thought and pressed Nicodemus further, "What do the agitators have to do with us? We've made no moves against Rome ..." Simon stopped and considered the words as they formed in his head. Thaddeus, James, Matthew, and Jesus turned— seemingly in unison—to face him and regarded him with stares and raised brows. *Are they waiting for me to finish? Do they expect to hear '... yet?'*

Simon was thinking it. *Is that why I stopped?* He couldn't be sure that a move against Rome was even part of Jesus' plans, elusive and unknowable as those plans seemed to be.

Is a move against Rome even what I want? He'd seen the treachery of the Zealots. *They might not be as bloodthirsty as the Romans, but we would merely be trading one oppressive sword for another.*

But then Simon remembered the recent months of traveling and healing. Even raising a dead man. *Is this what freedom* really *feels like?*

Is it time to be done with my own sword?

The whole room watched him with anticipation. He wasn't sure how long he had been lost in his thoughts. He gestured toward Nicodemus with an open hand and a nod and sat down without saying anything further.

Nicodemus resumed, "Rome might not care about a dead man being raised nor any of the other miracles that are being shared in the streets and the temple courts, but Caiaphas is insistent that they *will* care if he can't keep the people from following you. That's why he wants to stop you himself—to show Rome that he is capable of maintaining control."

"So Caiaphas is afraid of losing control himself," Philip spoke with just a hint of questioning. Other heads around the room nodded.

"So you see the problem then," Nicodemus nodded toward Philip as he continued. "When Caiaphas made his plea with the Sanhedrin, he said, 'It is better that one man should die for the people than the whole nation should perish.' And now that enough of the Sanhedrin has embraced his way of thinking, you are no longer safe here. I can warn you, but I am afraid my voice would not hold enough sway with the Sanhedrin to change their minds."

Simon thought of all the times that Jesus talked about dying and about all the encounters with the sick and dying they had all had since then, Simon, Jesus—all of them. Jesus had nearly amassed an army of followers. *But if he has no plans to give them swords and rally them ...*

A new thought occurred to Simon. *If Jesus expects to die, does he expect us to lead an army to avenge him?*

If only Jesus would simply tell us his strategy ...

"So we'll leave here," Jesus directed his response more to the disciples than to Nicodemus.

"You can't let the crowds follow you." Nicodemus held up a hand and added, "Dozens come to the temple daily, telling others where you can be found. If the *people* can find you, *Caiaphas* can find you."

Jesus turned to his disciples. "Gather the family members in your care. We will leave tonight."

Mary and Martha had pleaded for Jesus to stay. Matthew saw the compassion in his eyes, but Jesus had remained determined. Yet, despite their misgivings about Jesus' departure, the sisters had been kind enough to provide mules for the women to ride.

The night walk was slow. The disciples kept to a seldom-traveled route high on the mountain ridges. Once the temple was out of sight, they lit their own lanterns to guide their steps, but the increased light did not increase their speed.

Matthew stayed close to Simon and Thaddeus. "Would the Romans really be as severe as Nicodemus says?" Matthew asked as they walked.

"Yes. They wouldn't hesitate to sweep away every Galilean in Jerusalem if they thought it meant crushing all insurrection. But it doesn't matter what the Romans think. Caiaphas is the one who wants Jesus dead," Thaddeus responded.

"Also, consider what the Zealots have long known about the corruption in the Sanhedrin and their ties to the Roman regime," Simon added.

"So are they still a threat?" Matthew pressed his friends.

"The Sanhedrin?"

"The Zealots."

"We still don't know if Manaen is alive or dead. As for tonight's journey ... we won't encounter them on these high mountain roads."

"Wild animals, maybe ..."

Matthew walked alongside his friends in silence. Fatigue and darkness made the journey slow. They covered only half the distance they could travel by daylight—until they reached a well-traveled inland trade route.

"Teacher," Matthew called to the front of the group. "This route will take us to the coastal highways. We could travel much faster."

"We'll continue on this route. We'll reach our destination today yet."

Matthew couldn't imagine what destination Jesus had in mind. Both Galilee and Jerusalem had become too hostile. What destination was left for them that still gave them any purpose?

How can Jesus establish his kingdom if he is always fleeing?

As day broke on the horizon, they glimpsed the silhouette of a town. Even at their tired pace, they could reach it before the sun breached the sky.

"Matthew, Judas," Jesus called from the front of the group. "Go ahead and buy us food for the morning."

"Shouldn't we stay here? We've been traveling all night!"

"We'll eat and keep moving. Just for today."

Matthew took Judas and went ahead into the town. Fruit vendors and crafters were just reaching the marketplace and setting up carts for the day. They selected some figs and root vegetables. It was too early in the morning for bread.

They returned to the group, and after they ate, Jesus led them on a small well-worn path down the eastern slope.

After an hour that seemed like a full day of walking, the slope tapered out to a plateau. Trees were sparse. Only scattered shrubs dotted the otherwise rocky landscape.

A small settlement came into view. The houses were even more modest than the simple one-room structures that were familiar to so many of them from their lives in Galilee.

Matthew's thoughts returned to Jesus' teachings about his kingdom. *Does the rest of Judea even know that this tiny village exists?*

Despite the settlement's small size, they were able to find accommodation for their group. Without the stream of followers that they had grown accustomed to, their numbers seemed surprisingly manageable.

They filed into a boarding house and into a dining space that was just big enough to fit them all. Matthew collapsed to the ground as the others did the same. Despite the quickly-warming air as the sun shone in all its fullness on the stone walls, Matthew was asleep in minutes.

———

Mornings were quiet in Ephraim, far removed from the major routes. Matthew returned from a trip to a neighboring town— more amenable to commerce—with additional supplies. He went to Jesus' sleeping quarters but found only empty space. He visited the dining quarters, the garden, and the stable. At each stop, his companions engaged in various expenditures of restless energy, but Jesus was nowhere to be found.

No throngs of people waited, desperate for healing and purpose.

No crowds gathered on the hillside, drinking in every word of Jesus' parables.

Mathew had never experienced such quiet.

Too quiet for my liking.

"Do you know where Jesus went?" he asked when he encountered Philip and Nathaniel in the garden.

"He's probably out in the hillside. That's been his routine lately."

"It's been weeks, and it's getting unsettling."

"Unsettling? We spent months being chased by bandits, Pharisees, and everyone in between. It's been refreshing not to have to run constantly," Nathaniel responded.

"But what about the kingdom? You saw how the people surrounded Jesus when we were across the Jordan. Why couldn't we go back there, or even—"

"Don't say it."

Matthew threw his arms out wide and raised his voice more than he intended. "Say what?"

"We can't go back to Jerusalem. It's too dangerous."

"Well, I'm tired of doing nothing."

"That's why you get sent to the big city to buy supplies."

"I'd hardly call Bethel a big city."

"You'd really rather go back to Jerusalem? At least here, nobody is looking for us."

"That's my point!" Matthew yelled more than spoke. "Months ago, *everyone* was looking for Jesus. He was healing them; we all were! He was teaching them. We didn't need a big city. Crowds followed him everywhere. Now where are they? Have they forgotten about him?"

"We can be sure the Sanhedrin hasn't forgotten," Simon interjected. Matthew hadn't noticed his arrival.

"Are you suggesting we stay hidden, too? You've always been one for action!"

Simon held up a hand to Matthew. "I'm saying we can't go unprepared. We need to be ready for what comes."

"You can't be talking about raising an army again," Philip added. "Jesus would never allow it."

"Army or not, doesn't a king need to be protected? He has enemies."

"Some of which you've made for him." Nathaniel leveled his stare at Simon as he spoke.

Simon nodded as he responded, "Perhaps, but—"

"Jesus has asked us to meet in the courtyard," Peter interrupted as he approached from around the side of the boarding house.

They followed him to the front of the building where the others were already seated.

Upon seeing Jesus, Matthew realized that he hadn't taken a good look at him in weeks. Matthew had been busy with his errands, and Jesus often retreated to the wilderness alone.

He is slimmer—not gaunt and sickly, but a touch of his vigor seems to have faded. Perhaps I'm not the only one who has been affected by weeks of isolation.

"The time for Passover is approaching." Jesus' voice still carried the same strength and authority. Perhaps Matthew had misjudged the effect of their time in the desert.

"Then we must go back to Jerusalem. The law requires it!" James stood as he spoke.

Matthew nodded at his brother's excitement.

"Are you sure that is a good idea?" Judas added. "If we can believe Nicodemus—and *I* do—the Sanhedrin will have people looking for you."

"I believe him," Thaddeus responded. "But we will also have the advantage of going at a time when the city will be full of pilgrims."

"All the more reason to stay away!" Nathaniel was on his feet. "Once Jesus is recognized by *one*, it won't be long before he is surrounded by *hundreds*. We won't be able to hide from the Sanhedrin!"

Jesus stood and held out a hand toward Nathaniel while looking at him with his customary gentle eyes and hint of a smile.

"We are going up to Jerusalem. And everything written in the prophets about the Son of Man will soon take place."

Matthew looked around at the faces of his companions as Jesus spoke, searching for a hint of understanding. All eyes remained fixed on Jesus as he continued, "He will be handed over to the Gentiles. They will mock him, insult him, spit on him, and kill him."

Jesus remained calm, but Matthew's heart beat faster. The widened eyes of his friends told him that he wasn't the only one alarmed by Jesus' words.

How can he say these things in such a plain tone, as if he were simply telling a parable on the hillside?

Jesus continued, "and on the third day, he will rise again."

"What do you mean?" Peter asked the question that Matthew was sure they were all thinking.

"What prophets?"

"What was written?"

"What about the Sanhedrin?"

"And the Zealots?"

Matthew sat in silence as the others hurled question after question at Jesus. Jesus didn't respond. He simply held up a hand and waited.

When the chatter trailed off, Jesus added, "Prepare our things. We'll leave in the morning."

Maybe we would be better off staying here. Matthew was happy to return to the big crowds but couldn't shake his fear. *We're running out of narrow escapes.*

Chapter Twenty-Four

They reached the inland route before mid-morning and descended toward the Jordan Valley. Jesus had told them that it would be better to travel through the townscape than back over the ridge.

Simon wasn't sure he agreed.

He still kept the rope adorned with spearheads in his personal bag—a symbol of a promise not kept. He considered attaching it to the rear mule, but he concluded it would only attract harm. Instead, Simon kept himself positioned toward the front of the group, with his dagger holstered at his side.

At every crossing and in every town, Simon scanned for signs of recognition. Periodically he looked back to see if anyone followed them. *Nobody. So far.*

James and John walked alongside Jesus as he led the way. Their mother, a widow who had been riding one of the mules toward the back of the group, walked up to them during a rest.

"Are you going to ask him?"

"Mother, we talked about this," John pleaded with her.

"We did, and you're running out of time. So ask him already."

"Ask what?" Jesus had returned to the main road.

"Go on ..." the widow prodded.

James looked first at John, then to his mother. She nodded toward Jesus as she regarded her sons with open eyes and a clenched jaw. Jesus watched the trio patiently, until John broke the awkward silence. "We want you to do whatever we ask."

Simon stepped closer, with curiosity adding to his elevated alertness.

"What do you want me to do?" Jesus asked with sincerity and trepidation.

John looked back at his mother again, and she gave his shoulder a shove while holding her other hand toward Jesus.

"What my brother is asking," James added, "is for one of us to sit on your right and one on your left in your kingdom."

This is how every argument starts.

215

Simon turned to see if others were listening. The shocked mouth-agape expressions on several of the other's faces gave him his answer.

"You don't know what you are asking! Can you drink the cup I drink?" Jesus spoke sternly, but calmly.

The other disciples stepped closer and formed a circle around them as the conversation continued.

"We can," James and John spoke in unison, but Simon detected a lack of confidence in their response. He tightened his jaw to fight back his own outburst.

"You will drink the cup I drink. But sitting at my right or my left is not for me to grant. Those places belong to those for whom they have been prepared." Jesus stood in silence and let his rebuke hang like smoke in the air.

Simon used the opening to add his own thoughts. "Why this again? How many of these arguments must we have?"

"As if you haven't done the same thing?" Peter challenged him.

"And we've learned so much since then," Nathaniel said. He turned and faced James and John and added, "At least, most of us have."

James turned toward him and opened his mouth, but Jesus held up a hand. As one, the group became quiet. Jesus stepped away from the group and motioned for the disciples to come toward him. Their families waited among themselves with the pack animals.

"You know how the Gentiles operate. Their rulers lord their authority over their subjects. It can't be that way with you. If any of you wants to be great, you must serve. If anyone wants to be first, he must first be a slave to all. Even the Son of Man didn't come to be served, but to serve and give his life as a ransom for many."

Simon had no response. The silence in their circle told him that none of them did. He had tried not to dwell on the increased talk of death that came from Jesus lately.

Still, the closer they got to Jerusalem, the more certain he was.

Death is an increasingly likely outcome. Maybe even inevitable.

His thoughts turned briefly to Lazarus. *How can Jesus raise anybody if he himself doesn't survive? Give his life as a ransom for many? How would that even work?*

They walked on in silence while Simon tried to make sense of Jesus' latest talk.

———

The fortress tower at Jericho appeared on the horizon as the disciples descended toward the Jordan River. Travelers climbed up from the river crossing and entered the city. The tower grew more imposing as they approached Jericho. Just as Jerusalem was adorned to display radiance, Jericho conveyed strength. The city was framed by thick walls and buttressed with a solid stone outpost, almost as impressive as Jerusalem's Antonia Fortress.

Matthew took in the structures. They lacked the Roman opulence and excess of Tiberias—or even Sepphoris. Under prior regimes, Jericho was a hub of entertainment and respite. Under Rome, it had been stripped of its recreational appeal and outfitted for security in utilitarian fashion. Still, to that end, the Romans obviously spared no expense.

A new pang of guilt pierced Matthew's mind. Here, more than any place in Galilee, he understood the weight and magnitude of Roman oppression. He regretted the part he once played in it.

But is it Jericho or Jesus that opened my eyes to this truth? Not just my eyes, either ...

Matthew looked back at Simon, who took in the imposing military presence himself, but Matthew found no hint of bitterness in Simon's expression.

Matthew turned his sight back to the road, to the travelers entering the city from the east. One group that was still several hundred meters off began to point and talk among themselves. They were too far to hear, but Matthew was certain that they were pointing at Jesus, who led the way for his disciples. Two young men—barely beyond boyhood—broke from the approaching group and ran toward them. They awkwardly stepped into the brush off the side of the hard-packed road to pass other travelers.

The boys passed the city gate and seemed to be headed straight for Jesus.

"It's him! It's really him," one shouted as he grabbed his companion by the arm and shook him vigorously.

From behind Matthew, Simon abruptly made his way to the front and came alongside Jesus, hand on his hilt. Jesus held an arm out and looked over at him. "Stand down."

"We've spent months hiding, and now you've been recognized."

"It's like I told you, these things must now take place."

The boys reached Jesus. Matthew didn't recognize them. They could have been from any of the dozens of villages they visited in Perea.

"You've returned! The kingdom is finally here!"

Simon jolted and jerked his head back and forth with big eyes. He stepped between Jesus and the boys. "You can't shout these things here! This place is teeming with Romans!"

Jesus placed a gentle hand on Simon's shoulder and turned him back. Without a further word, Simon eased his stance.

The boys, meanwhile, had turned and ran back to their party, arms flailing as they shouted with excitement. "It's Jesus! It's Jesus!" The boys doubled back again and ran ahead of their group into the city.

People broke off from other groups and quickened their steps toward the city gates. As far as Matthew could see, travelers rushed to get ahead of others.

Their desert respite was over.

There will be no shortage of followers now.

As the men neared the gate, commotion rose behind the city walls. Voices and footsteps and excited shouts echoed off the solid stone of every structure. Several soldiers appeared on the wall and spread out. Some fixed their sights on the road; others looked back into the city.

None raised an alarm.

Their group met with inbound travelers from the east and was immediately slowed by crowds pushing around and into each other, squeezing toward the city gate. A dozen soldiers lined the road on either side of the gate, but they did nothing to keep the people from trampling one another.

They passed through the open gate. The sprawling fortress was twice as imposing on the inside of the city walls. Behind the fortress, steep mountains rose to the west, augmenting the city's girding. Soldiers lined the eastern wall, looking out across the valley beyond.

Matthew thought of Samchai and his hired muscle and their plundering of his estate.

Is this the sort of thing that my former wealth paid for?

Soldiers exited the barracks and filed into the street. It wasn't a full phalanx, but enough to deter whatever a stirring crowd might initiate.

The primary road ran straight ahead through the center of the city. People poured in from side streets and homes and lined the roadway on either side. Their modest dress contrasted starkly to a fully equipped Roman battalion.

Why do any Jews even choose to remain in the city?

The young men who had approached them on the road waited just inside the gate and fell into place ahead of Jesus. As they walked deeper into the city, the boys shouted.

"God's chosen one is here!"

"Come and see Jesus of Nazareth, who makes the blind see!"

The crowd swelled around them, and the soldiers made no effort to hold the masses back. Matthew had trouble discerning the shouts, but the tone was obviously celebratory. He pushed any lingering thoughts of danger from his mind and reflected with gratitude that he was privileged to walk with Jesus.

His attention was quickly drawn to a curious sight further up the road. A man had somehow become tangled in the low-lying limbs of a fig tree.

He studied the scene intently, trying to gain some understanding. Matthew absentmindedly tugged the sleeve next to him, not even sure whose it was.

"What is it?" Judas answered.

Matthew pointed at the tree. The man seemed to be struggling to find his balance in the branches.

"Someone got hung up in a tree?"

"I don't think so; nobody seems to be forcing him up there. I think he's climbing."

"It doesn't suit him." Judas shook his head.

Discussing the scene only enhanced its absurdity. As they approached, Matthew noted the man's embroidered coat, his receding hair, and his well-fed cheeks. The man grunted as his arms struggled to pull his girth over another branch.

A few of the crowd looked on with puzzlement, and the other disciples pressed in to get a closer look.

Most of the attention, though, was still on Jesus.

Children ran out and hugged Jesus' legs as he led his disciples through the crowd. When they reached the place where the curious man sat precariously balanced in the tree, Jesus stopped and looked up at him. "Zacchaeus, come down quickly. I will be a guest at your house today."

The crowd quieted as Jesus spoke. After a stunned pause, new chatter arose—with a new tone.

"The anointed one knows *this* man?"

"But he's a sinner!"

"The worst!"

"He is not worthy to host God's chosen one."

219

"Just another false messiah. A real savior wouldn't dare eat with a traitor."

As the people yelled, the man — Zacchaeus — twisted and fumbled for a hold to climb down. He clearly hadn't planned ahead for this part as he crossed an arm over his body and twisted at the waist.

Can he even breathe in such an unnatural position?

Matthew wanted to laugh at the madness of the scene, until he thought back to the time he hosted Jesus. *So many jeers and taunts.* Matthew had made so many enemies, and because of him more than a few people turned away from Jesus. Even Simon had left for a time.

Seeing the same scene again here, it was clear to Matthew who Zacchaeus must be. His heart swelled with pity for these people who lived under the cold and watchful fist of the Roman army. Unlike the extravagance and beauty of Tiberias, with all its luxuries, nothing in this stone fortress of a city could distract the citizens from the reality of their circumstance.

Matthew finally understood — more clearly than ever — why the people had despised him. He realized why Simon had fought him and regarded him with mistrust for so long.

How miraculous that Jesus could change me *— both of us — the way he had.*

It had cost him everything, but seeing the way the crowd despised Zacchaeus, he wished he had given it up sooner.

Zacchaeus emerged from the crowd and stood before Jesus, a full head shorter than the teacher. As they spoke, Matthew turned to his companions and squeezed past two of them to get to Simon. He pulled Simon into an embrace and said, "I understand now. Can you forgive me?"

Simon clasped Matthew's shoulders. There was no anger, no bitterness, no animosity in his expression. It was as if Simon was trying to mimic the tender gaze that they had all noted in Jesus' expression. He nodded. "All is forgiven, friend."

Over the agitated clamor of the crowd, a quivering, fearful voice cracked and grew louder. "Look! I declare now that I will give half of my possessions to the poor!"

Matthew turned back. Zacchaeus stood before Jesus, stooped over, holding out open palms. His brow arched with fear and pleading as he added, "And if I have cheated anybody, I will pay him back four times!"

A new roar rose as onlookers pressed from all sides.

They must all want to make a claim against that promise.

Jesus clasped Zacchaeus with two hands and addressed the gathered crowd. "Today, salvation has come to this house. This man, too, is a son of Abraham. For the Son of Man came to seek what was lost."

A few people cheered, but still others came close and shouted more accusations at Zacchaeus.

"Follow me," Zacchaeus said to Jesus. "My plantation is beyond the south gate."

As Zacchaeus led them deeper through the city, people continued to pour into the streets.

Matthew was relieved that the agitation had not been enough to prompt the Roman soldiery into action, though they continued to eye the crowd with dutiful stares.

As they neared the south gate, a call rose from behind the people lining the side of the road. "Jesus! Son of David! Have mercy on me."

Jesus and the others turned toward the voice. Several bystanders had swiveled around and shouted at someone to be quiet.

The voice called out louder than the first time. "Son of David! Have mercy!"

Jesus pushed toward the sound and placed a hand on a man's shoulder from behind. "Call him!"

The man turned and reached behind him, "Bartimaeus, take my hand and come up."

The people moved aside as a man seated by the road tossed away the cloak gathered in his lap. A few coins scattered from it, and children lunged to grab them. The man rose to his feet and stood on his own. His companion pulled him forward, and the man took short, deliberate steps. His eyes were milky and unfocused, but his face and body otherwise showed the vigor of a man still emerging from youth.

"What do you want me to do for you?" Jesus asked the man.

James and John looked around and hung their heads. All other eyes were fixed on Jesus.

"I want to see, Lord."

Jesus placed his palms over the man's eyes and said, "Receive your sight. Your faith has healed you." When Jesus removed his hands, the man's eyes glistened, and his hazel irises shone brightly.

The man held up a hand to shield the sunlight and blinked feverishly. After a moment, he looked back and forth until his eyes settled on Jesus. He pulled Jesus into a strong embrace and shouted, "Praise be to God!"

Cheers rose from the crowd around them.

Zacchaeus began sobbing. "Join us, Bartimaeus. You will also be my guest today."

The formerly blind man walked alongside Jesus as they followed Zacchaeus through the gate. Meanwhile, the still-cheering crowd swelled into the road behind them.

Jesus and his followers reclined at a large table in a dining hall that easily accommodated all of them with room to spare. It was obvious that Zacchaeus was no stranger to entertaining. They had passed several farms and estates on the approach from the main road, but none matched the size of the structure that surrounded them.

Zacchaeus must be at the top of the hierarchy. Simon was surprised at his lack of hesitation entering the tax farmer's house. *What is different now?*

As servants brought dried figs and cheeses, Zacchaeus confessed account upon account of greed and extortion to Jesus, who sat to his right. Bartimaeus, who hours ago had been a blind beggar, sat to his left.

Simon struggled to control the trembling in his hands as he listened to Zacchaeus. His stories of forcing young men and women into servitude, of pushing merchants and farmers out of their livelihood by extorting extra levies and taxes, and of padding his purse with protection money fed a long-latent anger that swelled to Simon's consciousness.

Simon recalled the stories his elders told him of a time he never knew. He thought back to the first time he saw the excess and indulgence that filled Tiberias and stained Galilee with Rome's defilement.

How much worse do the people of Jericho have it, with all their assets funding an imposing military presence that ensures they will continue to be crushed?

When Zacchaeus described his protection racket, Simon's thoughts turned to Manaen and Jeshua Bar-Abbas. Perhaps they were more like this tax farmer than he ever realized.

Perhaps I am more like Zacchaeus than I know.

Trading coin for dagger.

Does it matter which one I start with?

Oppression — under Rome or under the Zealots.
Bondage for bondage.

The realization didn't assuage Simon's anger. It merely turned his thoughts inward as his tremors of rage subsided into pangs of remorse.

He couldn't eat, but he couldn't stop listening either. He hoped that Jesus would cut in with some word of hope or encouragement that would ease his conscience.

Instead, Zacchaeus continued, "So I have many amends to make. And I'll start today with you, Bartimaeus."

The formerly blind man startled and looked puzzlingly at Zacchaeus.

"The palm plantation and balsam groves on the western end of my land once belonged to your father. He had to hire additional servants when you were young. The Romans were still just establishing their outpost here, during Herod's reign, and the pressure to fund them was great.

"They threatened to take the women for themselves if we couldn't raise enough. Timaeus was an honorable man, and he wanted to protect you and your sisters. So he paid whatever I demanded of him. He objected at first, but he feared the sword of Rome."

Zacchaeus choked, and his voice cracked as his eyes glistened. He inhaled deeply and blinked away tears before he continued, "One by one, he sold me tracts of palms, and the servants who came with the land. Each season, his holdings shrank. I let my greed — and my own fear of Rome — consume me. When he had no more land to sell me, he sold himself into servitude. You were all he had left, and he worked day and night to provide what little he could for you until he collapsed under his own exhaustion."

Tears ran down Bartimaeus' cheeks as he listened with wide-eyed attention.

Zacchaeus choked back another sob. "I can't bring Timaeus back. But the palms and the balsam groves are yours — as of today, Bartimaeus. I will have my scribes write the land transfers and calculate interest that I will pay to you out of my coffers so that you may begin operating *your* land immediately."

Simon noticed that Jesus had been shedding tears, too. He himself burst into a loud sob and got up and left the table.

Simon stepped out to the courtyard and sat on a bench. A moment later, a hand came to rest on his shoulder. He looked up to see Jesus standing over him, with Thaddeus and Matthew both behind him.

"I was so foolish. To think that I could simply take from those in power and ..."

"... and just hand it over to another power-hungry regime?" Thaddeus completed Simon's thought.

Simon nodded. "But this is real redemption. Not sword for sword. Just ..."

"Simon," Jesus placed a hand on his shoulder and stooped to meet his eyes. "You've heard me say that I came to set captives free. Now you, too, have received your sight."

Jesus stood and helped Simon to his feet. "Let's get back to our meal. We need to prepare to return to Jerusalem tomorrow."

At first light, they left Jericho. Zacchaeus stayed behind, having insisted on righting his past wrongs. Bartimaeus was eager to join the trip. "I finally get to lay eyes on the temple," he cried out when they passed the city gate.

Simon recalled his own visits to the temple in recent years— and his distaste for the corruption of the Sanhedrin that marred its beauty. *What would it be like to look on the temple with new eyes?*

A crowd waited outside the south gate and followed behind Jesus and the others as they began the steep climb to Jerusalem. They numbered at least 200, by Simon's estimation.

Pilgrims from the east broke camps and continued their own journeys. From the ascending road ahead to the approach from the Jordan behind them, dozens of caravans filled the road in both directions.

Hundreds of feet trampled the dry road to hardened earth and raised a continuous cloud of dust. Simon wrapped a cover across his mouth and nose and squinted to shield his eyes when a voice at his side interrupted the cadence of their steps.

"If only I had thought to respond the way Zacchaeus did," Matthew offered as he walked next to Simon.

"We've both made terrible mistakes. Funding Manaen and his Zealots was never going to help these people. Look at them. This is who they follow—the man who promises sight to the blind and life to the dead. This is what gives them hope."

"I only wish I had seen it sooner. I could have done more to make amends."

Simon placed a hand on Matthew's shoulder. "Yet, Jesus still keeps us around. Both of us."

They continued in silence as they slowed over a steep, rocky stretch of road. They followed the switchback paths, beaten into the ground by years of use. They reached a gently sloping length of road, and Simon resumed his conversation with Matthew. "I've never seen this many people—even for Passover."

"I've never seen them either," a voice called from behind Simon. "But thanks be to God and to His chosen one. I see them now!"

Simon turned, and Bartimaeus greeted him with a wide grin despite the dusty air. Simon couldn't help but smile, and he made no effort to suppress it. "That may be so, but still ..."

"Do you suppose they are all coming because of Jesus?" Matthew interjected. "Or because of all of the trouble that Pilate has caused?"

"There was a time when I would have been eager to get here just to slay a Roman and gain an inch of ground against Pilate and his cohorts." Simon turned and fixed his sight on Jesus, who led their party from the front. "But now, it's about following him wherever he goes."

"Even if the Sanhedrin tries to seize him again?"

"*Especially* if the Sanhedrin tries to seize him again." Simon kept his gaze fixed on Jesus.

Matthew said nothing, and Simon realized how dry his mouth had become.

The Mount of Olives came into view before midday, and the climb grew steeper. At several points in the journey, Simon had to help Bartimaeus secure his footing as they crossed rocky ground.

The road leveled to a gentle slope, and they followed the slight incline around the southern end of the mountain. The familiar town of Bethany was in their sights.

A small haven of safety in an otherwise hostile place.

Most of the caravans passed the town and proceeded toward Jerusalem. Tents and encampments covered the mountainside in all directions. Dozens of people emerged from the town, some running. They shouted with celebration at Jesus' arrival. The cheers were echoed by a new chorus of praises that rose up from hundreds who trailed their party, and people continued to pour out of the town to join the celebration.

A pair of heads adorned with blue mantles and phylacteries crested over the crowd and moved toward Jesus.

Simon tensed at the sight of the Pharisees and scanned the crowd for any sign of temple guards. He exhaled a deep breath that he hadn't realized he was holding when he recognized Nicodemus and Joseph as they reached Jesus.

"We weren't sure you were coming," Nicodemus told him. "The Sanhedrin is looking for you."

Jesus waved both arms out to the crowds around them. "Many are looking. But not all can see."

"I can see! Praise be to God!" Bartimaeus called from behind Simon.

Jesus and Nicodemus did not react. The Pharisee's expression grew stern and his voice curt as he added, "Not like this. The Sanhedrin has ordered your arrest. Some of them have even mentioned a reward. They're determined. And your friend Lazarus is not safe, either. The chief priests are all too willing to have him killed if it will silence your followers."

Jesus' expression did not change upon hearing the Pharisee's warning. "Then let's go see Lazarus."

A hand rested on Simon's shoulder, and Matthew addressed him. "So this is what it means to follow him anywhere."

Simon nodded, "Anywhere."

Chapter Twenty-Five

After Nicodemus and Joseph returned to Jerusalem, Jesus and the disciples reclined at the familiar table in the home of Martha and Mary. Lazarus reclined with them, as did Bartimaeus. Matthew's thoughts lingered on their stories.

These men once lost so much. How do you measure the gifts they received?

Voices carried into the spacious hall from outside as people pressed into the town, eager for an opportunity to see Jesus.

Martha served, aided by others that Matthew didn't recognize.

But where is Mary?

The second course began, and Mary entered the room, carrying a small jar. She circled to Jesus' seat and generously poured out the entire contents of the jar over Jesus' head and feet. A sweet, woody fragrance overwhelmed the room, and all eyes fixed on Mary as she poured out the last of the perfume over Jesus.

Judas jumped to his feet. "What are you doing? How could you be so wasteful? That has to be worth a year's wages." He turned and directed his impassioned speech at his companions. "Why wasn't that sold and the money given to the poor?"

Matthew was reminded of his own former fortune.

Wasted — now in the hands of Herod — or at least Samchai.

He contemplated responding, but before he found the words, Jesus offered his own reply. "Leave her alone," Jesus said in mild rebuke. "She has done a good thing. It was meant that she should save this perfume for my burial. You will always have the poor among you, but you will not always have me."

Matthew scanned the room in the silence that followed. His companions looked from one to another, every brow wrinkled, every jaw tightened. Judas quietly lowered himself as Mary left the room with her head held low.

Matthew looked to Lazarus, to Simon, and to Bartimaeus.

You will always have the poor among you.

He regarded the formerly blind man as he hung on Jesus' words.

Just a few days ago, he was a poor, helpless, blind beggar. Now he sits with us as a landowner with eyes wide open.

Matthew, by contrast, was left with only what he carried.

————

In the morning, Matthew and his brother, James, climbed a gently sloping road around the base of the mountain to the garden where Jesus had taken them to pray. The temple shimmered brightly over the Kidron Valley. Encampments filled the valley and dotted the land surrounding Jerusalem.

The brothers reached a small village at the base of a side road leading to the garden. The village was little more than a small scattering of simple one-room stone houses. Matthew assumed that the settlement was constructed as a convenience for the servants who tended the garden.

"That has to be the one." James pointed toward the nearest structure, which was slightly larger than the rest, but still small and simple.

Next to the building stood a young donkey hitched to a post. Two servants paid the pair no mind while they loaded a cart with empty baskets from a storeroom.

James approached the hitch and started to untie the colt without acknowledging the workers.

A servant dropped his baskets and ran toward him. "Hey! What are you doing?"

"You can't untie our donkey," the other added as he joined the first.

James did not look up as he continued to unfasten the donkey's rope. Matthew stepped between his brother and the servants and held up his hands, palms out, "The lord needs it and will send it back shortly."

"What lord? We don't know you."

A third man emerged from a building deeper in the settlement. The new arrival was not dressed in plain linen like the servants. By his dyed and modestly embroidered cloak, Matthew suspected he was the landowner. He approached with swift strides, and Matthew quickly recognized the youthful face.

John Mark.

The young man's eyes met Matthew's, and his expression changed from anger to sadness.

Our previous encounter must have left an impression.

"Friend," Matthew addressed John Mark directly. "You know what you have seen. Do as you will, but as I'm sure you realize by now, it was Jesus the Nazarene who sent us to retrieve this colt. He has promised that it will be returned when his need has passed."

John Mark looked down at the ground as Matthew spoke. When Matthew finished, the young man looked up and nodded. He turned to the servants and said, "Let them go with the colt." James untied the beast and led it to the road.

"Thank you, friend," Matthew responded. "You could still join us."

John Mark hung his head again and said, "Thank you. I have business to attend to." He turned and walked away.

The servants stood motionless and watched as Matthew and James led the animal back to the town where Jesus waited.

―――

Simon stood with Jesus and the others on the roadside just outside of Bethany. Residents and pilgrims alike crowded around them. Travelers broke camps and lingered along the roadside, adding to the anticipation. As new groups continued to arrive from the east, most stopped to see what had captured everyone's attention.

Simon, meanwhile, kept his focus on the road, watching for Matthew and James.

The brothers emerged from around a bend, leading a young donkey. They reached Jesus and placed their cloaks on top of the animal. Simon helped Jesus climb onto its back.

The crowd erupted with deafening shouts, and the masses waiting along the road proceeded toward Jerusalem shouting, "Hosanna." First it was a few voices, then dozens, until finally the cacophony of the crowd coalesced into a unified chorus. "Hosanna!"

A sudden yank on Simon's sleeve prompted him to turn around. Bartimaeus scanned the crowd with surprised apprehension. The swell of people gathered behind them encouraged them forward. Bartimaeus stumbled and almost pulled Simon down with him, but Simon caught him and helped him regain his footing.

Others pushed past Simon. When he resumed walking, Jesus was already several meters ahead of him, surrounded by singing and shouting.

Within the hour, the road brought them around the mountain. Then Jerusalem's temple came into view, rising above the city walls and the valley below.

Bartimaeus clung to Simon's sleeve and suddenly gripped his arm tightly with two hands. Simon looked over and braced himself, expecting to be toppled again. Neither man lost their footing, but the formerly blind man's eyes glistened with moisture.

"It is even more grand than I could have dreamed. Praise be to God," Bartimaeus said with a cracking voice as he took in the scene with the wonder of a child.

Simon fought off a pang of envy as he stirred up his own memories of the things that he had seen.

Bloodshed, corruption, hostility.

Crucifixion.

His own eyes filled with tears. The men continued around the mountain until they were directly across the valley from the temple. Simon looked out across the valley. Some of the crowd had run ahead and were already entering the city. Their shouts of *hosanna* echoed off the city walls and blended with the song of those nearby, who had not stopped signing praises since they had left town.

Simon looked at Jesus. He had stopped at the top of the crossroad that would take them into Jerusalem and into the temple. Jesus' shoulders heaved abruptly, and Simon pushed ahead toward him. Jesus' face was flush and wet with tears. He inhaled deeply and began speaking, but Simon couldn't hear him over the song of the crowd.

Slowly, the praises quieted as the people nearest Jesus realized that he was speaking. Simon continued to push ahead, despite being slowed by Bartimaeus, who still maintained a firm grip on his cloak. Finally, he got close enough to hear Jesus, "... not leave one stone on another because you did not recognize the time of God's coming to you."

Jesus gave a tug to his mount's rope, and the donkey stepped down the road into the valley. As soon as Jesus was on the move, the crowd erupted into a new song, even louder than before. People ran ahead and lopped branches from trees and covered the road with them. Some threw off their cloaks and placed them before Jesus.

Simon looked toward the city, where a new crowd emerged from the gate. They filed out and waited along either side of the road. Their *hosannas* filled the valley as Jesus descended with increasing speed.

Bartimaeus joined the singing, filling Simon's ear with his voice.

Simon's thoughts, meanwhile, rested with Jesus' words.

What stones will be toppled? The temple? The whole city?
Is Jesus rallying the crowd to tear down the temple?

They crossed the valley and climbed toward the gate. More branches and cloaks covered the roadway. Simon had managed to get nearer to Jesus and was relieved to find that Peter, James, John, and Thaddeus flanked him. Andrew, Matthew, and Matthew's brother, James, walked in front of him, while Judas, Philip, Nathaniel, and Thomas followed closely behind. They, too, were signing praises, seemingly undeterred by whatever Jesus had said earlier on the road.

Simon finally joined the chorus when they reached the columns of welcoming people outside the city gate.

"Blessed is the one who comes in the name of the Lord!"

"Hosanna to the king!"

So this is it. Jesus is finally allowing the people to proclaim him king.

They ascended the steps into the outer court of the temple, where hundreds more lined the way and joined the singing. Evening was near, and the usual commerce of the outer courts had ceased for the day. Still, the crowd swelled as people pushed past one another to get close to Jesus.

Simon looked across the outer court to the far corner, where the Antonia Fortress loomed over the colonnades in mocking defilement. Soldiers lined the fortress wall, every eye on the crowd. Bowmen stood atop the parapets on the near side, longbows strung and arrows unsheathed.

Simon's attention was drawn back to ground level when shoving to his left pushed a wall of bodies into him. Several people stumbled and fell, and his own foot was caught under a three-man pile that pushed and competed to be the first to stand again.

The crowd stirred and thrashed with fury until after a moment, three blue-mantled heads reached them. Simon did not recognize these Pharisees, but their expressions were flush with indignation.

"Silence your disciples, Nazarene!" the tallest of the three called out as he neared Jesus. Simon expected to hear authority and rebuke in his voice. Instead, the Pharisee quaked with desperate trepidation.

Simon looked again to the fortress. The Romans showed no signs of making a move for the crowd.

Safe. For the moment.

"Silence them?" Jesus shouted back with a hint of glee. "Even if they would keep quiet, the stones will cry out!"

The stones? Simon thought back to what Jesus had said on the road. *Was there something else about the stones that I missed?*

Several disciples positioned themselves between the Pharisees and Jesus. Simon examined the men who had gathered behind the Pharisees. A couple wore telltale priestly sashes and turbans, but no temple guards accompanied them.

This time.

The two Pharisees who hadn't spoken got in front of the donkey, seeming to block Jesus from moving forward. Matthew and James put hands up to hold them off. As they did, one Pharisee regarded Matthew with a look of recognition and stepped in close. Simon maneuvered to get a closer look, but he couldn't place the man's face in any memory from Galilee nor Jerusalem. After a tense moment, the Pharisees pushed back and turned away. Matthew clenched something in his fist. What it was, Simon could not tell.

Jesus looked around and said, "It is late. Let's go rest and return in the morning."

They crossed under the royal portico and down the stairs toward the south. They exited onto the main road, and Simon got his first look at the newly constructed aqueduct separating the upper city from the crowded living quarters below. On the escarpment above and surrounding the support columns below, Roman guards maintained an obvious — and heavily armed — presence.

Does Jesus even have plan for reaching the palace?

They followed the road south toward the Siloam Pool and a smaller pool beyond that sourced the aqueduct.

Roman might won out over zealous resistance after all.

They passed through the city gate, and a new sight caught Simon's attention. To his left, dozens of men approached the feeder pool from along the outside of the city wall. Most wielded daggers while a few carried hammers and ropes. Roman soldiers posted at the base of the pool moved ahead to intercept them, drawing their own swords.

The dagger-wielding men in the lead had no chance against the extended reach of Roman long swords. The first two were swiftly cut down.

Others came up behind them and climbed over the first two. One plunged a blade into a soldier's neck before toppling off the dying body beneath him.

Soldiers farther removed from the fray sounded an alarm, which was repeated before and behind them, carrying faintly into the city.

The skirmish between Romans and insurgents pushed closer to the pool. One rebel breached the line and began ascending the support tower, with a large hammer dangling from his waist. A Roman soldier pulled his sword arm back to take a swing at the man, but his elbow caught the helmet of his own man.

He shifted nearer the tower and started stabbing at the climber's heels with awkward jabs from below. The man kicked back and knocked the sword from the soldier's hand and continued to climb out of reach.

"No king but God!" the climber shouted as he continued his ascent. His accent was distinctly Galilean.

Simon instinctively reached for his own blade, and Thaddeus grabbed his arm. "Not here," his friend shouted as he pulled Simon away for the city. "Not like this."

They had moved only a few meters down the road when a column of soldiers emerged from the city's south gate behind them. The climber neared the top of the aqueduct. Beyond him, Romans trotted along the outside of the city wall behind the insurgents.

From Simon's vantage, the hopelessness of their situation was clear. He stood a moment until his friend yanked his arm a second time.

"Let's leave the city. We will return in the morning."

Simon walked while looking back over his shoulder. The climber reached the top and was promptly dropped by a Roman arrow. Soon after, the shouts of Galilean rebels faded, and only Roman voices could be heard.

Simon turned his attention back to the road and trailed behind Jesus and his other companions. As they continued toward the villages, they passed a dozen crosses lining the road.

The ominous threat of Rome, strategically placed to intimidate.

Some were empty and stained a deep brown. Two bore the near-skeletal remains of bodies that had been ravaged by sun and scavenger alike. The stench threatened to overwhelm Simon, and he held a sleeve over his nose and mouth.

Farther down the road, gasps and moans reached his ears from two more crosses. Simon saw the naked shame of two men—tied up and fully exposed—scorched by the sun and wind.

Their torsos were bruised and pocked where chunks of flesh had been torn from their sides. Despite their swollen eyes and lips, Simon recognized a familiar face.

Manaen.

Simon had no time to contemplate the relief that briefly crossed his mind. He might not be a hunted man any longer, but the scuffle at the pool behind him still reached his ears. He was certain that he was far from safe.

Not just me. All of us.

Simon turned away from his former mentor and set his eyes on the road ahead. He fixed his gaze on Jesus as he followed, hoping that his teacher had a plan.

Chapter Twenty-Six

"What did that Pharisee hand you in the temple courts yesterday?"

Matthew startled at the question. He turned with a jump and realized Simon had come alongside him. "It was strange," Matthew answered. "Just a time and place. Nothing else."

"A request to meet?"

"I imagine so."

"When and where?"

"Tonight, first watch." Matthew opened his pouch and pulled out a scrap of parchment. He opened it and continued, "Solomon's Colonnade, north end." He handed the note to Simon.

Simon took the parchment and looked it over. Handing it back to Matthew, he said, "This proves Nicodemus is right."

"Then why haven't they arrested Jesus? He was right there with us. And we're going back to the temple even as we speak!"

"Arrest Jesus?" The question came from Matthew's other side. He turned to see Judas had taken an interest in the discussion. Thaddeus caught up next to Simon as well.

"Yes," Simon interjected. "Remember the warning from Nicodemus?" Simon looked to the front of their party, where Jesus led them as they walked toward Jerusalem. "They must be getting desperate."

"So we're just letting Jesus walk into the temple to get arrested?" Judas asked with rising volume.

"No. Show him the note."

As Matthew retrieved the parchment from his bag, Simon said, "The priests are desperate, but *this* proves that they don't have cause to arrest him."

"I don't understand."

"They need witnesses," Thaddeus added. "Clearly, everyone who has seen what Jesus can do is celebrating him. The priests can't get anyone to say a word against him."

"That's why they're sneaking around," Simon added. He turned to face Matthew. "But I wonder, why you?"

Matthew stopped.

An accusation? After all that we've endured together?

"I have no idea! I've never seen that Pharisee before—nor any of them."

"What if we go and meet? Maybe it's something altogether different," Judas said.

"No!" Simon said with force. He inhaled and added with a calmer tone, "Thaddeus is right. This can only be an attempt to trap Jesus—or all of us! I still don't understand why the Pharisee picked you."

"Maybe he recognized Matthew as a publican," Judas offered.

Matthew shook his head at the suggestion and wrinkled his brow in contemplation. "The Pharisees wouldn't have anything to do with the Herodians."

"Maybe so. But they were accompanied by chief priests. And given the corruption in the Sanhedrin—" Thaddeus began before Matthew held up a hand.

"Corruption that the Pharisees are quick to blame on the Sadducees. Even so, the Herodians are no friends of Pilate."

"So we can't even be sure *who* is asking to meet." Judas added.

"This might explain something," Simon said as he pointed up the road.

Against the backdrop of the southern gate to Jerusalem, where they had seen empty crosses the previous day, Roman soldiers stood over several men in custody. The men were naked and bruised up and down their torsos. Gashes across their backs glistened and flowed with blood. They hunched on shaky legs, visibly struggling to bear the weight of the planks on their backs.

One dropped his beam, and the nearest soldier swung his short sword, meeting the man's temple with the flat side of his blade. The prisoner toppled over and wrestled to pick up the beam and right himself on his feet.

Beyond them, two soldiers fastened ropes to another man's wrists as he lay braced against a beam on the ground. The man's cries were cut short every time he coughed and rasped for air.

Matthew looked across at his companions. All of them had averted their eyes and looked down as they walked. When they passed the gruesome scene and approached the gate, a wall of soldiers stood to the right, forcing the road to narrow. The soldiers studied each face as the disciples passed, but they stood in still silence.

The disciples followed Jesus deeper into the city, past the merchants that lined the main avenue toward the temple. They reached the temple, ascended the stairs, and passed under the royal portico. The outer court was already teeming with people.

They struggled to keep up with Jesus as he turned toward the booths of the vendors and traders on the left. They passed fruit sellers and crafters. Matthew lost sight of Jesus several times as they wove through crowds that moved in all directions at once.

They heard the sounds of lambs and birds as they approached tented booths where caged carts stood nearby and pilgrims lined up clutching coin purses.

A crash beyond the nearest booths captured Matthew's attention. Through the crowd, he could barely see Jesus toppling a table. A man near him stumbled and brought down a booth on top of himself as he fell.

Onlookers pushed to get away, and coins scattered across the stone floor. Matthew stood motionless.

Do I try to get to him?

A man leading several calves by a rope tried to pass, but Jesus blocked his path and turned him away.

Matthew spotted Simon and Thaddeus nearby. "We have to stop him!" Matthew yelled to his friends over the shouts of vendors and the cries of animals.

Jesus continued to turn the tables of money changers — one after another — as they scrambled to move their strongboxes to their carts. Some succeeded, but most spilled onto the floor.

"I don't think we can," Simon answered. "This is how it all started."

"Then I suppose this is how it all ends, especially if the priests are looking for Jesus now," Thaddeus shouted back to them.

Jesus turned back toward the animal vendors, grabbed a cage full of doves, and toppled it. The birds scattered, and Matthew and the others ducked to avoid them.

"My Father's house is a house of prayer. You've made it a den of thieves!"

Matthew couldn't tell where the voice came from, but it was unmistakably Jesus.

He stood upright again as a group of Roman soldiers pushed through the crowd toward them. "Look!" he said to Simon and Thaddeus as he pointed them out and moved toward Jesus.

Simon reached Jesus just as Peter and Andrew emerged from elsewhere in the crowd. They surrounded him and were joined by the others as they crossed the temple court toward the eastern colonnades. They pushed past onlookers, and shouts of recognition took over as they moved away from the disruption behind them.

"Look! The Son of David!"

"Hosanna!"

Children pushed to the front and ran to Jesus. He slowed, but still moved with determination toward the porticoes. Others followed behind, and when they reached cover, Jesus sat in the place of the teacher while people led the blind and carried the crippled to him.

Matthew stayed in the back and watched as people surrounded Jesus. The song of the children grew louder. "Hosanna to the Son of David!"

Matthew stumbled forward when several bodies pushed past him. He returned to his feet and noticed three chief priests pushing through the throng toward Jesus.

The one in the lead—his face flushed and fixed in a scowl—pointed at Jesus and called, "Do you hear what these children are saying?" with the sharpness of accusation.

"Yes," Jesus called back.

What Jesus said next, Matthew couldn't tell as more shouts of *hosanna* echoed off the stone. The crowd closed in tighter around Jesus, wedging the priests away from him. The priests turned and left. As they passed, Matthew recognized them.

These are the same priests we saw yesterday. The Pharisee's message must be from them.

He found Simon and Thaddeus and pointed out the priests.

The three followed them away from the throng. Across the temple court, a concentration of Romans stood among the money changers and vendors who worked clumsily to reset their booths.

The three closed the distance and walked behind the priests. Matthew stayed behind Simon and Thaddeus as they continued toward the half-wall that partitioned the main temple from the outer court.

"It's impossible to stop him. You hear how all the people praise him," one priest said to the others.

"Nobody will say a word against him. There has to be a way to trap him."

"If we give him time, he will trap himself," the third priest said with a Galilean accent. "He can't stay away from the people. He'll be back again."

The priests crossed an opening into the inner court. Matthew turned to Simon and Thaddeus. "We should get back to Jesus."

The others nodded, and they turned and weaved back toward the eastern colonnades.

———

The mid-morning sun glistened off the temple wall as they returned to Jerusalem. They approached the south gate — and the too-familiar sight of dying men and withering corpses hanging over them.

The gruesome sight, putrid smells, and pained moans did not become easier to tolerate with exposure. Simon found that each time they passed, the assault on his senses was as fresh as ever.

But even more severe was the assault on his soul.

He pondered anew the brutality of Rome and the futility of the Zealots.

But how will Jesus' strategy of healing the crippled and angering the priests lead us to a better outcome?

As they passed the dead and dying, Simon forced himself to look up. He scanned the bruised, bloodied, and swollen faces until he found Manaen. His former mentor hung still and lifeless two days after Simon had first discovered his fate. Simon turned his focus back toward the front of his group, where Jesus led — as he always did. How would his present mentor fare?

Stoned by the priests? The people will never go for that.

Hung up with the insurrectionists? Even his disturbance in the marketplace yesterday hasn't attracted any unwanted Roman attention.

They entered the city, which was even more crowded than on the previous day. Simon couldn't recall a more heavily attended festival season.

Roman soldiers dotted the main avenue, not leaving a single meter unwatched.

As before, they passed by merchants and crafters and proceeded directly to the temple. They ascended the stairs and had barely emerged from under the royal portico when several priests encircled them. Simon recognized three from their recent encounters. Today they were joined by at least a half a dozen more and accompanied by their scribes.

"We demand answers!" one shouted as they stepped in front of Jesus, stopping him mid-stride. "By what authority are you doing these things?"

Jesus stepped to the side and continued toward the eastern colonnades. He regarded the priest with an open expression as he stepped around him.

The priest walked alongside Jesus while the rest followed, shouting as they went, "Tell us! Who gave you the authority to do this?"

Jesus looked ahead and kept walking as he responded, "Let me first ask you a question. John's baptism — was it from heaven or from men? You tell me."

The lead priest stopped and pulled the other priests and scribes aside. Simon and the others followed Jesus as he continued walking. Simon heard the priests discussing among themselves as he passed, "… if we say it was from heaven, he will ask why we didn't believe."

They passed the occasional Roman soldier as they walked.

An unusual presence, even in the unrestricted gentiles' court.

Simon scanned the crowd. Soldiers stood strategically posted as far as he could see. He looked back toward the money changers and found a similar — perhaps more concentrated — Roman presence. The priests and scribes still huddled in discussion behind him.

They reached the colonnades, where a small band of students stood and listened to a Pharisee in the teacher's seat. Jesus stood and waited. After a moment, the priests returned. The one who had challenged Jesus came to him and said, "We do not know the source of John's baptism."

Jesus turned and replied, "Nor will I tell you by whose authority I am acting."

The priest balled his fist as his face flushed and his brow tightened. His companions stood with mouths and eyes agape. Jesus had already walked away from them and moved toward the just-vacated teacher's seat.

He began to speak. "A man planted a vineyard …"

Simon looked to his right. Thaddeus, Matthew, and James stood nearby. He looked to his left where the priests stood, arms crossed, listening. Beyond them, bodies began to crowd under the portico and surround Jesus from all sides while he taught.

A familiar figure moved through the crowd, and Simon's heart skipped a beat.

Jeshua Bar-Abbas.

Simon elbowed Thaddeus and nodded toward the man. "He's here."

"Who is here?"

"Bar-Abbas."

"You mean, the one who ..."

"Yes."

Simon watched as Bar-Abbas slowly pushed through the people toward Jesus. He scanned the crowd continuously as he went.

Simon stepped sideways and shoved through bodies toward the man. A hand gripped his arm.

"What are you doing?" Thaddeus asked as he turned back.

"I have to stop him. I can't let him get near Jesus." Simon yanked his arm free from his friend's grip and shoved further through the crowd, toppling onlookers.

Jeshua Bar-Abbas slowly worked his way closer to where Jesus sat. Simon reached him while they were still several meters away from the front. He no longer heard what Jesus was saying as he turned over his next words in his own mind.

He reached out and grabbed Jeshua with two hands, "Your attempt to kill me failed!" He was almost nose-to-nose with the man.

"I could plunge a dagger into your belly right here. But I'm willing to let your debt go. I see the value your teacher holds. I understand why you follow him."

Simon released one of Jeshua's shoulders. Gripping the other firmly, he turned the man and pushed through the crowd toward the open air of the temple courts.

When they were beyond the sound of Jesus' voice, Simon stopped and turned Jeshua to face him. "So you've changed then? You believe now?"

Bar-Abbas chuckled, "The people love him. He holds a special sway over them. More importantly, he makes the weak strong. He could be useful to us."

"To us? I'm done with your movement! It didn't work out too well for Manaen."

"So you saw him, then," Jeshua said with a tinge of remorse. "That means you have seen the brutality of our Roman oppressors. Now it is time for them to answer for it."

"I refuse to trade one brutal regime for another."

"Simon, it won't be like that—"

"Your men hunted me like an animal and tried to kill me while I slept! Jesus is the reason that I still live. Whatever you are planning, I won't be a part of it."

"You mean *Manaen's* men ..." Jeshua let the statement hang in silence before he continued. "Still, your Jesus has done us a great service. I heard about his tantrum with the money changers. Look around you."

Jeshua waved an arm with a flourish toward the open-air court. Simon followed the gesture with his eyes and scanned the scene.

More people than ever. But what is he getting at?

"And now," Jeshua continued, "full patrols all around. The fortress is nearly empty. The Romans are not leaving a single meter unwatched. But look closely at them."

Simon scanned the crowd again. This time he understood what Jeshua wanted him to see.

Romans. All throughout the crowd.

"They're separated from one another. Now is our time." Bar-Abbas grabbed Simon by the shoulders and bore into him with a fierce gaze. "Tell your teacher to follow my signal. If he does, others will follow, and we'll succeed."

"Signal?"

"He will know it when he sees it."

Bar-Abbas let go of Simon's shoulders and stepped away. The crowd closed between them, and Simon lost sight of the Zealot. He turned, and the crowd seemed to move around him with dizzying speed. His blood ran cold, and he walked back toward the porticoes where Jesus taught, barely aware of his own steps.

———

Matthew's attention was diverted away from Jesus when Simon took off into the crowd. Thaddeus lunged toward him, then stopped. Matthew grabbed his friend's sleeve and asked, "What's happening?"

"Simon says he saw Jeshua Bar-Abbas."

"The one who tried to kill him?"

He scanned the area where he had lost Simon in the crowd. There was little movement from those closest to Jesus; the people stood with rapt attention. Matthew looked out toward the open-air courts. *Just the usual bustle of the crowd.* There were no signs of a struggle nor confrontation.

A loud cry of objection rose behind him and yanked his attention back to the portico. The priests who had challenged Jesus earlier shook their fists and yelled at him, "How dare you speak these things!"

"You have no authority over us!"

The priests and their scribes turned and exited the portico. Matthew watched them leave, then turned back to Thaddeus. "We need to find Simon!"

"I don't think we can. Not in this crowd."

"Then we at least need to get to Jesus."

They moved toward the front, competing with others who brought crippled and blind people to Jesus. Everyone he touched was restored. Matthew stumbled more than once as the crowd pressed tighter. He wasn't sure that he was even making progress.

Peter and Andrew stood next to Jesus and tried to maintain order. Philip and Nathaniel helped the healed people out of the area to make room for others to get to the front.

Matthew forgot about the threat to Simon as he watched. The way compassion freely flowed from Jesus to all these people moved him.

This is all I have left to give.

He quickly went to work, helping more blind and sick people toward the front.

Matthew had no idea how long this went on—how many came and went. Songs of praise echoed off the walls and ceiling as more people were healed. They poured out of the portico shouting praises as quickly as new people poured in.

A group of four or five well-dressed men pushed toward the front. They seemed well and able bodied, and they stopped within a couple of meters of Jesus. Matthew pushed closer to the front and looked toward the men. One looked familiar. He had seen the man at parties hosted by Samchai, but never learned his name.

Beyond them, the priests who had challenged Jesus—including the Galilean that Matthew assumed had arranged the meeting request—stood several meters back, watching closely.

Matthew's attention was torn from the sick and the lame who still trickled into the colonnade. The other disciples were still moving people toward and away from Jesus, but the lines of people seeking healing finally dwindled.

"Teacher," a voice called. Matthew turned and confirmed that the speaker was Samchai's man. "We know that your teaching is of God—"

Shouts of *amen* and *hosanna* echoed off the stone around them.

"Is it right to pay taxes to Caesar?" the man asked.

Matthew's heart sank as the crowd quieted and waited.

The priests stepped closer but did not speak.

So this is the trap.

Matthew knew the Herodians well.

They won't hesitate to petition for the arrest of anyone who defies the taxing authorities.

Authorities that the priests — for their own adherence to the law of Moses — refused to acknowledge.

Matthew wanted to get to the front, pull Jesus from the teacher's seat, and flee. Twice he escaped stoning from this very place.

There's no way he can escape a third time in such a full crowd.

"Show me a denarius!"

Jesus is answering! Why?

Jesus pointed toward the questioner as he spoke. "Whose portrait and inscription do you see?"

"I see Caesar," the man replied as he held up a coin.

"Then give to Caesar what is Caesar's," Jesus said. He turned toward the priests who continued to move nearer, "and give to God what is God's."

The priests stood in silence, mouths hanging open. After a moment, the people resumed pressing Jesus with questions.

Matthew spotted Simon returning to the colonnade. He pushed through the crowd to meet up with his friend. "Are you okay?"

"I am. But we need to get Jesus out of here." Simon looked to his left and right, then got closer to Matthew and spoke as quietly as the surrounding chaos would allow. "Bar-Abbas is planning something. Whatever it is, we need to be away from here when it happens."

"But what—"

"I don't know. But I can only assume there will be bloodshed."

Matthew looked back toward Jesus. He stood now, his hand full of movement as he spoke. The crowd remained silent, fixated on him with dumbfounded expressions. "Let's get to him then." He pressed toward Jesus while Simon followed.

They struggled through the crowd as they were packed tight under the portico, listening and unconcerned about the shoves from behind.

They finally got close enough to hear Jesus saying, "… a little while longer. Walk while you have the light, before darkness overtakes you."

Simon grabbed Matthew and said, "We need to get him and go while *we* still have some light."

Someone nearby hushed them, "Let the teacher speak!"

They listened more as they slowly made their way forward, "... while you have it. So you may be sons of light."

Jesus stepped away from the teacher's seat into the crowd. Peter, Andrew, and the rest followed while Matthew and Simon pushed toward them, meeting them where they emerged from the portico.

They crossed into the open-air court, and a cry went up toward the north end, beyond the temple structure. Several helmeted heads moved toward the source of the commotion. One dropped into the crowd, and a wave of bodies tussled around that spot.

They continued toward the royal portico. Another shout went up. "No king but God!" This one was closer—straight ahead where the money changers stood. Another immediately followed. Then two more.

More bodies pushed toward the exit, and they slowed as the crowd converged. Looking back, Matthew saw that scuffles— at least seven or eight—dotted the crowd and raised swords converged on those spots. As they moved with the swarm toward the stairs, Matthew had a clear view of the Antonia Fortress. A mass of bodies moved in every direction at once below the fortress, and soldiers emerged on the wall above with bows in hand.

Simon had stopped and was watching the scene. Matthew grabbed his friend's cloak and yanked him through the crowd and toward the exit.

Chapter Twenty-Seven

"Do you wonder what is happening in there right now?" Simon asked as they sat in the now-familiar olive grove. He looked across the valley at the temple, the light of the mid-morning sun reflecting brightly off its gilded facade.

"Well, the temple is still standing, if that's what you're asking," Thaddeus answered.

"But for how much longer? He said that Jerusalem's enemies would topple every stone."

"What about yesterday?" Matthew added. "Did you hear what he said on the road? He said he'd be handed over to be crucified!"

"Are you suggesting that the Romans will blame yesterday's uprising on him?" Judas asked with a panicked tone as he stood.

"The Romans aren't even looking for him," Thaddeus said with a wave of his hand.

"But the chief priests are!" Matthew was on his feet now.

"The priests wouldn't hand him over to the Romans!" Judas' voice grew louder.

Simon stood and stepped to the edge of the clearing where he could have a more direct view of the temple—the whole city.

The gates were open. People were coming and going. Hillside camps bustled with meal preparation, and travelers filled every roadway.

It's as if nothing happened yesterday.

"Don't overlook the corruption of the priests," he said without looking back at his companions. "But there is also something that Jeshua Bar-Abbas said. He told me that Jesus did him a favor when he upset the money changers' tables."

"How?"

"You spoke to Bar-Abbas?"

Simon turned and faced Judas. "It was a chance encounter. He saw an opportunity to eliminate a few Romans, so he arranged it."

"So what does this have to do with Jesus?" Matthew asked.

"Don't you see? If Jeshua is captured, he can say he was following Jesus' lead."

"That won't save him from Roman retribution," Thaddeus said.

"You're right," Simon added. "But it would still give him the revenge that he sought against Jesus — against *us* — in the end." He turned and gazed at the temple again.

"Maybe the priests can help him."

Simon shook his head and started to turn but stopped when Thaddeus said what he was thinking, "No. The Pharisees tried to stone him twice. And the Sanhedrin has put out a demand for his arrest."

"So what do we do now?" Judas yelled more than spoke his question.

"We rest today. Tomorrow, we celebrate the Passover."

Simon turned at the sound of Jesus' voice. His mentor and friend stood at a trailhead. His face was reddened, and his eyelids were puffy, but his characteristic benevolence still defined his gaze. Peter, James, and John stood behind him.

"Let's return to the village. There's more to be done," Jesus said and walked down the path toward the main road. Simon and the rest followed behind in silence.

———

The next morning at first light, Simon accompanied Jesus and the rest into the temple. The vendors had moved to the north end of the outer courts, where animals could be brought in from the pastures as needed.

They rounded the inner court toward the north side and passed under the imposing towers of the Antonia Fortress. Lines of soldiers armed with bows spread across the fortress walls, watchful of the crowd below.

By curious contrast, there seemed to be no Roman presence on the temple concourse — not even in the outer courts.

If the vendors recognized Jesus when he approached the carts, they showed no sign. Judas paid for a lamb, and Andrew carried the animal around to the inner courts, where lines of priests waited with knives and bowls to complete the required sacrifices.

Simon kept his attention on the outer courts. Even as the sun climbed higher and brought more pilgrims to the temple grounds, the Romans stayed out of the crowds, watching from the security of their elevated position.

When the sacrifice was complete, they took their slain lamb and exited the temple grounds under the arches leading to the upper city.

The morning sun reflected off the palace that rose along the western wall of the city. Even from the temple, Simon could see the concentration of soldiers surrounding the structure.

Pilate is taking every precaution. It's a wonder he hasn't sent his troops to trample their defilement across the Passover festival.

"Why are we going this way?" Simon asked. "Bethany is beyond the south gate."

"We'll be the guests of a family in this section today. I sent Peter and John ahead to make preparations. We'll meet them there shortly," Jesus answered.

Jesus led them down streets that wove between the two-story houses of the priests and landowners. Between the buildings, Simon caught glimpses of the densely packed Galilean quarters in the lower city.

The pretense in this part of the city must be blinding.

He fought to suppress a wellspring of bitterness.

Just returning to Jerusalem — and to the temple — for the first time since their hasty exit two days ago left Matthew feeling unsettled. And now, Jesus led them into the upper city, where the priests and other influential types lived under the protective watch of Rome.

Who here could have invited us as guests?

Are we walking into a trap?

From the comfort of the olive grove the day before, the temple was a beacon of magnificence, a reflection of the presence it contained. Now, as they walked with the temple behind them, the royal palace dominated the horizon. Though not as grandiose as the temple, the size and gilding of the palace stood as a visible reminder of the extravagance of Herod the Great and his legacy.

No doubt, Pilate has all the comfort he demands behind those walls.

The palace walls, guard towers, and — most importantly — visible and ample presence of Roman soldiers, provided the prefect all the security he could need, even in such a volatile season.

The houses in the upper city were several times the size of the packed dwellings in the lower tier. Matthew estimated that as many as ten houses could fit into each of the estate-sized structures before him.

They followed a winding street to the farthest corner of the upper city until they reached a two-tiered structure where a well-dressed merchant met them. The merchant was accompanied by an adolescent who Matthew promptly recognized.

Did he come back and speak to Jesus after our first meeting?

"Your friends are ready for you, and they have a fire ready for the lamb. Come this way," the merchant said. He turned to the boy and said, "John Mark, join us." The man led them around the side of the building to a staircase leading to a smaller second tier that itself was the size of four lower-city dwellings.

Andrew and Thomas carried the spitted lamb across the balcony to where Peter and John tended a fire in a stone pit. The merchant directed the others through a doorway into a spacious room with windows on three sides. "My son will show you in."

Tables and couches were arranged in the center of the room. The center table was set with herbs, water, unleavened bread, apple paste with cinnamon sticks, and four cups of wine.

"Your place is prepared," John Mark told them, "and the house is clear of leaven. This should be everything you need."

Matthew wondered how John Mark's family came to host this feast.

Was this the father's doing, or the son's?

His thoughts turned just as quickly to his own fatherly remorse — to the daughter who he had lost after barely realizing that she was even there.

"Will you be joining us for the feast?" Matthew blurted the question almost impulsively.

"No. My father will host our family's feast in the main dwelling below. But he is happy to provide a place for your teacher." The boy didn't look up when he answered, and he exited with his head still hung low.

He can be your teacher, too, if you let him.

Matthew thought back to his earliest encounters with Jesus and allowed himself a moment to relive the conflict and shame of those days over again in his mind.

———

While the lamb was roasting, Jesus walked around the table and reclined toward the farthest wall, and the others followed his lead.

"I've longed to eat this Passover with you before I suffer," he said as he looked each of the twelve eye-to-eye, one-by-one. "I tell you: I will not eat this meal again until it's fulfillment in the kingdom of God."

Simon met Jesus' eyes; his teacher did not hide his sorrow. *Sorrow, but no fear. Never fear.* He thought of all the times Jesus spoke about dying. *Was he ever worried? Was he ever panicked?*

Simon couldn't recall a hint of wavering ever in Jesus' words. Despite the sorrow in his tone, Jesus' words still carried the familiar air of conviction and purpose. Simon reflected on the city outside, embroiled in conflict. Passing by crosses daily, seeing a familiar face ...

Passing through the upper city, where Pilate's palace cast its pretentious shadow over the homes of the rulers and priests ...

And all Jesus can talk about ... is dying ...

"Take this and divide it among you." Jesus' voice pulled Simon from his reverie. He looked over and saw that Jesus had taken the first of the cups.

"I tell you: I will not drink the fruit of the vine again until the kingdom of God comes."

Jesus passed the cup to Peter, who took a sip and passed it on.

One-by-one, they drank and passed. Simon received the cup from Thaddeus and took a drink, praying that doing so might give him some understanding, or even settle his growing trepidation. *Nothing. It still doesn't make sense. What am I missing?* He passed the cup to James and looked down at the table.

When the cup returned to Jesus, he set it down and promptly stood. He shed his coat and crossed to the entrance. Simon shifted his weight to his other arm and watched with curiosity while Jesus retrieved a towel hanging near the door and fastened it around his waist.

Jesus took one of the earthen wash jars and filled a basin with water, then he turned and carried the basin toward Peter.

"Lord, are you going to wash my feet?" Peter's voice rang with alarm, and his eyes opened wide with horror as he asked the question. The outburst startled Simon.

"You don't realize now what I am doing, but later you will understand."

Simon nodded silently. *There is still plenty that I would like to understand.*

"No!" Peter began to pull himself up to his feet and protested, "You will not wash my feet."

Jesus stood and answered him calmly, "Unless I wash you, you have no part of me."

Peter exhaled deeply and sank back to his seat. "Not just my feet," he said, "but my hands and head as well."

Jesus proceeded along the back wall to where Peter reclined and answered him, "A person who has bathed is clean; only his feet need to be washed. And you are clean, but not each of you."

Now what does he mean by that? Who does he mean by that?
Jesus knelt at Peter's feet, ladled water over them, and dried them. As he did, he spoke in soft tones. Simon couldn't hear him, but the expression on Peter's face softened as Jesus spoke.

Jesus moved over to where Andrew sat, and Simon looked around the room. Matthew also scanned the room, confusion and introspection apparent on his face. Simon was sure—perhaps for the first time—they each understood exactly how the other felt.

Most of the others looked down at the table. Judas and Thomas fixed their sights on Jesus, seemingly unable to turn away.

Jesus continued around the table. As he washed Thaddeus' feet, Simon heard an indiscernible whisper. He gave a quick, self-conscious glance toward his friend, who nodded softly as his eyes moistened.

Jesus came to Simon and poured water over his feet. Simon couldn't bring himself to even look at Jesus as his heart grew burdened. He wanted to kick the bowl aside and lift Jesus to his feet, to raise him up on their shoulders and carry him to the palace, to complete the procession that started just days ago when Jesus rode into the city to shouts of *hosanna*.

Instead, he found himself unable to move while the man who rode in as a conqueror now stooped low before him like a servant.

Jesus looked up at him and said, "Simon. Hold on to what I have taught you. Love your enemies. Pray for them. Bless those who curse you. Then you will be a son of your heavenly Father."

Simon remained speechless. He didn't understand what Jesus had planned, but he knew that he trusted Jesus. And that made him want to proclaim him king more than ever.

———

Matthew watched in awe while Jesus went around the room washing feet.

A home of this size must have servants. Any one of them could have been called to do this.

Had this been Matthew's home, he would have insisted on it. But his home was long gone.

This was his life now. Traveling—sometimes fleeing. Living in borrowed spaces. Owning no more than what he could carry.

When Jesus rode into the city, Matthew expected the crowd would usher him straight to the palace and demand he be enthroned. *Instead, this man who could be king – should be king – is washing feet.* Jesus finished drying James' feet and placed the wash basin in front of Matthew. Matthew looked on puzzlingly as Jesus poured water over his feet. There was no sign of shame nor resentment in his expression. Jesus looked completely at peace, full of contentment. *It's as if this is what he wants to do.*

He gently shook his head in confusion as Jesus continued. When Jesus took the towel, he looked up and met Matthew's eyes. "Remember what I have taught you, Matthew," he said with quiet calm. "Moth and rust cannot touch what you possess. Where your treasure is, your heart will also be. Store up your treasures in heaven as you prepare for the coming kingdom."

Matthew closed his eyes and thought about all that he once had, and about the truth that Jesus spoke now — *nothing more can ever be taken from me.*

Yes, Jesus could be king — should be king. Instead, he stoops to wash our feet. What did that say about Matthew — about all of them — that Jesus would so willingly humble himself and exalt them?

And what does he plan to do next?

Matthew didn't know, but for the first time, not knowing what came next brought him peace. He allowed himself a moment to rest in a security that he had never known before.

"Do you understand what I have done for you?" Jesus' voice jolted Matthew from his reverie. He opened his eyes and listened while Jesus addressed the room. "You call me 'Lord' and rightly so. Now that I, your Lord, have washed your feet, you should do for one another as I have done for you. No servant is greater than his master."

Matthew looked around and realized that the lamb had been brought in and placed on the table.

When did that happen?

He looked to the windows; darkness had overtaken the eastern sky.

What else did I miss?

Matthew turned his attention back to Jesus, who was still speaking, "... One of you is going to betray me."

What?

Matthew scanned every face in the room. Each of his companions did the same. Murmurs of "Not me," and "You don't mean me," filled his ears. Peter motioned to John, who sat next to Jesus. John looked over and asked, "Lord, who is it?"

Every eye was open wide, and every mouth silent as they all waited for Jesus to answer. The thought that any of them would betray Jesus turned Matthew's stomach inside out. He thought back to the priests who approached him in the temple courts.

The note! Where did it go? He looked to Simon, then to Thaddeus, but they stared at Jesus and did not notice Matthew's imploring look. He noticed that others had glanced his way and realized that his expression must be panicked. He forced his body to stillness and his face to calm, even as his heart raced and his stomach churned.

"It's the one who takes this bread," Jesus broke a piece of bread and dipped it in the salt water. He held it before Judas, who slowly raised his own hand and took it.

With a weak voice, Judas asked, "Surely, it isn't me?"

Jesus nodded, "Yes. What you are about to do, do quickly."

Judas pushed up from the table and stumbled over the others' feet. Matthew watched his friend walk briskly toward and through the door without looking back.

Matthew's heart sank, and he hung his head. Judas had seen the message. *Did he go? Did he meet with the priest?*

Matthew thought back to their hasty retreat from the temple and back to Bethany. *Was Judas with us then?*

He could not recall.

The disciples began cutting off portions of meat. Matthew followed their lead, but struggled to eat as he silently wondered what he could have done differently.

─────

The eleven followed Jesus out of the city and across the Kidron Valley to the olive grove. They spoke little as they walked. Simon turned over the events of the past few days in his head.

Bar-Abbas. The priests.

Both wanted Jesus to capitulate to their demands.

Both were unable to see how impossible it was to sway him.

Simon had tried, with all of Jesus' talk about death. But first came Lazarus. Then came the words that Jesus had spoken to him just a few hours ago, *"Repay evil with kindness."*

Simon felt exposed whenever Jesus spoke to him. Just as he felt exposed now, having left his sword behind — something he had not done in years.

"Why do you think he is bringing us out here now?" Simon asked Thaddeus as they walked.

"I've stopped trying to discern his reasons," Thaddeus responded. "He always seems to know what will happen. That's why I trust him."

"Yes, he does seem to know." Simon stared absently at the ground. "That's what I am afraid of."

"Afraid?"

"He keeps talking about dying. And where has Judas gone?"

"Never mind Judas. Remember Lazarus? Or even Bartimaeus."

"Great victories, indeed." Simon forced confidence into his voice and added, "But he waited and let Lazarus die. What else has to happen? Do you know what he said to me tonight? 'Repay evil with kindness.' Something is happening soon, and he *knows* it."

Thaddeus stopped and clasped Simon's shoulders. "And what will you do when it happens?"

"Die. Unarmed. It was the only way I could ensure my own obedience."

Thaddeus nodded in silence, and they resumed walking. They passed the gardeners' village as they approached the grove. A young donkey sleeping just behind the stable gate caught Simon's notice. He pointed at the donkey, leaned toward Thaddeus, and said, "Hosanna!"

"Hosanna."

They entered the grove. Jesus stopped at the far end and turned to face the others while they all fanned out in front of him. "You will all fall away," he told them.

Simon looked over at Thaddeus, who was himself looking around at the others. Before he could collect his thoughts, Peter's voice cut in, "I will not!" The forceful tone jolted Simon.

"Peter," Jesus responded with his customary calm. "This very night, before the rooster crows, you will deny me three times!"

Peter's volume rose. "I will never disown you! Even if I have to die with you!"

Others added their own voices to the call. "We are willing to follow you anywhere."

"To prison."

"To death."

"We are with you!"

Simon took a deep breath and called, "I am ready to die for you!" His hand reached to his waist and groped for a hilt that was not there.

When the grove was quiet again, Jesus said, "Sit here while I pray." He motioned for Peter, James, and John to join him, and the four followed a path deeper into the garden.

Simon sat and rested his back against a tree. The burden on his mind was outweighed only by his eyelids.

Chapter Twenty-Eight

"Are you still sleeping?"

Matthew opened his eyes and looked in the direction of the voice. The sky was dark, with no sign of the sun rising anytime soon. Matthew's eyes adjusted to the dim light of the group's lanterns, and Jesus said, "The time has come! Get up! Here comes my betrayer."

Heavy footfalls approached. They were muffled and distant. It was impossible to tell how many approached. Matthew untangled his cloak from his legs and staggered to his feet. He looked around; his companions were as disoriented as he was.

Light emerged from the path, and the footsteps grew louder. Matthew put up a hand to shield his eyes. His sight adjusted to reveal Judas flanked by two of the chief priests' personal guards. Dozens more followed, carrying lanterns and clubs, with swords slung at their hips.

Matthew staggered toward Judas. "What have you done? You know that—"

The lead guard grabbed him and hauled him to the side before he could complete his thought.

"He's not the one," Judas said. The guard let Matthew go, and he stumbled back and fell to the ground.

Judas approached Jesus, who stood between John and Peter. Judas clasped Jesus' shoulders, said, "Rabbi!" then kissed his cheek.

As Matthew returned to his feet, the two guards moved toward Jesus. Peter drew his sword and sliced toward the man nearest him, the same guard who had pulled Matthew aside.

The guard brought a hand to the side of his head and screamed.

"Enough of this." Jesus reached and touched the servant's head, where blood flowed between the fingers that pressed tight against it. Two guards hauled Jesus to his feet and pulled him away from the first guard.

The man withdrew his hand. There was no blood and no wound. The guard quieted his scream and looked, shocked, at his own hand.

Twenty-Eight

To the men who held him, Jesus asked, "Am I leading a rebellion that you would arrest me with swords and clubs? Every day I was with you in the temple courts teaching, and you did not arrest me."

The guards did not answer Jesus. They bound his hands and turned to lead him back to the city.

The other guards stood watching at the trailhead. As the arresting guards passed them, one said, "Seize the others."

The men, wielding clubs, filed into the clearing and spread toward the disciples. Matthew retreated into the trees and stumbled over roots, orienting himself as best as he could by slices of lantern light weaving between the trees. Footsteps and snapping branches echoed from every direction. He carefully stepped between trees toward the gardeners' village. The lead guards were already taking Jesus down the path, and some other guards followed, seemingly giving up their pursuit after the disciples.

Matthew spotted a figure carrying a lantern and wearing only a linen nightshirt.

That's definitely not one of the soldiers.

Matthew stepped closer until he recognized him.

John Mark.

"We have the one we came for!" a voice bellowed from the path. "Let's return. Time is short."

The guards scattered about the clearing and found their way back to the path and filed out.

Matthew followed as direct a route as the roots would allow him toward the path. He watched in silence as John Mark stepped beyond the buildings and walked toward the first grove. Two guards emerged from the trees on the far side of the path just in front of him and lunged for the young man. One grabbed hold of his garment at the shoulder, and John Mark jerked back and lost his footing. His head disappeared into his shirt, and after a brief moment, the guard stood upright, regarding the empty tunic in his hand with bewilderment.

Matthew turned and briefly spotted a naked form retreating behind the buildings.

The guards left. Matthew waited until they were out of sight before stepping onto the path and making his own descent.

Thomas, Simon, and Nathaniel emerged from the trees nearby. When they reached the village, Matthew turned past the stable and toward the building where he had met John Mark just days ago. The others followed.

Matthew pushed on the door and found it barred. "It's Matthew," he called through the door. "The threat is gone."

From inside came muffled footsteps and a low scrape. The door opened, and lamplight revealed John Mark, standing in his coat.

"How many of you were seized?" he asked.

"Only Jesus, I think," Matthew answered. "But we're not all accounted for. May we shelter here?"

"Some of the servants' quarters are empty. Most of them are back at the house for the feast."

"Thank you. We'll wait here and watch for the others."

"I should return to my house," John Mark said. "My family doesn't know that I'm gone."

"You followed us out?"

John Mark nodded.

"Why?" Matthew asked.

Before John Mark could answer, Philip, James, and Thaddeus came through the door.

"I had to know," John Mark said.

"Know what?"

"What would happen if I really followed Jesus."

"You chose an interesting time to make that decision," Matthew said as he shook his head and looked down. "Let's wait here for the others to find us. We'll return to your family's home before sunrise."

Chapter Twenty-Nine

"Are you in there?"

Shouts and thumping roused Simon abruptly from his sleep. His eyes burned as he opened them and took in his surroundings. *Where am I?* A faint predawn light slipped through the shutters. Simon surveyed the room; his companions were also stirring from their sleep.

With a heavy head and heavier eyelids, he returned to his rest.

Another thump — louder than the first. "Andrew! Are you in there? Philip? Thomas? Anyone?"

Simon's head jerked upright, and he forced his eyes open despite the sting. He blinked tightly and glanced around in a futile attempt to orient himself.

A soft column of light entered the room. Simon turned toward it. Andrew stood at an open door with Peter and John on the other side. Simon took advantage of the new light to survey his surroundings. The table, the cups.

This is where we ate the Passover feast the night before.

"They've handed him over," Peter said as he stumbled into the room.

"Who? How?" Philip asked as he stood up.

"The Sanhedrin. They've taken him to the palace to make charges before Pilate!"

"Pilate? Shouldn't they have tried him under our law?" Nathaniel asked.

"They did! At least, they made a *show* of trying him."

Did I sleep all day?

Simon looked out the door to see the sun rising in the east. "There was no time for a trial," he added. A new thought crossed his mind. "What about Nicodemus? Couldn't he stop them?"

"He wasn't there. And neither was Joseph," Peter responded.

The eleven remaining disciples regarded one another in silence for a moment. Thaddeus was first to speak. "So it was never really about the law ..."

Others nodded.

"What do we do?" Thomas threw his arms out wide.

"There's still a chance," Peter said. "Pilate is examining him now. Maybe if we go to the palace—"

"The palace?" Simon rose to his feet. "Pilate crucifies so many Jews that he doesn't even care if he records their names correctly! Do you really think he'd give Jesus a fair trial?"

"We have to try," Peter said with a cracking voice.

"What about the chief priests?" Simon pressed. "They'll have us rounded up, too."

"I'm not accustomed to seeing you back down from a fight," Thaddeus said.

"A fight? This is walking into a trap!"

"It's a walk we all promised just last night that we would take," Matthew said. "I've done a lot of dishonest things. But today, I need to keep my word."

"Yes, please," Peter implored. "I've already failed him once today. I can't do it again."

Noises rose from the street below. They stepped out the door and looked down. People poured from their homes and walked toward the palace while a crier walked down side streets.

They put on their cloaks and sandals and descended the stairs. They filed into the street and mixed with the swarm. Despite the exhaustion—a feeling Simon was sure they all experienced—they walked briskly and passed dozens of others. The palace loomed ahead. A crowd was already gathered at the far end, where Pilate stood above them on the parapet and addressed the crowd.

Simon couldn't hear what Pilate was saying and forced his legs to carry him faster. When they reached the already gathered crowd, heavy with priests and Pharisees, he spotted Jesus standing before Pilate.

Jesus' face was bruised, and a crown of thorns was set tightly around his head. Blood ran into his hair and face and stained the already deep purple robe that someone had draped over his shoulders.

What have they done to him?

Pilate addressed the crowd, "I've examined this man who you say incited a rebellion, and I have found no basis for your charges. Neither has Herod, so he has sent him back to me. He shall be punished and released."

"Crucify him!" The shout came from a cluster of chief priests. People continued to fill the streets.

"What about your custom?" someone shouted. Simon could not tell where the call came from. "It is the feast. Release the prisoner to us!"

Pilate set his jaw and inhaled deeply. "Very well, I shall release the one who you are requesting—"

"Release Bar-Abbas!" Simon recognized the voice. It was the same Pharisee who had approached Matthew days before.

"Release Bar-Abbas!" More calls went up, first from the chief priests, then spreading through the crowd.

Simon shouted for Jesus, but he couldn't even hear himself over the chant of the crowd.

Pilate turned and spoke to an official, who then disappeared into the tower. After a few minutes, he returned with a soldier leading a bound Bar-Abbas out to stand beside Jesus.

No bruises. No blood.

Why did they single Jesus out for such harsh treatment?

Pilate signaled for the crowd to quiet. The noise settled, and Pilate continued, "Do you want me to release the King of the Jews to you? This Jesus, who you call the Christ?" He paused. "Or do you want me to release Jeshua, who is called Bar-Abbas?"

"Release Jesus!" Simon called with all his strength. He screamed over and over until his voice was hoarse and he coughed dust.

Again, the chant rose around him. "Give us Bar-Abbas! Give us Bar-Abbas!"

Simon's stomach knotted with the realization that Bar-Abbas would get his restitution.

And at the hands of Rome, no less.

Simon's knees buckled, and he collapsed to the ground. Tears welled up in his eyes, and he struggled to draw air into his tightened chest. He felt one arm around his waist and another under his shoulder. After a moment, he was standing on shaky legs, supported by Thaddeus and James.

Simon looked up. Jesus, Pilate, and Bar-Abbas were already gone. The people had begun to disperse. His friends turned and led him back to the house.

———

"What do we do now?" Panic laced Peter's voice.

Jesus was condemned, and the one who betrayed him had disappeared. The remaining disciples sat sullen and still, with gazes fixed on the floor of the spacious room. Only Peter was on his feet, pacing.

The power of the previous evening—Jesus' words as he washed their feet and shared their meal—seemed a distant memory to Matthew.

Fear flooded his mind. They were old fears, the kind that he knew before he met Jesus, but didn't know that he knew. The kind that were always there, informing every decision.

The fears that Jesus helped him to see.

And to overcome.

Only now, he was painfully aware of every fear.

He thought back to Samchai and the others in Capernaum.

They carry on without a care—or even knowledge—about what is happening here.

He could never return to that life, not after what Samchai had done.

But how can I remain here now?

His mind searched for a strand of peace to cling to. He thought of the miracles.

Blind Bartimaeus.

Zacchaeus.

John Mark.

Lazarus.

Lazarus!

"We have to do something!" Peter's voice cut the silence in the room.

Matthew straightened. "We have to go and tell Martha, Mary, and Lazarus," he said.

"The priests wanted Lazarus killed, too. Do you suppose he was also captured?" Philip asked.

Peter stopped pacing and turned to him. "We can't be sure. But what I saw at the high priest's house suggests that they were focused on Jesus at the moment."

"Then there's still time," Philip added as he stood.

Matthew caught a glimpse of Simon as he stood. *I've never seen him looking so weak and defeated.*

They descended the stairs and followed the streets through the lower city and out the south gate. The people seemed to have returned to their daily routines.

They passed the same crosses they had encountered all week. What few bodies hung on them were still and lifeless, most well pilfered by scavengers.

Simon fixed his eyes on one in particular, a corpse that was little more than bones. He heaved and began sobbing.

Matthew and Thaddeus moved to either side of him.

"It wasn't supposed to be like this," Simon said as he gestured toward the corpse. "Manaen earned this. And I would have, too, if I kept following him. Jesus never raised a sword, and this will be his fate, too?" Simon's face contorted as he pushed the words out through gritted teeth.

Matthew choked with compassion as he grappled for words — any words — to console his friend.

Simon inhaled and continued, "How could I think that he would be crowned king without fighting for the throne?"

"We have all had to think in new ways," Matthew said, unsure if he believed it himself. "My old life is gone for good. Samchai made sure of that." Matthew turned and looked back at Manaen's body. "And it looks like you can't go back, either."

"But Bar-Abbas goes *free*?" Simon's voice rose as he spoke.

"Doubtful for long," Thaddeus answered.

They walked in silence a moment longer, then Simon said, "He kept saying he would die. And we all followed him anyway. But now … it's happening, and we can't do anything to stop it."

"He *refused* to let us stop him," Matthew offered with as much consolation as he could muster.

"Didn't he also say he would rise?" Thaddeus asked.

"You mean in the great resurrection?" Simon countered.

Several dozen people approached them on the road ahead. Leading the way were two familiar faces, framed in the blue mantles of the Pharisees. "No," Matthew answered as he pointed down the road, "like Lazarus."

Peter broke into a run toward them. Matthew stopped and waited. The others stood with him. John Mark came up from behind him and stood with them. *How long has he been following us?*

Nicodemus and Joseph led the crowd closer. Behind them were Martha and Mary, Lazarus and Bartimaeus. The women's faces were streaked with dirt and tears. All eyes were red.

Peter walked alongside Nicodemus as they met up.

"When we learned what was happening, we went looking for you," Nicodemus said. "But Martha told us that you never returned."

"We feared that you had been taken as well," Joseph added.

"We came close," Matthew said. "But we found shelter nearby." He looked over at John Mark and offered a strained smile.

"What did you see?" Simon asked Nicodemus.

"We had gone to begin our day, and when we arrived at the house of the high priest, they were already taking Jesus to the palace."

"A trial at night?" Nathaniel asked. "How is that lawful?"

"It isn't," Nicodemus responded, "and neither is excluding us. They know that we're sympathetic to Jesus. They have no interest in fairness nor legality, only their own standing."

"Just like Rome," Simon said.

"Well, we can't stay here," Peter said. "We should go back."

"And do what?" Simon asked.

"Trust," Matthew responded, not fully realizing what he had said.

They turned back toward Jerusalem, and the sun climbed higher in the morning sky. As it neared its peak, they passed the crosses leading to the south gate. They entered the city and turned toward the upper tier, away from the commerce that lined the main avenue toward the temple.

They passed the house of John Mark's family and returned to the palace. The crowd was gone, but soldiers remained on the parapets and palace walls, watching dutifully over the streets below.

They passed the palace and proceeded out the western gate toward the valley beyond. Hundreds of crosses dotted the hillside and lined the road leading out of the city as far as they could see.

Matthew sickened at the sight. "So this is the price of power," he whispered.

"A price the powerful never seem to pay themselves," Simon added.

Matthew startled. *Did I say that out loud?* He caught sight of activity on the slopes leading up toward the city wall. The hill was littered with bones that snapped under booted feet as Roman soldiers wove in and out among the crosses. Above them hung three men who labored against their restraints as they pushed against outstretched arms with each breath.

Two of them, Matthew did not recognize. They were not from among Jesus' followers.

The third could hardly be recognized as a man at all, much less identified. Still Matthew knew, more from the events of the morning than by the sight before him, that this had to be Jesus. He had been bloodied from head to toe, but Matthew could still discern where clumps of hair had been ripped from his face, and chunks of flesh torn from his abdomen.

He doesn't deserve this.

Peter, John, and several of the women had already descended to the valley and begun ascending the other side, where Jesus hung. Matthew looked toward Simon, who stood motionless with clenched fists and a firm jaw.

Matthew turned to Nicodemus, who hung his head and whispered. He turned toward John Mark, who had been secretly following them all week.

The boy quivered, eyes wide with horror. Matthew stepped toward him and clasped his shoulders. "Following Jesus cost me everything," he told the boy. "I've had my doubts along the way. I don't know what happens next, but I know I can never go back to where he found me. I would never want to."

The boy met his eyes and nodded in silence.

The sun reached its midday peak and a shadow moved across the brightness. Matthew looked up and saw no clouds, only a sky that grew dimmer and dimmer until it was completely dark. A hand gripped his sleeve—he assumed it was John Mark—as he looked to his left and his right. The darkness was so deep that he could not see even those nearest him.

"Light a lantern," somebody called.

"Nobody carries a lantern in the daytime."

The murmurs continued. As long as they did, Matthew knew that he wasn't alone. So he decided to stand still.

Perfectly still.

And wait ...

———

Simon turned and looked in every direction. Not a glimmer of light could be seen anywhere. No sun, no lantern, no fire.

He wondered how far the darkness spread.

All of Jerusalem?

Judea?

The whole empire?

He thought of the cross where Jesus hung — *the one that Bar-Abbas evaded.* He wondered how far Bar-Abbas could have gone before the darkness caught up to him, too. Perhaps the darkness would cause him to lose his way in the wilderness and be eaten by wild animals long before reaching Galilee.

Repay evil with kindness.

The last words that Jesus spoke to Simon pounded his brain from the inside.

Bar-Abbas tried to have him killed. Yet, the Zealot instigator ran free while Jesus hung on the cross that should have been his. Jeshua Bar-Abbas deserved whatever fate the darkness thrust upon him.

Repay evil with kindness.

They had once been brothers-in-arms against a common enemy — Rome — whose brutal oppression was felt by all of Judea. Rome's sadistic cruelty even now stretched Jesus with a torturous death.

Jesus, who knew only love, compassion, and kindness.

Bar-Abbas or Rome.

Evil for evil.

That had always been his way, too. *I earned this darkness.*

They all had.

All but one. All except the embodiment of kindness, who even now paid for Rome's power and the Zealots' vengeance.

Repay evil with kindness.

Simon sat, buried his head in his hands, and began to sob.

The murmurs and the gasps finally quieted. Matthew wasn't sure how long he had been standing in the darkness. His knees grew stiff, and he shifted his weight, which only reminded him where he was hurting.

Perhaps the darkness is some kind of divine mercy.

He couldn't see the one who he had given everything to follow hanging in shame, brutalized and humiliated.

He couldn't watch his friend die.

Nothing got through this darkness. If the sun was still there, Matthew could neither see nor feel it. The opulence of the palace was now hidden. The temple — with its blindingly bright gilded walls — had no light to reflect.

Blindingly bright.

Matthew thought back to his home outside Capernaum. His lamp always had oil. His table always had food. His storeroom was never bare.

I had all I ever needed.

Until it was all taken from him by one whose home was even more grand, whose servants were more numerous, whose storeroom of gold shone even brighter.

Blindingly bright.

For years, Matthew had been blinded by the bright things of the world. When they started to slip from his grasp, he gripped them tighter, but it wasn't enough.

And now, in the darkness, he finally saw clearly.

Treasures in heaven. Where moth and rust cannot destroy.

He had lost everything. But in doing so, he had gained everything.

How many others fumbled in this darkness, scared and lost, hoping to hold on to anything that would help them find their way?

He thought of young John Mark, who reflected the blind fear that Matthew once knew. *Are his eyes as open now as my own?* He hoped so.

Still, the world was blinded by greed and power. Rome's insatiable desire to conquer. The Sanhedrin's tightening grip on their control. *All to possess and cling to whatever they have in this life.*

They squeezed so tight that—even now—their pride, envy, and greed squeezed the very life out of the one who never took, but gave freely.

Because they are blind to who he is.

Matthew opened his eyes wide and took in the blackness before him. He knew that for the first time he was seeing clearly.

He saw nothing.

He needed nothing.

Nothing can ever again be taken from me.

Matthew sat on the ground and laid back, looking up at nothing.

———

"My God, my God, why have you forsaken me."

The cry was faint but unmistakable as it reached Matthew's ears.

Even more unmistakable was the bright sun—suddenly visible in the sky above. Matthew turned and threw his arm over his eyes. He knocked into someone as he scrambled to his feet. The murmurs and thumps around him assured him that his companions were having similar difficulty.

He had barely picked himself up on one knee, the ground a blur to his still-adjusting eyes, when he heard the voice again—a little louder this time.

"Father, into your hands I commit my spirit."

The voice of Jesus.

The ground shook, and cracks louder than thunder rang in Matthew's ears as he toppled to the ground face first.

After a moment, the shaking stopped, and Matthew righted himself. He looked around and was relieved to see familiar faces:

Simon, Thaddeus, Lazarus, Martha. Even John Mark was still with them.

Across the valley, Jesus' head slumped over his shoulders as he hung—unmoving—on the cross. The men who had been crucified with Jesus still pushed up weakly and gasped for air.

A centurion at the base of the crosses nodded to his men, and they picked up hammers and approached the crosses.

Two swung their hammers into the legs of the men who still gasped for breath. Even from across the valley, the crush of bones assaulted Matthew's ears. The men's screams were cut short as their bodies drooped.

Peter and John stood near the crosses. The women with them shielded their faces and turned toward them as a soldier lifted his hammer in front of Jesus. He stopped and gazed up at Jesus for what seemed a long moment, then he dropped his hammer and retrieved a spear. He thrust the tip into Jesus' side and turned away as blood poured out over him.

"Is there no end to their brutality?" Simon asked.

Matthew looked over. His friend's tear-stained face was fixated on the scene before them both.

"He deserved a more noble end than this," Matthew said as he looked back across the valley at Jesus' lifeless body.

"I will go to Pilate," Joseph said to them. "We can at least lay him to proper rest in my family's tomb."

Matthew nodded in silence, still unable to look away while Joseph and Nicodemus left toward the gate and the palace.

Chapter Thirty

"What happens when the feast is over?" Peter posed the question to the thirty or so gathered.

The feast and its rituals were far from Matthew's mind. Just a few days ago, he sat in this very room—at this same table—breaking bread with Jesus.

And now, Jesus had been taken from them.

This feast was little more than an excuse not to think about what came next.

"I have nothing to return to back in Galilee," he answered. "When I came here, I simply followed and trusted that Jesus would tell us where we were going. Now, I don't know."

"My family could hire you as an administrator," John Mark said directly to Matthew, who was seated beside him. "We've expanded our growing operation and could use the help."

"That is a kind offer. I'll discuss it with your elders."

"All we've ever known is fishing on the Galilee. We could still go back to that," James answered.

"If we don't get captured on the way," Nathaniel countered. "The priests will probably still be looking for us. We already know that they've issued an arrest order for Lazarus. They won't be convinced that Jesus has been silenced until we are *all* silenced!"

"I should return to my family and our estate," Lazarus said.

"So I suppose some of us are returning to Galilee?" James pressed the group.

"Pilate might have no jurisdiction in Galilee, but the Sanhedrin has influence in the synagogues even that far north," Nathaniel continued.

"That's assuming we can even make the trip without getting caught," Andrew added. "We should travel at night."

"No," Simon spoke up but kept his head down, staring at the floor. "Bar-Abbas is out there, no doubt traveling at night himself to avoid the Romans. He knows his release was never meant to be permanent. And you might recall, he tried to kill us before. Given the opportunity, I'm sure he'll try again."

Most heads in the room nodded in silence. Matthew had no intention to return to Galilee—ever, but he appreciated the young strategist's thoughtful assessment.

Simon added, "The safest travel will be when the festival breaks. We leave with everyone else and hide among the crowds and caravans."

"So we hide here until the week passes?"

"You're welcome to stay," John Mark insisted.

A rattling door, followed by rapping on the window shutters, interrupted the conversation. Several of the younger men jumped to their feet while Matthew merely jumped where he sat.

Simon had already drawn his sword and stood near the door. Other young men took up similar positions at the windows. A household servant moved toward the door. The rattling continued.

A muffled sound—indistinguishable to Matthew's ears—came from the door. *Probably not soldiers. They would announce their presence more loudly.* Still, he remained motionless as he watched.

The servant lifted the bar and opened the door slightly, then calmly opened it the rest of the way. The women who had left at daylight to anoint Jesus' body spilled into the room, stumbling and out of breath. Matthew chuckled at their uncharacteristically haphazard demeanor.

A Magdalene woman named Mary, who had followed Jesus since their time in Galilee, was first through the door. "I have seen the Lord," she said between labored breaths. The other women entered, and the servant swiftly closed and barred the door behind them.

"You went to his tomb. Of course you saw him."

"No! I saw *him*. Alive. His grave clothes were there, but his body wasn't. I was scared, and I cried because I thought they had stolen him." Mary gasped loudly and broke into a sob. Through gasps and wails she added, "I was scared, but then he was there, and I didn't know it was him, and he said my name and then I knew."

Mary let out another sob, inhaled deeply, and continued, "He said that he's returning to his Father and that he's going to Galilee and that he will see you there and that I should go and tell you."

Matthew looked at Lazarus and watched him breathe.

And dared to hope.

"This is all hard to understand," Thomas said. "It's too much to believe."

Peter stood. "We've all seen things that are hard to believe, haven't we?"

Matthew couldn't turn his gaze away from Lazarus, who himself wore a look of deep introspection.

"There is only one more thing to do, and that is to see this miracle for ourselves." Peter lifted the bar from the door and was through it before Matthew realized what he had said.

A young maid helped Mary, who was still drawing deep breaths, to a seat. Simon looked out the door for a moment, then pulled his head in and shut the door. As he reached for the bar, Andrew added, "A few more of us should go. It is not good for Peter to go out there alone." He stood, and about a dozen others stood with him.

"I agree," added Thomas as he rose. "We should see this for ourselves." He followed Andrew and the others through the door.

———

It had been hours since the women returned and the others left. There had been no further talk about returning to Galilee. Simon didn't want to think about going back, but he couldn't avoid it.

What would he do if Bar-Abbas knew he returned and came after him? *Could I even raise a dagger in my own defense after all that has happened in these past weeks?*

His best hope would be the swift recapture of Bar-Abbas. But that just meant the man would be subject to the horrors of Rome's cross.

Is that a just wish?

There was certainly no justice when the Romans hung Jesus up to die.

Just as quickly, his thoughts returned to Jesus, to the brutal torture he had suffered and the images seared into Simon's mind. Jesus, whose condemnation—strangely—set Bar-Abbas free.

Did he mean to?

Jesus had done nothing to stop any of this.

Why?

He had spoken so often of dying, and that's exactly what he did. *Could all his talk about resurrection have been just as real?*

Peter, Mary, and the others seemed to think so. There was no point in planning a trip back to Galilee until they returned with their report from the tomb.

Simon wasn't sure how many times his thoughts had gone around this singular loop, especially because sleep had been so elusive the past few days.

A rap at the door brought his attention back to the moment. "It's Peter," the voice on the other side called.

Simon recognized Peter's voice. He stood and removed the bar from the door.

Peter came in. "It's true. What Mary said is true. The linens are there, but the body is not. I went out and wandered. I'm not even entirely sure where, but the Lord found me."

"Did anyone else see him?" Nathaniel asked.

"I don't know. I was alone at the time. I saw some of our number. I told them what I saw. But I had to hide and go around the walls on the way back here. The guards had put out alerts, and I didn't want to pass by the palace."

Simon nodded his appreciation at the strategic decision. He wanted to ask questions, but another rap at the door redirected his attention away from Peter. He opened the door cautiously and saw Cleopas and Ananias, two of the men who had left with Andrew.

"Where are the others?" Simon asked, sensing a heightened risk that they might have been captured.

"We split into groups after we got to the tomb and couldn't find Peter," Cleopas answered.

"You did find me," Peter answered.

"Later, yes. Then we fled on the northern road when we saw that guards blocked our route back here. We were almost to Emmaus when we met a man who revealed himself to be Jesus!"

"What do you mean he *revealed* himself?" Thaddeus voiced what Simon was thinking. "We all know Jesus!"

"It's hard to explain. He walked and talked with us, but it was like we couldn't *see* that he was Jesus — until he broke bread with us. Then we saw."

Simon's mind went back to the Passover meal a few nights before.

To the miracle loaves on the shores of Galilee.

The bread of life.

"So where did he go?" Nathaniel asked. "And where are the others?"

"We don't know. After we saw him, he was just gone."

"Well, this doesn't make it any easier for us to plan for what comes next," Simon said as this new information clashed with the thoughts already swarming in his head.

"Peace be with you." The words came from behind Simon. He drew his sword, turned to the voice, and saw Jesus standing there. His sword fell to the floor, clattering loudly in the silence.

Simon reached to the door and felt the bar — in place as it should be — without taking his eyes off Jesus.

"How long have you been here?" Simon asked.

———

Matthew froze where he sat. He wanted to crash through the door, but he was unable to move. It was like that night on the boat in Galilee with nowhere to go. Only this time, the waves were stirring inside of him.

"Why are you troubled with doubt?" the phantom spoke.

Matthew couldn't explain it any other way. He didn't come through the door or even rise from a seat in the corner.

What cruel spirit could be toying with our minds?

"Look at my hands and feet. Touch me and see. What phantom has flesh and bones?" He looked around the room before taking a step toward Matthew. Nobody else moved, and Matthew wondered why he had been singled out.

Matthew shivered, and tears welled in his eyes. Fear had gripped him that night in the boat, but the phantom who walked on the water turned out to be no ghost at all.

Is it possible?

A smile began to form on his face, even as he still shook. Other faces in the room showed similar conflicting thoughts.

Matthew didn't know what to believe.

I want to believe. Help me in my unbelief.

"Do you have anything to eat?" The figure standing among them asked. John Mark turned toward a servant, who retrieved a tray of broiled fish and brought it forward. The man took a piece and ate it. Relief flooded Matthew's mind.

Before Matthew realized what he was doing, he jumped to his feet and embraced Jesus. He let go, and Peter threw his arms around Jesus next. Then most of the people in the room were on their feet. Simon had even stepped away from his post at the door to be near Jesus.

"This is what I told you," Jesus said. "Everything that was written about me had to be fulfilled for it says that the Christ will suffer and rise from the dead on the third day."

"Why did Mary tell us that you were going ahead to Galilee?" Andrew asked.

"Because I am," Jesus answered.

"I suppose we should all plan on going then," Simon said.

Matthew turned toward him as he spoke, then looked back to Jesus for further instruction.

He was gone.

Everyone looked to their left and right with big eyes that Matthew was sure matched his own.

"I can't go to Galilee," John Mark said as he wrinkled his brow.

"I now know that I *must* go," Matthew put a hand on the young man's shoulder. "But it's okay if you stay here."

"I agree," Andrew added. "Those of us who were there from the start in Galilee need to go back."

"We should still wait until after the festival when everyone else is traveling," Simon added.

A rap at the door startled Matthew. Simon stepped to the door and threw the bar without saying a word. Matthew braced for an intrusion, but only Thomas stepped through the door.

"I saw the empty tomb and the grave clothes," he said. "But I searched everywhere, and I could not find the body nor Peter."

"I've already returned," Peter said.

"And he's not the only one," Matthew added.

"What do you mean?"

Chapter Thirty-One

"We're leaving at first light." Peter addressed the room. "Let's make sure everything is ready."

"If we leave now, we can gain ground under cover of darkness and be ahead of any officials who are still looking for us," Nathaniel countered.

The same argument every day.

Simon stood and repeated the point that he made every time, "Jeshua Bar-Abbas will be traveling by night, and he might even be days ahead of us. We will be vulnerable if we run into him. Our best chance at traveling safely is to go when the masses go and hide among the crowds.

"The officials in Jerusalem will be focused on the city. If there are no more incidents before we leave, we can expect to get out without being stopped. After last week's events, they will probably be relieved to see all the pilgrims leave — especially Galileans."

"What do you suggest we do if we encounter trouble? If you draw your sword, you're going to get us all cut down." Nathaniel pressed the issue with Simon.

"That's why we're going at a time when we are least likely to encounter trouble," Simon answered.

"Besides, Jesus is going ahead of us to Galilee. The Lord will see us there safely," Peter added.

"You keep saying that, but I am still not convinced," added Thomas.

"Peace be with you!"

Simon's heart skipped a beat at the interruption. Just as before, Jesus stood before them in the center of the room. Simon confirmed the door was still barred, then turned back to Jesus.

Jesus walked over to Thomas, who wore a frightened look and shook visibly. He held out his hand. "Put your finger here." There was no harshness in his tone, only compassion.

Thomas sat unmoving, his expression unchanging.

"Reach out your hand," Jesus continued. "Put it into my side. Stop doubting and believe."

Thomas took hold of Jesus' hand, then collapsed to his knees in front of him. "My Lord and my God," he said from his face-down position on the floor.

Jesus lifted him up. "Because you've seen me, you believe. Blessed are those who have not seen and yet have believed."

Simon scanned the room. The whole gathering looked as taken aback as he felt. He double-checked the door. *Still barred.* He turned back to Thomas.

Thomas stood alone.

Every head in the room looked left and right. Simon checked the door a third time.

Still barred.

"I thought he was going ahead to Galilee," Nathaniel said.

"I'm sure he'll be far ahead of us by the time we leave at sunrise," Simon answered and sat down with his back against the door.

Chapter Thirty-Two

"So what do you think? Are you ready to take up fishing?" Peter asked.

"I don't know. It might be more appealing if we actually caught something," Simon answered.

It was only their first night back in Galilee, but the fishermen had been eager to get out on the water. Simon joined them in the boat because of a need—a compulsion—to stay together. He was grateful that Thaddeus had reached the same conclusion.

"Some nights are like this, but usually we get better results."

"Still, are we really supposed to just come back to what we were doing before?" Nathaniel asked. "Does it make sense, after all that has happened?"

"Maybe we just need to lay low until things quiet down," Simon answered.

If any of can ever really experience "quiet" again.

"I don't know," Thomas added. "The empty tomb is going to keep the Romans and the priests talking—and looking for us."

"The Romans have probably already silenced the guard who was at the tomb," Simon said, surprised as his own thoughts turned briefly to sorrow. The guard didn't *fail* to keep Jesus in the tomb, but he still paid the penalty—a penalty that he didn't earn.

Just like Jesus when they hung him on Rome's cross.

The first light of dawn glowed over the eastern mountains.

"I guess there is nothing more to do tonight," Peter said. "Let's bring the boat in."

Peter and Simon pulled up the net while James and John took hold of the oars. They turned the boat toward shore. With their first heave, a voice called from behind them, "Friends! Do you have any fish?"

Everyone in the boat turned to face the shore. A man, visible only in silhouette, stood on the shore in the dim morning light.

"No! Nothing," John and Peter called to him.

"Throw your net on the right side," the man shouted back. "Then you will find some."

Simon turned to Peter and waited silently for instructions. The brothers James and John had stopped rowing and watched him patiently, too.

"I guess it doesn't hurt to try," Peter said as he lifted one end of the net and gestured for Simon to grab the other. The pair tossed the net into the water. As they pulled its cords to spread it, the boat heaved. Simon reached back for something to hold on to. His hand came up empty, but he managed to stay in the boat when a strong pull on the net brought him to his knees. His abdomen caught the side of the boat, interrupting his breathing. Still, he gripped the net tight, not knowing what else to do.

Simon's breath returned, and he turned to Peter and asked, "Does it normally get this heavy when you throw it in the water?"

Peter grabbed the other end of the net while Thaddeus and Thomas took hold between them and pulled. The boat listed heavily toward their side.

"There's too much here. We can't haul the net in," Peter said as they all fought against its weight.

"It's the Lord!" John said. "What other explanation could there be?"

The net yanked at Simon's arms again, and he looked up in time to see Peter splash down into the water and begin swimming for shore.

"You two hold the net as best as you can," James said. "Nathaniel and Thaddeus, help us with the oars."

Simon held on with both hands as the boat lurched slowly across the surface. The net hit the sea floor, and the jolt sent Simon tumbling backward into the bottom of the boat. He climbed out and followed the others, wading toward the shore.

John was right.

Jesus sat on the shore, tending to some fish roasting over burning coals.

He went ahead to Galilee, just like Mary said he would.

As they reached the shore, Jesus said, "Bring some of the fish you've just caught."

Peter turned and waded back to the boat. "I'll need some help with this one," he said. Simon and Thaddeus followed.

"To answer your earlier question, no," Simon said. "I don't plan to take up fishing."

"That's too bad," Peter said as they reached the boat and he untied the net. "We're just getting started."

The three dragged the net to shore while John and James led the boat aground.

"This will take all morning to count," Peter said.

"You have 153 fish," Jesus responded with a visible grin. "Come and have breakfast."

Simon took the fish and bread that Jesus offered him, and he thought of the crowds on the mountainside and the baskets of leftovers.

So much has happened since then.

They wanted to make him king.

Rome crowned him with thorns.

How many of the thousands who ate the bread were there to see his "coronation"?

"What happens now?" Nathaniel asked.

"Get the other four," Jesus told them, "and go to the place where you first received your instructions."

They stood, and Nathaniel took a step toward the road. He motioned for Simon to join him. The fishermen tended to their catch. Thaddeus and Thomas were already on their way down the shore toward the mountain.

———

"Why didn't you go out to fish with the others?" Matthew asked.

"I'm not sure," Andrew answered. "Being back in Galilee, in the house that I have always known, no longer feels like home. And it makes me wonder what exactly I should be doing."

"I understand. I am *certain* this is no longer home. Samchai saw to it that I have nothing left here. It will be good to get back to Jerusalem and begin something new."

"So you don't want to try your hand at fishing?" Andrew asked with a raised brow and slight smile.

Matthew chuckled, "You've seen how well I do in a boat."

The door opened, and Nathaniel stepped in, followed by Simon. "Jesus is here. He wants us to meet him on the mountainside."

"How could he have gotten here so quickly?" James asked, seeming to still be waking from his sleep.

"Come now, brother," Matthew answered. "After all that we've seen, you wonder how he made the same journey that we made? It isn't difficult, even if you dismiss the signs."

"We should go," Simon said. "The rest are already on their way up the mountain."

They left and followed the familiar route around the outside of town, away from the shore. Matthew thought of the times they walked this path surrounded by crowds.

Desperate people.

Hopeful people.

Angry people.

He had been shunned, insulted, pushed, and threatened.

I understand them now.

Even after all Matthew had seen, he knew if he were given a chance to go back and make a different choice in his early life, he would have done so.

Then where would Jesus have found me?

His brother, James, walked in front of him in silence. As a young man, he had made very different choices than Matthew, rejecting wealth and comfort, cutting himself off from much of society on purpose.

Now, thanks to this miracle worker from Nazareth who somehow even defied death, they both walked among friends.

All of us are so different. Yet we each were found by Jesus.

They reached the place where Jesus first brought them together. Most of the others were already there, waiting. Matthew didn't feel worthy to be called then, and the feelings — with all their questions — flooded back.

Why would Jesus bring us back here, to this spot?

"Where is Jesus?" Nathaniel asked. "I thought he was with you."

"He sent us ahead while he's speaking with Peter," Thomas answered.

"Did he say what we are doing here?" Matthew asked.

"Does he ever?"

John came up the path from the shore and joined them in the clearing. Jesus and Peter followed a few minutes later.

Matthew wasn't sure if it was the setting, the presence of Jesus, or both together, but an irresistible compulsion drove him to his knees, face down on the ground.

"Get up. Gather around," said the familiar voice. Matthew pushed to his feet and realized that he was not alone in his reaction. Jesus was seated on a large boulder, just as he had been three years before when he turned their lives upside down.

"All authority on heaven and earth has been given to me. Go and make disciples of all nations, baptizing them in the name of the Father, the Son, and the Holy Spirit."

Matthew tried to make sense of Jesus' words. *Go to the nations? What does he mean by the "Holy Spirit"?*

"… I am with you always, to the very end of the age."

It took Matthew a moment to realize that Jesus had stopped talking. The collective silence of the group assured him that he was not alone in his confusion.

"What do you mean by baptizing in the name of the Holy Spirit?"

"Which nations are you sending us to? Not the pagans who hung you on a cross!"

"You'll receive more instruction when it is time. For now, return to Jerusalem, as we did the last time."

"Are you coming with us?" Matthew asked.

"I must do other things. But go ahead and bring the faithful together. Gather Bartimaeus, Lazarus, John Mark, and the rest."

Andrew looked to Matthew and said, "I suppose we don't need to figure out what to do next after all."

Matthew nodded, his heart hopeful with anticipation of a return to Jerusalem.

Anticipation of a new purpose.

Chapter Thirty-Three

Matthew was glad to be back in Jerusalem, in the very room where he had shared some of the most impactful moments with Jesus and his friends.

Finally, they were together again, eating as they had before. It still amazed Matthew that just weeks ago, the man now sitting across the table was hanging on a cross.

Now, he is enjoying a meal with us once more.

Matthew considered the empty seat where their friend Judas once sat. He allowed himself a moment of sadness over his friend's departure — and the betrayal behind it.

Still, even that memory could not rob him of the joy of the moment, in the company of Jesus, who was dead yet now lived.

Like Lazarus.

Like all of us.

Ever since Jesus healed his injury years ago at the tax booth, He had been infusing Matthew with life that he never realized he could know.

"I know you all have many questions, and I promise you'll receive answers in time," Jesus told them. "Don't leave Jerusalem. Wait in the city until you receive what my Father has promised. You'll be clothed with power from heaven."

"How will we know?" Nathaniel asked.

Matthew recalled his earliest encounters with Jesus — that day at the tax booth when he knew he was in the presence of indescribable power. The power had compelled him to walk away from the only life he had ever known.

Pressed to *describe* that power, Matthew would not be able to do so. Perhaps Jesus was preparing him — all of them — for another moment like that one.

Like Nathaniel, Matthew didn't know *how* he would know, but he trusted that somehow he *would* know.

Jesus was still speaking, "… in a few days, you will be baptized with the Holy Spirit."

Thirty-Three

No matter how many times Jesus mentioned the Holy Spirit, Matthew still didn't quite understand. He looked forward to making sense of it all.

"But for now, there is something else I need to show you."

They followed the mountain path to the olive grove that had seen its share of prayer and excitement. Matthew thought back to the last time they were here and was saddened again at the loss of Judas.

They passed the stable where they had borrowed the donkey.

"Is it now time for you to restore the kingdom of Israel?" Simon called to Jesus as they walked. Matthew turned and smiled knowingly at him.

Jesus shook his head as they continued past the stable and the servants' house, into the garden. "It's not for you to know the days and times my Father has set," He said without looking back.

The men entered the grove. Jesus turned to face them and said, "You will receive power when the Holy Spirit comes on you. And you will be my witnesses in Jerusalem.

"And in Judea.

"And Samaria.

"And to the ends of the earth."

Questions swirled in Matthew's mind. *Samaria? The ends of the earth?* His thoughts of settling into a simple administrator's life seemed impossibly far now.

He opened his mouth to ask, but no words came out. The air—even the light around Jesus—seemed to shimmer and move. Matthew reached out and set his hand on the nearest tree to keep from toppling over at the dizzying sight.

Jesus was somehow above them now, but not floating in the air. His presence was real, but ethereal. A gossamer aura surrounded him and brightened.

Matthew lifted his arm over his eyes. When he looked again at the air, the grove, the trees … everything was normal. His friends looked left and right, up and down. Jesus was gone.

Again.

"Do you think we'll see him again?" Matthew asked no one in particular as he examined the sky above.

"I don't think so," Andrew answered. "This time definitely seemed … different."

"Men of Galilee." Matthew was startled by the voice behind him. He turned. Simon had already taken up a place in front of the intruders. Peter stepped forward and placed a hand on the young man's shoulder, and his stance slowly relaxed.

The strangers — two of them — were dressed in plain white cloaks, as clean and dust-free as Matthew had ever seen.

What path could they have taken that wouldn't leave them at least a little dirty?

"Why do you stand here and look into the sky?" one asked. Without waiting for an answer, he continued, "This same Jesus who has been taken from you into heaven will come back in the same way you have seen him go."

The disciples exchanged glances with one another.

Peter said, "And he told us to stay in Jerusalem. Let's get back quickly."

Heads nodded in agreement, and they turned to leave.

The visitors were already gone.

Chapter Thirty-Four

Simon was glad to be back in the temple courts. The feast of Shavuot was underway, and the outer court filled with pilgrims from everywhere as they prepared to celebrate the harvest and the law.

He appreciated the cover that the immense crowd provided. The mood was a welcome contrast from the tumultuous events of Passover. Still, Simon remained wary and watchful as he observed his surroundings carefully. Despite the celebratory atmosphere, visions of all-too-recent events seared his memory.

Money changers.

Bar-Abbas and his insurrection.

Priests and their conspiracies.

The Roman patrols along the outer wall were more numerous than before, no doubt to deter a repeat of the events of that week.

If only these Romans could understand the true magnitude of that week.

Simon and his companions were gathered under Solomon's porch along the eastern wall of the temple courts, eager to avoid arousing new conflict.

"All these Romans," Simon said. "Do you suppose any of them are still looking for us?"

"Not likely," Nicodemus answered. "Jesus' empty tomb was a gross embarrassment to them—and to the Sanhedrin. Some of the elders even bribed the soldiers to claim that you all stole the body."

"The soldiers wouldn't promote that story. Rome executes soldiers for far less serious failures."

"Of course," Nicodemus added. "The bribes would have to flow to those who would give such orders as well."

Simon nodded, "The corruption runs deeper the higher it goes."

"But what do you do about it?"

"I'm done taking up the dagger of the Zealots," Simon answered. "Even Galilee showed signs of quieting. Of course, I doubt Bar-Abbas ever made it back. The Romans were never going to let his release be permanent."

"But if the sword is all you know ..." Nicodemus answered. To Simon's ear, it sounded more like a question.

"The sword *was* all I knew. Now I know healing. Justice. The coming kingdom. Rome's sword killed Jesus ... and even that didn't stop him. I don't know how it all works, but Jesus said to wait for power."

"Wait for what kind—"

Nicodemus was still speaking, but Simon could no longer hear him. The low whistle of a fierce wind—the kind that portends a storm in the Galilean caldera—filled the colonnade.

Simon lifted his hood over his head, only to realize the air was not moving. He dropped his hood and looked across the open court beyond the colonnade. The crowd searched for the source of the sound.

He looked for his companions and flashes of light distorted his vision. More than just the brightness of sunlight on a clear day, these flashes emanated from cracks in the very sky, surrounded by the same shimmer that took Jesus from them just days ago.

What did the man in white say?

The lights separated and spread out. They appeared as long tongues of flames that grasped for the heavens, but seemed unaffected by the movement of the air. They danced over the heads of the crowd until they rested, one by one. First above Peter, then James and John. Then Philip and Andrew. A spark split from the nearby light and raced toward Simon.

He ducked, perhaps unnecessarily. The light did not descend, but rather it stood above him. It was not supported by a wick, and it gave off no heat. Simon moved toward the others, and the light followed him, showing no danger of being snuffed out.

Without giving it any thought, he began to recite the *shema,* "Hear o Israel. God is our Lord, God is one ..." His friends did the same, and they had captured the attention of all who could hear them.

"How do these Galileans speak our language?" one onlooker asked a companion.

Simon had no answer.

"Clearly, they've had too much wine," another suggested.

Peter stepped to the teacher's seat and faced the crowd. "These men are not drunk, as you say! It is only midmorning! What you see here is what was promised by the prophet Joel. 'In the last days, God says, I will pour out my Spirit on all people.'"

Thirty-Four

Simon remembered Jesus' parting words.

You will receive power when the Holy Spirit comes on you.

This is the promised power of heaven.

The baptism of the Holy Spirit.

The otherworldly lights that danced over their heads were beautifully strange, but Matthew's attention was seized by the power of Peter's words.

There would be no more hiding. Not for Peter, as he proclaimed to those listening—thousands, by Matthew's estimation—that Jesus had been raised from the dead. Just as the Psalms foretold.

Across the entire outer court, the crowd moved as one toward where Peter stood. The same throng who just weeks before shouted, "crucify him!" now eagerly absorbed every word Peter said.

The Roman soldiers patrolling the porticoes from above watched, but they made no move.

Their cross did not stop Jesus.

And now everybody knows it.

What more could Rome do?

What more can I do?

He recalled what Jesus had told them.

Promised them.

They would be his witnesses. In Jerusalem. In Judea. In Samaria. To the ends of the earth.

Nothing could stop Jesus. Not even death.

And certainly not Matthew.

His plan to settle in Jerusalem, to return to a life of records, administration, and pushing coin around was not to be.

Where will I go?

He had no answers.

He only knew that just as Rome and the grave could not contain Jesus, neither could Jerusalem.

Neither can I.

"Brother, what must I do?"

"What?" Matthew turned to the voice that drew him from his own thoughts. An unfamiliar man with an accent that he didn't recognize clasped his shoulders and pleaded with him.

"Brother, tell me what must I do?"

A similar din rose across the crowd, and Peter's voice cut through. "Repent and be baptized. Every one of you."

"Yes," Matthew said to the man. "Do you want to be baptized?"

"I do. Yes. I believe."

Matthew crossed the court to the southern steps, with the man clasping his sleeve and following close behind.

Matthew led him down the steps and to the *mikvah*, the ceremonial pool. Simon and Thaddeus were already in the baths baptizing people, just as John had done in the Jordan River years ago.

Matthew tossed his cloak aside, took a place beside them, and helped his new companion into the pool. The man looked at him in eager silence.

"Do you repent of your sins?"

"I do!"

"Your sins are forgiven in the name of Jesus the Christ. I baptize you in the name of the Father, the Son, and the Holy Spirit." Matthew plunged the man backward into the water. The man did not resist. He fell into the water freely with a splash, and Matthew pulled him to his feet. "Go forth, believing and proclaiming Jesus of Nazareth, whom God raised from the dead."

Peter, John, and the rest joined them in the ritual baths, and lines of people flowed up the steps into the temple courts as far as Matthew could see.

As soon as one was baptized, another stepped in to take his place. All day, Matthew baptized dozens, then hundreds. If he was tired, he didn't feel it. Only when the sun fell behind the palace to the west and the shadows grew long did the line of people diminish. The disciples caught their collective breath and exchanged knowing glances.

"All these people will soon return to their homelands," Matthew said to the group. "To Egypt and Arabia and Syria and everywhere else. What happens then?"

"The message goes out with them," Nathaniel answered. "And perhaps so do we."

"Where would we all go?"

"For me," Simon said with the widest grin that Matthew had ever seen on his face, "Anywhere beyond the reach of Rome."

Matthew smiled and nodded.

Epilogue

Naddaver, Ethiopia, 47 AD

Zaroes stood in the center of the spacious royal bedchamber, whispering incantations over the still form of Euphranor, the crown prince. One cobra coiled around his shoulder and another around the neck and shoulder of Arfaxat, who sat nearby in a meditative trance.

For years, the two sorcerers had enjoyed their status as chief magicians to King Aeglippus. Now, Zaroes was consumed with worry. If they failed to bring the king's young son back to life, what would their fate be?

Since the first light of dawn hours ago, they worked their magic over the prince to no avail. The cobras were uncharacteristically calm. The crystalline likeness of Arwe, the ancient serpent-king, stood cold and silent between the sorcerers. No incantation, incense, or oil had produced even the faintest response from the idol.

If we fail, the king will have us exiled. Or worse.

Zaroes recalled the dazzling colors and whispered words that he had coaxed from the statue in the past. He had spent years perfecting his magic until he finally earned a place in service to the royal household.

Then, everything changed when a strange visitor from the north introduced foreign gods.

That's when the dragons went silent.

The king's breathing intensified, and Zaroes feared he was losing patience. He added incense to the censer at the base of the statue and began his incantation again.

"I have heard your refrain over enough to repeat it myself," King Aeglippus said with a terse tone that did not mask his growing discontent.

"Your majesty," Zaroes began, "with respect, I ask that you not disrupt Arfaxat's med—"

"There is nothing more to disrupt!" The king stepped forward as his volume rose. "You have tried every incantation you know. Either your gods are incapable of restoring my son's life, or you are incompetent to petition them!"

Arfaxat rose from his meditation, and the serpent around his neck gently tasted the air. He turned and addressed the king. "Your majesty, with respect. I see that your grief is heavy. But you must know that Prince Euphranor has been taken among the gods. They are his home now. Let us honor his passage by building an image and a temple, so that we may burn incense to him."

Queen Euphenissa let out a sob and buried her face in the king's chest.

Zaroes could not take his eyes off the king as fear of an outburst gripped him.

"Your majesty, with respect," said an attendant standing against the far wall, "forgive the interruption. With your permission, there is another in the land who may be able to raise your son. If you wish, I would summon him."

"Who is this man? And why would he succeed where my best sorcerers have failed?"

Zaroes stifled a shiver as a new chill ran through him.

"He is Matthew, a servant of the Judean Jehovah God. He proclaims the resurrection of Jesus of Nazareth, who he says is one with Jehovah. This Matthew witnessed the death of Jesus, yet saw him raised three days later."

"How did you learn of this Matthew of Judea?"

"I first met another Judean, Philip, who opened my eyes to the words of the prophet and the resurrection of Jesus of Nazareth. He baptized me into their way and was taken away miraculously. That's how I know his words were true."

"And what of Matthew?" the king prodded, as an advocate would examine a witness at trial.

"He arrived recently in our land. I have seen him heal the sick and injured—even from the poison of serpent bites."

"Serpent bites?" King Aeglippus directed his inquiry to Zaroes.

The sorcerer's stomach knotted. *He means the man who tamed my dragons.* "Your majesty, with respect. The Judean god is a god of darkness. Moses and his prophets were deceivers. Their own scriptures tell that they rejected the likeness of Arwe. This Jesus is a fraud, and this Matthew a deceived fool."

"So you say," the king responded, "yet I ascertain from the testimony here that your dragons have been powerless since his arrival." He turned to the attendant and added, "Go and summon this Matthew. Make haste."

Zaroes nodded to Arfaxat, and the pair returned their cobras to their cages.

"You two will remain here." King Aeglippus said. "If this Matthew is the charlatan that you claim, surely you will want to be witnesses to his debunking."

Zaroes was unable to hide his shaking. He stepped away from the prince's bedside and took a seat with Arfaxat.

After an hour that felt like an eternity, the attendant returned with the Judean. His hair was white, and deep lines rested under eyes that sparked with vigor in contrast to his otherwise obvious age.

"I present Matthew of Judea, servant of Jesus of Nazareth," the attendant said when they entered.

"Matthew of Judea," the king began, "my attendant claims that you have the power to perform miracles, cure the sick, and even raise the dead. My own trusted magicians have failed to raise my son." The king indicated the prince with a wave of his hand. "Why should you succeed where they have failed?"

"Your majesty, with respect," Matthew answered. "The prophet says,

"Those who make idols are nothing,
and their treasured things are worthless.
The ones who would speak for them are blinded;
they are mere fools, to their own shame.
Who crafts a god and casts an idol,
which can accomplish nothing?'

"And the Psalmist has more to say of these idols, declaring, *'They have mouths, but cannot speak, eyes, but cannot see.'*

"The one true living God has opened the king's eyes to His truth. He has shown you that a serpent made by human hands has no power at all, much less the power of life and death."

Zaroes welled with rage. Only fear of the king's retaliation gave him strength to resist an outburst.

Matthew continued, "To prove that what I say is true ..." Matthew stepped to the prince's side, took his hands, and bowed, "... Our Father in heaven, you alone are God. You hold the power of life and death. In the name of Jesus of Nazareth, whom You raised from the dead, breathe life into this boy again."

The room was silent. Zaroes held his breath and fixed his gaze on the prince. After a moment, the boy's eyes opened, and Zaroes felt a chill in every corner of his being. He glanced toward Arfaxat and saw fear wash over the younger magician's face.

The boy sat up. Queen Euphenissa raced to his side and threw her arms around him. Sudden weakness came over Zaroes, and he hunched over his serpent cages.

"Matthew of Judea, your god is the true God," the king said. "What must I do to worship Him?"

"Repent and believe in his chosen one, Jesus, the Christ whom He raised from the dead. Be baptized in the name of the Father, the Son, and the Holy Spirit, and be filled with the Spirit."

"I will do all you have said. When my son has regained his strength, we shall be baptized — the whole royal house. And from now forward, we will worship only Jehovah, and His Christ, Jesus of Nazareth."

Zaroes collapsed to the floor and shook with growing fear.

The king continued, "We shall rid the land of all idols and magic. They are powerless and deceitful. Take these sorcerers away to be executed."

"Wait!" Matthew interjected. Zaroes mustered the strength to look up at the Judean interloper as he spoke.

"These men need not die. In the name of Jesus, I bring a message of life." Matthew turned to face Zaroes. "You, too, can repent and be baptized."

Zaroes stood and looked toward Arfaxat, whose own expression revealed sadness mixed with anger.

"We reject your god, and you with him. We would rather die and unite with Arwe than live in your way." Zaroes closed his eyes and inhaled deeply, waiting for a sword to pierce him right there.

"Nevertheless," the king added, "Matthew is right. Today we worship the God who gives life. There will be no bloodshed. But you must leave our land by sundown and never return."

Zaroes and Arfaxat, without a word, without looking back at the king or at Matthew, collected their serpents and their statue and exited through doors the attendants had already opened for them.

Northern Persia, 50 AD

Zaroes stood across the table from General Varardach, commander of the Babylonian army. High-ranking military officers surrounded the table while Arfaxat stood beside Zaroes.

Together they regarded the map laid out on the table, with stones marking known positions of army units — Babylonian and Parthian.

"Go ahead, sorcerer," General Varardach said. "Petition your gods to reveal the outcome of our next engagement."

Zaroes set a flame to the incense that Arfaxat had already prepared and placed in the censer at the base of the crystal serpent. He spoke an incantation over the statue — just as he had dozens of times since joining the general's service.

He finished his incantation and waited. The statue stood as cold and silent as an ordinary chunk of rock. Zaroes turned to Arfaxat. The younger magician gave him a shrug, obvious concern playing across his face.

Zaroes fidgeted as the silence lingered.

Only one has ever silenced Arwe. Could it be ...?

The officers shifted on their feet and exchanged glances while the general's breathing grew deeper and louder. "Do your gods have no answer?" The general's piercing stare matched the displeasure in his tone.

"Sir," Zaroes began, "this is an anomaly for sure. Arwe must sense a threat that preoccupies — "

Arfaxat's eyes grew impossibly wide as he turned to Zaroes and shook his head.

"If your god is threatened," the general interrupted, "then perhaps we could petition whatever greater power causes him such fear!"

"Sir, I don't — "

"General!" A young sentry burst through the entry curtain. "Messengers have arrived in the camp. They come from the west."

"Our enemies are in the east. Who are these messengers?"

"They call themselves servants of Jesus the Christ. They say they bring news of salvation."

With a familiar knot in his stomach, Zaroes fought in vain to suppress his fear. General Varardach turned to him but said nothing.

Whatever question the general would have asked, my face must have answered.

Varardach nodded to the sentry, "Bring them in."

Two men entered, neither of whom Zaroes recognized. They were slimmer and younger than the Jesus-follower who cost him his homeland, but not by much. The lines on their faces and the gray streaks through their beards put these men just a little past their prime.

"I present General Varardach, commander of Babylon's armies," the sentry said.

"I am Simon of Cana, and this is Jude Thaddeus," the taller of the two visitors said. "We come in the name of Jesus of Nazareth, the Christ whom we serve."

"This Jesus," the general asked, "he is your king? I have never heard of Nazareth, nor of Jesus."

"Jesus is a king like no other," the one called Jude Thaddeus replied. "His kingdom is not of this world. He was sent by the living God, maker of heaven and earth, and He is one with God. He rules over all the earth from His heavenly throne, and it is by the power of His Holy Spirit that He has brought us to your presence."

"Sorcerer," the general addressed Zaroes. "Does your god know this Jesus? Is this the threat that makes your god cower in silence?"

"Sir, I have heard of this Jesus, but I do not presume that it is he who compels Arwe to silence." Zaroes hoped his lie was enough to stall the general.

"If I may, general," Simon interjected, "our scriptures answer your question. Our psalmist writes,

'Not to us, Lord
 but all glory to your name,
 because of your steadfast love.
Why do the nations ask,
 "Where is their God?"
Our God is in heaven;
 he does whatever he pleases.
But their idols of silver and gold,
 Are crafted by human hands.
They have mouths, but cannot speak,
 eyes, but cannot see.'

"Clearly, a mere object made by men is incapable of answering your question."

"But Arwe has spoken—many times!" Zaroes protested. "Sir, you have heard him yourself."

"To this," Simon answered, "our prophet reminds us that,
'Those who make idols are nothing,
and their treasured things are worthless.
Men who would speak for them are blind;
they are mere fools, to their own shame.'"

"So," the general addressed Simon, "what you servants of Jesus are saying is that my sorcerers and their serpent-god speak only ignorance?"

"It is not what we say, but what the One who sent us says."

"Very well. Then I shall pose my question, and *any* god who wishes to answer may do so. Our enemies gather their army in the east. Before we go on the offensive, I wish to know the outcome of a direct military engagement."

Arfaxat gestured silently to the statue. Zaroes spoke an incantation over the crystal figure.

And waited.

"It appears that your god remains silent," the general observed.

"Spirits tremble in the presence of Jesus, because all authority is His," Jude Thaddeus answered. "To show that what I say is true, in Jesus' name," he turned to the statue, "I command you to speak."

Smoldering incense sparked and cast a pale green glow, the color of illness and death, through the crystal serpent. A cavernous voice emanated from the statue. "You will face a long and hard-fought war. Many on both sides will suffer and die. Now set us free and let us leave the presence of these servants of the most high God."

A high-pitched shriek escaped the statue as it split lengthwise and fell in two pieces to the floor, then shattered into fragments.

Zaroes collapsed to his knees, scooped a handful of crystal shards, and squeezed them until his palms bled.

While Zaroes remained hunched over the ruined statue, Simon responded, "The idol has lied to you, general. Tomorrow at this very hour, your adversary will come to you seeking peace on your terms."

"You have given me conflicting reports," The general said. "No matter what I believe, if I believe wrongly the results will be costly. We will do nothing more today. I want all these men held tonight. Tomorrow, we will see who has spoken the truth. The fate of everyone will be decided then."

Strong hands lifted Zaroes from his prone—almost fetal—position and led him to a smaller tent where he was left with Arfaxat while guards stood outside the entrance.

"Where will we go if Arwe was wrong?" Arfaxat asked.

We won't live to decide.

"Arwe will not be wrong," Zaroes answered. "We'll sleep now and prepare to be vindicated tomorrow."

At first light, two guards entered the tent and led the sorcerers back to the command tent. General Varardach and his senior officials were already present. A man Zaroes didn't recognize—eastern, judging by his complexion and attire—was with them. After a moment, another pair of guards led Simon and Jude Thaddeus into the command tent.

"Now that everyone is present," the general began, "we have received an envoy this morning from our adversary, who has come to negotiate peace terms."

General Varardach turned to Simon and Jude Thaddeus. "Your god has revealed truth to you, and the king is prepared to reward you generously and appoint you as royal advisers in his court."

"We need no reward. We have all we need from the One who sent us. We only ask that you and your king give ear to all we have to say about Jesus the Christ and salvation in Him."

"Very well. You are free to go, and you may remain in our camp as our honored guests as long as you choose." The general turned to Zaroes and Arfaxat. "As for you. Your god spoke lies that would have brought immeasurable harm. You are hereby relieved of your duties and your lives. Take them away!"

Cold fear washed over Zaroes, and he trembled as guards seized him.

"Wait!" Simon said. "We came to give life, not to destroy it. Jesus has overcome death. For His name's sake, we plead with you to spare these men their lives."

"Very well," the general nodded. "See them to the edge of the encampment."

As guards led them beyond the tent village, Arfaxat leaned to Zaroes and whispered, "How many more times must we encounter these Jesus followers?"

"If we encounter them again," Zaroes answered, "it will surely be for the last time."

Author's Note

Some of you might wonder how this story came to be. More specifically, you might wonder why I chose Simon the Zealot and Matthew the Tax Collector as the featured disciples around whom to center this tale and why I chose to feature *both* instead of focusing on just one or the other.

I chose Simon and Matthew because, more than any of Jesus' disciples, they force us to wrestle with contrast and division. They represent the opposite extremes of their society and culture, so getting to know them sheds a helpful light on the division that defines our present society and culture.

We divide ourselves into tribes, nations, and people groups. We seek out belonging and identity in our heritage, our borders, our education, our economic classes, our politics, and even our sports teams.

The division that we experience so acutely in twenty-first century America is nothing new. It is part of our fallen nature. When humanity broke fellowship with God back in the earliest pages of Genesis, we broke our capacity to experience full fellowship with one another.

I wrote this book because our societal division has infiltrated the church (a danger that C. S. Lewis warns against in *The Screwtape Letters*). Too often, our remedy to division—even within the church—is to surround ourselves with like-minded people and plead for others to embrace unity by becoming more like us.

But that is not the solution that Jesus calls us to embrace. Jesus calls *all of us* to a new way of thinking—a renewal of our minds (Romans 12:2). He doesn't do this by helping us to find the right spot on whatever continuum our society uses, but by calling us to follow him and live on a different axis entirely.

That is the core message of this book, and that is why I chose to feature Simon and Matthew side-by-side. No matter where each of us starts on society's continuum, Jesus invites us to orient ourselves toward him.

Jesus challenges every manmade ideology—often all at once. Just as often, we try to become more like "the other side" or make them more like us in order to achieve some appearance of unity. But when we achieve "unity" of this kind, the results can be disastrous. As believers, we must instead be open to the work of the Holy Spirit that conforms us more into the likeness of Jesus.

Speaking of Jesus, his presence in this book is both prominent and necessary. I recognize that portraying Jesus in fiction carries inherent risks. Though much of this book takes place in the "white spaces" of the gospel narrative, it necessarily intersects with scripture throughout—and increasingly as the story progresses.

Where I relied on gospel scenes directly, I made every effort to do so in a manner that is consistent with the Biblical account. Similarly, I was careful not to put words in Jesus' mouth that the Bible doesn't already reveal. Every teaching spoken by Jesus in this book comes from his words recorded in scripture.

My goal is not to reinvent Jesus but to honor him, as he is revealed in the Bible, by exploring his impact on the lives of both Simon and Matthew.

Though I was careful to stay true to the words of scripture, the fact remains that I am a human author, and this book is a work of fiction. So if any part of my book conflicts with or contradicts the Bible in any way, trust your Bible.

That said, even while staying true to the Biblical text, I had decisions to make along the way about the order of some events, their locations, and—in one notable case—their frequency. These are topics that scholars passionately research and debate, and sincere believers may disagree on these points. But for the sake of a complete and cohesive story, I had to make a choice in these matters, and typically I chose to depict what I believe to most likely be correct.

Perhaps the easiest example to identify is Jesus confronting the money changers. Did he do this once or twice? Scholars are divided on the answer, in part because John places this event in Jesus' first visit to Jerusalem and the synoptic gospels (Matthew, Mark, and Luke) place it in the Passion week. Through my research, I concluded that these tellings depict two distinct but similar events, and that is the approach I used in this book.

It is beyond the scope of this writing to examine all the reasons for my choice—perhaps I will explore this in a future blog entry. But for our purposes here, I point this out simply to provide an example of something on which believers may disagree without it having any bearing on our understanding of scripture or our relationship with Jesus (and with each other).

Finally, one truly fun aspect of writing this book was discovering so many "one-liners" in scripture that refer to off-page events without elaborating on the events themselves. I hope you spotted a few of them and enjoyed them as much as I did.

How did Mark know the Pharisees and the Herodians were plotting together to kill Jesus (Mark 3:6)? How did John learn of the plot by the chief priests to kill Lazarus (John 12:10)? And who were the eighteen men who died when the tower in Siloam fell on them (Luke 13:4)? These are a few of the "writing prompts" that came directly from the pages of scripture.

As you encounter these scenes, my hope is that they might prompt you to mine more of these hidden gems on your own. Not just because it is fun (which it is), but because engaging with and immersing ourselves in scripture has life-changing power that deepens our faith, strengthens our hope, and compounds our joy. And that is what I hope and pray you experience.

Peace,

Jac

Acknowledgements

Thank you, first and foremost, to my God for calling me to new life in Jesus, opening the doors to my writing opportunities, and directing this project over the past two years.

Thank you to my wife, Angela, and my sons, Kyle and John Mark, for your unrelenting support and contributions.

Thank you to Jennifer and the team at Bright Communications for all your hard work and insight throughout every phase of this project.

Thank you to my early readers, my church family at Christ Community Bible Church, and the crew at Bucks County Free Library for your continued encouragement.

About the Author

Jac Filer is a lifelong resident of Bucks County, Pennsylvania, where he presently lives with his family and his dog. Since 2020, he has been enjoying a second career as a freelance Christian writer, and he is an ongoing contributor to multiple blogs, websites, and devotional apps. Coin and Dagger is Jac's first novel.

Printed in the USA
CPSIA information can be obtained
at www.ICGtesting.com
LVHW012037130124
768908LV00004B/159